The Memory of Elephants

The Memory of Elephants

Boman Desai was born and raised in Bombay, but has spent most of his life in Chicago. He has degrees in Psychology and English, both from the University of Illinois in Chicago. He has published stories and essays and a novel, *Asylum, USA*. He has worked in various capacities including farmhand, bartender, dishwasher, short-order cook, secretary, musician, bookstore clerk, telephone operator, auditor, and teacher. His memory is not what it used to be.

The Memory of Elephants

Boman Desai

The University of Chicago Press
Chicago and London

The University of Chicago Press, Chicago 60637
The University of Chicago Press, Ltd., London

Copyright © 1988, 2000 Boman Desai

All rights reserved. Originally published 1988
by Andre Deutsch Limited
Published by Sceptre Books 1990
Published by Penguin India 1992

This edition first published by HarperCollins
Publishers India 2000
University of Chicago Press edition 2001

Printed in the United States of America
09 08 07 06 05 04 03 02 01   1 2 3 4 5
ISBN: 0-226-14381-3   (paper)

Library of Congress Cataloging-in-Publication Data

Desai, Boman.
    The memory of elephants : a novel / Boman Desai.
      p.   cm.
    ISBN 0-226-14381-3 (pbk. : alk. paper)
    1. Iran—History—To 640—Ficton.   2. Zoroas-
trianism—Fiction.   3. Pennsylvania—Fiction.
4. Scientists—Fiction.   5. Parsees—Fiction.
6. Memory—Fiction.   7. India—Fiction.
I. Title.

PR9499.3.D466 M46   2001
813'.54—dc21
                                          2001027807

For Soonamai and Granny

Seervai and Cama Family Trees

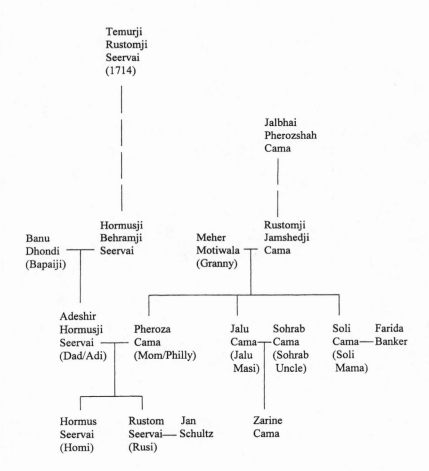

Contents

Acknowledgments	*ix*
Prologue	1
BAPAIJI	25
Navsari	27
Adi Ghadiali	37
Hormusji Behramji Seervai	53
The Mother	63
The Emancipation of Women	72
Maharani Is Coming	79
Simply Cleaning House	87
Between the Mosque and the Temple	94
GRANNY	101
The Long Dining Table	103
Cambridge	113
Like Cambridge	119
Nawaz	128
Rustomji Jamshedji Cama	131
A Midsummer Night's Dream	136
A Legitimate Heir	151
The Episode of the Vase	164

MOM AND DAD   171

Froglegs   173
Edinburgh   183
Ratilal   192
Baksheesh, Seth, Baksheesh   195
Land of Forefathers   199
The Two Girls Huddled Together Like Monkeys   206
First Class! Absolutely A-Number One-First Class!   217
Joyride   227
Her Mona Lisa Smile   239
The Greater of His Two Loves   253
Nehru and Lady Mountbatten Had an Affair   267
The Towers of Silence   283

RUSI   289

Maybe If I Had Been a Quadriplegic   291
Stupid Bloody Bawaji Bastard   302
You Think This Is Bloody Communist Russia
    You Can Just Walk into My Room   311
Look at His Hair, Like a Gollywog   317
Chicago   322
Jan Schultz   333

HOMI   347

Penny   349
Penny: Corollaries   360
Aquihana   364
Va-Va-Va-Voom   375
Manasni, Gavasni, Kunasni   380
On the Wings of a Dragon   389

Epilogue   405
Glossary   408

Acknowledgments

Thanks to Cheryl Rozycki for the use of her house, her Apple, and her countless cups of tea — thanks also, to Mom, for the translations and the time — and to Anil Dharkar, editor of *Debonair*, in which earlier versions of "Ratilal" and "Baksheesh, Seth, Baksheesh" were first excerpted, whose support came at a time when it was much needed. "A Midsummer Night's Dream" was also excerpted in a different form in *Another Chicago Magazine*.

Prologue

I am a bawaji, the son of the son of and so on and so on of a bawaji; but as my bapaiji, my paternal grandmother, whom everyone (including her son) called Bapaiji, as if it were her name, recently said to me: 'You are a bawaji, Hormusji (she spoke ironically, using the exalted form of my name, Hormus — or Homi as everyone called me), but you do not know what it means to be a bawaji. You should be ashamed.'

I was not ashamed; I was too ignorant to be ashamed; but I was bewildered. I thought I was going crazy. I was watching Candace taking off her clothes — again. I had lost count of the number of times I had watched, but I watched again as if for the first time. I wanted to see it through without interruption as I had not been able, inexplicably, the last few times. I recognized again the azaleas in the deep green pot, the columns of roses climbing the wallpaper, and the worn blue rug against which shone the rhinestones which studded her leather jacket and slippers of gold. She had shucked off her jacket and kicked off her slippers as soon as we'd entered the room at the Come Back Motel. I had switched on the lights, but she'd dimmed them and pushed me gently backward, onto my back, in the bed, from where I had watched her strip to the Bee Gees singing "How Can You Mend a Broken Heart" on a car radio outside.

1

It wasn't much of a strip; she hadn't much to take off; rhinestone jacket, gold slippers, blue miniskirt, red panties (primary colors, as primary as my excitement and fear), and she was naked, undulating lilywhite limbs and torso in my face to the music.

Bad enough she was more experienced than I was, bad enough she was beautiful, bad enough she was naked, but her appearance was compounded by factors of which even she was not aware. For a mere undergraduate from Bombay, India, such as I was, a Jane or a Doris or an Anita from Aquihana, Pennsylvania, U.S.A., such as she was, was far more exotic than an Asha from Ahmednagar or a Mehroo from Mysore or a Vimla from Vijayavada. Her name alone, Candace Anderson, would have been enough, but she had also the blond hair, blue eyes, creamy skin. I had never stood a chance; more than a woman, more even than a woman of the occident, she was a woman of the silver screen and golden celebrity as much as Jane Fonda, Doris Day, or Anita Ekberg, the only American women in my Indian world; associated with them by name, race, and pedigree; as exotic, and as internationally acclaimed. I spent just one night with Candace, not even an entire night, but I'd been lost even before I had started, lost not even knowing I was lost. I had never stood a chance.

A rose deodorant filled the room and bouquets of pink roses adorned the pillowcases matching the columns of roses climbing the wallpaper. The bed was wide, its counterpane blue. Outside, the Bee Gees yielded the airwaves to Carole King singing "I Feel the Earth Move" and Candace's undulations, adjusting to the earthier music, yielded to bumps and grinds. Her breasts jumped as she danced and she steadied them with her hands. Her face became impassive as she caressed herself, squeezing her breasts, pinching her nipples, highlighting various parts of her body with her hands. "Sweetie-pie," she said. "If you wanna get something outta this, you're gonna have to do something. Otherwise, it's not gonna be any fun."

I might have been stung, but her voice was as dulcet as a choir of cellos. I looked out of the window again, not daring to hope that I would see once more what I might reasonably have expected: a Pennsylvanian vista, mountains lush with evergreens and waterfalls, perhaps the town in cross section, perhaps a steel mill, perhaps even just the parking lot where we'd left her Thunderbird — but no, once more my memory was interrupted, once more I saw the desert.

A desert! I felt heat from the window, but I knew it was fall. I could see the sun in the hot white sky, but I knew it was after nightfall. I could see drifting oceans of sand, but I knew we were in Aquihana, Pennsylvania, U.S.A., maybe twenty miles from the Susquehana River, a hundred miles northwest of Philadelphia, a hundred and fifty southeast of Lake Erie. Where was this Great Pennsylvanian Desert?

I looked back into the room and saw to my relief Candace again, still staring impassively, my chance still ahead of me — but looking outside the window again, I saw Arabs mounted on camels, their swirling white haiks dirty with the desert billowing like sails behind them, appearing through the heathaze like a mirage, tall and slender and shimmering, congealing before my eyes into figures painted by El Greco, sculpted by Giacometti.

Let me be clear: I had lost count of the number of times I had watched Candace take off her clothes, but she'd taken off her clothes for me just once; I had watched her countless times, but I'd always watched the same performance, exactly the same performance; rhinestone jacket, gold shoes, blue miniskirt, red panties, all came off in the same order, exactly the same order; I heard the songs, first "How Can You Mend a Broken Heart," then "I Feel the Earth Move," leaking through the window at the same times, exactly the same times; I even saw her from the same angles, exactly ... but you get the picture. It was as if I were seeing a movie, a movie I had seen so many times that I could trace its progression as if with a template — hell, I could have made the template.

Let me be clearer: It wasn't even a movie as much as a single scene, a single scene which I had played repeatedly through the memoscan — at first, and for countless times, successfully, to its conclusion — but, increasingly, the memory disintegrated into hallucinations. Yes, hallucinations. There was no other explanation. Back in the room, I saw naked Candace; back outside, camelbacked Arabs; back and forth, back and forth, Candace and Arabs, Arabs and Candace, both hostilely, increasingly hostilely, staring at me, glaring at me. When the images began to merge, my command finally slipped away and I surrendered to the madness. The lips of her vagina grew larger, more wrinkled, grey, an elephant's trunk and tusks emerged from the folds, elephant ears sprouted like wings on her back. I think that was when I started to scream.

★

What was happening? A vagina was flying on elephant ears, dragging trunk and tusks behind. Worse, I saw the dead (Bapaiji, Granny, Dad) and the living (Mom, Jalu Masi, Sohrab Uncle, Soli Mama, Rusi, Zarine — Myself!) as if they were acting out the scenes of their lives by my bedside. Worst of all, I saw armies, hordes and phalanxes of warriors, Arabs and Iranis, on foot, on horseback, camelback, elephantback, engaged in battle, showers of descending arrows, a constant swarm of adverse activity as might be witnessed when rival ant colonies or galaxies collide. The fantastic merged with the real, the ancient with the modern, naked Candace, airborne on elephant ears, mounted on an elephant's trunk and tusks, split into a hundred similar images, and the flight of Candace angels soared to meet squadrons of flying monkeys approaching from the distance. The landscape was littered with rhinestone jackets, gold ballet slippers, blue miniskirts, and red panties. Sometimes the images appeared in closeup as if through a zoom lens, sometimes from afar as if through a wide angle, in short bites of motion as if in a badly edited movie, all to the accompaniment of a relentless atonal symphony. I was not ashamed, but I was in terror of imminent insanity.

I wanted to get up, but I couldn't move. I might have been bound like Gulliver by the Lilliputians even to his hair twined around stakes hammered into the ground, but my hair was not that long. There was a throbbing in my head as if threads were being drawn by needles from right to left, from left to right, sometimes in both directions at once, sometimes in more. My conscious states blurred with my unconscious like everything else happening all at once. "Hello, Homi? Can you hear me?" People in white stood all around me, some faces grim, others anxious.

"Yes. Who are you?"

"It's Dr. Edward Horvath, Homi. You are in good hands. You are getting better. Can you tell me exactly how you feel?"

I tried to focus on the voice but couldn't. "My head hurts."

There was a shuffle. A new face loomed in the foreground. "Homi, do you know who I am?"

I recognized the voice, even the face though it had a heavy black beard. "Rusi, my brother."

The face smiled. "Yesyes. How are you feeling?"

"My head hurts."

He couldn't stop smiling. I must have been unconscious a long time. "They will give you something for that. Are you hungry?"

"Yes."

"What would you like?"

"Anything. Tell Mom I want sali boti for dinner."

"Mom isn't here. We are in Aquihana General. I flew in from Chicago when they said you were sick. Mom is still in Bombay. They have a choice of beef stew and baked chicken in the hospital today. What do you want?"

"Chicken."

Someone left for the chicken. I was still in Aquihana, still so near and so far from Candace, still where I had accepted the scholarship from Aquihana University. I could have gone to Harvard, I could have gone to Yale, I could have gone to Princeton, all had offered scholarships and others had too, but they were not for me. I preferred the low profile; I preferred to create my own prestige; I preferred, if you wish, to be a snob in reverse. William Faulkner flunked out of highschool; his grandson went to Harvard. You figure it out.

"Can I get you anything else?"

"Rusi?"

"Yes?"

"I want to go home."

Home? Yes, not to leave Candace, no, never, but to lick wounds, discretion the greater part of valor, running away to pursue my Candace another day.

"When you are better I will take you home myself."

"When?"

"Soon."

A nurse gave me pills to swallow, a glass of water. I went through the motions of drinking, when the food arrived of being fed; with all the movement I continued to feel as if I were immobile, but the throbbing in my head subsided. Rusi pushed his scraggly black hair behind his ears; they were long like Bapaiji's ears, and as I watched Bapaiji materialized in entirety, as if from his ears, where Rusi had been standing. "Hullo, hullo, Bapaiji! Tamhe kem chho? How are you?"

"I am not Bapaiji. I am Rusi. Bapaiji is dead." The voice was Rusi's.

"Arre, listen to me, no? It is Bapaiji only. I may be dead as you know the dead, but I am trying to show you something. Look now, pay attention. Just look what I am showing you." I couldn't see clearly, I couldn't believe I was talking with

Bapaiji — who, as Rusi said, and as she herself said, was dead — but though the voice was deeper than I remembered it was unmistakably Bapaiji's. The throbbing in my head returned as I looked at what she wanted to show me.

★

The desert appeared again, and the Arabs on camelback approaching at a leisurely pace through the loose stones and thickets of thorny bush that grew around them. Behind them the earth was arid, dirty yellow, without even brush to be seen. Before them stood two sentries, spears held ready, guarding a bridge. To left and right of them stood other sentries, similarly ready, guarding adjacent bridges. It was spring and the river — a canal, actually, from the Euphrates River — was full. When the summer reached its zenith the canal receded and could be forded easily, even at its fullest, on horseback. How did I know this? Do not ask; I was not in control; I was learning. Trees full of figs, pomegranates, oranges, dates, and lime grew on the Irani side of the river before the walls of the city of Madayn. The foremost sentry waited for the caravan to stop. When it was almost upon him and showed no signs of slowing down, he shouted, "Halt!" and the camels were reined to a halt. The sentry counted their number, fifteen, to himself, before he shouted again. "Dismount!"

The Arabs commanded their camels to their knees and sprang off unwrapping the white flap of cloth across their faces. They were hardier, bred in the desert, than the Iranis, taller with gaunt faces, sand encrusted stubble, thin noses like beaks, and eyes narrowed by continual squinting against the wind and the sun; the space around the eyes was more wrinkled and darker like a mask owing to the lesser protection provided the eyes by their cowls.

When the last Arab had dismounted the sentry spoke again, still shouting. "State your business!"

One of the Arabs, standing ahead of the others, spoke with scarcely concealed contempt. "Do not shout. We are bedouin, and we are expected, a deputation from our Caliph Omar to your King Yezdigard III. My name is Noman Makarin."

The sentry knew they were expected. He had been appointed to stand by the gate because his life as a soldier had acquainted him with a little Arabic. "Yes," he said, lowering his tone to conversation level, "you are expected. We will escort you to the throne room of King Yezdigard III — but you must leave behind your camels and arms."

One corner of Noman Makarin's thin mouth curved sharply downward. "Has the great Irani empire been so debilitated by its wars with Byzantium that it now fears the arms of fifteen bedouin?"

The sentry's face grew tense as if he'd been slapped. "You must leave behind your camels," he said, shouting again.

Noman Makarin smiled and raised his arm to gather the Arabs around him. One of the Arabs stayed with the camels; the others were escorted across the bridge by the sentries. They walked with long measured strides and the old Irani sentry was struck immediately by their difference from the Arabs he had known, a skulking subservient nomadic people, lacking culture, lacking education, barely above the rats of the desert upon which they fed, but these bedouin walked as if they were nobility, as if they were conquerors (faces as smug as the faces of their camels), as if the Iranis were lackeys.

They entered the city of Madayn through an arched brick gateway guarded at each end by giant stone dogs — a legacy of the legendary Irani hero, Jamshed, whose dogs' vision had been powerful enough to drive away demons invisible to men. The houses within the walls were of brick, some with flat roofs of timber and packed earth, others with domes of vaulted brick. The walls around the doorways were plastered, painted shades of tan and blue; the wealthier homeowners had pillared porches;

fire temples stood apart from the residences, square buildings of limestone blocks embedded in mortar, roofed by domes over four arches, built for the worship of Ahura Mazda and His prophet Zoroaster, their entablatures supported by winged bulls with human faces. The Iranis, sleek and oliveskinned — the men in colorful blouses open down the front fastened by girdles and breeches reaching their knees, the women dressed similarly but in longer wider garments with blouses closed down the front except for a slit at the breast — gathered to make fun of the curved scimitars of the Arabs, their dirty burnooses, weatherbeaten features. Someone suggested, to the crowd's immense amusement, that they acquire new clothes, make distaffs of their bows and spin flax. There were enclosures with horses, donkeys, cows, camels, and fat tailed sheep; goats, dogs, and cats roamed freely; a brightly clothed juggler thrust his rump at the procession juggling oranges between his legs. The Arabs remained inscrutable, looking neither left nor right, appearing oblivious even to the magnificence of the palace ahead.

In the desert they might have imagined the palace a mirage, it was that sumptuous. The entire face of its main staircase was covered with sculptures in low relief, of Irani guards, armed with spears, swords, shields, others carrying bows and quiversful of arrows, lions attacking bulls, hunting parties, mythological beasts combining lions and bulls and eagles and men, and more. A border of rosettes adorned the parapet on which was carved an inscription commemorating the founder of the palace, the Great King, Khushrow II, shahanshah eran ud aneran, the king of kings of Iran and nonIran. The tall, wide, central arch, which provided the main entrance, had a shallow tip. On either side of the arch the facade, divided into string courses and pilasters, was ornamented. Inside were huge square rooms with barrel vaults of baked bricks which opened one into the other, the largest of which, the Great Hall, the throne room, was in the center, large enough to hold thousands of ministers, noblemen, guards, and attendants. The interior walls were stuccoed and ornamented with paintings, embroidery, and hanging weapons glittering with jewels. The Paradise carpet, seventy cubits long and sixty broad, which provided the backdrop for the golden throne, was richly embroidered, seeming like a garden with walks of gold, streams of silver, meadows of emerald, and trees, flowers, fruits, and birds of diamonds, rubies, sapphires, and pearls. The crown, encrusted with gems, was so heavy it had to be suspended over the head of the Great King, Yezdigard III.

The throne was set on a platform behind curtains embroidered with gold. Knights and princes stood thirty feet to the right of the throne, governors and tributary kings in residence a similar distance farther, and jesters and musicians a farther distance yet. Guards stood on the left; but despite the remoteness of his throne, despite his fine trappings, Yezdigard III, the grandson of Khushrow II, could not appear to be more than he was, a boy king with a thick cluster of black curls, the more barefaced for the men of his court with well trained beards tied in knots below their chins. His necklace of stones only accentuated his pearly face, his ruby cheeks. Since the murder of Khushrow II in 628 A.D. by his son, there had been a succession of eleven rulers, two of them women, in the span of four years, before Yezdigard's accession had been masterminded by the Irani general, Rustom, who'd removed Purandakht, daughter of Khushrow II, from the throne. The regal bearing of the Arabs despite their beggarly raiment surprised him. He knew they'd taken Damascus from the Byzantines and won decisive battles against them, but the Byzantine forces had been enervated by his own wars against their emperor Heraclius. He knew the Arabs had won some battles against even the Irani forces, but he couldn't think of them as more than jackals harrassing an old lion. Something had happened to give the Arabs their uncustomarily dignified bearing.

The sentries escorting the delegation prostrated themselves before Yezdigard, but the Arabs remained standing. "Down, fool," the old sentry whispered sharply to Noman Makarin, "if you wish to live."

Noman Makarin said nothing. He did not look at the sentry. He had ignored all the wonders of the palace concentrating instead on his purpose, fixing Yezdigard with his stare from the moment he had entered his presence. He made his obeisance without servility, waiting to choose his own moment, with deference to etiquette more than the threat of the sentry, and the other Arabs followed.

The Iranis were known for their humanity; vanquished kings were dealt with honorably, enemy towns were left unmolested, their ranks welcomed into the services of Iran, and land given them to administrate. Zoroastrianism was the religion of the royal house of Iran, but Judaism, Christianity, and even paganism were tolerated with equanimity. Yezdigard assumed the Arabs wanted clemency for their excursions against the Iranis, permission to mingle, and perhaps some land. He officiated the ceremony by satisfying his curiosity about some of their accouterments. The old sentry continued to serve as interpreter. "We call this *burd*," said Noman Makarin when the sentry asked what they called their cloaks. Makarin's eyes never left Yezdigard's while he spoke and the boy king felt threatened because the Irani word *burdan* meant "taking." Similarly, when he asked about their whips and sandals Makarin said *saut* and *na'l* whose homonyms in Irani, *sukhtan* and *nalidan*, meant "burning" and "lamenting." Yezdigard blanched, then spoke angrily because Noman Makarin continued to appraise him inscrutably, imperturbably. "What is it you want, then?"

Noman Makarin replied: "Allah has commanded us, by the mouth of His prophet Mohammad, to extend the dominion of Islam over all nations. This order we obey. We invite you to become our brothers by adopting our faith — or pay tribute if you wish to avoid war."

Yezdigard knew of the prophet Mohammad. The prophet had died in the year Yezdigard had come to the throne, but he had not felt the power of the prophet before. He was outraged that the representative of a people who had no precedent for organizing, holding, and ruling an empire, who were acknowledged in the common parlance as desert rats, would dare to speak as Makarin had done to the shahanshah eran ud aneran. His eyes flashed, his hand went to the gem encrusted hilt of his sword, he almost rose from his throne — but he fought to regain his composure and spoke calmly though with his hand still on his sword. "Your minor victories have made you bold indeed — but Byzantium has fallen, and if Iran sets aside her internal dissensions for only a day she will drive you deep into the desert again with the rats and the snakes upon which you feed. You have been known to bury your daughters to avoid sharing food with them, you have been known to feed on carcasses and drink blood. Of all the world's nations you are the poorest, the least united, the most ignorant, the most estranged from the arts. Who are you to dictate what Iran should do? If want and misery have driven you from the desert, if you open your eyes and cease deceiving yourselves, we will give you food and clothing and freedom of worship. We have welcomed Jews to live peaceably among us, we have welcomed Christians — and we will welcome you, for that is the way of Iran."

Noman Makarin remained silent for a moment as if with respect, but when he spoke his tone was condescending as if he spoke to a child. "What you have said about our former condition is true. We ate lizards, we buried our daughters, we drank blood, such was our state — but Allah, in His mercy, has sent us His prophet Mohammad, and through the organ of His prophet has instructed us that He is the only God, that the earth belongs to Him, that we are to spread His dominion, to exact tribute from those who would keep their faiths, and to exterminate all others."

The Arab stopped as if to appraise his effect. "This is our destiny. Those of us who fall will obtain Paradise, those who survive, victory. Now it is for you to choose."

Yezdigard recognized it would be hopeless to talk further. "If I had less respect for your offices as emissaries," he said, "I would have you instantly deprived of life." He ordered a bag full of earth to be given to Makarin. "This is all the tribute you will get from me," he said. "Return to your Caliph and tell him that my general Rustom will bury his general and his entire army in a few days at Qadisiya."

Yezdigard did not understand why Makarin accepted the earth so eagerly, but his general, Rustom, understood immediately that he had taken it as a pledge of future success. Rustom ordered the bag retaken as soon as he learned what had happened, but the Arabs had made good their escape. Makarin deposited the bag before his general, Sa'd, exclaiming, "The soil of Iran is ours."

★

Yesyes, verynice, palace and throne and crown and everything; suitably impressed I was though still full of incomprehension — but where was Candace? when was I going to see Candace again?

"Candace Schmandace!" Bapaiji said, her voice still deeper than I remembered, and still unmistakable. "Look, no, what I am showing you? What is this Candace? a hair in your history. Pluck it out, throw it away. Bigbig brains you have got, but little little sense. Just look, no, what I am showing you?"

If Candace was a hair in my history, she was the only hair that mattered, the rest was silence, shantih shantih shantih, but you didn't talk back to Bapaiji. "Yes yes," I said. "I am looking. Show me, no, Bapaiji? Show, no, what you want? I am looking."

"Look, then, and enough of this bukbuk. Look, and maybe my big brain, little mind, lost in America, American grandson will at last learn something."

I looked. What I saw was as hallucinatory as what I had seen already, but I was no longer afraid. Bapaiji, dead or alive, was there to protect me.

On the edge of the desert there was a village, Qadisiya, with a fort, some cultivation, and palm groves. It lay within a plain bound on the west by a stream and the east by a canal from the Euphrates. Sa'd, the Arab leader, and his troops camped by a spring near the desert; Rustom and the Iranis camped by the canal. The Iranis were weary from their long wars with Byzantium; they had forty thousand men to the Arabs' thirty thousand, but Rustom didn't want to attack as long as the Arabs could escape into the desert and attempted negotiations instead to determine the Arabs' grievances, their ultimate goals, and their reasons for raiding Irani frontiers but to no avail. After four months, against his wishes, Rustom opened the battle.

I heard the scrunch of marching feet, the thud de-de-thud de-de-thud de-de-thud of galloping horsehooves, a slow soft heavy regular pad, pad, pad, which, as the glorious horrific spectacle unfolded in front of me I realized were elephant steps. The plain was flat, and the sun cast long shadows in the haze of early morning. The Irani cavalry wore helmets, coats of mail, buskins reaching up to their knees; they wielded swords, shields, lances, maces, bows, and arrows; even their chargers were protected by armor not unlike the chargers of medieval knights. The sun grew brighter picking highlights from the abundance of metal in the field so that the charges resembled a turbulent glistening river. Archers, trained to shoot with accuracy and rapidity from behind wattled shields, formed the most important part of the infantry; the rest of the infantry supported the archers with spears and swords. Vaults of arrows flew like monster predatory birds casting ominous shadows on the ground before arrows and shadows converged on their prey. The Arabs in desert robes with only shields for protection were easy targets; the numbers of their dead mounted quickly and their bodies held clusters of arrows like pincushions. Men squealed like children, scurried like trapped animals, struck blindly at one another. Two mounted Arabs squeezed Rustom's mount between them. One held him so the other might find a vantage point for his blade, but Rustom spurred his horse forward breaking the first Arab's hold, held his shield against the second Arab's scimitar, and swiped backward with his sword slicing the first Arab's face from the crown to the chin. Someone else swung at the second Arab so that his head flew through the air with wide white bulging eyes. Rustom smiled, nodding a quick acknowledgment to his compatriot.

More effective than cavalry or infantry, the Irani war elephants scattered the Arab horses and threw their riders in the air. The victory for the first day belonged to the Iranis and Sa'd sent for reinforcements from Syria. If the Iranis had followed up their advantage through the night they might have checked the Arab expansion for all time, the moving finger might have written a different history, but the numbers were still great on both sides and they returned to their camp instead.

On the second day the field was cluttered with the bodies of the dead, stuck with arrows, appearing like porcupines, and the ground still damp and dark with blood. Rats and snakes gnawed at the bones of corpses, and the stench of rotting flesh got stronger as the day deepened into a hot suffocating afternoon. The Arab leader, Sa'd, with two arrows in the back of his left shoulder, felt as if his arm would fall from its weight alone. He wanted to leave the field to have his shoulder bound, but that would have undermined the Arab morale. He was grateful for whatever lack of foresight had prevented the Iranis from bringing their elephants onto the field again, but he couldn't tell which way the battle was going yet. His arm was almost too heavy to hold up much longer when Syrian reinforcements arrived. Sa'd rallied, fastened his arm within his girdle to relieve its weight, and shouted the taqbeer, Allah Akbar, God is Great. The reinforced Arabs, renewing their onslaught, won the second day.

On the third day an elephant plucked an Arab from his mount and held him high with his trunk, but before he could throw him to the ground the Arab drove his lance firmly into the elephant's eye. The elephant gored the Arab into the earth with his tusks, and stamped his body into puddings of flesh, but he couldn't shake the hateful shaft protruding from his eye. Dark red blood spread like a wash across his armored trunk. Trumpeting his rage and pain above the cries of the battle he invited a volley of Arab arrows to be fired at his good eye. The blinded elephant went berserk, and wheeling madly around charged the Irani troops disrupting their center. The Arabs pushed them back with renewed cries of Allah Akbar, not letting up even when the night fell. The armor of the Iranis worked to their disadvantage in the close quarters of the night, weighing them down though there were no more arrows to deflect; a sandstorm blew in their faces; more reinforcements arrived from Syria. By the fourth day the Iranis had been driven against the canal, their forces disorganized, Rustom killed.

For two months the Arabs rested and rejoiced, then Sa'd led them on to Yezdigard's capital, Madayn. The bridges across the canal to the city had all been destroyed. When the guards saw the Arabs they ran through the city shouting, "The devils have come! The followers of Ahriman have come!" Yezdigard had already fled to the east with a retinue of four thousand noncombatants including secretaries, cooks, women, children, old people and as much of his treasury as he could manage. Madayn fell after token resistance and the wealth of Iran passed into Arab hands — carpets, dresses, arms, jewels, a horse of pure gold. Fifty thousand Arabs, many of whom had never seen gold before, never lived in more than a tent, wandered as if in a dream through the palaces and gardens taking whatever they wished. Each received a booty of twelve thousand dirhams (one thousand dollars, Bapaiji translated). The prophecy of the prophet, that the treasure of the Khushrows and the Caesars was destined for the Arabs, was coming true.

Above the looting Arabs, as high in the sky as eagles, flights of Candace angels flapped mightily with squadrons of winged monkeys, soaring gracefully into the sun.

★

"Did you like the fish?"

The whitefish, served with a lemon sauce with French beans, hadn't been bad, but I wasn't partial to fish; neither it seemed were most of the residents of the hospital — they'd run out of the alternative, roast beef with a baked potato, before noon. "I like chicken," I told Rusi.

"I know. I'm sorry — but there was no chicken on the menu today." His tiny snubbed nose wrinkled with regret in his tiny oval face fringed by his wild black hair and beard. "Maybe tomorrow."

"Rusi?"

"Yes?"

"I want to go home, Rusi."

"Yesyes — soon. The doc thinks you should rest still. You have to build up strength for the trip."

"I am well. I feel well. Look." I sat up in bed. I tried to get out but he stopped me. "I am fine. We can go tomorrow."

Rusi pushed me gently back again by my shoulders. "Homi, you must be patient, only a little longer. Let me tell you what the doc said. Can you follow what I'm saying?"

I was the older brother; it was strange to have him speak to me as if I were a child. "Yesyes, of course I can follow you. Why shouldn't I follow you? What do you mean?"

"Listen carefully," he said, observing me for my reaction. "You've been in the hospital for a month now and the doc says you're recuperating well — but your system has had a severe shock and he wants to be sure there will not be a relapse. He's given you all the tests and the results have all been negative — but, as you know, it's a unique situation because of the nature of your experiment. He doesn't know what is best because he doesn't know what exactly is wrong. The only thing we know for sure is your memory has been damaged, something to do with the memory machine you invented, a memoscan I think you call it. At least we don't have to feed you intravenously anymore like when you were unconscious — but even when you're conscious you don't remember what you've eaten or even whether you've eaten at all."

My memory? damaged? I was recalling things I didn't even know I knew — in vivid detail!

"The doc thinks there might be permanent damage to your longterm memory as well because you keep talking to Bapaiji as if she were still alive. He thinks that if I took you back to Bombay the familiarity of childhood associations might be the best thing to spark your longterm memory — but he wants to be sure you're well enough for the trip. Otherwise, you might slip back into your coma. Are you still following me?"

I think I nodded. I wanted to say Yes but I couldn't. I understood what he was saying — but there was so much I didn't understand about which I couldn't even begin to ask. How did I know what I knew? see what I saw? hear what I heard? when it was so evidently fantastical? How could I possibly recall scenes in such vivid detail that I'd never witnessed? that I couldn't possibly have witnessed?

Rusi segued once more into Bapaiji. "Arre, but my dear Hormusji, what is so very fantastical about this? You said no, yourself, that you are the son of the son of and so on and so on of a bawaji? So sonorously you put it — and what is a bawaji but a name we Parsis call ourselves? and what are Parsis but the people driven from their homeland to India by the Arabs? The Europeans called the homeland Persia, after the province Parsa, to represent the whole of Iran, and it wasn't until 1935 that the Europeans began calling Persia by her true name, Iran, land of the Aryans, at the request of the Irani government, but by then it had been too long the home of the Arabs, nonAryans of nonIran, desertrats, the Mussalman as we Parsis call them.

"The Mussalman did not allow freedom of worship like the Iranis, and all Zoroastrians, Jews, and Christians had to pay an extra tax after which they were marked with lead seals to advertise their inferior status. They were not allowed to ride, carry weapons, drink wine openly, show signs of their religion, wear Mussalman clothing, speak to Mussalman women, nor build houses taller than Mussalman houses. These Iranis were your ancestors, and many left as you know, first chance they got, sailing to India, to their old trading partners, and most of their descendants, whose numbers have now fallen to below ninety thousand, live in India today, mostly in Bombay.

"The battle of Qadisiya in 636 A.D. which I showed you, which the Arabs called the umm al-ma'arik, the mother of all battles, was the beginning of the end of the Irani empire, of the Sassanian dynasty, which had flourished for four centuries, of which Yezdigard III was the last monarch. It was also the end of the ancient world, and the beginning of the modern. First, the Iranis escaped to the coast, then to the island of Hormuz in the gulf, then finally across the sea to India with whose people they had once traded. Yezdigard raised armies wherever he could, but lost battle after battle, Jalula in 637 A.D., Nivahand (Victory of Victories for the Mussalman) in 642 A.D., and finally his life, murdered in Merv by a miller in 652 A.D.

"But enough bukbuk. Showing the story is the best way of telling the story. Let me show you so you can see for yourself. Looklook, this is how it happened."

I looklooked and sawsaw a silhouette of ancient ships, their masts, spars, yards, booms, and rigging, rising like sleek black spires against a rising sun, against sleek streamlined clouds over the horizon, their underbellies filling with gold. Around the ships the sea was still, but in the distance fishermen cast nets into the water.

There was a Turneresque stormscape-on-the-sea mounted on the hospital wall in front of me — which suddenly appeared to spill out of its frame, merging with the tranquil early morning seascape Bapaiji had presented, submerging it along with my hospital bed as if someone had edited a strip out of a movie reel. The water slapped the floor around me, sharp as the crack of gunfire, rising, spiraling, sucking everything into its vortex. Through the black walls of water I saw the ships being tossed like toys — one, capsized, its hull dancing madly as nerves of lightning struck it from the sky; another, lying on its side, its oars sticking helplessly into the air like the legs of a giant dying insect; still others, bobbing like buoys, occasionally thrown clear into the air. Within the hulls, sailors and passengers, clinging to rafters, benches, posts, kneedeep in rank water and debris, had long given up attempts at guiding the ships, when the hull of one ship came to a scraping jarring sudden stop against an abrupt rise in the sea floor, sending a number of its inhabitants into orbit. Other ships passed the first, but came to a similar stop. Some of the voyagers lay unconscious where they'd fallen, some slept, but the hardiest ventured onto the decks and stared at a long white beach, bright with the sun, and a soft green forest beyond. Birds skimmed the sea, driftwood approached, blackfaced monkeys screamed from tall swaying coconut trees, and brown skinny fishermen with white loincloths stared back at them from the shore. To their left a bay held an armada of dhows, sails furled. The fishermen launched canoes, climbed into them, and paddled noisily toward the ships. The Iranis girded themselves at first for an attack, noting, despite their travails, the advantage of their war weapons over the fishermen's harpoons, knives, and paddles — but the first canoes greeted them like heroes with hosannas, flowers, coconut milk, invited them ashore, and provided shelter and food, a feast of rice, fish curry, and toddy.

★

"Listen, Homi. Great news!"

"What?"

"The doc thinks you're well enough to go home. We're going home tomorrow."

"Home? Where? Aquihana or Bombay?"

"Tomorrow, Aquihana — in a week, Bombay. You still need a lot of rest. You move around too much even in your sleep. The doc says your dreams are too vivid, but he thinks the best thing for you is to be in secure surroundings. The sooner we get to Bombay the better."

They thought I was dreaming — you stumble over a vine in a lime green jungle and your leg twitches in your hospital bed, that sort of thing, but I said nothing. My tales of Arabs and elephants and shipwrecks might have been interpreted as a relapse into dementia.

"Tell Mom to get an airconditioner ready."

"I did already. You never stopped asking for it."

I didn't remember asking for it, but I said nothing.

"Actually, your timing is perfect," Rusi continued. "Jan is two months pregnant. What do you say, Homi? You are going to be an uncle in seven months."

I'd never met Jan, his wife. "Jan is here? Where is she? I want to see her."

"Nono, she is not here. She is still in Chicago. She is enrolled in a course for the summer, but like I said, your timing was perfect. If you had got sick next semester I would have had to drop out, or Jan might have been ready to deliver — but your timing was too good."

"Tell me about Jan."

"She is looking forward to meeting you. She can't wait to meet you."

"That's nice," I said. "I would like to meet her. Have you got a snapshot?"

"Yesyes, hold on a minute." He dug into his pocket, pulled out his wallet, pulled out a picture. "She looks even better in real life. She hates pictures — but here. Take a look."

I looked, but instead of Jan I saw Jadhav Rana, the rajah of Sanjan, the fishing village where the ships had beached. A darbar was being conducted on a large maidan; a month after their arrival the rajah was finally meeting the Iranis officially. He wore a long violet satin robe, red satin slippers, and a diadem of gold with a ruby centerpiece. He sat on a covered throne with embroidered drapes surrounded by noblemen in satin and velvet robes and turbans, and guards in white with spears glittering in the sun. He raised his hand; the Iranis were brought to the center of the assembly and invited to tell their story. The seniormost of the dasturs, the priests, each of whom wore a white turban and robe, had been elected spokesman. Jadhav Rana sympathized with the Iranis, but was uncomfortable with their warlike appearance. "This is a sad story," he said when the dastur was finished. "What you wish — a place to stay where you may worship freely, where you may cultivate the soil so that you are not burdensome to others — is fine and honorable, but it is not that simple. Let me show you how it is."

He clapped his hands twice and a jug of milk, filled to the brim, was brought out. "Sanjan is like this jug of milk," he said. "There is no room for more."

The old dastur brought a coin out of his robe. "Your Highness," he said, holding up the coin, "if I may be so bold."

Jadhav Rana frowned, puzzled, but nodded giving his permission.

The dastur slipped the coin carefully into the jug without spilling a drop. "Your Highness, we Iranis will be as the coin is in the milk. You will not even know that we are here."

The crowd applauded the dastur, but Jadhav Rana didn't smile. "This is well," he said, "but a coin is tribute, and the hospitality which can be bought with a coin is not the hospitality of Sanjan. How will you repay our hospitality?"

The dastur dropped a pinch of sugar into the milk, taking care once more not to spill a drop. "Your Highness," he said, "as the sugar sweetens the milk so shall we endeavor to sweeten your lives with our industry."

Members of the crowd jumped as they cheered. Jadhav Rana smiled finally, gave his consent, but also named five conditions: the Iranis were to give him a full explanation of their religion, they were to adopt Gujarati (the language of Sanjan) as their own, they were to adopt the local forms of dress, they were to surrender their weapons, and they were to conduct their ceremonies after nightfall to avoid influencing the Hindus. The warriors among the Iranis hated to give up their weapons, but the priests said it was more important to win the trust of their hosts, to start a new life. "We have come through the long tunnel of war," they said. "What use have we now of weapons?"

BAPAIJI

Navsari

Seen from above Bombay is a doglegged peninsula jutting into the Arabian Sea. It is hot, as much of India is hot, but were it less of a peninsula, were it landlocked like Delhi, it would be at least less humid. Delhi is hot, but dry. In Bombay, no sooner had you taken a bath than the last drops of water, no matter how cool, mingled with the first drops of sweat; the most absorbent clothing became immediately damp; and the green of the landscape appeared a denser green as if swollen with the humidity, refracted through the lens of the air.

I hated the hot season, but that was not the only reason I insisted that Mom buy a new airconditioner before we arrived. When we were young, Rusi and I would lug the mattresses from our beds every night during the hot season to Mom and Dad's bedroom because it was airconditioned. We laid the mattresses on the cool tiled floor between Mom's bed and the Grundig radiogram. The black rubber insulating strip around the doorframe, clearly visible to me on the floor, insulated us even more cozily from the outside world. Sometimes, after the lights were out, I would listen quietly as Mom and Dad talked; sometimes, Rusi and I would join in; it made us feel grown up. The low hum of the airconditioner, the clean cool clear air, the

warmth of the blanket, and the friendly darkness with Mom and
Dad nearby, lulled me into a deeper sleep than I would get in
my own room.

Mom had got rid of the airconditioner soon after Dad died,
by which time I was in Aquihana. She'd always mistrusted it
as she mistrusted anything that hadn't been part of her childhood, from the Grundig radiogram to the pocket calculator Rusi
brought her from the States — she preferred to do her hisabs
in longhand.

The new airconditioner meant more to me than relief from
the heat, more than a return to what I had before the womb.
How can I explain it? Sealed into my airconditioned room, with
its millennial thrum, I imagined myself at the controls of a
rocket, with the ability to fastforward or backward in time and
space — but of course the control was never mine, and I might
more accurately have imagined myself in the belly of a primor-
dial beast, journeying through an amniotic ocean as ancient as
an Indian age, beyond what elephants could remember, to the
dawn of creation.

The first time Bapaiji "spoke" to me she said, "Arre,
Hormus, my lost-in-America-grandson, this is your bapaiji
speaking, not your mamaiji — or are you too much American
now to remember what little Gujarati you so eagerly learned
from me?" I recognized her immediately by her irony: I hated
Gujarati. I hated it because she was the only person with whom
I spoke it and that was the only reason I had to learn it. She
should have learned English if it meant that much to her to
speak with Rusi and me. We spoke English with everyone who
could, Hindi with everyone who couldn't; Bapaiji could speak
Hindi, but wouldn't.

Still, Bapaiji lived in Navsari, a small town about two hundred miles north of Bombay, where we visited her for just two
weeks during Christmas every year, and Mom said it wasn't too
much to ask to humor her during that time. So I sat with Bapaiji

in the long enclosed front verandah, black slate in my lap, chalk pencil in hand, for an hour every morning of our visit. Rusi was exempted from these sessions because he was at first too young (actually, just a year younger than me), and by the time he was old enough Bapaiji had realized what I could have told her all along: it took more than two weeks a year to learn a language.

In the afternoons I would be in the same verandah with Mom, she on the bench swing, I with my cane (because of my polio) on one of the innumerable seats, with my *Fundamental English* text, reading stories of the Bargery family, except now I would use a notebook and a lead pencil, and after my tenth year a fountain pen. Bapaiji slept in the afternoons; otherwise, she might have objected; she hated to waste anything, even paper when I could have used a slate.

I remember her house, Hill Bungalow, best for its countless chairs and photographs. Chairs of all kinds, rockers, recliners, uprights, upholstereds, Morrises, Windsors, with cushions, without, couches, settees, sofas, loveseats, benches, stools, footrests (my favorite was an upholstered elephant's foot, two feet tall, with toenails, just my size through my growing years), crowded the large sittingroom and verandah. Bapaiji's favorite was a cane recliner with slats under its arms which slid out to provide leg rests so she could lie back as if in a hammock. There was a part of the verandah which was never used, always shuttered, where the seats were always covered with dust. Once, when I was five, I wrote my name in the dust of a wooden stool — in English. I erased it immediately thinking Bapaiji would have wanted me to write it in Gujarati, but suddenly the rocker was too clean, and I was afraid I would have to dust the entire section of the verandah to hide the evidence of my crime. I needn't have worried; the seat went unnoticed and by the end of our visit you couldn't tell it had ever been disturbed.

For every seat there were at least five photographs on the walls, each bordered by an elaborate wooden frame, of *all* our relatives (which meant *all* the Parsis in Navsari; all Parsis in Navsari have photographs on all their walls of all the Parsis in Navsari), single portraits, duos, trios, quartets, quintets, larger ensembles, at navjotes, weddings, other functions, standing glumly like schoolchildren in single file along stoops, seated like prophets on the innumerable chairs in their sittingrooms, arranged in studios with dramatic backdrops (jungles, ruins, storms), men in white ceremonial dress with high collars (satin daglas, cotton daglis), and ceremonial headgear (paghris, fehntas), women covering their heads with the sashes of their saris, gazing into the distance as if considering weighty matters, children with the large eyes of cartoon animals. The space between the frames and walls was thick with dust and cobwebs.

Bapaiji knew her irony about my affinity for Gujarati wasn't lost on me. "I was only kidding," she said, "as you Americans like to say." She cleared her throat loudly, like a man, and spat. I wondered what she'd spat into; I still couldn't see her clearly. In Navsari, she'd kept a tin plate under her bed full of ash into which she spat periodically through the night.

"Don't be surprised you understand me so clearly," she continued. "I know as much English as you know Gujarati, but here language means nothing. Whatever is said, in whatever language, is clear, by magic, hocus-pocus, abracadabra, to whomever it is addressed. You would understand me if I spoke Zulu."

What surprised me was not that I understood her, but that I *heard* her. My problem was not a language barrier but a sound, overcoming my delusion (what else could it be?) that she was speaking to me — but she continued speaking as if she'd read my mind.

"Just to put you at your ease," she said, "to convince you this is really me, though dead as you know the dead, not someone playing a trick, let me remind you of the time of your operation."

I knew immediately that she was referring to my first tonsillectomy. I'd been four; I'd been given an injection; the doctor had asked me to count to ten; I'd counted down from a hundred instead because what he'd asked appeared too easy; the doctor had been surprised; Mom had said brightly, "He's a *very* intelligent child." The next thing I remembered was a clock striking five, a pendulum clock, across the room from my bed, which struck just as I regained consciousness. Everyone was smiling; the doctor said I shouldn't say anything unless there was something I wanted; he showed me my tonsils in a glass, saying everything had gone well; there was all the ice cream I wanted because it was good for my throat; but all I wanted was to gargle. "Kogra," I said, or tried to say, to Bapaiji, the Gujarati word for "gargle," but she kept shooing away a crow cawing at the window thinking it was bothering me: the Gujarati word for crow is "kaagro." The charade was repeated tirelessly until she realized what I wanted. The incident had never ceased to amuse her, particularly since the crow had proven so stubborn. She repeated the incident once more to prove to me that she was Bapaiji.

"Things seem different here," she continued, "but they're not. Everything is spirit. I don't mean souls are flashing around like fireflies. Everything is just like you want, but nothing is tangible. I am a man here, I wear pants like a man, I walk like a man, straight, direct, forward, one-two-one-two, left-right-left-right, not that sideways motion like a woman, waddling one-side-two-side-one-side-two-side. I talk like a man, you can hear me, deepdeep bullfrog voice, not highhigh like a koel or a sparrow. You know I always wanted to be a man, to do the things men did — but, and here is the irony, I did more in Navsari as a woman than I can do here as a man. Here I have no effect, only illusions. It makes you think, what is important, what is not, not to waste wishes like Aladdin.

"Your mamaiji is here, Granny you called her, my English-American grandson, but she has her own illusions. Here you can have anything you want — anything, as long as it doesn't interfere with what someone else wants — and what does she ask?

A house with high ceilings, crystal chandeliers, custommade furniture, paintings on the wall, a verandah just like the one from which she stared at Bombay everyday — the same house, Zephyr, in which she lived so much of her life, even the same dust.

"Your pappa also is here. You know how much he loved U.K. Here he dresses like he never left, like he was always going to the the-YAY-tah, wearing top hat and tails, twirling his stick, thinking he is English. When I first saw him in London I laughed so hard that my sides hurt. After that he didn't put on airs with me. He even hid his stick behind him thinking I would not notice. I noticed, but I said nothing. I had made my point.

"Worst of all, he dances like a nautch girlie, but wearing a kilt, and playing bagpipes. I hate that music, snakecharming music — and the trouble with kilts is you don't wear anything underneath, and I could never stand show-offs.

"It is strange, Hormus, when you know everything about everything but you can change nothing. I am a man here, but without the power that goes with being a man. Your mamaiji thinks she has got what she wants, but it is the same as what she always had. Your pappa chooses to be in the U.K. to be far away from me, but he is closer to me now than when he was in Bombay. Be careful what you ask; it is not always the same as what you want.

"But still I am not getting through to you. Still you are fighting me, still you are thinking I am a delusion. I thought it would be clear to you by now, but for a scientist you are not thinking very clearly. When you plugged yourself into your memomemomachine, whatever you call it, you cut into the Memory of the Soul. You have said yourself, the brain is like an iceberg, the tip holding the living memory, the submerged the Memory of the Soul, the Memory of the Dead — the Memory of Everything Else! Everything is known, little is realized. A drop of water can become lost in the ocean — or it can become the ocean. I am giving you a chance to become the ocean, Hormus. For one time, look properly, use your bigbig brain."

I began to understand, to recognize the importance of the memoscan. It can be used to scan the traces of memory recorded in convolutions of the brain rather like a movie projector can be used to scan a movie on a screen, speeding it up, slowing it down, moving forward, moving backward, until the required episode has been located, until the required memory has been located to be relived as if it were occurring for the first time — but there is a catch: the memory traces are recorded on convolutions of the brain; the deeper the convolution the more vivid the memory, and the more frequently the memory is replayed the deeper the convolution becomes. The process can be repeated an indeterminate number of times depending on how vivid the memory is to begin with — how deep the con- volution is to begin with — before the depth of the convolution becomes like an incision in the brain. Beyond that point, brain cells decay with, as you can imagine, deleterious effects on the rest of the body.

2

A man in baggy white pants, a smooth white dagla, and shining black fehnta, sat on a cane chair, leaning aggressively forward, one arm outstretched, hand resting confidently on the head of a walking stick. The polished brass tip of the stick rested by a black, polished, leather boot. The cuff of the pantleg was high enough to reveal a sagging white sock, but not skin. The other hand rested in a fist on the man's waist. His face was fair, with the skin of a young boy, but his expression, particularly the barely perceptible lift at the corners of his wide mouth, indi- cated a deeper, broader experience, but I could not determine his age. I didn't know who the man was but I'd seen his face, certainly his mouth, before. I recognized his surroundings more easily: he was seated in Bapaiji's sittingroom with the chairs and photographs; the wooden clock behind him weighted with pine-cones on chains, housing a cuckoo behind one of its two tiny doors, a German boy fiddler behind the other; to the left of the clock the swing doors one might expect in a wild west saloon leading to the diningroom; and to his right the old Murphy radio in its wood and glass case broadcasting the news in Gujarati. The man smiled as if he knew I was watching him, held up his walking stick, and switched off the radio. I recognized Bapaiji's walking stick as soon as I saw the ivory knob of its handle; its body, I remembered, was of sandalwood.

The man's smile deepened, as if he understood my deepening comprehension. "You are doing well, Hormus, very well. Your faith is stronger than I thought. You can see me now as well as hear me. It only took a little rest, a little trust. Don't be so surprised. I told you I was a man here. I told you we can have whatever we want here as long as it does not interfere with what someone else wants — so, here I am. Take a good look. How do you like my fehnta? You think it is just another fehnta, but you know so little. All fehntas were made individually, so much care was taken — but now there are no more fehnta makers, there is no money in it. Men are all wearing paghris now instead which they buy from the store. What they gain in money they lose in majesty — but take a good look, no, at my dagla, at my pants. Convince yourself who this is. No rush. After all, this is not the first time I have worn pants — but look, no, look, let me show you. I was the first woman in Navsari to wear pants."

The panorama changed even as I looked. An unseen camera appeared to pan from Bapaiji's face to the window, to mango and tamarind trees outside, to a ragtag bunch of children playing Catch, among them one girl, a child Bapaiji! recognizable even then by her sharp wide jaw. As I watched, one of the boys lunged at her and she fell. That was when I saw the other girl, standing to the side, pretending not to see, appearing more embarrassed

than Bapaiji as Bapaiji's dusty skirt rode up her bony thighs.
"Come on now, Banu," the second girl called. "Food is ready.
Mamma is waiting. Come on, all of you, Jamshed, Jehangir,
Savak, Kavas. Food is ready. It will get cold."

Bapaiji laughed, punching the boy who'd knocked her down,
who tagged her again so she'd chase him. "Are you coming or
no, Banu?" the other girl persisted, her brow furrowing with
annoyance. "Food is getting cold."

"Then let it get cold." Bapaiji tagged the boy again, laughing
so she was almost out of breath.

The game was over. The others started going home. "We
are going, Banu," the girl said, her hands on her hips. "If you
are coming, then come now."

"Comingcoming, no, Dhunmai? Wait, no, you all? I am
just coming."

Bapaiji caught up with the others walking back to the house.
"I swear, Dhunmai, sometimes you are like an old woman."

"At least, I have some shame," Dhunmai said, her voice
shaking. "Just wait until Mamma hears about this."

"About what?"

"Just wait."

"About what?"

"I said no? Just wait."

Bapaiji mimicked Dhunmai. "I said no? Just wait."

Dhunmai remained obstinately, ominously, silent after that
as they walked home through narrow wadis, over mud roads,
past mango trees, peepul trees, coconut trees, past stray chickens,
dogs, goats, cows, clouded by the farmyard scent of dust, dung,
hay. Bapaiji and her brothers ignored her, but Dhunmai's silence broke as soon as they got home. "And she was just lying
there with her skirt up and all the boys laughing at how shame-
less she was." Her brothers said they were all just having fun,
no one thought about shame, but Dhunmai wasn't finished.
"And who has to keep the time while everyone is having fun?

Who has to go and call them when food is ready as if I don't have something better to do? Who does all the work while everyone is playing the fool?"

"Wahwah," Bapaiji said, shaking her head primly. "As if only you do work around here. Who puts the dung on the floor in the morning? Who lets down the mosquito nets at night?" Dhunmai was too squeamish to line the floor with dung which was purchased everyday for two or three pice a basket from vendors at the door and mixed with sand from the talao, or to kill the mosquitoes within the nets at night as Bapaiji did clapping her hands so they became splotched with blood.

Dhunmai began to scream. "And who does the sweeping every morning? And who fills the matkas with water from the well? And who puts the chalk on the doorsteps? You think we can afford dubras to do all the work or what?" All were chores done by the women before the men awakened. Their mother burned sandalwood in the looban, took it around the house, and kept it burning all day so the house would always be full of its scent.

Their father looked unconcernedly at their mother. His primary interest was his work, the experiments he conducted as a perfumer and chemist discovering new cosmetics and medicines which made most people avoid him because he smelled constantly of chemicals; discipline was the mother's responsibility. "Be quiet now, Dhunmai," she said. "What is all this screamingscreaming? And, Banu, you are not to play with boys. You are a girl. You have to wear skirts. You must have more shame. You cannot do the things boys do. Now, everyone, be quiet. Food is getting cold."

The next day Bapaiji wore her closest brother's pants, bunching her dress into its waist, making more holes in the belt to make it fit, rolling up the cuffs to shorten it. The boys laughed; Dhunmai scowled; their mother smiled; their father was in his workroom pouring a bubbling green liquid from a beaker into a test tube.

Adi Ghadiali

Bapaiji took a deep breath and crossed the line into the dusty combat zone of the game, saying "Hu-tu-tu-tu" in a barely audible tone. The object of the game was to step across the enemy line, touch one of the enemy, and return to your own line without losing your breath. You kept up a low "Hu-tu-tu-tu" to indicate you were holding your breath. The enemy couldn't touch you until you had crossed their line, but once you had crossed they could grab you to keep you from returning to your team. Bapaiji had her eye on Adi; if she could get away with touching him it would be a coup. He pretended not to care about the way he looked, but took a lot of trouble to look that way; he never cut his hair, but washed it and oiled it and combed it to make it look as if he had just been in a fight; he had no brains, but all the girls liked him because he was the tallest person in Navsari, almost six feet, and the school's best athlete. The girls' parents liked him because his father was rich, a sweets merchant, the owner of *Ghadiali ni Mithai* in the Mota Bajar.

Bapaiji knew all these things, she had even seen Dhunmai staring at Adi when she thought no one was looking, but Bapaiji liked Adi most for his delicate woodworks, frogs and snakes and landscapes in relief for picture frames, and figurines of bears, tigers, buffaloes, camels, elephants. He was never without the burlap sack in which he carried whittling knives and wood, and set to carving at every opportunity.

Bapaiji was wearing Kavas's pants as usual, but she no longer moved as easily. Her hips were still skinny enough to fit into a boy's pants, but her breasts were larger and hurt when they bounced. The boys too had changed, spoke to her less, touched her more, and more roughly, particularly when they dragged her across the home line, but she didn't know what to do about it. It was becoming increasingly difficult, even for her, to ignore her encroaching womanhood.

Adi maintained a warrior's stance, ready to dodge her but no less ready to grab her if she touched him first. His eyes narrowed under the mat of curly black hair plastered with sweat to his forehead, but she couldn't be sure that he concentrated only on the game. "Tu-tu-tu-tu-tu-tu," she continued under her breath, an inch away from the enemy line, an armslength away from Adi, feinting at him, a caterpillar of sweat beading her upper lip. Once she'd stepped across the line she'd lose the element of surprise and have to move quickly to touch one of the enemy and get behind her own line, but the longer she waited the sooner she'd be out of breath. She looked at Adi, sizing up her chances, but found herself admiring instead his glossy skin, sleek eyebrows, red tongue sliding over pink lips. He puckered his lips, "Tu-tu-tu-tu," mocking her, but she saw in his lips the promise of a kiss, puckered her own firmly, raised her voice, "TU-TU-TU-TU," but didn't want to cross the line; that would signal the others to grab her again. She couldn't say when she'd begun to resent their touch, as if a favorite shirt had grown suddenly too small, as if this game she'd enjoyed had developed an undergame which made her queasy, what had once been fun had developed into a pretext for something else. "TU-TU-TU-TU-*TU!*" She spat the last syllable at Adi and walked away from the game. "I don't want to play anymore."

Both sides were bewildered: "Arre, but you must finish the game"; "Arre, but you are our best player"; "Arre, but we were just winning"; "Arre, but what is the matter, no?" She said nothing was the matter, she just didn't want to play, she was going home. Adi said he would walk her home; then the game could go on with one less player on each side. She said, "Okay." On the way he said, "It is still early. Let us walk by the Lunsi Kui Talao." She said "Okay" again. She'd become quiet and quiescent since he'd offered to walk her home. The gulmohor trees seemed more orange than she remembered, the lotuses on the talao more pink, and the vines under the surface more green. Adi asked if she wanted to go farther, into the forest. There were monkeys in the forest, and jackals and snakes, but she said, "Okay." The animals would not bother them, not in daylight, not unless they were bothered first. She stumbled over the underbrush following Adi along a narrow beaten path until they came to a large banyan tree. The thick vines and widespread roots provided a cozy enclosure, inviting them as if into a room.

"I come here when I want to be by myself," he said. He seemed shy, unable to meet her eyes, as if he were showing her something private and precious.

She nodded. "It is very peaceful."

He pulled a knife from his pocket, a piece of roughly carved wood from his sack, and began to work. She saw it was a squirrel but said nothing, sat on a root, watched him work, listened to the song of the koels and sparrows and mynahs and bulbuls and crows. She didn't notice the passage of time until he suggested going home. As they approached the town again he said, "Would you like to come to the forest again sometime?"

"Okay." She was thrilled, but spoke nonchalantly, without looking at him, without even a smile.

When she saw him again the next day in the school playground he kept his hands behind him. "I have got for you something," he said. "What is it, do you think?" Bapaiji tried to dart behind him, but he was too quick. "You must guess," he said. "Sun chhe? What is it?"

Bapaiji ran around him again, chanting the foolish rhyme of children:

Sun chhe?	What is it?
Saru chhe.	It is fine.
Danda leke	With a stick
Maru chhe.	I'll break your spine.

Adi eluded her easily again, but didn't make her guess anymore. "It is a walking stick. I carved it myself."

Bapaiji had chanted the rhyme only because she hadn't known how to show her pleasure that he'd brought her something. When he showed her the stick she grabbed it from him, still nervous, and walked around him, bent and hobbling like a cripple. "Why is this? What is all this?" she said, walking and talking so quickly he could hardly follow her. "Are you thinking I am an old woman for giving me a stick? Is that what you are thinking?"

"Nono," he said, laughing at her craziness. "It is for clearing the underbrush when we go to the forest. Look, no? It has got a metal stop at the end. And look at the handle. It has got a fine grip. Try to swing it. You will see what I mean."

Bapaiji looked at the stick more closely. The bottom was stopped with iron, the body sandpapered smooth and cylindrical, the handle carved like a snake's head with grooves along its neck for a firm grip. "It is beautiful," Bapaiji said, stealing a quick look at Adi. "Thank you." He was smiling. She touched his cheek with her hand.

They said nothing about their meetings to anyone and no one said anything to them. Bapaiji's parents were too preoccupied — her father with his experiments, her mother with the household — to keep a lookout on each of their children; but Dhunmai's suspicions were aroused and she came into the forest once to look for them. "Are you there, Banu?" she called.

"Food is getting cold." She hadn't meant to call out loud, wanting to surprise them, but as she got deeper into the forest she got scared and wanted their reassurance, so she called telling herself she didn't want to embarrass them catching them unawares. "Are you there, Banu? I thought I saw you going in."

They were not far when they heard her call. Adi threw everything into his sack and jumped into the tree, Bapaiji on his heels. They didn't mind being found together, but didn't want to give Dhunmai the satisfaction of finding them. Too late they realized they'd left one of Adi's whittling knives on the ground. There was a chance Dhunmai would not see it, but sometimes when the shadows changed in the wind the steel glinted in the sunlight.

Behind Bapaiji, in the thick foliage, hung the tails of three monkeys. She would have ignored them; there were hundreds of monkeys in the trees, tails hanging like furry brown ribbons; but not this time. She grabbed all three tails and yanked — hard. The idyll of the forest was slashed as if by lightning: the monkeys shrieked *oop-oop-oop-oop*, setting other monkeys shrieking, birds screaming, a wolf howling in the distance as if it were night; and woven into their screams, as brilliantly as the centerpiece of a peacock's fantail, was Dhunmai's screech as she turned and ran. The monkeys continued to shriek, *oop-oop-OOP-OOP-OOP-OOP!!*, baring their teeth, whooping around Bapaiji and Adi as if the trees had suddenly grown too hot to touch. Bapaiji bared her own teeth, whooping back. Adi laughed so hard he fell out of the tree; when Bapaiji reached to catch him he pulled her down with him; the fall knocked the air out of them and they choked, unable to stop laughing.

2

The forest was denser in Bapaiji's time than when I was growing up. The talao is still full of lotuses like a floating pink and white

garden, but Navsari is more industrialized today. The ground was
more thickly matted with leaves and grass than I remembered,
and there were more wolves, water buffalo, snakes, reptiles, and
wild birds — but whereas the animal kingdom was very much
in retreat in my time I still remember the blackfaced monkeys
and one rather frightening incident associated with them.

There is a fountain in the park near the Lunsi Kui Talao with
frogs on lily pads, warty toads, tadpoles, and goldfish. I enjoyed
watching them and playing with them so much, pushing my
cane after them in the water, that I invariably gave Rusi's Goanese
ayah, Julie, a difficult time when it was time to leave. She was
almost too patient, so much so that on one occasion we were
the last to leave the park. We had to cut across a forested area
to get to the main road. It was twilight and there were no lights
along the narrow beaten path, but we could see the distant street
lamps toward which we were headed. Rusi clutched her sari
walking alongside; I hobbled along her other side suddenly
subdued by the encroaching dark, the solitude, the sound of
crickets, and the gaze of perhaps a hundred monkeys gathered
on either side of us as if we were rulers parading for subjects.
I felt their hatred as if they knew we had diminished their forest.
It was a relief to be on the road again. It was even more of a
relief when, at a later date, the monkeys were exterminated (as
the forests shrank they'd become bolder, stealing things from
houses, leaving their odor in the rooms) — my imagination,
running amok, had conjured a monkey revolution in which
they'd all chased the wicked lame boy who'd chased goldfish
with his cane.

3

"Still young you were when Dhunmai died, but you must
remember her. You must at least remember the kharia party
when you told the Fox story as I taught you." Bapaiji's voiceover

faded; the panorama of herself and Adi laughing, out of breath
from their fall, undulated like a backdrop, until that too faded
and we were back in her sittingroom with the photographs and
chairs. A boy holding a cane stood with his right leg in calipers
(myself!) among maybe twenty guests, some still on the grey
stone floor finishing their kharia and chori. I was smiling, barely
able to stand still while Mom wiped my mouth and face still
sticky and brown from the kharia. When she was finished I was
ready, pink tongue peeking from the corner of my mouth,
pacing my four foot square of podium, telling my story as if it
were a revelation.

I remembered the story easily as I watched myself tell it:
Once upon a time, Sri and Srimati Fox were hungry but had
no firewood with which to cook puris. They visited Tiger Sahib
in the forest promising to make him a puri if he would give
them firewood. Tiger Sahib gave them firewood, the Foxes
made three puris, but were so hungry that they ate Tiger Sahib's
puri as well. When Tiger Sahib came for his puri, Sri and
Srimati Fox hid themselves in baskets of straw. While Tiger
Sahib was prowling about their house the Foxes had to fart
(puris will do that to you), and they cautioned each other to fart
quietlyquietly. Srimati Fox farted quietlyquietly, but Sri Fox
could not. He had to fart *BOOM-BAANG FATAANG!* The
straw baskets in which they were hiding exploded so violently
that Tiger Sahib jumped out of his skin, the Foxes had a tigerskin
for their bed, and lived happily ever after.

My antics created an even greater stir than the story. When
the baskets of straw went *BOOM-BAANG FATAANG!* so did
I, crouching first as far as my knee would allow, then exploding,
arms and cane flailing dangerously in arcs overhead, repeatedly,
as often as I was encouraged, the company shrieking with laughter, rushing for shelter from my explosions, until Mom said,
"Okay, okay. Enough now, Homi, enough! We get the picture,"
after which I was allowed one more explosion.

"You had told the story many times," Bapaiji continued, "but at the kharia party you added a twist." She started laughing at her own reminiscence. "When Srimati Fox farted, you said she farted quietlyquietly — like Dhunmai! And when Sri Fox farted, he 'farted *BOOM-BAANG FATAANG* like Bapaiji!" Everyone laughed out loud, but Dhunmai sat with a smile like a rubber band.

4

The man in baggy white pants, smooth white dagla, and shining black fehnta nodded approvingly, as if he understood that I now understood how things were, and turned into a sulky child Bapaiji sitting on a low wooden stool in the kitchen with her mother who was bent over a woodburning stove. "Give me the matches," she said, poking at the faggots with tongs.

Bapaiji threw her a box of matches.

Her mother flashed her eyes. "I said to give the matches, not to throw! Did I say to throw?"

When Bapaiji remained silent, she lit the wigwam of sticks and fanned the flame with a square of cardboard. "Banu, listen now. I am having something to say. I have warned you, no? how Navsari is, like a newspaper? Everybody always talkingtalking, everybody knowing everything about everybody else."

Bapaiji knew the discussion was to center on Adi, and resented the intrusion. "So why we should care what people say?" Bapaiji said. "We have done nothing wrong, no?"

"Give the sali boti."

Bapaiji passed the dekchi of sali boti. "Tell me, no, Mamma?" she said. "We have done nothing wrong, no?"

Her mother shook her head. "You are not understanding me. Never you are understanding me. Already people are talkingtalking. For your own sake, I went and talked with his motherfather."

Bapaiji raised her eyebrows. "You went to Adi's motherfather? But why?"

"Banu, you are sometimes stupid like a nanny goat. Why do you think? You have to marry before you lose your reputation more. Otherwise, who will marry you?"

Bapaiji bunched her skirt between her knees. "You went and talked with his motherfather about marrying? What they said?"

"They said what always they were going to say. They said they were Ghadialis, of the priestly class, we are only Dhondis, common people. They are too good for us. I said to forget it, we are not interested."

"You said I was not interested! What for you said such a thing, Mamma? You should not have said."

"Khabardar, Banu! I am warning you! Do not give me what-for! You are not an English. I am your mamma. Give the spoon."

Bapaiji passed her a ladle, and her mother stirred the sali boti. "I have found another man, somebody better, also in the priestly class. They are not thinking they are too good to marry Dhondis. You will be a fool not to marry."

"But Mamma, I am not interested in anybody else just now. I am not even interested in marrying Adi. We are only having fun."

Her mother shook the ladle at her. "Still you are talking like a nanny goat. If you are not interested now, soon no one will be interested. Already you are sixteen years. I was six months when I married. I was fourteen when I was widowed —"

Bapaiji slapped her knee impatiently. "I know, Mamma, I know — and you were fifteen when you married Pappa. You have told me one hundred times. You have told me one thousand times. What that has got to do with me?"

"What that has got to do with you! Arre, already you are sixteen. How much longer your highness is going to wait? Whole of Navsari is lining up for you to marry?"

"How long I am going to wait is between me and Adi, nobody else."

"Adi is not marrying you. His motherfather have spoken. He is not going against them. Forget Adi. I have talked with the

Seervais. They have a fine boy. He has even got a law degree from a Bombay university. They are richer even than the Ghadialis. Emperor Aurangzeb himself gave them land for their services to his court."

I remembered that story (Aurangzeb, the sixth Mughal emperor, had rewarded my great great great great great great grandfather, Temurji Rustomji Seervai, in 1714, with land in Navsari and all the revenue that went with it, for services rendered his court) because Dad always coupled it with another story, more horrific, probably apocryphal: Aurangzeb's father, Shah Jehan, the fifth Mughal emperor, who had built the Taj Mahal, mausoleum for his dead wife, Mumtaz Mahal, had cut off the hands of all the builders of the tomb so they could never replicate the feat. Nevermind that Aurangzeb had killed his three brothers to gain the throne; nevermind, also, that he had imprisoned his father for seven years until he died in a cell from which the Taj was visible in the distance; mind only that he had gifted my grandfather, great to the sixth degree, with land.

"Mamma," Bapaiji said, getting to her feet, "why I should care one snap about Aurangzeb?" She snapped her fingers. "He is a dead man. He died long ago. If I have got to marry, I will marry Adi. I have got to talk with him first, that is all."

"Talking will not benefit. I know. I have done already talking with his motherfather."

"I have got to do myself, in my own way. I have got to see for myself."

"Gogo! See for yourself. No good will come, but I am tired of all this bukbuk."

Bapaiji stamped out of the kitchen, unable to understand her mother's lack of sympathy when her own case had not been much different. She had married her father, the family apothecary, against the wishes of her own parents. He was only a tinkerer, they'd said, not a real doctor, but it had made no difference to her mother.

5

A young girl in a thin bright shortsleeved dress, white socks, and dusty heavyheeled brown shoes, rapped sharply on the frosted glass of a sliding window on which was printed:

DHONDI
DISPENSARY

She felt her heart pound as loudly as she'd rapped on the glass. She chewed the tip of one of her pigtails absently admiring the tiny pink ribbon she'd tied into a bow at the end. When the window was slid to one side she looked first at the weathered bricks in the wall in the back, visible where some of the yellow powdery plaster had cracked.

"Yes? What is it?"

The voice behind the window was gruff, but it was one she frequently played back for herself. Looking into the narrow rectangle of the open window she saw his thin long face with the sparsely cultivated goatee, the hurricane lantern hanging from the ceiling behind him, and handed him a folded piece of paper. "My mamma is sick," she said.

He took the paper, hardly unconscious of the low blue neck of her dress, her fingers caressing the pink silken ribbon in her hair, turning away to hide his smile as he recognized the prescription on the piece of paper once more. He'd lost count of the number of times she'd brought him the same piece of paper. He'd mixed a compound into a harmless solution with water each time, and returned the prescription each time because he didn't think she knew how to write and he wanted her to come back. He'd followed her on more than one occasion, watched her pour the solution by the roadside when she thought no one was looking, and been intrigued enough to find out more about her. There was no one else in the dispensary when he gave her the solution that day. He didn't know when he might get another chance. "Wait," he said. "Don't go. I am having something to say."

"What?"

"Wait. I will come out."

When he came through the door she was surprised how short he was (there was a step going up to the dispensary), but it made him more approachable. There was a smell of chemicals about him, but that only made him different. He didn't waste time. "Will you marry me?" He'd thought it· through. Most parents found his interest in perfumery too eccentric a hobby to be tolerated in a son-in-law. It demanded too much of his time and affection and might adversely affect his ability to provide for a family with both love and money — but this girl was compromised too. Her chances were no better than his because she was a widow — but she'd pursued him, flattering him, allowing, however discreetly, for no misunderstanding of her intentions.

The girl smiled, but turned away, blushing as if she, not he, had proposed. He touched her for the first time, by her waist with both hands from behind. She turned again to face him, her face full of light. "Yes," she said. "Yes, I will marry you."

6

Bapaiji went on a fast to change her mother's mind. On the third day of the fast she arranged to meet Adi by the banyan in the forest to talk things over. If they kept up a strong front their parents could do nothing, but Adi was less sure. "If our parents are against it, then it is hopeless," he cried.

"Why? If we just get married they will come round to our way of thinking. Once it is done they are not going to hold a grudge for the rest of their lives."

"They might do that, no? What we will do then?"

"What is to do? We will have each other, no? We will have our friends, no?"

"But they will cut me off from the sweet shop. What I will do then?"

"You will start another sweet shop. You will do whatever you want to do."

"But *Ghadiali ni Mithai* has been going a long time. If they keep me I will be able to open more shops. I will be able to go to Surat and Bombay and Delhi and Srinagar on business. I will go to U.K. for a holiday."

Bapaiji knew then his mind had long been made up. She said, "If we want to do something we can do it, whatever comes in the way," but she knew it was a losing battle.

"But there is no guarantee," he said. "This is a guarantee."

Bapaiji saw how he was, saw she'd been fooling herself. "There are no guarantees," she said. "Only cowards live by guarantees." She felt a sudden emptiness. Adi waited as if for her blessing to leave, but she was too angry to give him what he wanted. "Gogogo, no? Why you are still here? Go to Bombay, go to U.K., go where you want, go to hell — but do not look for me again. I will not be here. Go, no? Why you are not going? What is there for you now?"

He left with a forlorn look, as if she'd misunderstood him, wronged him. She waited until she could no longer see him, then thrashed the trees and bushes around her with her stick. Her rage had just begun to die when she realized she'd knocked a cobra from its rest. The snake raised its small black hooded head to strike. Bapaiji was transfixed momentarily by the wicked glinting beady eyes, the narrow flickering ribbonlike tongue, but she struck first with the snakeheaded handle of her stick, hitting the cobra on the side of its head, and again where it fell on a rock. She smashed its head with her second blow, but kept on beating it until the head of her stick broke off and rolled behind the rock. The snake was dead, but continued to move amid the carnage of its own dark blood and white flesh. Bapaiji hit it two or three more times to be sure, then threw away the stick. She went home, broke her fast with a slice of bread and jam and a drink of toddy, and told her mother she was willing to marry whomever she wanted.

7

Things become clearer: In the evenings Bapaiji and Mom went to the club together in Bapaiji's green cycle rickshaw, which then returned for Rusi and me (it only seated two). The evenings were uncomfortable for us because we spoke little Gujarati and hated the fuss the old ladies made over Bapaiji's grandchildren when we arrived or during their turns as dummies at bridge. Bapaiji and Mom, intent on their games (canasta, samba, rummy, whatever), hardly noticed us then. Eight card tables and two carom tables were arranged every evening behind the club by the badminton courts, or, if it rained, on the verandah in the back.

The club was a long brick bungalow with a stone floor and a gable roof, long verandahs in the front and back, a long room in the middle with two table tennis tables set lengthwise, cupboards along the walls for the decks of cards, badminton racquets, shuttlecocks, table tennis racquets and balls, draughtsboards and draughtsmen, caromboards and carommen, and Bapaiji's portrait conspicuously in the center of the wall (she was president of the club), a library on one side of the room, a den and bathroom on the other. One caretaker, Thakor, a bony, hollowcheeked man in a white Nehru cap, who said "Yesyes, ofcourseyes" to anything Bapaiji asked of him, managed everything.

I spent much of my time on the swings because they were farthest from the club, or reading a book in the library. Rusi would either join me on the swings or play badminton or table tennis. We never ceased to procrastinate when it was time to go to the club. Often, to the chagrin of our rickshawwallah, we would ask him to take us via detours, around the Lunsi Kui

Talao or through the Mota Bajar. The bajar was always crowded;
bicycle bells rang and motor rickshaws hooted incessantly; people,
cows, goats, and dogs moved around the stalls, shops, and
caravans of vegetables, fruits, clothes, stationery, luggage, tools,
and the homes of the hawkers who lived behind their shops.
From above, the ensemble might have resembled a continuously
shifting kaleidoscope, the occasional tonga, victoria, or auto-
mobile parting the crowd like Moses parting the Red Sea.

On one such occasion the rickshaw developed a puncture;
Rusi and I waited while the rickshawwallah fixed it when a tall
man with a long face called us into his sweet shop. He was the
tallest man I'd seen until then, but his face was even more
memorable, full of regret, perhaps for innumerable lost opportunities, and old with a bristly white stubble as if he'd lost
interest in his appearance. He looked happy to see us, but it was
a transparent happiness that might have dissolved had someone
questioned its cover. He said nothing, but got behind the glass
cases filled with pyramids of sweet round laddoos, fat pendas,
and squares of burfees ornamented with spangles of silver paper,
large puddings of red and green and orange and yellow halvahs,
brittle khatais wrapped in tissue paper with the ends twisted like
the ends of party firecrackers, balls of ghulab jamans and white
rasgullahs in thick honeyed syrups, interlocking concentric circles
of gleaming orange knotty deepfried jalebis with sugary casings
and syrupy centers, and white suttarfanis like flattened birdsnests
with badams and pistas — and began heaping the various sweets
onto plates for us. We ate the sweets as much to please him as
ourselves. He might have cried had we refused.

I remember the shop best for the wood carvings of animals
on exhibition: monkeys, elephants, camels, buffalo, deer, even
dogs, cats, and mice. When he asked me which piece I wanted,
I picked a walnutsized sandalwood elephant (Rusi picked a
tiger). I kept the elephant for good luck even after the veneer
came off when I accidentally washed it along with the pants

from which I'd forgotten to remove it in a washing machine years later in Aquihana, but I gave it finally to Candace Anderson (it might have been just last month, but I cannot be sure of such things anymore) as a token of my love.

When the rickshaw was ready to leave, he filled two tins with more sweets and insisted we take them with us. We tucked the tins under our arms (mine with a picture of the blueskinned Prince Rama drawing his bow, voluptuous Sita by his side; Rusi's with a picture of Hanuman, the monkey god, ripping open his chest to reveal the picture of Rama and Sita engraved in his heart), and muttered thanks, but at a discreet distance from the shop we gave the tins to the rickshawwallah for his family. Bapaiji would have scolded us for accepting food from a stranger (she scolded us even when we accepted refreshments from her friends because, so she said, they'd think she didn't feed us enough — which she didn't, doling out portions at dinner as if we lived in a Dickensian workhouse) — except now he appeared less of a stranger.

Hormusji Behramji Seervai

A montage of images followed, not unlike those sped up in silent movies, culminating in a series of bushybrowed club-footed men and sourfaced hunchbacked women followed by the most horrific of all: a baby, crying, so small it was nestled in the palm of someone's hand, being immersed in a bucket of milk, barely the suggestion of a struggle as the hand held it under, just bubbles of air breaking the surface of the milk for less than thirty seconds before the surface appeared undisturbed again.

"Do not be so shocked. The baby was made to drink milk. It was illegitimate; it was unwanted; it was the accepted way to get rid of such babies. A Seervai would not have married a Dhondi if something wasn't wrong with him. In the centuries after the Parsis settled in Sanjan to escape the Mussalman they wanted only citizenship and commerce, no more war. In Sanjan they stayed three hundred years; their numbers increased; they became farmers, weavers, carpenters, fruit growers, toddy planters; they spread to Cambay, Variav, Ankleswar, Navsari, Surat, Udvada, Bulsar, and finally Bombay. You know already how the Seervais got their money from Aurangzeb. For generations they married only their first cousins because they were so exclusive now — which accounts for all your deformed

ancestors you just now saw. Your bapavaji, your paternal grandfather, my husband, Hormusji Behramji Seervai, was better
looking than the other Seervais, but he too was married first to
his first cousin — but she had a baby by someone else, the
marriage was annulled, and the baby was made to drink milk.
After that there was not much to be said for Hormusji's prospects: he was older than other eligible Navsari bachelors because he had been married for three years and spent four years
before that in Bombay getting a law degree. More important,
there were no first cousins left to marry and his name had been
touched by scandal after the annulment so that the Seervais
were willing to allow even a Dhondi into their family."

2

When Bapaiji moved in with her in-laws I had a clear picture
of the house, Hill Bungalow, with which I was familiar, but the
in-laws themselves, whom I'd never seen, appeared gnarled,
gnomic, seated in chairs at isolated points in the front compound, clattering their teeth, khut-khut-khut-khut, and shaking
twisted walking sticks in the air, reminding me of the Mother
Goose nursery rhyme I'd played frequently on my old, blackbox,
windup, HMV gramophone, whose needle had to be changed
every six 78 r.p.m. records:

> There was a crooked man
>   and he walked a crooked mile.
> He found a crooked sixpence
>   beside a crooked stile.
> He bought a crooked cat
>   which caught a crooked mouse,
> And they all lived together
>   in a little crooked house.

Bapaiji's house was not crooked (the images and rhyme
come to mind because of the clubfoots and hunchbacks in the

family), but it was not well planned either. It looked fine: ground floor and first, brick walls, stone floors, hip roof, teak balustrades with cordate and paisley motifs in shades of tan and chocolate enclosing verandahs on each floor; but there were no hallways and often the only way to get from one room to another was through someone else's bedroom.

The toilet, four feet square, with its hole in the center and collapsible wooden seat, was even stranger, built apparently as an afterthought, in a tower twenty feet from the house connected by a covered passageway to the first floor. A wicker basket at the bottom of the hole in the tower was emptied every morning by one of the dubras, and a matka of water stood in the passageway with a tumbler to be filled and used for cleaning. When someone farted, or when shit hit the basket, the gamut of sounds reverberating along the column ran from PAAARRP to SPLAAATT to BLOOOPP to BOINNNGG depending how full the basket was, how heavy the load.

In front of the house was a pond, with lily pads, goldfish, frogs, tadpoles, and snails, among other pond creatures, built around a fountain which spouted from a single metal stalk in the hand of a two foot Cupid on a pedestal. Dragonflies and mosquitoes hovered constantly over the pond. A narrow beaten track passed by one side of the pond coming up a gentle incline (the hill in Hill bungalow). On the other side was a gravel path wide enough for the rickshaw.

Beyond the paths, on either side of the compound, slimleaved mango trees stood like sentinels. Sometimes, stray cows and goats slipped through an unlatched gate and grazed until Bapaiji was sent to turn them out again. Bapaiji had not anticipated the many ways in which marriage would make a woman of her. Being the youngest female in the house she was expected to stay home all day, cook everyone's meals, wash their clothes, keep the house clean. She had the help of the dubras, but the responsibility was hers if something went wrong and she hated it. The only time she had to herself was at the end of the day when the work was finished and the old people talked before going to bed. They would not miss her then until someone wanted something — a pillow, a glass of water, a newspaper, slippers, to close a window, to close a door.

On one such evening Bapaiji sat upright and crosslegged on the long wooden swing in the front verandah pushing herself lightly from the wall, her sari bunched in her lap, a shawl wrapped around her shoulders, waiting for Hormusji to come home from his club. I waited with great anticipation myself; Hormusji had died before I'd been born, and I had never seen him, my grandfather, except in snapshots.

Bapaiji had brought a kusti with her to weave and a hurricane lantern for light. She hoped Hormusji would get home before his father realized she was sitting out with the lantern and told her not to eat up all the oil. She was beginning to trust Hormusji; he made no demands on her, he taught in the school, he went to the club, he was polite. She disliked him only for the awe he continued to hold for his father; she felt it made him less of a man. She kept her ears tuned for the sound of Hormusji unlatching and latching the gate as he came in but all she could hear, interspersed with the sound of the crickets and the frogs, was the BOINNNGG BOINNNGG of her father-in-law in the toilet tower whom she recognized by the loudness and the rhythm of his BOINNNGGs and his PARP-PARP farts. She missed the sound of Hormusji at the gate, but his lanky frame soon emerged from the dark incline by the pond into the light of her lantern. "Arre, you, Banu, here, all alone?" he said. "Are you not getting cold?"

It was November. Bapaiji pulled her shawl more tightly around her shoulders. "Arre bawa, what is a little cold? I am not cold. Sitsit, no? I want to talk first before you go in."

He came up the stone steps and sat beside her on the swing. She liked how handsome he looked in his shirt, sweater, coat, and puffy long white pants. She liked even better the concern in his eyes which narrowed behind the black round frames of his spectacles and his forehead furrowed beneath the sharp black rim of his skullcap. I was pleased with the way he looked myself, finely chiseled face, trim moustache, reminding me of the pictures I'd seen of Dad as a young man, also of myself. "What is it?" he said. "Something has happened?"

"Nothing has happened. That is the trouble. I need more money for the house. That is all. You must do something."

Hormusji shook his head slowly as if he spoke with regret, as if he'd given the matter much thought. "That is out of my hands. For that you will have to talk to Pappa."

"But why? It is your money, no? You have earned it, no? Why you must give it all to him?"

"He is my pappa. He has spent on me all of my life. I cannot be so ungrateful."

There was a BOINNNGG-BOINNNGG from the toilet tower, but they both ignored it. "So give him, but don't give him everything. Give him for his needs. Keep the rest for ours."

"But he is my pappa. He expects me to give everything."

Bapaiji hated that argument, but kept her patience. "My pappa has got four sons," she said, "but he expects nothing. He knows they would give if needed."

There was a PAAAARRRPP, but again they ignored it. Hormusji remained silent. He looked unhappily away from his wife. "I hate to ask him for money," Bapaiji said, "but I need for the house. If you give it to me it will be the same thing, but I will not have to ask him all the time for it. Why you cannot trust me? I am your wife, no?"

Hormusji shook his head. "It is not done. I cannot do it. But you are making more money from the kustis now, no? Mamma has shown you how to make them? That is more money, no?"

"That is ten annas for one kusti, but you know how much time that is taking?" Her voice rose as she spoke. "But that is

my money — for my work. Why I should spend that on the
house when I have a husband who also works?"

She lowered her voice again. "Today was your payday, I
know," she said, squaring her shoulders. "If you give me the
money now it will be the same thing, no?"

Hormusji shook his head. "I cannot do it. He is my pappa.
I am his son."

Bapaiji picked up her things, swung her feet from where she
was sitting into her slippers on the floor, and got up as if she
couldn't argue anymore. "He is a donkey who loves to bray,
ghonchi-ghonchi-ghonchi, and you are a goat going ben-hen-
hen-hen all the time." She stamped away and was almost gone
before Hormusji could compose himself to say something, but
as she turned the corner of the house to the main entrance on the
side there was a loud BOINNG-SPLATT-BOINNG, followed
by a trumpetlike PARP-PARP-PARP-PARP-PAARRRPP! She
turned back to Hormusji right away. "See? What I told you?"

She spoke so triumphantly that he had to laugh. She'd never
heard him laugh so loudly. It made her smile. He motioned her
with his hand to come back. "Wait, no, Banubai? You are always
in such a hurry. Whose life you are going to save? I also have
something to tell. Come. Sitsit."

She came back, a little shy. He had never criticized her
before. She sat where he patted the space beside him on the
swing. "What?"

He clasped his hands in front of him and spoke more
seriously. "I am thinking of going to Bombay. I am a solicitor,
but there is no need for solicitors in Navsari. Here I can be only
a schoolteacher. Do you think that is a good idea?"

She was flattered he had asked her. Men did not ask women
such things. He was giving her the same respect as to a man.
"Yes," she said. "I think that is a great idea. I think that is the
best idea. I think we should go tomorrow. I think we should
go this night only, but I have got to pack up still."

As the two of them went into the house the soundtrack provided by Bapaiji's father-in-law reached a crescendo, accompanied by images of fireworks blazing like comets, a rocket shot from the roof of the toilet tower, convincing me that Bapaiji was dramatizing what she showed me to her own advantage. Perhaps her in-laws were not the clutch of hobgoblins and hooligans she presented — but perhaps also her exaggerations provided a more instructive truth, otherwise too plain to be seen: how she felt about them, and how she chose to reveal her feeling, was no less a part of her truth.

3

In Bombay, Hormusji slept on a wooden bench in the verandah of his great uncle's huge house on Grant Road. It was cold in December, but he took two blankets and stayed there because he wanted to please Bapaiji. He knew she had not wanted to marry him, there was only one bed in their room, and he wanted to make it easy for her. He didn't know that Bapaiji sometimes came to the verandah to look at him while he slept. One clear night she studied his face in the light of a million stars; it was long, thin, and smooth except for his moustache so narrow it might have been penciled; his cheeks, brow, and temples were composed of flat planes like the facets of a crystal. When he wore his stately black fehnta he was tall enough and imposing enough to turn anyone's head — except Bapaiji's. She had walked with Adi, the tallest man in Navsari; for the longest time Hormusji's purely physical charms had been wasted on her; but his tenderness had made an impression; and that night, in his starlit sleep, his face appeared so noble, so sad, she wanted to hold it, snuggle it, caress it, but she didn't dare.

She herself, as she readily acknowledged, was no beauty. Her jaw was wide and sharp like the edge of an axe, her ears were long, her lips thin, but her breasts were huge and she enjoyed the attention they commanded — but Hormusji, inexplicably, looked at her only from the neck up. They'd had separate beds in his father's house in Navsari, and he hadn't touched her once except socially even though they'd slept in the same room now for a year. At first it had been a relief because he'd been more an intruder in her life than a husband, but once she was secure that he wouldn't touch her she wondered why he didn't, then curiosity led to anxiety that he found her unattractive, and then to frustration because she had too much pride to tell him what she wanted. She'd thought things would change in Bombay, particularly when she'd seen the single bed in their room, but now he slept in the verandah and she sometimes stood watching him. On the starry night she watched him for two hours before going back to her bed.

The next night Hormusji's great uncle heard a noise in the sittingroom. He suspected it was Bapaiji because he'd seen her the night before looking at Hormusji in the starlight, but she must have heard him coming because by the time he was in the sittingroom she was back in her bedroom. He'd seen her on other nights too, but said nothing because he was a shy man himself who'd never found the courage to marry, but now the situation was getting strange and if he didn't say something he was afraid it would get stranger. He woke Hormusji from his sleep. "What is this, Hormus?" he said. "It is cold. The bench is hard. Why you are sleeping here?"

Hormusji blinked his eyes like an owl. He was too astonished to speak.

"You should sleep with your wife, Hormus. You should sleep inside where it is warm. Here you will only catch cold."

"I am not cold. I am comfortable. I am all right, really, Motabawa."

"What you mean you are not cold? You are shivering like a rat in a trap."

"It is okay, Motabawa, really. I am all right. I am not cold."

"No, it is not okay. I do not like people to sleep on my bench. A bench is for sitting. You should be with your wife. Go to Banu, no? She is waiting for you."

"Tomorrow! Tomorrow, I will go to Banu. Tonight I will only disturb her."

"How you will disturb her? You are her husband, not a killer. You must go tonight. This is all nonsense."

Bapaiji heard the entire exchange, but pretended to be asleep when Hormusji approached her bed loaded down with the blankets and pillows he'd brought from the verandah. "Banu, you are sleeping, yes?"

She was turned away from him and groaned as if she were deep in sleep. He asked again if she was asleep, but she was enjoying herself. She groaned again, more loudly, turning to face him, but still saying nothing.

"Motabawa does not want sleeping on the bench. The bench is for sitting only he says."

Still she said nothing, simulating instead a breath that was perhaps too deep for credibility in an attempt at a breezy snore. When Hormusji remained quiet for a while she cracked her eyes just enough to see what he was doing. He had unrolled his blankets on the floor beside her and was puffing up his pillow getting ready to lie down. "Hormus," she said, opening her eyes. "What you are doing?"

"Motabawa says there is no sleeping on the bench. And I did not want to disturb you."

"Arre, comecome, no? Sleep in the bed. What is this sleeping on the floor? You will catch cold." She moved to one side of the bed, making room for him.

He looked at her uncertainly from the floor. "It is all right? I will not disturb you?"

"Arre, disturbdisturb! What is to disturb? I am your wife, no? What is to disturb? Come, no? Sleep, sleep with me. You are my husband."

He would have been happy enough just to sleep in the bed beside her, but she put a hand behind his head and pulled him to herself, reassuring him all the while, "It is all right. I am your wife. This is how it should be."

Bapaiji would have shown me everything; she had no shame about these matters; once, when I had accidentally surprised her in the act of dressing, found her naked from the waist up, she had made no effort to cover herself, shown no embarrassment aside from an unfathomable smile; but I wasn't quite as willing a voyeur as she might have supposed — or wished. I hid in the only place in the room from which I couldn't see them — under the bed, on the cold mosaic floor, watching two sets of slippers, while the wooden slats of the bed rattled above me telling the story I dared not see for myself.

When the slats stopped rattling, Bapaiji was disappointed that she'd had to take all the initiative. "Hormus," she said, "if I had said nothing, you would have slept all of the night on the floor?"

Hormusji suddenly smiled as if he had a secret. "No," he said, offering no more explanation.

"What you would have done? Tell me, no?"

"I would have waited. I knew you heard everything. You were smiling all the time I was talking. I said, Let her have her fun. I will have my own."

Bapaiji was surprised, delighted, with his playfulness; he was different away from his parents. "Thief!" she said fiercely, pushing him out of the bed, "You stole your way into my bed."

"I stole nothing," he said, pushing her back. "This is my bed also. You are the thief for keeping it all these nights."

Soon, the slats started rattling again and I kept my focus on the black rubber slippers again in front of my face on the floor.

The Mother

Bapaiji was determined with the first stirrings in her womb that her son would be in the railways (if she had a daughter, she swore she'd make it drink milk herself). Motabawa was an engine-driver and made nine hundred rupees a month (it was a new profession then) and Hormusji, a solicitor, made only ninety, most of which he sent his father. Bapaiji was able to persuade Hormusji to keep at least enough for tramfare to and from work, even though his father thought he should walk as he had done in Navsari. "Bombay is not like Navsari," Bapaiji said, "where you can walk everywhere, jut-phut, in one minute."

As she developed her intimacy with Hormusji, she prevailed more frequently over his father. Hormusji had seen how efficiently she managed the thirty-five rupees Motabawa gave her monthly for their household expenses and felt confident trusting her with his own money, particularly when she spoke about saving it for their son.

They stayed in Bombay less than a year because there was no one but Bapaiji to care for the baby there, and she didn't want to be cooped up with it all day in the house. She insisted that the baby would be named Adi, after her sweetshop sweetheart whose family had refused her before; it was her way of finally resolving the situation. Hormusji didn't mind though his father wanted the baby named after himself, but Bapaiji stayed with the baby at her parents' house (it was the custom for a mother to stay with her parents again until the baby was at least six months old, though Bapaiji didn't stay even six months), and after that it was too late to call the baby by another name. Hormusji returned to his parents and taught once more at the same school at which he'd taught before they'd left for Bombay.

When Adi was born Bapaiji's mother yanked his arms and legs fiercely, methodically, turning his head one way, then the other, until it seemed he would never stop crying. When Bapaiji had first voiced her objection to marrying Hormusji by recounting the deformities in the Seervai family her mother had said, "Gogo, you are making only excuses," but now she wanted to make sure herself.

The baby was fine and Bapaiji let her mother and Dhunmai take care of it. She'd hated the pregnancy and she hated motherhood; it was just one more way, perhaps the most diabolical, of tying down a woman. It was not that she didn't love her baby, but she resented having to show it in the conventional womanly ways, and with both sides of the family making such a fuss over the baby there was no need for her to do anything — if anything, someone needed to be strict just to strike a balance. She let the baby stay with Dhunmai most of the time, even at night, to make her point.

One afternoon, when Adi was three months, Bapaiji found Dhunmai nursing Adi at her breast. She had a smile on her face as if she were the mother. Bapaiji strode up to her and pulled the baby away. "What you are doing?" she said.

Dhunmai looked embarrassed. "I have milk. It happens with sisters like that sometimes."

"What milk? Where you have milk?" Bapaiji tweaked Dhunmai's flaccid nipple sharply with her fingers, digging with her nails. "What lies you are telling."

Dhunmai screamed, the baby started crying, their mother came rushing. "Now what is it? What is all the noise?"

Bapaiji related the story in outraged tones, rocking the baby to make it quiet, while Dhunmai covered her breast and quietened down. To her surprise, their mother said, "So what is the fuss? Even if there is no milk the baby is quiet, and what is the harm?" She felt sorry for her youngest daughter who would never marry. This was the closest she would come to motherhood. She didn't want to take that happiness from her, particularly when it was clear how much Bapaiji resented her own motherhood.

Dhunmai smiled again; the baby was still crying and reaching for her. "Give him here," she said. "I know how to make him quiet."

Bapaiji turned her back on Dhunmai. "Sometimes it is better to let him cry," she said.

"Banu, think, no?" her mother said. "You have got bread, but you want butter also. You should be thanking Dhunmai for how much time she is spending with Adi."

"I am not thanking her for anything," Bapaiji said, rocking the baby violently to keep it quiet. "She is stealing away my baby. I am packing up and going back to my husband tomorrow." She strode from the room, rocking Adi as if to stun him into silence.

Strange to see, but easy to believe: Bapaiji never stopped stunning Dad into silence, thwarting him at every stage of his life, for which he never forgave her.

2

Things didn't work out as Bapaiji planned. The Seervais weren't willing to overlook the six month period, but when she said, "I will die on the roadside first of hunger and thirst with the baby with me," they took her back on the condition that she wasn't to step in the house itself but stay in the room where the women went during menstruation. The room was adjacent to the house but had no direct access to it. During menstruation the Seervai women were isolated in the room, their food was cooked separately, they used separate utensils and an outhouse which was a few yards from the house. Bapaiji would have to stay there for the remainder of the six months.

She hated her life during that time. She hated living in cramped quarters with bedbugs, spiders, cockroaches, lizards, and mice. No matter how much she cleaned the room it remained muddy and full of cobwebs. She could hear wolves howling in the sugarcane fields. She felt unsafe because the door had a faulty latch and she slept with a string tied from her wrist to Adi's cradle. Often, she cried herself to sleep.

One night she heard a twig crack as if something large had stepped on it. She immediately got a firm grip on the thick wooden stick with the weighted knob at the end which she kept by her side. There was a furtive tapping at the door. "Who is it?" she said in a loud voice.

"Do not shout. It is only me." It was Hormusji. "Let me come in."

She unlatched the door. He had brought a thin rolled mattress and pillow with him. "Why you are bringing all this?" she said. "I already have."

"Not for you," he said. "For me. I am staying here for the night."

"But why?"

"I heard you crying before."

"I was not crying."

"I wanted to be with you."

"But why? You will be with me tomorrow."

"You are my wife."

"But this room is only for women in their menses."

"So what do I care?"

She liked the way he looked in the dim light of her candle.

She liked the way she felt, isolated with her baby and her man and the sound of the frogs and the crickets outside. She wanted him to stay, but she liked what he was saying and would have continued the conversation except for a sound in the back of the room. She turned and swung her weighted stick without warning, striking three times before she was satisfied. She smiled; she could see, even in the flickering light of the candle, that Hormusji had turned pale. He was afraid of mice and continually amazed at how easily she killed them. "I killed my first mouse when I was four," she'd told him. "I don't even remember, but Mamma said." She picked up the dead mouse by its tail and flung it with a swing from the door. "Still you are wanting to stay?" she said.

"Yes."

"Then let us go to sleep now. It is late."

He unrolled his mattress across the room from where she had killed the mouse. She watched him as he prepared for the night, facing the candle, saying his prayers as he wrapped his kusti around his waist in three loops, and lying down at last to sleep. She wanted to cry then because he was going to stay with her all night in that room even though he was afraid of every little thing that moved. Her heart felt big and she sat by his side for a while caressing his face in the dark.

The next morning he was gone with his mattress and pillow before anyone could miss him in the house — he was even more afraid of his father than of mice — but he was back the following night and every subsequent night until it was time for Bapaiji to enter the house again.

3

Bapaiji's violin teacher was a Mussalman. He wore a red fez with a black tassel and a coat which he buttoned to his neck even in the hottest weather. He had a face like a chicken with a tiny beak of a nose and no chin. It was ten o'clock on a Tuesday morning and he stood in the Seervai sittingroom with his violin case under his arm, waiting for Bapaiji, almost afraid to sit down because the other Seervais glared at him like tigers as they passed in and out of the room without saying a word. When Bapaiji came he took a deep breath. "Are you ready, Maiji? Shall we begin?" He had his violin out of its case in an instant.

"Wait, no?" Bapaiji said. "You would like something to drink? some water, no?"

"No, it is all right. It is not so hot today."

There were trails of sweat running down his thin brown face to where his chin should have been. "It is no trouble," Bapaiji said. "Mamma," she called loudly, "get some water, no, please, for me and the teacherji? It is so hot today."

Her mother-in-law shouted from the kitchen. "Today there is no water."

"What you mean there is no water? Bring us water, no?"

Her mother-in-law appeared at the door, bent, stout, ferocious. "What I said? I am talking to the wind? There is no water. You want some oil to clean your ears?"

Bapaiji was furious but the violin teacher said, "It is all right. I am not hot. I have got to go soon. I have got another lesson far away at half past eleven."

During the lesson the Seervais talked loudly to one another. At one point Bapaiji's father-in-law shouted to Bapaiji that she and her teacher were making too much noise. Bapaiji bit her lip, but when the lesson was over she wasted no time. "What is it with all you today? What is this business Today there is no water? We are living in the Sahara Desert or what?"

Four bent old frowning women, tapping sticks angrily on the floor, responded like four Jacks-in-the-Box:

"How you can let a Mussalman in our house?"

"We could get diseases from him."

"We do not want to keep a separate glass for his water anymore."

"Also, he smells."

Her father-in-law spoke last. "Give up this vilin-filin, Banubai. We do not want Mussalmans in our house all the time. Adi could get germs from him."

Bapaiji knew what the real issue was. Everyone liked to play with the baby but no one wanted to mind it. She had started violin lessons to provide herself with a regular respite from the baby for herself, but they'd seen through her scheme. "All right," she said, "from next week I will go to teacherji's place myself instead. I am not so afraid of diseases like you are."

They said nothing to her, grumbling among themselves instead, but the next Tuesday, when Bapaiji was ready to leave the house she found herself alone with Adi. The others had left, jut-phut, as Bapaiji might have said. The image she provided was memorable: dozens of gnarled old men in wheelchairs wagging twisted sticks and hunchbacked women with long noses and chins on broomsticks ejecting themselves like rockets from the doors and windows of the house, blazing behind them trails of fire, clouds of smoke.

4

After lunch on Sunday afternoons the Seervais napped. Bapaiji rarely napped, preferring to read or weave kustis. The money she made from the kustis she saved for Adi. She'd just settled herself with a kusti on the swing in the verandah one afternoon when her mother-in-law came to her with Adi in her arms. "Our lion has gone to the bathroom in his pants," she said. "He is needing to be changed."

They called him the Lion, the King of the Jungle, because he received so much attention in the house. "So change him, no?" Bapaiji said coolly without looking up from her kusti.

With her hunched back, her mother-in-law was no taller than Bapaiji on the swing. "I have to clean myself," she said, her voice low, threatening to turn ugly. "Who is the mother?"

"Who is the grandmother?" Bapaiji said. "A grandmother is not helpless."

"A mother should not leave her son dirty," her mother-in-law said, and left without waiting for a response.

"And a grandmother should leave her grandson?" Bapaiji shouted, but she knew the old lady would not come back. Adi was crying. She flung her things on the floor and picked him up roughly. He was just an excuse for them to tell her what to do.

On the evening of the same day her father-in-law lay in his armchair in the sittingroom, his legs raised on the slats which slid from under the arms of the chair, his pajama bottoms pulled up so that his calves were bare, playing with Adi. He liked the armchair because it was good for his elephantiasis to rest his legs up high. His legs were swollen and pierced at points so that they seemed ready to ooze pus. Adi liked playing on his grandfather's huge torso, particularly to reach up and squeeze his lightbulb nose, but on this occasion he was crawling from his stomach toward his knees when Bapaiji picked him up without a word and took him to her room. "Arre, Hormus," the old man shouted. "Your wife is gone crazy at last. She has snatch my grandson from my own hands. What she is thinking? Go and bring back our lion from her clutches."

When Hormusji went to see what was wrong she said, "Adi will catch a disease from his legs. If Pappa will not keep the bandages on his legs like the doctor said, then he cannot play with Adi."

Poor Hormusji, caught between his love for his wife and his fear of his father, relayed the message. "What?" his father shouted, sitting up in his chair. "What she said? To me? In my house? Tell her to send Adi at once! You hear? At once!"

For once, Hormusji didn't jump to his father's command. He replied in a small voice. "Pappa, why make such a big fuss about such a small matter?"

The old man said nothing at first. His mouth opened, his lightbulb nose appeared to shine as it did when he was angry, and he looked at his son as if he were someone else. After a long silence he smiled, sank into his chair again. "So, the goat has finally climbed the hill." He seemed to shrink then, as if there were no need for him to appear so large anymore.

The Emancipation of Women

A series of images followed: a skinny six year old Dad in khaki uniform trotting to school, buying chana and singh from a streetvendor which was forbidden because the foodstuffs were polluted; bending over Hormusji's desk in his office for a caning for setting a bad example as the headmaster's son; unrepentant, buying bhelpuri, more polluted than chanasingh — a skinny fifteen year old, recognizable as Dad from snapshots I'd seen, walking with friends along Bombay's Chowpatty Beach from Wilson College where he was studying; skipping in a kilt with bagpipes in a room with a fireplace and a view of a castle near the University of Edinburgh where he studied engineering; leaning on a walking stick, wearing tails and a bowler in Piccadilly Circus, waiting for Bapaiji — Bapaiji laughing at Dad ("What is this ganda-gehla? what is this khenkotuck? what is this nonsense? for what you are needing this stick? you are an old man?") until he stopped carrying his stick; Bapaiji in the cabin of the *Strathaird*, lying on an unmade bed, staring in wonder out of a huge porthole at the choppy water striking the hull barely a few feet below her, over a pile of sweaters on the wide curving sill — the two of them at the Folies in Paris, Dad smiling at Bapaiji's wide-eyed admiration of the nude kaleidoscopic formations on stage; the two of them sprawled luxuriously on the plush green seats of the privileged quarters of a railway engineer as a steam engine pulled them through a flat dry Indian landscape — Dad, back in Bombay in the uniform of an army captain, a young woman on his arm as sleek as a freshwater fish, standing by a jeep in the driveway of a palatial house — Bapaiji, back in Navsari, addressing a group of men from the head of the long wooden table at which they sat; Bapaiji again, behind a nucleus of microphones in an auditorium, addressing an audience, behind more microphones in a maidan addressing a crowd.

Bapaiji was easily recognizable behind the microphones; she loved making speeches, loved the attention, telling people what she thought, and I had seen her often enough behind lecterns, podiums, at heads of tables, on daises, stages, platforms, even standing once on a chair, to recognize her stance as easily as her features. Even the image immediately prior to Bapaiji at the head of the table was familiar. The woman, sleek as a fish on Dad's arm, was Mom, recognizable from the snapshots I'd seen of their engagement, head and shoulders encased in the calyx of her sari which swirled from the width of her hips to a strip at her knees before swirling again to a fantail covering her feet, providing her lower body with the cast of a mermaid. Bapaiji had said it was her low center of gravity, nothing else, that had attracted Dad, but she was happy enough with his choice because Mom was the great niece of Jalbhai Pherozshah Cama, the industrialist, capitalist, and philanthropist, who was in all the history books. Jalbhai had been born in Navsari, but gone to college in Bombay and stayed there, but his sister, Tehmina Cama, had started the movement for the emancipation of women in Navsari. I had heard of her but knew little of what she'd done because she had died long before I'd been born and her accomplishments had been overshadowed entirely in the history books by those of her brother. I moved backward through the images until I found the one I needed, Tehmina Cama unlatching the door within the gate leading up to Hill Bungalow, Bapaiji and Hormusji reclining on the verandah talking to one of the dubras, the older people inside the house, sitting by the windows, praying, eating, talking among themselves, to themselves. It was morning, it must have been Sunday for everyone to be at home, chalk patterns had been laid in the damp mud in front of the stoop, two goats grazed in the compound to the side of the house, the two-foot Cupid on his pedestal spouted water from the stalk in his hand into the pond. "Look," Bapaiji said, rising from her chair, "someone is coming. They came in a ghora gari."

Hormusji stopped talking to the dubra but did not get up. "In a ghora gari they came? Who is it?"

"Waitwait, no? Let me put on my spectacles." Bapaiji raised her full moon, wire rim spectacles to her eyes. "It is Tehmina Cama."

"What? You are sure?"

"No, it is the king of England. Of course, I am sure. I have seen her before, no?"

Hormusji got out of his seat and came to the front of the verandah.

"Nagin," Bapaiji said to the dubro. "Go make a plate of sweets from the pinjda, little bit of everything. Go now." Bapaiji kept sweets, wafers, and khari biscuits in glass jars for just such occasions in the pinjda with its legs planted in earthen saucers filled with water to keep away termites.

Mrs. Cama was within earshot as Nagin disappeared. "Arre, Mrs. Cama," Bapaiji said, "it is good to see you at our house. How are you?"

"We are how we are," Mrs. Cama said with a smile. "So nice a day we are having, no? And how are you, Mr. Seervai?"

Hormusji opened the balustered gate as Mrs. Cama came up the steps. "Nothing to complain," he said. "The day is very nice, yes. Comecome, inside the house."

Mrs. Cama preferred to stay on the verandah because it was

such a fine morning, so the three sat again. "We are always hearing great things about your brother," Bapaiji said. "How he is doing?"

"Jalbhai is always okay — but I have my own business to conduct. That is why I have come. I cannot stay very long."

"Arre, staystay, have some food, no? Have some water. Nagin, bring food, no, for our guest?"

Mrs. Cama protested she'd just breakfasted, would soon be lunching, but Bapaiji insisted she eat something, "just to make your mouth sweet, nothing more," and Mrs. Cama complied nibbling on a single long stem of jalebi while she got to the point of her visit. Her organization for the emancipation of women needed a solicitor to draw up their constitution and not only was Hormusji the only solicitor in Navsari but he had a reputation for being sympathetic to the cause of women.

Hormusji's older brother, the first of the inmates to find the courage to present himself to Tehmina Cama, made his appearance on the verandah as if he were about to leave the house on an errand, but his ruse was painfully transparent when he sat instead beside Hormusji and gaped foolishly at Mrs. Cama. "Go, no," Hormusji said, "if you have got something to do."

"It is nothing," the older brother said with a silly smile. "It will take only a very little time."

"Mrs. Cama and I have got important things to discuss," Hormusji said. "If it will take a very little time, then go and come back. We will still be here."

The older brother left but then Hormusji's hunchbacked sister appeared, smiling, then his mother, then an aunt. The older brother kept waving from the gate, the others sat smiling in chairs around Hormusji eating the sweets Nagin had brought for Mrs. Cama.

"Everyone, listen," Hormusji said. "We have got business to do with Mrs. Cama. Please go inside, everyone of you."

His mother was the first to protest, pointing at Bapaiji.

"Why she is staying if you have got important business to discuss? Who is the mother? Who gets the respect?"

Bapaiji said she would go inside if everyone else went with her and, grumbling to themselves, smiling at Mrs. Cama, they followed her in. Hormusji concluded his business quickly. Too shy to do much for himself he'd always encouraged Bapaiji to express herself, and was ecstatic at this chance not only to be working as a solicitor but also to develop Navsari. When Jalbhai himself later offered Hormusji a job in Bombay as an industrial solicitor at a much higher salary, Hormusji declined. He often said he preferred to work for the rights of women than the wrongs of industry — but would immediately profess his admiration for what Tehmina and Jalbhai were doing for both women and industry, both were necessary for emancipation from the English.

He was pleased with his new responsibilities, but when he asked Bapaiji if she would like to be on the governing board she turned him down. Adi, already in college in Bombay, no longer made demands on her time, but fifteen years of domesticity had tamed Bapaiji to the point of questioning a woman's role outside the home. She was embarrassed to discuss it with Hormusji, but she asked their closest neighbor, Framroze, what he would do if his wife started working outside the house. "I would throw her out of the window," Framroze said. "Throw her out of the window and forget it." When she presented this argument to Hormusji, Hormusji put on his black coat and fehnta, picked up his stick, and strode to Framroze's house, an inflated Ichabod Crane, a rooster fluffed with wrath, his customarily twiglike frame appearing to swell as his customarily limp arms became bowed and firm, and his customarily white pencilthin face turned puffy and red.

When Framroze recognized the source of Hormusji's rage he capitulated easily. "Only a joke, it was, Hormusji, an empty joke, nothing more. I am sorry." Hormusji felt foolish after his majestic entry, but drawing himself to his full height he said, "If you throw your wife out from the window then you don't deserve her in the first place."

Bapaiji was inspired. Hormusji's selfesteem had been lacerated by his first wife's infidelity, for which the baby had been made to drink milk, and for himself Hormusji might remain a mouse for the rest of his life, but for her he had risen like a giant.

2

Bapaiji sat silently on one side of the table where the Committee of Eleven had met to vote on the subject of a dance workshop. She knew there were men at the table who would have voted differently had they not been intimidated by the chairman, Mr. Patel, a tiny brown man who chewed paan constantly and scowled. She was afraid to say anything herself but if she was to be more than a token woman on the committee she knew she would have to assert herself. "Wait," she said, "I think before we put this subject to rest we must think about something else."

Mr. Patel spoke impatiently. "What is it, Bapaiji? What you are trying to say?"

"I am saying," Bapaiji said, looking around the table, "that we should have a secret ballot. Otherwise, people do not vote what they think."

"What nonsense is this, Bapaiji?" Mr. Patel spat the red paan spittle into a dish full of ash on the floor by his chair. "You are wasting time. The matter has been settled."

"Waitwait, Mr. Chairman, Mr. Patel. Let me suggest a different issue for voting. Who over here thinks we should keep the vote open like it is now, raise your hands."

The men looked from Mr. Patel to Bapaiji. "What you are all looking at?" Mr. Patel said. "Raise your hands, no? whoever agrees."

Eight hands of the eleven went slowly up.

"Now I will pass this box around," Bapaiji said, picking up a shoebox from a windowsill behind her. "Write on a piece of paper what you think, Yes or No, and then let us see."

Nine ballots voted for a secret ballot. Mr. Patel fumed, "That is not the way, Bapaiji," but he'd been thwarted. The dance workshop was voted in with the next ballot.

3

More images: Bapaiji in the newspapers; Hormusji compiling a scrapbook of clippings of Bapaiji; Hormusji, one of his last appearances, fine white hair like webs of gossamer in his ears, stepping with Bapaiji from the back seat of our chauffeur-driven Ford at the gate of Hill Bungalow, the first car in Navsari, draped in marigolds, surrounded by throngs of openmouthed townsfolk, presenting it to Dad in his Captain's uniform and Mom on his arm on the occasion of their fifth wedding anniversary; finally, Hormusji dying of cancer, Bapaiji holding back tears by his bedside.

Maharani Is Coming

Bapaiji settled in her favorite armchair in the verandah of Hill Bungalow, resting her feet on the slats, to read the daily, *Jam-e-Jamshed*, the six page Gujarati newspaper she'd cofounded with Tehmina Cama almost thirty years ago. She was proud of the newspaper as she was of so many of the projects sponsored by the Women's Committee. They had classes in sewing, dance, music, drama, embroidery, Hindi — whatever someone could teach someone else wanted to learn. The Maharajah of Baroda had attended one of their annual conferences (for which Bapaiji had written a skit), and been impressed enough to initiate an annual donation of five hundred rupees, making it fashionable to donate to the cause of the Women's Committee, which enabled them to build a library and a club for the women. Bapaiji was the club's first president and remained so until she died. She wished Hormusji could have been with her for the next day's event, when the Maharajah of Baroda would award her a solid gold medal embossed with her name and new title, Rajya Ratna, Jewel of the State; he had been so proud of all her honors and medals. She wished Adi would come with Pheroza; the ceremony was to be held in the school compound where Hormusji had been the headmaster, Adi a pupil, but her relations with Adi were not like they'd been with Hormusji. Adi resented everything about her that Hormusji had encouraged. He'd even chosen a docile, eager to please, pretty wife, everything she was not — but if Pheroza had been more like herself they might have had arguments about everything. There wasn't room for more than one Bapaiji in a family, and Pheroza was wise enough to understand that, but Bapaiji wished she understood Adi's discontent better.

The pendulum clocks in the different rooms whirred and struck almost simultaneously, the cuckoo called once to mark the halfhour, the German boy fiddler in the door next to the cuckoo's played the first two lines of his quatrain. It was half past eight. I heard laughter from the diningroom past the wooden swing doors off the sittingroom. Mom and Dad were finishing breakfast. Dad was eating scrambled eggs; Mom stood behind him, hands on his shoulders head lowered, nuzzling his face, as close as Siamese twins — or, to phrase it with Bapaiji's customary irony, Siamese cats.

Bapaiji cleared her throat to warn them of her presence. Mom jumped immediately away, her face suddenly pink. Dad continued as if nothing had happened, but his shoulders became rigid and he kept his eyes on his breakfast. Bapaiji felt something shrink inside her as if a screw were being tightened. She saw they'd bought an extra loaf of bread when she'd told them one would be enough; she had even sacrificed her own two slices that morning, but Adi had to have four slices with each egg and Pheroza had to slice them four fingers thick as if she were afraid to cut herself. Bapaiji sat heavily at the head of the table. "Who is drinking this tea?" she said, pushing away the cup and saucer in front of her.

"I was," Mom said, approaching the table again, "but I'm finished. I'll clear it away."

"First, finish it," Bapaiji said. "There is still at least two annas of tea in it. We are not all rich like Camas here. We cannot afford to waste."

Mom sat next to Dad. She said, "Yes, Bapaiji," but made no further attempt to take the cup.

Dad looked up suddenly. "There is nothing to waste. There is not even two pice of tea in the cup — but why not just let it be now, Bapaiji? Too much has been said about it already."

Bapaiji took a deep breath. "Arre, yesyes, too much has been said. I will let it go. You have bought an extra loaf of bread also, do not think I have not seen, but I will let that also go. But one thing I must ask you again." She paused to inject gravity into what was to come, to allow her querulousness to smooth into plaintiveness. "Will you not please just reconsider about tomorrow, no? How it will look if my own son is not there when the Maharajah presents me with the Rajya Ratna? What I will say when people ask, Arre, but Bapaiji, where is Adi today? You only tell me what I should say then?"

Dad paid more attention to his eggs than to Bapaiji as he replied. "Say the truth. Say he has work in Bombay. Say he has his own sons. Say he cannot come everytime his Bapaiji is given a medal. Otherwise, he would have to live in Navsari only."

"Arre, but Son, there will be pehlwans. They will do wrestling and gymnastics and weightlifting. Come, no, to see them if not for me? There will be Kolah's ice cream. You like ice cream, no?"

Dad spoke, still without looking at her, his voice shaking with anger. "I am not a child, Bapaiji, that you can bribe me with ice cream and pehlwans. Besides, the pehlwans are for you only. I do not care about pehlwans. I do not like ice cream so cold like you like it." When Bapaiji began having trouble with her teeth she'd had them all removed, and now she liked her ice cream so cold that it chilled everyone else's teeth. "I have got work in Bombay to do," Dad continued. "Let us leave the subject now, let us just leave it."

"It is still about the gate, no? You are still angry about the gate money, no? That is what it is, no?"

"It is not about the gate. If I did work I should have been paid, but that is all over. Just say I had work in Bombay."

The school gate had been in need of repair. Bapaiji had volunteered to donate the money if she were recognized for her donation with a plaque bearing her name mounted on the arch over the gateposts. Her way of cutting costs was getting Dad to engineer the project. When he'd asked what he was to be paid she'd said, "We will see." When he'd submitted his first design she'd said she wanted a much larger plaque with her name in bolder letters so it could be seen from a great distance; the extra cost meant nothing. Dad completed the job, even when he realized he wouldn't be paid because he felt obligated professionally to finish what he'd begun and to obey his mother. Besides, as she never ceased to remind him, it was his old school, where his pappa had been the headmaster, where he had been a pupil; and she was his mother, not just a client; but he continued to feel she'd used him again as she'd used him times before.

Bapaiji knew she'd taken advantage of him, and knew she'd continue as long as he allowed her. How else would he learn? She received no satisfaction from besting him, only frustration. He knew how she was; he should have refused the job or settled the money problem from the beginning. "Why you cannot understand?" she said. "Everything I have is yours only. What difference it makes if I pay you? For who I am doing this? For me?"

"Yes, you are doing it for you — but even that is not the point, Bapaiji. You know that is not the point."

"Then what is the point?" She waited for an answer, but when he remained silent she said, "Never mind. What is done is done, but stay for tomorrow, no? What difference one day will make? Bombay will not fall into the sea. Stay, no, my son?"

Still, Dad shook his head. He understood vaguely that he was refusing her now to make up for his earlier inability to refuse to design her gate and other occasions when his sense of duty had overawed his common sense, that his irritation was directed as much at himself as at her, that leaving her on this important day would give him no more satisfaction than it would her, but he couldn't help himself. "No," he said. "I have got to go. I have got business in Bombay."

Bapaiji might have said more, but the doorbell rang. "That will be Thakor," she said. "Think what I have said, no? Just think. I am asking nothing else."

After she left Mom spoke. "Perhaps one of us should stay, darling," she said, stroking Dad's head. "It would mean so much to her to have family there."

He knew she was right, he knew he should stay himself, but he said, "Perhaps you're right, Philly. Would you mind very much staying by yourself? I would, but you know how it is. I have so much work in Bombay."

They both knew how it was; there was no work that couldn't wait; but the sacrifice of a night apart would ease Dad's conscience and enhance Mom's sense of her worth. "Not at all. I'll be happy to stay. It will make Bapaiji so happy."

Bapaiji had already forgotten them on her way back to the verandah, thinking instead of the things she had to tell Thakor. Thakor arrived about that time every weekday morning. He always stayed in the verandah unless he had brought something to be put in the house or Bapaiji needed something moved or fixed, but mostly she needed him at the club to set up the card tables, board games, badminton courts, sweep the floors, dust the furniture, fill the matkas with water — in short, he was indispensable.

He was always dressed the same — white Nehru cap, white shirt, baggy white pants clamped at his ankles so they wouldn't get in the way of his bicycle chain, black leather chappals, a grey sweater in the winter. Even his appearance — hollow cheeks, hair shining with Brylcreem, a few longish hairs on his chin which he called a beard, constant sweet boyish look — remained the same, except that in time his hair became greyer. When he saw Bapaiji he bowed his head immediately. "Saebji, Bapaiji, saebji. Tamhe kem chho? How are you?"

Bapaiji nodded her head. "Saebji, Thakor. We are fine."

"Everyone is fine? Seth? Bai?"

"Everyone is fine."

"Goodgood-verygood."

"Some things I want to do first, Thakor. Then I will say what you must do when the Maharani comes tomorrow."

"Yesyes, ofcourse-yes, ofcourse-yes."

Bapaiji knew he worshipped her and she loved it. After she'd run through her regular list of errands she said, "The Maharani is coming First Class in the Baroda Express tomorrow at half past eleven. She is coming here for lunch. The Maharajah will come later straight to the school. He is too busy before. You must keep a ghora gari ready for the Maharani and bring her here straight away. I will be waiting for you."

"Bachubai said she will send her motor. After all, she is a Maharani, no?"

"She is a Maharani, but we are ordinary people. We will show how ordinary people live. Tell Bachubai to keep her motor-fotor. Bring our Maharani in the ghora gari."

Bapaiji's democracy delighted Thakor. He gave one of his locomotive laughs which seemed to go on forever. "Hyuh-hyuh-hyuh-hyuh-hyuh! Yesyes, ofcourse-yes, as you say only, it shall be as you say only. Hyuh-hyuh-hyuh-hyuh-hyuh!"

When Bapaiji had concluded her business, Thakor stayed, an embarrassed look creeping into his face. "There is something else?" Bapaiji asked.

"Actually, yes, one thing."

"What is it?"

"It is like this. I have worked for you now how many years?"

"Arre, Thakor, who is counting? We are all getting old."

"I have a wife, three daughters, one got married, but I need dowries still for two, or who will marry them?"

Bapaiji understood what he was saying. "Everyone needs money," she said. "I had a son. I sent him to U.K. to study. You think I pulled money from the wind? I had to live within my means. It is the only way to learn the meaning of money."

Thakor looked embarrassed as if he'd somehow appeared ungrateful, but his mouth set in a pout.

"Arre, Thakor," Bapaiji said quietly as if to persuade him to reason, "if wishes were wings, elephants would fly. Think, no? Elephants would fly! But it is not so."

Thakor could think of nothing to say; after thirty years, working for her had become his life; she was no more able to do without him than he was able to leave her; there were no jobs for an old man in Navsari, and no one else would work for Bapaiji at the rates she paid; he needed her as much as she needed him; but she was being unfair and he remained stubbornly, silently, where he was.

"I will do one thing for you," Bapaiji said realizing how he felt. "When I go to the cinema you can come with me — for free. Three times a week we can go to the cinema. Comecome, now, what do you say? That is fair or no?"

She knew she'd won even before the big grin broke on his face. Hill Bungalow was on Station Road, near the Navsari railway station, ideally situated for the three cinema houses to advertise their movies. She'd struck a deal with the cinema houses: she allowed them to mount posters on her compound walls; they allowed her and all her guests free admission at all times. Thakor realized the arrangement did nothing to help his daughters with their dowries, but he was too much a cinemaphile to think beyond the next movie. Besides, Bapaiji said he could bring his family too — but most often he came alone and sat a few rows in front of Bapaiji in the balcony. On the occasions we accompanied Bapaiji to the movies we enjoyed his company even from the distance in the dark; his laugh, hyuh-hyuh-hyuh-hyuh, was more infectious than the movies.

2

The next day, if not for Mom, the wooden table in Bapaiji's diningroom with the cracked leathern oilcloth, rolled in a stiff uneven scroll at the edges, would not even have been wiped of the spills of the day before — not that Bapaiji was a slovenly housekeeper; she'd long accepted the humdrum in life; but as much as she enjoyed being feted by Maharajahs and Maharanis, her zeal for democracy required her to exhibit mostly her cussedness. The table was laid with the same old grainy dishes, their patterns of swallows and tulips barely discernible, that she always used, the tall brass tumblers for water; the boi fish was served without the heads removed, and chapattis. Mom tried to persuade Bapaiji to remove the heads in the kitchen as in later days she would try to have them removed for Rusi and myself. "This is nothing to do with democracy, Bapaiji. This is only making things easier for your guest. At least put knives and forks on the table, no? In Bombay we always use knives and forks. That is how educated Indians eat now." Still, Bapaiji refused, and when the Maharani asked for a fork and knife and to have the head of her boi removed, Bapaiji complied without a word, eating her own boi with a new relish, sucking repeatedly on its severed head and beady eyes. Later she grumbled to Mom: "Arre, she thinks she's an English, saying What-phot and Howdo and all. Eating with hands is not good enough for her now."

Bapaiji didn't show me much of the ceremony that followed, I suspect, because Dad wasn't there and she didn't want to reveal how she felt about it, but she did show me a smiling picture of herself in the next day's *Jam-e-Jamshed*, standing in front of a pyramid of pehlwans with a caption that read: "Wahwah," says Bapaiji, "look, no, everyone? What muscles!"

Simply Cleaning House

I recognized Bapaiji among the pehlwans; it was how she'd looked through my childhood; but the Bapaiji who shuffled now along a long dark corridor, shuffling through papers in her hand, dimly illuminated by bulbs hanging on long wires from the ceiling, looked frail, bones of matchsticks. She shuffled through her papers as much to organize the papers as to organize her thoughts. The nurse guiding her by her elbow said, "It is the next room, Bapaiji. Room 34. Remember, he is not to be excited."

A fan whirred slowly in the room on its long spindle from the ceiling. Flies drifted lazily by the window. Dad lay in the only bed in the room, attached to an IV. He made no movement when Bapaiji entered. I imagined he wasn't well enough to greet her, but it was more complicated. Bapaiji waited for the nurse to leave before leaning over one side of the bed. "How you are feeling, Adi?"

"I am dying," he said, in a disinterested voice, "thanks to you."

Bapaiji shook her head wearily. "Adi," she said, and her voice shook as I'd never heard it shake, "you are my son."

She stopped as if she couldn't go on, but Dad stared straight up at the ceiling as if he hadn't heard.

"You are my son," she continued finally, with an effort, "and I love you."

Again, she stopped, her mouth trembling too much for words, and again Adi continued to stare at the ceiling. She'd never said such things to him before.

"I have made one big mistake in my life," she continued finally, with more control. "I see that now. I have made one big mistake in my life and I could not have made a bigger. I have had a son, but I have not been a mother. I have never been a mother."

Dad spoke finally. "Bapaiji, it is too late for all this. What are you asking? Forgiveness? I don't want to hear it. Really, now, I have had enough."

Bapaiji shook her head vehemently. "Nono, Adi, you *must* listen. I am not asking forgiveness, but you *must* listen. For both of us it is important that you listen."

When Dad said nothing she continued as if she couldn't stop. "Arre, Adi, my son, you know how I am. I hated being a woman. Always I rejected the woman's role because that was just a way men had of controlling women — and I did not want to be controlled. Your pappa, my Hormusji, God bless, where would I find such another in whole of Navsari — in whole of India, maybe even in whole of the world — he understood how I was. He let me do the things men did without feeling shame — he *pushed* me to do the things men did. He was proud of what I did, he kept a scrapbook of my accomplishments — but in rejecting the woman's role I also rejected the mother's role, and that was my big mistake, my biggest mistake in my whole life — but I did not know how to reject the woman's and not the mother's."

Again, Bapaiji stopped. Again, Dad stared at the ceiling. Again, Bapaiji started. "When we sent you to U.K. you were only seventeen. Your pappa said you were still young, but I said we must find courage and send, sooner the better."

Bapaiji shook her head. "What was the hurry? Where was the fire? What I could not understand was after you had gone

I could not stop crying. I was so ashamed, but I could not stop crying. I could not understand where the womanish tears came from. Hormusji said they were a mother's tears — but I said I was the mother, and the mother, not the father, had sent the son away. I was rejecting the woman's role, but you must have felt I was rejecting the mother's role. You must have felt I was rejecting you."

Bapaiji looked away from Dad. "Between the woman and the mother I could never make a distinction. I should have had more humility; then I might have had the love of my son. I should have learned something from your pappa. With his humility you could fill the Indian Ocean."

Bapaiji paused, and in the pause I could hear what she was thinking: How to explain I do not know; after Adi Ghadiali gave me up for his sweetshop I never loved anyone the same way; simple, but who to tell such a thing?

"Look," Bapaiji said suddenly, holding up the papers she'd brought. "I have made everything out to you. You do what you want. That was what you wanted, no? That is what we have been fighting over so many times, no? It is all yours now."

"It is too late, Bapaiji. It is too late now for me for anything. I am dying."

"Arrerere, Adi, what you are saying? Nobody is dying. We are simply cleaning house. That is what we are doing. We are simply cleaning house. We can start again."

"I am dying, Bapaiji. It is too late. You could have made my life easier if you had listened before. When we had difficulties you could have helped, when I could not get jobs, when we needed money which you could have easily given, but you were too stingy, but it is too late now. This means nothing now, only so much paper."

Bapaiji clutched the papers tightly in her hand. "Arre, my son, my son, what you are saying? You were so goodhearted you never learned the value of money. You would have spent it all.

You would have let people take it from you. In my time, Adi, prices remained the same over generations — but today the same kusti costs one hundred rupees which cost ten annas when I was a girl. That is a hundred and sixty percent increase —"

"Bapaiji, when I want a lesson in economics, I will ask for it. Just leave me alone now. Please go."

"Adi, son, my love, please, just listen, no? Let me finish. Then I will go. I will leave you alone. All I am saying is I saw the first electric lights, the first engine trains, the first motor cars, the first aeroplanes, but nothing like this inflation. That is all, Adi. I wanted to protect you. That is the truth. Believe what you want, but that is the truth."

Dad looked suddenly more alive, as if he'd been waiting for the conversation that was developing. He would have got out of bed if the IV hadn't restrained him, but even so he gestured with his free arm as he spoke. "If I had spent it, it would have been my fault — but you never gave it, and that is your fault. I was not asking for your money, only my own money which was to come to me after you died, but you would not give it. What is the use now?"

Bapaiji appeared to acquiesce. "Maybe you are right, Adi. Maybe I was stingy, maybe it was my fault — but for who I was doing it? only to protect you, from your own nature. For who I was saving? For who I was living like a mendicant? Did I spend even one pice? Everything is still here. Everything is still yours. That is the truth. Believe what you want."

Dad clenched and unclenched his fist. "Arre, Bapaiji, what was I? a baby of six months or a man of sixty years that you were protecting me? What are you saying?"

"Adi, think, no? When it was time for Homi-Rusi's navjote, how I spent. I was stingy then? Think, no? I made mistakes, that is what I am saying, but when it was necessary, I spent like a fountain, no?"

"That was different."

"How it was different? It was still money. I spent it for you, on your sons. Otherwise, you would have had to spend."

Dad slapped his forehead resoundingly. "Bapaiji, please, I really do not want to talk about it. We have talked about it enough. Please leave me alone. My blood pressure is going up. I can feel it going up. Everytime we talk it goes up. Please, now, please, just leave me alone. Let me just die in peace. Please, just go away. Please, please, go away."

Bapaiji got up. "I am going. You are getting too excited. For your own good, I am going. If you want anything, you have only got to ask for it."

"I only want you to leave me alone. I only want you to go away. I will nevermore ask for anything else from you. Please, just go away from me, just get out of my sight. That is what I want. Get out of my sight. Please!"

Bapaiji wanted to kiss him; the impulse had never been stronger, but she knew how it would upset him. "I am going, my son. I am going. So sorry, I am. I am so sorry. My son, my son. Goodbye."

Still she waited, afraid it might be her last goodbye; she knew he was dying, had heart trouble, diabetes, high blood pressure, many other things. Dad finally raised himself on his elbow, began to shout. "My God, is the old woman never going to leave me alone? Am I not even to die in peace? Will someone not get this damn woman out of my sight?"

She left then in a hurry, tears flooding from her eyes, spilling in sheets over her cheeks, as she hustled into the dimly lit corridor and walked out unaided, hands stiffly to her side, papers clenched in a fist.

2

The man in the dagla whom I'd come to know as Bapaiji knelt on the grey stone floor of one of the bedrooms in Hill Bungalow, winding up a clockwork chimpanzee wearing a red cap with a bell at the tip and cymbals attached to his hands. He put it on the floor and watched it bob, clashing its cymbals, jingling its bell. A clockwork train ran around the chimpanzee, a clockwork bear lumbered by the tracks moving its head slowly from side to side, a clockwork frog leaped over the train. Other clockwork toys (I recognized them all) crawled and scurried and rang and tooted. Bapaiji had bought them during her trip to Japan and wound them for us simultaneously on special occasions. The man she'd become shrugged as I watched, as if he'd perhaps been forced to show me the bedroom scene with Dad, and her regret burst like a flood: I never went back, he did not want me. It was not right, a mother should die before her son, the son would then have understood her better, he would not have borne grudges against the dead, he would have respected the dead, but he died first, with his resentment swollen to the fullest. How I regretted, not what I had done but that he died first. I had not thought dying would be so complicated, I was taking care of my own business, I was expecting eternal unconsciousness, but when he died first I knew there was more, that could not be the end. First I said there was no God, but if there was no God there was no point in living. There was still something for me to understand, something to atone, and for that I had to go on living. I gave myself to Him, in Christianity they say Thy Will Be Done, same thing: His will, not mine. Your mamma said he remembered me in the end with love. If she was lying, God bless her; if not, praise God.

The chimpanzee was slowing down, but instead of winding him up again Bapaiji put him on a table among other toys in the same sequence that I remembered them from our navjote when they'd been on permanent display. Yes, Bapaiji was stingy — a greased needle wouldn't have made it through her purse strings, Dad liked to say — but it had never affected my admiration for her, and the occasion of the navjote, an investiture ceremony, was grand for Rusi and myself. Some of the rituals were embarrassing (dealing with cow's urine, bathing in milk before an audience of women, chanting ancient prayers with ancient priests on an open stage before a thousand guests), but the personal embarrassment was greatly compensated by the festivities.

A tent large enough to hold a circus was erected in the compound in the back with eight large woodburning fireplaces to hold the huge smoke-darkened dekchis — and what a menu! Wafers, chapattis, pickles, chutneys, eggs fried with potatoes, fish wrapped and baked with spices in banana leaves, lamb cooked with fruit, sweet juicy murrabba, rich kulfi with pistachios, soft drinks, seconds of everything. Rows of tables with white tablecloths were arranged to the side of the compound for the guests, food was served on banana leaves, to be eaten with hands, in three seatings. Rusi and I were free to roam the tent and sample whatever was available; when I was full I hung around just to sniff the air.

The Rander Takor Khana played Indian classical music on a sitar, sarod, sarangi, harmonium, and tablas. I didn't care for the music, neither did Mom nor Dad nor Rusi, we were too sophisticated, too westernized, neither did Bapaiji who preferred the Hindi music of the movies, but the people who knew about such things assured us it was sublime. It was certainly, as Bapaiji constantly reminded us, expensive. In Bombay we might have had the music we preferred, Goody or Nelly on accordian with their bands playing Western popular music, "The Cuckoo Waltz," "Wonderful Copenhagen," "Goodness Gracious Me," but Bapaiji had undertaken the expenses conditionally (the navjote had to be performed in Navsari), and Dad hadn't complained. There'd even been accommodation for friends from Bombay, which provided welcome secular overtones to the sacrament.

Between the Mosque and the Temple

Bapaiji was awakened every morning by the crowing, kuk-re-ku, of the rooster. She was out of her four poster bed almost as soon as she was awake. The dubri Pemmy, who had lived with her husband for years in a single room abode with walls and roof of mud and corrugated metal in Bapaiji's back compound, was already sweeping the floors. When Bapaiji got out of bed Pemmy folded the blankets and raised the mosquito net. As she got older Bapaiji relied increasingly on Pemmy, not only for household chores but companionship.

The sun would be rising as Bapaiji said her kusti prayers, and the other morning birds, koels, sparrows, bulbuls, announcing their presence. One morning she said an extra Ashem Vohu prayer because she was anxious about the outcome of the day.

Ashem Vohu	Blessed Is Virtue
Vahistem Asti	The Highest Good
Ushta Asti	The Greatest Happiness
Ushta Ahmai	He Who Loves Virtue
Hyat Ashai	For Its Own Sake
Vahishta Ashem	Will Find Virtue Is Bliss Untold

As Chairman of the Sanitation Committee Bapaiji had to settle a dispute between a Hindu and a Mussalman faction about the placement of a rubbish bin. The Hindus said it was too close to their temple and wanted to move it farther away, but the Mussalmans said it was already too close to their mosque and wanted to move it closer to the temple. The Collector, who was responsible for the collection of revenue for the Seervais in the surrounding wadis, had warned that a bloodbath might ensue if she weren't careful. It wasn't safe for a man, let alone a woman, but Bapaiji had said she was the chairman and set a day to examine the site.

After saying the extra prayer Bapaiji put on a plain cotton blouse, a plain sari with a plain border, and plain black walking shoes with plain brass buckles to look more businesslike. The accouterments of women, bangles and rings and tilas, she never wore. She breakfasted on one egg, one slice of bread, one cup of tea which she slurped from the saucer because it was too hot, while listening to the news on her Murphy radio. The Collector sent a car to pick her up, but she sent it back. She had chosen to walk because it wasn't far and she wanted to show the people she was just like them; but she was glad the two committee members who had come with the car stayed with her. They would have been little help in a riot but she was glad for their moral support.

The day became hotter as she set out and she held up the sash of her sari to shield her eyes from the sun. Along the way a group of students from Hormusji's old school recognized her and said, "Saebji, Bapaiji, tamhe kem chho? How are you today?"

Bapaiji stopped. "Sari kani, I am well, but we have got some important work to do. We cannot wait around for chitchat."

"Where you are going, Bapaiji?"

Bapaiji smiled suddenly; a thought occurred to her. There were Hindus and Mussalmans among the students. She re-membered Gandhiji's salt march during which Hindus and

Mussalmans of both genders and all castes and ages had united in a show of solidarity against the English. "Comecome, see for yourselves. We are not going far. Everyone, come."

The students followed her and, as they walked, more people joined them, three women with baskets of vegetables on their heads on their way to the Mota Bajar, two men carrying a crate of tiffins between them on their heads on their way to the college, chanawallahs doing business as they walked, other hawkers, begging children, an acrobat, street animals, loafers. "Comecome," the students said as if they were on a picnic. "Come, see what is going to happen."

Soon the Collector's car approached them again and the Collector himself got out. "Why you didn't want the car, Bapaiji? It would have been better, do you not think?"

Bapaiji called him with her hand. "Come with us. See for yourself."

The Collector understood. The retinue Bapaiji was building for herself was more impressive than a Rolls Royce. The populist way was always more effective than the aristocratic approach. He took his place by her side.

Bapaiji led the parade, the men mostly in white, the women more gaily dressed, with dogs and goats and chickens, along the dusty wadis, the dirt paths, the cobbled streets, past the tiny huddled shops of cobblers, tailors, potters, other artisans, around phlegmatic cows swishing tails at flies, past pyramids of dry dung, amid a constant ringing of bicycle bells and honking of scooter hooters. When a white cow stood in their path, Bapaiji genuflected and others did the same. She was enjoying herself; if she somersaulted she was sure the others would have followed.

When they got to the rubbish bin the Hindu and Mussalman spokesmen and their followers stared with their mouths open, not just at the crowd but that the chairman was a woman. The Hindu, a fat man with a red handkerchief knotted at its four corners on his head, a kurta, a dhoti, and chappals, said, "Maiji, Maiji, you are the chairman? Maiji, you are the chairman?"

"Yes," Bapaiji said. "Why you are so surprised?"

"Nothingnothing, but you are the chairman?"

The Mussalman was much darker, wearing a red fez with a black tassel, a brown jacket buttoned to his neck even in the heat, and brown tailored pants which revealed red socks at his ankles over worn dusty brown shoes. He said nothing, but his brow was wrinkled in puzzlement so that his eyebrows became one long ridge.

Bapaiji got straight to the point. "The solution is simple," she said, "but we have all got to be reasonable. We have got to find the place *exactly* between the mosque and the temple. I want you both to walk with me from the mosque to the temple and count my footsteps."

Bapaiji spoke with such assurance that a passerby might have thought she had rehearsed the event. A rope was held from the mosque to the temple for accuracy and Bapaiji walked alongside holding the rope. The Mussalman walked grudgingly, stiffly, to one side as if he were not with them, his brow still wrinkled as if he were thinking important thoughts, counting in his mind. The Hindu walked with Bapaiji, counting aloud in a singsong voice as if he were learning numbers in school. The crowd counted along just to add thunder to the proceedings.

They counted exactly two hundred and thirty-two steps to the temple. "Now," Bapaiji said, turning to the enthusiastic crowd. "What is half of two hundred and thirty-two?"

A number of cheerful voices replied, "One hundred and sixteen, Maiji. One hundred and sixteen."

She asked them to count with her again as she walked back to the mosque and stopped at a hundred and sixteen. "This is the middle point," she said. "This is where you must put the bin." It meant moving the bin closer to the temple and farther from the mosque. Bapaiji was relieved because she'd felt the Hindu would give in more easily than the Mussalman. "This is the best place," she said. "This is the fair place. What do you think?" She looked squarely at the Hindu.

The Hindu looked at his followers who nodded. He beamed. "It is fair, Maiji. It is fair." The Mussalman did not smile, said nothing, but nodded his approval without even looking at his faction. Both thanked her, said it was a wise decision, they were in her debt, if she ever needed anything she had only to call and they would come.

"Anyone could have provided the solution," Bapaiji said later, "but it helped that so many came with me, also that I was a Parsi, not a Hindu or a Mussalman — and it helped even more that I was a woman. That just surprised them too much to argue."

2

When George Bernard Shaw was feted on one of his nonagenerian birthdays, he presented himself apologetically as just an old man instead of the legend some might have expected. The self-effacement was probably tongue-in-cheek, but his appearance was unmistakably frail, disbelieving, tentative, selfconscious, even timid — in one word, humble. Bapaiji was not much different in her last days. She spoke of death with curiosity more than resignation or fear as if readiness were everything. She had outlived her generation, even her son; those who remained admired her, wished her well, took care of her; Thakor, who now went to the cinema alone though still as her guest, still visited her in the mornings; Pemmy, with a family of her own in the compound behind the house, was always a bellpush away; Mom, who had doubled their salaries on the sly to allay Bapaiji's fear of inflation, stayed with her almost constantly; friends, associates, acquaintances, visited in the evenings; but none, of course, could give her back the world she had known. Like Shaw, she appeared unbowed but grateful, aware of her debts as much as her triumphs.

On Bapaiji's ninety-fifth birthday, the Collector organized a function in Seervai Wadi where speeches were made in her honor, a lifesize photograph was unveiled, and a purse was presented of one thousand, one hundred, and eleven rupees. Bapaiji made a speech in an old froggy voice, but instead of recounting public triumphs as was her custom she credited Hormusji with making the triumphs possible. She slept that night with my birthday card, received the same day, under her pillow, the largest card I could find so she could read it easily. She appeared so frail she might have snapped if you'd held her. The next morning she was dead. Mom found an unfinished letter addressed to me on her writing desk:

My Dear American Grandson, Hormus,

It has been a great day, but more than anything else I am so happy that you remembered my birthday. I know you are a busy man with your experiments and college and life in America, but I am happy that you did not forget an old woman's birthday. Your mamma was also there. She has been with me since your pappa died, God bless him. And God bless her. She has been my greatest comfort in this difficult time. I could not manage without her. I wish I had been more like her sometimes. My gifts, such as they were, were more selfish. But I am more tired than I thought and I have still got to say my prayers. I will finish this letter tomorrow....

The letter was the only indication that she had not anticipated death; otherwise, she had blotted the letter, capped the fountain pen, put the squat bottle of Quink ink in its box and into its corner in the drawer, arranged her thicklensed, fullmoon spectacles neatly on the page, said her prayers, turned out the light, arranged her slippers neatly by the bed, they might have been on exhibition — and lying on her side, clutching my birthday card under her pillow, whispering God's will be done, passed directly into sleep.

GRANNY

The Long Dining Table

I saw Bapaiji dead, fragile as an unwrapped mummy, lying on her side in her black four poster bed, green nightlight and switch embedded in its headboard, snug within the mosquito net, one hand under her pillow touching my card — and the needles in my head temporarily ceased their activity.

The fantastic turned into the familiar. I recognized my childhood bedroom in Mayo House on Cooperage Road as my eyes, now open, became slowly comfortable with the daytime darkness induced by the drawn curtains. I recognized the red bookshelves still holding the entire James Bond series in the flexible Pan bindings, and Perry Mason and Agatha Christie Pocket Books sporting the kangaroo and cardinal emblems. I recognized also the black elephant bookends with ivory tusks, and below the shelves pinups of Brigitte Bardot and Sophia Loren alongside pictures of Einstein, Pasteur, Newton, Madame Curie, Alexander Hamilton, Edward Jenner, Jonas Salk, and Albert Sabin. My desk with the elephant lamp lined one wall, so did the Telefunken stereo. The electric clock we'd brought from Hong Kong, a gift from my incomparable Sohrab Uncle, was mounted overhead, a miller and his dog hiking toward a windmill with spinning vanes on the clockface.

Dr. Horvath knew what he'd been talking about; the rec-
ognitions were already providing a balm; I couldn't wait to
rediscover my old possessions. I got up and walked slowly to
the cupboard to browse through my record collection and other
artlessly variegated, newly meaningful, rosebuds: Dinky Toys,
Matchbox cars, Rolleicord camera, magnetic compass, coin
collection, stamp collection, Chemistry set, Bayko set, Meccano
set, skittles set, Odhams Encyclopedia, Collins Dictionary, Gray's
Anatomy, Photoplay magazines, navy blue schoolties with di-
agonal red and white bands across the center, and prize books
for my scholastic achievements: *Oliver Twist*, *Robinson Crusoe*,
Swiss Family Robinson, *Lamb's Tales from Shakespeare*, *The Three
Musketeers*, *Lorna Doone*. Each recollection set off a hum of
rediscovery countering the drum in my temples, as if I'd unexpectedly recognized an old friend.

I was distracted by the cawing of crows, a harsh nasal sound.
There is a time in the evening before twilight when they call
incessantly, ritualistically, to one another. I'd seen them gather
in the hundreds once in a maidan, flying and cawing over a dead
rat; they might have been disputing a point of etiquette or law.
I'd been momentarily frightened thinking I'd underestimated
the intelligence behind their cruel black faces. Their cawing
more than Sohrab Uncle's Hong Kong clock told me it would
soon be dark and I stepped into the verandah to catch what I
could of the evening.

My first awareness was of heat, then of people. I never felt
entirely alone in Bombay; even with no one else in the flat the
bustle of the city stayed with me. You didn't walk as much as
elbow your way through Bombay crowds; and by night there
were always people on charpoys, even just sheets, in the streets.
When I saw my first deserted street in Aquihana (it wasn't even
night), I wondered what had happened to the people.

I could feel the heat reminding me I was unwell, but if I
could only make it to the railing of the verandah, just a few feet

from the door, I was sure I'd be all right. I almost tripped over a bathstool in the way; the ganga must have forgotten to return it to the bathroom after she'd hung the clothes on the line. I ducked to avoid the clothes swaying in the slight warm breeze. Above the clotheslines Mom had rigged a wire trellis and entwined it with mani plants so the ceiling was invisible for the leaves.

By the time I reached the railing I was tired. Below me (we lived on the third floor) was the same rubble gathered around the brick wall where it had collapsed five years ago. The wall separated our parking spaces from the spaces for the adjacent building. Fiats, Ambassadors, and Standard Heralds were parked on either side of the wall around the rubble as they'd been five years ago, incorporating the rubble into the overall design.

To my right, behind the house, were the Back Gardens, a large triangle of space, occasionally grassy, occasionally sandy, occasionally earthy, with swings, a slide, a jungle jim, two tennis courts, and a banyan in the center so large you could have lived in its vines. Narrow alleys, infested by rats, filled with refuse, dung-encrusted, led from the corners of the triangle to the main streets.

The triangle also provided recess grounds for the Campion School for Boys (my high school, a tall, bright, imposing, red and white building) and the Fort Convent School for Girls — but our recesses were staggered so there was no mingling. It was also the ground for morning assemblies, PT classes, ACC drills, scout meetings. The scouts gathered every Saturday morning behind the banyan for a glimpse of Cecilia, the prostitute, who sometimes appeared in a black negligee at her third floor window with her lover of the night before, frequently a balding man, smoking a cigarette, wearing a sleeveless undershirt, and they'd smile and wave and kiss for our benefit. I swore I'd someday rescue Cecilia though she'd never revealed signs of distress.

No such compunction had assailed me when Dad had taken me (to show me the world) to The Cages on Lamington Road where the prostitutes stood behind bars soliciting men, inviting them into the rooms in the back. They were different from Cecilia who could have passed for any of the Goanese Christians I'd known among my teachers and ayahs, even among Mom's friends — but the women in The Cages, some of whom might have been no older than thirteen, were too gaudy in their appeals for my sympathy, their saris too bright, faces too heavily rouged and powdered, hands ornate with mehndi, ears and noses weighted with rings, wrists jangling with bangles, wearing the anklets of slaves and prisoners. Besides, they called too loudly, too eagerly, to arouse desire, and their cages were not unlike those of the monkeys at the Victoria Gardens Zoo.

I was fascinated, but hardly aroused — but Cecilia was different. Derek D'Souza, who'd carried an FL in his wallet for three years ("Arre yaar, you never know when it might come in handy"), gave her his highest rating: ten jhing-jhangs, while the girls in The Cages rated only one jhing-jhang apiece, owing more to the kindness of the scouts than merit of their own. Derek's Trojan, to complete that story, came to the same end as all Trojans of that time: filled with water it burst at one of the scout camps.

To my left, across Cooperage Road, behind the corrugated metal walls of the Cooperage Stadium, was a function, the overflow of which spilled onto the road. It was where Campion School had its annual Sports Meet. I couldn't tell what the function was from the crowd — perhaps a hockey match, a football match, or something else, none of which held much interest for me. Crowds gathered around the bhelwallahs, chanawallahs, bhajiawallahs, ice cream wallahs; men lit cigarettes and bidis from slow burning ropes hanging by the hawkers' stalls lit by hurricane lanterns and petromaxes; others chomped paan spitting reddened saliva everywhere. The theme from "Come September," arguably the most popular of Western hit records in Bombay alongside "Spanish Gypsy Dance" by Edmundo Ross and His Orchestra and "Walk, Don't Run" by the Ventures, played over the loudspeakers.

I'd begun to come alive recalling the early memories, but "Come September" affected me like a cliché, made me tired, aware of the heat wrapping itself around me like a wet blanket — of the flies, two of which cavorted boldly on the railing by my hand, one astride the other, a third rubbed its forelegs, a fourth buzzed overhead like a bee.

We'd become experts with flyswats, Rusi and I, during Sunday afternoons at Granny's, between chicken lunches at one o'clock and teas with pastries from Bombelli's at four, massacring flies by the dozen. We took pleasure in our skill, the taut give of the swinging swat, the bloodless kill. It wasn't unusual for us to tally a hundred flies each in Granny's diningroom with the long oak dining table, covered with the white linen tablecloth, set with a slender frosted blue vase holding sunflowers from the garden. Ten stately chairs attended the table, crystal chandeliers bathed it with light — but the ceilings were so high, the wattage of the bulbs so low, that the rooms and corridors seemed cavernous, and the ceiling fans needed the longest spindles. The flies camouflaged themselves against the speckled tiled floor, against the dim grey walls holding prints of Watteaus, Fragonards, Constables, and Turners, and against the stiff, long, heavy, gold drapes — but in vain.

When we were done with the flies, I'd lie in the Morris chair in Soli Mama's room. Soli Mama, Mom's kid brother, had lived with Granny until he'd married and moved from her flat on the first floor to his own on the ground. While I slumped in Soli Mama's chair Rusi jumped on his bed until Granny, waking from her nap, asked him to stop before he broke the springs.

She hated to prohibit us from anything, and to compensate for the prohibitions gave us three rupees for comics (*Superman,*

Spiderman, *The Flash*, *Justice League of America*) from Warden
Book Store, Kamal Book Store, or Shemaroo, circulating librar-
ies near her house. In the mornings we might have started a
game of Monopoly with Cyrus Mehta from the second floor
and Anand Patel from the fourth, the game to be interrupted
when we left for lunch at Granny's, resumed when we returned
— though not until Cyrus and Anand had first digested the
comics. We rarely completed a game of Monopoly.

Strange: I saw less of Bapaiji than of Granny but I knew her
better, perhaps because during our two-week stays in Navsari
I was swept entirely into Bapaiji's world having none of my
Bombay ties to distract me, but during our Sunday afternoons
with Granny I was continually aware of the discontinued
Monopoly game from the morning, and Cyrus and Anand
awaiting our return with the comics. Granny's world was not
as sweeping, she spent much time alone, shunned physical
contact, was uncomfortable with small talk, screamed readily at
her servants, and toward the end she had kind words for only
her children and grandchildren.

Bapaiji's activities were never a secret (her morning prayers
awakened us, Rusi and me, her stories of Sohrab and Rustom,
of Rama and Sita, and of Aladdin, Sinbad, and Ali Baba put us
to sleep), but I couldn't imagine what Granny did with her time.
I knew she read because she received *The Illustrated Weekly of
India* and *Eve's Weekly*, but she was always finished with them
by the time we arrived, so it was hard to imagine her actually
reading them. We saw her eat, nap, and play endless games of
patience, but that was almost all.

I knew also that she took drives along Marine Drive because
I'd seen her once through the crowd of strollers — groups of
teenagers, families with baby carriages, people walking dogs,
couples holding hands, hawkers shouting wares, black smoke
drifting from the chulas of the chanawallahs keeping warm their
mounds of chana and singh, columns of paper cones wedged

alongside. She sat in the back of her huge creamy Studebaker (the tiny Fiats and Ambassadors never suited her) with one of her cardplaying friends, the back door open to let in the sea breeze, while her uniformed chauffeur squatted on the sidewalk in his Captain's hat. I'd waved my cane from the distance (I was with Rusi and Anand and Cyrus and didn't want to hold them up), but she didn't respond. She might not have seen me (her eyesight was deteriorating); she might also have questioned the propriety of my gesture, hailing her so commonly through a crowd — but having seen her just once by the sea, I found it hard to relate that image to the person with whom we lunched on Sundays.

Sadly, the image of Granny in her car by the sea corresponded with what we learned of her later, cruising Warden Road in her chauffeur-driven Studebaker looking for a ganga to sleep with her overnight because she was afraid to sleep alone. She couldn't pay the servants enough to stay because she screamed at them for the least thing. Soli Mama said there was nothing to fear: he lived downstairs from her and there was a chowkidar at the gate all night. When she continued to solicit strange women for the night, Mom began sleeping over. When Dad objected, she sent me and Rusi over to spend the nights. When it interfered with our homework, Mom found a servant she trusted to stay overnight.

"Come September" had weakened me and a renewed tug of voices in my head weakened me further. I left the railing to sit on the bathstool, my face in my hands. Granny's voice was in ascendance. "Homi, this is Granny. Please listen carefully. I have been waiting a long time to talk, but you know how Banubai is. There is no stopping her once she gets started."

Granny insisted on calling Bapaiji by her real name. "She's not *my* bapaiji," she said, which of course was beside the point. It was her nickname as much as a sign of respect, but they were entirely different: Bapaiji preferred to eat with her hands scrap-

ing even fishheads clean with her teeth, Granny preferred an
entire table setting whether or not she used it; Bapaiji's cycle
rickshaw was a symbol of the proletariat, Granny's Studebaker
of the aristocracy; Bapaiji wanted to make a difference, Granny
wanted to maintain the status quo. Granny admired Bapaiji
openly, even envied her, but never understood her well enough
to be comfortable. Perhaps she insisted on calling her Banubai
as much to maintain her own identity as to confuse Bapaiji's.

"I know how exhausted you are, Homi, I know how sick,
but I have to say just one thing first; then, when you are rested,
I will say the rest — but first let me say it, I love you, my Homi,
my dearest, I love you. This will sound strange to you because
I never said it before, but I should have said it, I should have
said it often, because it is the truth, because it would have been
good for us both. I would have shown it more but things
happen, disappointments make you brittle, afraid to break. It
happened to me. It could happen to you. I shall do what I can
to prevent it. Where shall I begin?"

Granny seemed to have forgotten, but she'd told me once
she loved me, at one of our Papeti lunches at the long table with
Mom, Dad, Rusi, and Soli Mama. We had sweet buns with
butter, patrel, mince pattices, baked chicken with cherries, and
a strawberry souffle. Rusi and I were too young to follow the
conversation, and too interested in the food to care — but I was
hardly as invisible as I'd imagined. The cherries in the chicken
dish had been pitted, but I came upon one that had not, and
slipped the pit back into the serving dish not wishing to clutter
my plate, but Granny noticed though at first I couldn't be sure.

"Homi," she said, cutting through the conversation at the
table (she was at the head, Mom to her right, then Dad, then
Rusi, Soli Mama to her left, then myself), "you are a very good
boy, my oldest grandchild, and I love you."

I'd braced myself for a reprimand, but she'd said she loved
me. I didn't know what to expect next. I didn't have to wait long.

"When you were born I was so happy I didn't think it was possible. When you developed the polio I prayed for three hours everyday for a month. It's better now but I still remember you in my prayers everyday that someday you will be completely cured."

I was beginning to relax though I didn't understand what had precipitated her reminiscence. The others looked on curiously. "Then we learned you were a genius, not just intelligent, but a genius. I was so proud — and I am still proud. There is almost nothing I wouldn't give you if you wanted it."

Even Rusi had stopped eating. I was so taken by her encomium I'd even forgotten the pit. "But don't you think," she continued, "it was naughty of you to put that pit back in the serving dish?"

I wanted to crawl under the table. I reached to take the pit back, but Granny said, "Leave it now, but don't do it again. It was not a nice thing to do." She explained what had happened while I looked appropriately chastised and woebegone. I said "Sorry" when she was finished and the matter was ended. What strikes me now more than my embarrassment at the time is the length to which she'd gone to soften her reproach. She screamed so easily at the servants that her tirades might just as easily have been directed at me, but I needn't have worried; she never shouted at her grandchildren; I don't think she could have lived with herself if she had.

We never learned what killed Granny; she was sick but refused to visit the doctor, refused to have the doctor visit her; she did not want to live, and the doctors wanted only her money, so she said. At least, she didn't die alone, but surrounded by her three children, Mom, Jalu Masi, and Soli Mama, in her bedroom, talking in her chair. Her head drooped midsentence. I'd felt no remorse when Bapaiji died; she'd been in readiness, she'd slept with my card under her pillow. Granny was the less responsive grandmother, appeared to need less but needed more;

I wished I could have sent her off with a card or letter to hold in her lap, but when she stopped replying to my letters I stopped writing. If I'd continued writing she might have died more happily and I'd have received the news with more equanimity. There were times I'd thought of her as Miss Havisham sternly directing Pip and Estella to "Play," but now she and other members of my family, dead and alive, seemed more like characters constructed by the Ghost of Christmas Past, and I an ever unlikely, increasingly curious, increasingly penitent, Ebenezer Scrooge.

Cambridge

Granny sat at the head of her long dining table, but not as I'd ever seen her, wearing a dress, not a sari which was all I'd seen her wear, her features smooth as porcelain, without the grandmotherly lines I knew. Her chin, cheeks, mouth, and eyes were so tiny, so finely sculpted, and tinted (except for her nose, too thin, too long, too shiny even in a dim light), that they brought to mind the sharp toylike elegance of freshwater fish; I could see Mom in her face like a palimpsest. I couldn't see her legs, under the table, but her arms suggested they would be thin and supple with the spring of an antelope rather than thick and muscled with the kick of a pony. I recognized her by her expression (haunted, afraid something or someone were about to grab her) and the cards she had spread before her (Lion and Unicorn on the back, decks she'd brought back from Cambridge). I recognized also the stately chairs, the chandelier, the showcases with the *Venus de Milo*, crystal goblets, china dishes, cutglass vases, porcelain figurines, but I wasn't prepared for the sight beyond the balcony at the far end of the room: elm trees, bare and bowed with snow, a hare in midjump, hindlegs motionless as if caught in a photograph, blurry against the flurry of snow kicked up by its feet. Snow! In Bombay! I looked more closely, for something to discredit my fantastic notion, but found instead something to verify it: a fireplace behind Granny, where the doorway should have been, enhancing the cavernous appearance of the room.

"Homi, no, you are making a mistake. Yes, an understandable mistake, but a mistake. Yes, this *is* Zephyr, yes, my Bombay house, but, no, it is *not* in Bombay. I had a choice. I could put it anywhere I wanted. Banubai has already explained it to you so I won't go into it again, but it was unfair of her to make fun of me for wanting to stay in my house. Maybe there is more to life than chandeliers and paintings, but that's what I was accustomed to and that was what I wanted — and she's hardly in any position to criticize me. She should take a sharp look at herself before she says anything about anyone else. In those baggy white trousers so short you can see her ankles she could pass for someone's bearer. She makes fun of your pappa's walking stick, but she still carries the stick her fancy man gave her, with the snake head. She still clings to her fantasy of him.

"It was a good thing she had so many interests; a commotion of people and events keeps you from imagining things, it keeps you from going crazy. Not that it matters, of course, once you're here; it's not as if you can change anything. So if she chooses to be a man, and I choose to situate my house in Cambridge, why does she have to make an issue of it? Yes, that is snow outside, Cambridge snow — Cambridge, England — and yes, the elms are Cambridge elms, and yes, the hare is a Cambridge hare. The years I spent in Cambridge, chaperoning your Soli Mama while he was at King's College, were the happiest of my life. I resided at The Queen's Arms, not far from the Great Bridge over the Cam from which Cambridge got its name, where I met some of the staunchest bridge and bezique players — Agnes McGuiness, Muriel Fitzwilliams, Sarah Allsop, Nora Bomford, Iris Masters — most of them widows like myself. All of them had been married to armywallahs and spent some time in India. Hence, our amity.

"They called me Mary. Meher was too difficult. They kept calling me May-her, accenting the first syllable so ponderously that I had to correct them every time. Finally, Agnes McGuiness said, 'Why don't we just call you Mary, my dear, if it's all the same to you.' Actually, I preferred it. It made me feel like one of them though they always deferred to my opinion when we dined at the Koh-i-noor or the Taj Mahal despite their own vast experience with Indian cookery, and I continued to wear saris — I hadn't worn a dress in so long I'd have felt uncomfortable. Besides, it's true what Edith Sitwell said about Englishwomen, that they dress as if they'd been mice in previous incarnations, or hoped to be in the next.

"Still, despite their appearance the English are the most splendid people. Their very rectitude is charming. Muriel Fitzwilliams never lost the opportunity to tell a new acquaintance her story about the wife of a senior officer, a burra mem. It seems they were to go shopping together and Muriel arrived to find the mem's bearer straddling her in bed massaging her back with the gravest expression on his face. I won't tell you what she was wearing because she wasn't wearing a thing, not a stitch, but she said without an iota of embarrassment: 'Quite all right, my dear. Quite all right. I find this works wonders for the digestion.'

"These were marvelous women and they made marvelous friends, whether we walked along the puntfilled river shaded by willows to Clare Bridge or shopped along the narrow lanes of Market Hill lined with stalls. I still remember how Clare Bridge looks in a dim light — a fog or a late evening — how the arches of the bridge kiss their reflections in the water creating lovely orange shapes between them. And one of my favorite walks was along Magdalene Street to the Bomford House amid a row of stately old homes with bay windows, projecting storeys, and steep russet roofs. I must admit that I don't much care for walks, much prefer drives, but the English are the

greatest people in the world for walks, and I obliged them
mostly out of friendship.

"They looked out for me too. Being a foreigner I took the
utmost care not to give offense, but there were times I needed
rescuing. I was shopping for flowers once with Agnes when one
of the shopkeepers held an undergarment with laces and stays
in my face and barked, 'Ere yer are, lidy, jest whatcher want fer
yer figger! Ten bob and it's yers — it's a gift — who says ten
bob?' I don't think he meant to thrust it in my face. He was
just holding it up and I just happened to turn around, but all
of a sudden there we were, frozen in that wretched tableau, with
everyone in Market Hill watching — at least, that was how it
seemed to me. I was embarrassed as much for the undergarment
in my face as my inability to follow his accent, but Agnes was
quick to intercede. 'My dear man,' she said, taking the garment
from him, 'what this lady wants for her figure could be had for
nothing, because it's nothing short of nothing she wants.'

"Everyone smiled, but I turned directly to a flower girl and
bought a dozen violets. Later, when Agnes told me what the
man had said, we both laughed. I thanked her, and she said it
was nothing.

"When they found out I'd once played the sitar, Nora
Bomford got me one that her husband had brought back from
India as a souvenir and said I could keep it as long as I stayed
in Cambridge. 'Much better to have it used, my dear,' she said.
I hadn't played the sitar since I'd been married because your
grandfather, Rustomji Jamshedji, whom you unfortunately never
met, said it was a servant's instrument. Good Parsis played only
the piano or the violin. It was so silly, this pilgrimage to all things
Anglo, but that is how it is with us Parsis. Jehangirji Kawasji
Daboo named his daughter Bachubai Guinevere Pestonji insisting that her great aunt, a few times removed, had been an
Englishwoman. He was too obsessed with his notion to recognize how the ridiculous juxtaposition of names had exposed his

despair that he wasn't English himself. Anyway, I was delighted to have the instrument and I played for them and even gave Nora some lessons, teaching her what little I knew about ragas and talas.

"Those were halcyon days. I chose the Gogmagog Hills, southeast of Cambridge, for the new site of Zephyr because between the east and west balconies of the house I can see King's College, the pinnacles and cupola of its gateway, the buttresses, and the wonderful backs. If I use my telescope I can see the heraldry, the woodwork, the window tracery, the ducks by the river when the season is right, even the striped awnings of the stalls on Market Hill. Of course, I don't need a telescope, even with the Gogmagog Hills some five miles from the town. As I've said, as you know now, one can have what one wishes here merely by wishing it so long as it doesn't interfere with someone else's wishes, but I don't wish to leave the house, and the telescope adds to the reality of it all.

"Winter is my favorite season. I keep it snowing much of the time and my fireplace crackling. I like the warmth of a fireplace in winter more than the warmth of summer. It's toastier, I don't feel the obligation of walks in the sun with friends — and best of all, unlike the summer, I can turn off the heat. Besides, I like the winter scenes better; the snow becomes a motif for the entire landscape: adults shoveling pathways to their doors, children throwing snowballs, animals leaving deeper prints — and, of course, the fireplace in winter deepens the luxury of tea and hot buttered toast — or scones, or buns, or eclairs — or later in the day, of glasses of sherry with olives, or sausages, or cheese straws.

"Next to the snow I like the rain. Its patter on a windowpane enhances the spell of the fireplace while enveloping the landscape in its own intrinsic personality: glistening streets, dripping elms, a rustle of raincoats, and, with the radiant arc of a rainbow, the crystalline song of a thrush.

"Unfortunately, the rainbow heralds the sun, and I have never liked the sun. At its best it is warm, but it is too often too bright, too hot, for comfort. The sun exposes more than enhances life. It forces one to squint, adding lines to one's face. Of course, goggles are available for those so inclined, but goggles are for actors, who live on the words of others, and for other such lesser luminaries who parade themselves for the same superficial attention. Worst of all, of course, the sun darkens the skin.

"Perhaps I should add that I recognize my affectation, I recognize my minority status as a cloud worshipper, both for obstructing the sun and heralding rain; even Muriel and the others wore goggles when the occasion warranted, but not me, not ever, never wishing to call attention to myself, no matter what they said. Even your Soli Mama wore goggles when he thought I wasn't looking, and pranced in the sun in his corduroy slacks and tweed jacket like a sheep gone mad. More than anything else I liked Cambridge, all of England for that matter, because it was a town, a country, that found such little favor with the sun."

Like Cambridge

Everyone said Cambridge had changed Granny. She smiled more easily, her eyes were brighter, with a constant sheen. Mom said she might have fallen in love. I was nine the summer she and Soli Mama returned from Cambridge and we holidayed in Darjeeling. Granny chose Darjeeling because she wanted a place, like Cambridge, with an airconditioner in the sky; because she wanted to visit the home of the Darjeeling tea she'd consumed in such quantities in Cambridge; and because two of her bridge companions were going to be there as well. Dad had to work so there were just Granny, Soli Mama, Mom, Rusi, and me — and Julie, Rusi's ayah. My ayah, Mary, had been left to mind Dad; she was also afraid to fly, and we had to fly from Bombay to Calcutta, Calcutta to Bagdogra, before taking a van up the foothills of the Himalayas to Darjeeling.

I was so struck by the change in Granny during the Indian Airlines flight to Calcutta that I said, "Why is Granny smiling so much?" The air hostess had just passed around cotton wool for our ears and sweets on which to suck during the ascent, and asked us to fasten our seatbelts. "It's because she's happy," Mom said, seated on my left. "Darjeeling is as close to Cambridge as she can get in India." Mom had said once that Granny had almost wished Soli Mama would fail his examinations so they'd have an excuse to stay longer in Cambridge. "Now, hush — and remember to swallow." It relieved the pressure to swallow, and I clutched a second sweet in my hand in case I swallowed the first whole by accident.

The first difference I noticed between Bombay and Calcutta were the rickshawwallahs. There were none in Bombay. Bapaiji had a cycle-rickshaw, but these were hand-drawn, like the ones I'd seen in Hong Kong. These rickshawwallahs, as Soli Mama explained, couldn't afford bicycles. Otherwise, the gauntlet of taxiwallahs, tongawallahs, hotelwallahs, and brown spindly deformed begging children was hardly unfamiliar. The doubledecker buses were the same, the electric trams, and the congestion of people, cows, dogs, cats, goats — but my pity was newly evoked for the begging children. I'd heard some parents deliberately broke their children's arms and legs to give them a headstart as beggars. Being a visitor I felt I couldn't take the same things for granted that I had in Bombay. I wanted to give them money, but Soli Mama assured me that was not the way to be rid of them.

I didn't argue, anxious to be settled for the night. The air was fetid, infested with flies; the ground uneven, full of puddles. We had to shout down the other arrivals for coolies, bargain for rates, beat our way through the crowd, and find a large taxi (with a meter; otherwise, we might have been cheated) to take us to the Great Eastern Hotel on Old Court House Street. Our flight for Bagdogra left early the next morning, leaving us without time to sightsee in Calcutta, but Granny made sure we drove past the Howrah Bridge and Hooghli River because I'd studied them in Geography.

Congestion was everywhere. Rickshaws weaseled past our taxi through the tiniest openings. The windows were broken, couldn't be raised, and beggars pawed through them until Soli Mama yelled at them to leave us alone. I understood he was right, but couldn't get them out of my head until later when

I was overwhelmed by the automatic lifts of the hotel, the airconditioned rooms, the giant glass doors manned by a uniformed doorman leading to the Chinese restaurant with guests in evening dress — and the next morning it was still dark when we boarded the plane for Bagdogra.

It wouldn't be too gross an exaggeration to say that the Bagdogra Airport was almost as large as the town itself. The town doesn't need the airport, but travelers to Darjeeling, Kalimpong, and Sikkim do. A van took us from Bagdogra to Darjeeling. Along the way Soli Mama read from a guidebook. Darjeeling had been forested, barely inhabited, before the British had built roads, houses, a sanitarium, and hotel, started the renowned tea plantations, and constructed a Toy Train to transport supplies — which now also transported tourists. Granny said she'd never get on such a train; it seemed too small for adults; but Soli Mama said it was actually a narrow gauge railway, had been in use since 1881. We saw the train along the way, its little blue engine puffing smoke, tugging carriages through forests and tea gardens, reminding me of The Little Engine That Could.

Darjeeling is built in a series of steps carved from the side of the mountain, seven thousand feet above sea level. As we went up I kept my eyes open for monkeys, leopards, jackals, bears, otters, hares, deer, even elephants, which, according to the guidebook, inhabited the area, but had to be content instead with ponies and their riders. It was raining when we entered the marketplace on our way to the hotel on top of the hill, the Oberoi Mt. Everest, and Granny stopped the van to send Soli Mama to buy umbrellas for us all, even for Julie. Mom said one umbrella would be enough for Rusi and me, but Granny said we were old enough to have one each. A small blue Fiat slid alongside as we waited. "I thought that was Soli leaving the van," said someone in the Fiat, lowering her window. "How was the trip, Meher? We've been waiting for you."

They were Granny's friends. Everyone said hello, the trip was fine but we were all tired, hadn't had a chance to rest in Calcutta. Soli Mama returned with the umbrellas. Rusi's and mine had vanes of bright colors. "Arre, man, Homi, these are great," said Rusi. "I thought umbrellas were always black."

Granny's other friend, sitting at the far window of the car, had hardly spoken, but now she said, "Is that how they teach you to speak in school, Rusi? in slang? like a babu?"

Perhaps she'd meant it as a joke. I'd met her in Granny's house, but couldn't recall her name. Granny's friends all looked the same and none seemed comfortable without a handful of cards. They always went directly to the card table in the verandah, and when the game was over directly home. While they played they caught up on conversation and ate the confectionary and drank the sodas and Kalvert's Rose Syrup that Granny ordered for the game. They hardly looked at one another, or at anyone else, so when her friend made the remark from the car I think she might have embarrassed herself as much as anyone else because now all attention was focused on her and Rusi. Granny's smile disappeared, her eyebrows narrowed in a way I'd almost forgotten. She hated us to speak less than perfectly, but couldn't have liked her friend for reproving her grandson in her presence. The rain seemed louder during the moment before Rusi answered. "No. I just never saw such rainbow umbrellas."

The smiles that followed might have put the issue to rest, his use of a metaphor, but Rusi wasn't finished. Some days later, Granny and her friends had been at a game all morning in one of the hotel rooms, when Rusi stopped me outside the room within earshot of the players. "Arre, Homi, man," he said, "this is a great hotel, no? What do you think, yaar?"

I understood what he was doing. "Arre, man, of course. It is the absolute best, yaar. Tip-top! All red roofs and cream walls, just like in England, man." Without Rusi's instigation I wouldn't have been so bold, but we were on holiday and I didn't like the old lady any more than Rusi.

"It is *just* like in England, man, this carpet, and all these fireplaces, man."

"And the walls and the ceilings all so high, yaar. This was a chateau once, you know, man?"

"I know, yaar. Who would have thunk it? Like a maharajah's palace, yaar, just like a maharajah's palace."

I wasn't sure what to expect when Granny called us to her side after lunch that day before going to her room for her nap, but she smiled and gave us each a bar of Cadbury's Milk Chocolate. "I just want to say that I think you are both very good boys, and you both speak very well." Darjeeling had worked greater wonders on her even than Cambridge. Rusi wasn't surprised. "Gran's not stupid, yaar. She knows what's going on."

No one could stay disgruntled long; Darjeeling was too idyllic. We were too young to appreciate the beauty, but the grownups were charmed, and that made things easier for everyone. The air was so clean it looked washed; the people never looked less than cheerful; Granny said it was the climate — cool enough for work, but warm enough for leisure. I wasn't easily impressed, not by the Lloyd Botanical Garden (flowers bored me), not the Happy Valley Tea Estate (scenery bored me), not the Natural History Museum (old things bored me), not even the Mountain Zoo (Bombay's Victoria Gardens Zoo was better), but even I appreciated the view from Tiger Hill despite my grumpiness at being awakened at four in the morning to be harried from my snug refuge under four blankets into a cold jeep for a forty minute ride to a concrete pavilion where we sat shivering under blankets, sipping tea and coffee, waiting for the sun.

A sunrise, always beautiful, becomes even more memorable for what it reveals. Within ten minutes the panorama turned from black to gold; during the interim a rusty incandescence hung upon the clouds, the eastern sky turned brilliant with streaks of pink and red, the blue-grey mountains turning brighter reflected the brilliance so that the snowy peaks merged with the clouds and the horizon was lost. The sun rose, a translucent shimmering orange orb against a cerulean backdrop. To the northwest lay the Kanchenjunga range; Mount Everest, in the distance, was pointed out to me. Unlike the Howrah Bridge in Calcutta which inspired pride, Mount Everest inspired humility; the bridge created a buzz, the mountain a hush; one invited comment, the other introspection.

Darjeeling might have sustained the spell of Cambridge for Granny, but what happened in Bagdogra during our return to Bombay broke it forever. She lost her smile, the sheen in her eyes, and resumed her conviction, forgotten when she'd embarked for Cambridge, that "they" were out to get her. The regression wasn't apparent at once. When we first learned our flight to Calcutta had been delayed by a day she said nothing, but as the discomforts mounted (there were no good restaurants in Bagdogra, no hotels, there were no private quarters at the airport, no baths, there was nothing to see, nothing to do, there were cockroaches, beetles, and spiders among other assorted bugs in the airport, there were lizards, there were rats, there were jackals howling through the night in the wilderness beyond the runways) you could see her color rise like mercury in a thermometer with its bulb over a flame.

Mom and Soli Mama bought bread, butter, cheese, tomatoes (most of the food either too hard or too soft) for sandwiches from the Bagdogra market which was a fifteen minute walk from the airport, boiled eggs for breakfast the next morning, and filled two thermoses with cold drinking water.

We were the only passengers at the airport that day, our flight was the only flight. When Mr. Prasad, the official who'd told us of the delay, went home, the rest of his staff followed. We had the entire airport to ourselves. Rusi and I were excited, especially when the jackals howled after nightfall, but Granny didn't like it at all. Soli Mama pushed couches around to construct a fortress in the center of the vast and otherwise empty hall. Granny wanted all lights left on all night.

The next day Mr. Prasad didn't arrive until ten-thirty, but called Dum Dum Airport in Calcutta on the radio (there were no telephones) and assured us that our plane would arrive at three-thirty that afternoon as promised.

Rusi and I spent much of the day on the runway, exploring the hangars, watching mechanics at work, pushing the ministaircases around on their castors, pretending to board planes to Kenya, California, Sweden, Peru. We were warned not to go beyond the runways into the tall grass; jackals might be lying in wait.

At three-fifteen Mr. Prasad emerged from his office to say the plane had been delayed another day. He was almost as tiny as Granny, and in his uniform that was too large he appeared even tinier. He extracted something laboriously from his left nostril and studied it on his thin delicate finger before flicking it away. We were still the only passengers at the airport. Granny stamped her tiny foot in its grey patent leather shoe. "I don't need the brains of a turnip to see what's going on," she said. "You're waiting for more passengers to make up the flight — but we had tickets for yesterday!"

"Yesyes," Mr. Prasad said, smiling, eagerly agreeing, and "ofcourse-ofcourse," but it was evident he didn't credit Granny with the brains of a turnip because he reversed himself immediately, "and also nono. Even now they are repairing the aeroplane. Even now they are working on it. Tomorrow it will be ready."

"Arre, but that's what you told us yesterday." Soli Mama's forehead was creased, his arms were crossed, but he spoke civilly. "How do we know you're telling us the truth now?"

Mom, who hated confrontations of any kind, said, "Arre bawa, now let it be. If we have to wait one more day we can wait one more day."

Soli Mama uncrossed his arms, stood like a fivepointed star with his fists on his waist. "And if I *don't* have to wait another day, I *won't* wait another day. How do we know he's telling the truth now? This could go on till the cows come home."

Mom, embarrassed, smiled and looked away. "Well, of course, if *that's* how you feel about it...." I felt sorry for Mr. Prasad, picking his nose again, lost in his uniform, withered still further by Soli Mama's indignation, though it was evident he was lying. Perhaps the plane had indeed been out of commission; perhaps they'd withdrawn the flight owing to cancellations; in either event it seemed unlikely the airlines would schedule a flight for just the six of us. The most plausible scenario indicated that we'd be staying at the airport until the next scheduled flight which wasn't for two more days. Perhaps Mr. Prasad knew that, and knew that we knew it too, but he was following orders, had to maintain the integrity of the airline. "It is the truth now," he said, still smiling to keep his dignity. "You will see. Tomorrow, you will see. Goodgood, verygood." He turned abruptly and walked stiffly back to his office.

The next day he stayed in his office, but Soli Mama went to him only to learn the flight had been delayed yet another day. I could hear him shouting, but found it too depressing to stay. I knew Granny would start yelling when he returned so I hobbled onto the runway again with Rusi. When we returned Granny was still yelling: "They're doing it to me again, the swines. They're always waitingwaiting, plottingplotting. They pretend not to understand but they're sly, so sly. They're waiting to see how much she can take, the old woman, they're just waiting to see me crack."

Soli Mama seemed as annoyed with her as with everything else. "Nothing of the sort," he said. "No one's doing anything to anyone. They just don't know how to organize anything. Just wait till I find out who's in charge of this two-bit operation."

The next day Mr. Prasad didn't show up at all, but about eleven-thirty other passengers arrived bound as we were for Calcutta, precluding Soli Mama and Mom from making yet another trip to the Bagdogra market for bread and cheese. We were sure the plane would arrive now, and it did, which was just as well because Granny had been awakened that morning by two geckos who'd fallen from the rafters onto her out-stretched hand. Her face had become slowly distorted; from her brow to her eyes to her nose to her mouth to her chin her face flattened, stretched, wrinkled, as if a demon were descending, scrambling, snaking its way into her body. I felt sad, thinking that no number of shots of Cambridge could help her now. Bapaiji wouldn't have been bothered by mere lizards. She'd severed the tail of a gecko once for my edification beating it off with a walking stick; the tail had wriggled around by itself, independent of the lizard; the lizard, Bapaiji explained, would soon grow another tail. Granny, unfortunately, was never to grow another temperament.

Nawaz

A montage appeared before me: child Granny with clean skinny limbs skipping rope in a bedroom with another taller girl; laughing at a party with Indian, English, and Anglo-Indian friends; playing London Bridge, Musical Chairs, Pin the Tail on the Donkey, a Tisket a Tasket; singing in a choir, "All Things Bright and Beautiful," in her grey and white convent uniform; reciting "O Romeo, Romeo, wherefore art thou Romeo?" with perhaps too much vivacity before a school audience; picking among books, *Little Women*, *Black Beauty*, *Jane Eyre*, *Wuthering Heights*, *Oliver Twist*, *A Tale of Two Cities*, *The Count of Monte Cristo*, in a library; sitting at a wooden table pasting pictures into a Queen Victoria scrapbook; wedged on the wide sill of a window opening from her bedroom into a porch, her back against one jamb, her feet against the other, lost in a clothbound, illustrated volume of *Alice's Adventures in Wonderland* so large that she almost dropped it everytime she turned a page.

In the last picture she looked perhaps twelve years old, sitting up in bed in the dark, wishing she could sleep. Usually, the pendulum of the sea outside, rocking her in its rhythm, made her drowsy, but not tonight. She got out of bed imagining a glass of water might help. The floor was mosaic and uneven; by day she saw pictures in the tiles; by night she walked unsteadily as if she were on the deck of a ship. The waves outside didn't help. She was careful because she didn't want to wake her sister, Nawaz, asleep in an adjacent bed, but a movement in the corner of Granny's eye made her cry out, "Who is it?" and Nawaz was soon awake.

"What is it, Mehru? Why are you out of bed?"

Granny laughed softly. "It's nothing. I was just getting a glass of water when I thought I saw something move — but it was only my own reflection in the mirror. Sorry I woke you up, Nawaz."

Nawaz spoke sleepily, yawning. "Such an imagination you have."

Granny marveled that Nawaz was generous even in sleep, crediting her with imagination when she was just a scaredy-cat. "Not really, but anyway, now that I'm up, would you also like a glass of water — or some Horlicks?"

Nawas turned on her side, pulling the sheet over her head. "No, not tonight."

"All right. Goodnight."

"Goodnight."

Granny tiptoed to the kitchen, poured herself water from the matka, tilting the glass so the water would pour on its side and not make a noise, and made her way back to bed. She was soon asleep, but almost as soon awake again. She sat in the bed in the dark, the sheet like a tent at her knees, her tiny hands holding it up to her mouth so that her shiny nose appeared like a knuckle flanked by bony white knuckles, her eyes fixed to what she saw reflected in the mirror. A patch of moonlight fell on the floor from the open window leading to the porch, il-luminating a swirl of white and blue mosaic pointing toward the bed. She prayed that the image she saw reflected in the mirror was a nightmare from which she would wake, after which she would wake Nawaz, tell her what she had dreamed, and the two of them would go to the kitchen, switch on the light, make some Horlicks, sip it slowly, talking in whispers until the sun came up.

She was too terrified to make any noise or movement, but her eyes flashed across the room to where her father stood transfixed in the doorway in his sadra and pajama bottoms. Their eyes met and she knew his fear as clearly as she knew her own and she knew also his shame for his fear, but still he did nothing. A man was smothering her sister in her bed and they both behaved as if it were a movie and they were waiting for the horror to pass, he staring as if to punish himself for his fear, she looking away as if to deny what she'd seen. Slowly Nawaz's struggles ceased, a white twitching foot became still in the moonlight in the corner of Granny's eye, but the man continued to press the pillow hard on her face. Then her mother came into the room in a grey faded gown and began beating the intruder on his back with a rolling pin.

The man fell immediately on his knees, breathing heavily, shaking and crying and begging for mercy. She stopped beating him, she recognized his voice. She turned to Nawaz to see how she was, screamed, and continued beating the man until he lay unconscious on his side on the floor. Granny's father switched on the light.

Granny learned much the following week. Nawaz was her half sister. Their mother had come from a wealthy family; her father, a doctor, had graduated from Oxford, a rarity in those days for an Indian; but she had fallen in love with a bounder who'd left her with a child. No man of consequence would marry her, and she'd married Granny's father, a nice man of limited means, physical, emotional, and financial. They'd made a good life despite the ostracism of her family, Granny and Nawaz had a happy childhood, but if she'd married a bolder man Nawaz might have lived her natural life. The man who killed her was her natural father. Why he did it, what he wanted, where he'd been all those years, no one ever knew. By that time he was crazy.

Rustomji Jamshedji Cama

Child Granny stood on the rough stone floor in her convent uniform and rang her doorbell. I knew nothing of Granny's parents, but guessed from the name on the brass plate, Motiwalla, that her father was a jeweler. Granny switched her satchel of books from her left to her right shoulder, swung the narrow wooden flap marked LETTERS back on its hinges, and peered through the slot until she saw her mother's slippered feet approach. Her mother had trouble with the latch and Granny shouted impatiently. "Push with your knee, Mamma. Then open." Her mother did as she was told and the latch slid easily.

The flat consisted of a central corridor which held an ironing board, two cupboards, and suitcases, the front door at one end, the bathroom at the other; the two bedrooms were adjacent to the bathroom, and the sittingroom was across the corridor from the diningroom and kitchen. If her father had friends Granny would slip by quietly so they would leave her alone, but on that day there'd been too much noise. To her annoyance her father called her, introduced her to his friend. "Meher, this is Mr. Rustomji Jamshedji Cama. I am sure you have heard of him."

I watched Mr. Rustomji Jamshedji Cama carefully. I knew he was to be our other grandfather, mine and Rusi's, after whom Rusi had been named, whom I had never seen either except in

snapshots, who'd died, like Hormusji, before I'd been born.
Hormusji was the better looking man, Rustomji was already
losing his hair, but Rustomji was the more dapper. He wore a
white suit, a neatly knotted cream tie, and a straw hat lay on the
marble table over which they'd been conducting business. He
was the nephew of Jalbhai Phirozshah Cama, the industrialist —
which interested me more than Granny because I'd already seen
Jalbhai's sister, Tehmina Cama, approach Hormusji in Navsari to
draw up the constitution for the emancipation of women.

"Yes, of course I have heard of him," Granny said, and held
out her hand, greeting him as she would any other of her
father's friends. "Hello, Uncle."

Mr. Cama put aside his pearlhandled cane, got up from his
chair, shook her hand. "Nononononono," he said. "What is this
'Uncle'? I am not an old man. My name is Rustom."

It was unprecedented for one of her father's friends to
object to being called "Uncle." She looked at him, still
unsmilingly, but with interest. "Yes, Uncle — I mean, Rustomji."
She couldn't call him just "Rustom" even then.

He was holding her hand. "She is such a pretty girl," Mr.
Cama was saying, "but such a sad little face."

Her mother had entered the room and stood smiling behind
a chair holding its back. When Granny returned to her room
she looked at her face in the mirror. Mr. Cama was right: it was
a pretty face, but sad. After Nawaz died she'd lost interest in
things, cultivated her sadness, proud that it set her apart. She
was flattered he'd noticed. He was not an old man, just closer
to her father in age. She was only sixteen, but when she thought
about him she found herself filling with hope.

2

I was not prepared for what I saw next: it looked like Big Ben
— but with a row of swaying coconut trees alongside, no Houses

of Parliament, no Westminster Bridge, no Thames. I shouldn't have been surprised (if Granny could move her house from Bombay to the Gogmagog Hills in Cambridgeshire, she could just as well have moved Big Ben to Bombay), but the explanation was simpler. When I looked again I realized I'd let myself be deceived. Big Ben was actually the Rajabhai Tower, the Big Ben of Bombay, which hardly seemed incongruous among coconut trees. I hardly recognized the maidan (the Oval, where my classmates from Campion School had played cricket and football and hu-tu-tu) in front of the Tower because there was only water where I'd been accustomed to seeing the Eros Theatre, Churchgate Station, and Marine Drive. I was looking at Bombay before the reclamation from the sea. There was a function in the Oval, a celebration of the marriage of the Prince of Wales, Prince Albert Edward, the future King Edward VII, the second child and eldest son of Queen Victoria and Prince Albert, to Princess Alexandra of Denmark. A crowd had gathered, Indians and English, for a display of fireworks. The rows of rickety wooden chairs had long been filled, but hundreds of Indians were content merely to squat at the perimeter of the grounds. Within the select enclosure of chairs an altercation was taking place: a tall, gangly, uniformed English official was trying to remove a chair "for one of the English ladies who just arrived" he explained, while a young Parsi in a dagla and paghri held on to the same chair. "I'm sorry," the Parsi said, "but this chair is reserved. My friend will be back in a moment." The Parsi was smaller, but with the thick density, the quick strength, of a dwarf in his body. He spoke politely, but his face was stern. "In fact, here he is now," he said without turning away, as his friend came up beside him.

"Let go the chair," said the Englishman.

"No," said the Parsi. "It is you who must let go."

The Englishman looked from the Parsi to his friend and back. "Who are you to speak to me like this?"

"We know our rights," said the Parsi with the same politeness, the same unswerving gaze.

The Englishman might have backed off then if he could have saved face doing so, but it was too late. "I could have you confined for the night," he said.

"That is a risk I will have to take."

Fortunately for everyone, a second uniformed Englishman called from a distance, "It's all right, Ian. We've got all the chairs we need."

The first Englishman thumped the chair down without looking at the Parsis and walked away. The Parsi put the chair calmly back where it had been, explaining what had happened to his friend. The first rockets flashed in the darkening sky, fountains of flame erupted in the heart of the enclosure.

3

"Homi, that young man, to whom you so charitably granted the density of a dwarf, was Jalbhai Phirozshah Cama, your grandfather's uncle, the first major industrialist of Modern India. Of course, you know who he is from the history books, but there are some things that bear repetition, especially when they concern the honor of one's family. Cama Enterprises was the first to institute an eight-hour working day and paid holidays when such things were unknown even in England and America. He instituted a provident fund, accident compensation, medical aid, maternity benefits, profit sharing, all long before they became required by the law. Grandfathers and fathers and sons and grandsons worked for the Camas as if they worked for their own families. Jalbhai himself said that without the human touch all work, composing a symphony or digging a ditch, became drudgery, and no success could transmute that lead into gold. Fortunately, many of his successors understood that well enough to keep up the momentum. Unfortunately, your grandfather,

Rustomji Jamshedji Cama, was not among them. I should have known it on the night I saw the Bombay Players do *A Midsummer Night's Dream* at Cama Hall, but I was only a girl, still only eighteen, and my mother and father both liked Rustomji Jamshedji so much they thought I was a fool for not being as excited as they were. Actually, I was; he was special, and his interest made me special, but a girl has to maintain her dignity. Rustomji Jamshedji came at least once a week, my father was the excuse, Rustomji wanted a necklace setting, a ring cleaned, but it was no secret he was coming to see me. We didn't go out, it wasn't done. We were never without a chaperone even at home, but people talked about us so much — mostly because he was a Cama, very rich, and still an eligible bachelor — that my mother said he would have to make up his mind soon because people were talking, I wasn't growing any younger, and there was my reputation to consider. So he invited us all to the play. He thought it would be a good way for everyone to meet."

A Midsummer Night's Dream

Rustomji Jamshedji sent his carriage to pick up Granny and her parents on the day of the play. It was a pleasant fifteen-minute walk from their house along Napean Sea Road (first along a quiet residential street, then along the beach) to Cama Hall, but they'd have got their best clothes dusty. Besides, it might have rained, they might not have felt like walking, so many things might have happened — and Rustomji Jamshedji wanted to be sure they would come. Her mother had wanted Granny to wear a sari; it seemed wanton for an eighteen year old to show her ankles and calves, but Granny insisted on wearing a dress because she didn't want the English to think she was oldfashioned, and since she hadn't seen her so excited about anything in so long she let her. Her mother, wearing all her jewels, her finest shimmering sari, was pleased to be riding in a carriage as if she were being vindicated for the misfortunes her family had heaped on her for her marriage. Her father in a twice-washed dagla and white pants, black paghri and shining black shoes, was also pleased but nervous. These were not his people, but they had been his wife's, and he wanted them to be his daughter's.

Rustomji Jamshedji did not live in Cama Hall. He was a Cama, but uninterested in commerce preferring instead the life of a gentleman though some called him a dilettante — he painted portraits inspired by the work of Sir Joshua Reynolds and had written two novels about corruption in commerce and immorality in high places creating a minor scandal in Bombay when his readers associated his characters with members of his family and circle of acquaintances. He was not popular among the Camas, but they'd established a generous fund for him because it would have been even more of a scandal had they disinherited him — besides which they'd have provided him with fodder for a third novel. Granny and her parents had visited him occasionally on Sunday mornings in the past two years in his house, Cama Mansion, in a cul-de-sac near Kemp's Corner. They'd been impressed (her mother less than her father) with the least thing, but even his house, lavishly built and furnished though it was, could not compare with Cama Hall. As the carriage passed through the high iron gates and made its way up a winding hilly driveway to the high colonnaded entrance, marble steps leading into the mansion, her father became glazed with wonder, her mother smug as if indulging a secret pleasure, and she herself so bright with excitement that everything around her seemed colorless. Their feelings of privilege were heightened when a uniformed usher seated at a desk by the steps found their names on a roster, issued them tickets, and directed them through the house to the back where a living area projected like a proscenium onto an oval terrace which descended via marble steps in wide arcs like ripples toward the lawn.

The terrace, easily accessible from both house and garden, was ideal for theatrical productions. If necessary, the lawn immediately before the terrace could have been used as a second stage. Rattan chairs had been arranged in rows for the guests, and carefully landscaped beds of roses and hedge enclosing picnic tables bound them on the sides. The coconut and mango trees had been strung with fairy lights so that one might have imagined Oberon and Titania and Puck and Peaseblossom and the rest even without the aid of the Bombay Players. Far to the back stood a gazebo with a domed top like a giant pearl, and behind the gazebo, past a narrow stretch of sand, lay the sea.

They found their seats without talking to anyone, but her father kept pointing out the luminaries he recognized in the Cama firmament; the brightest, Jalbhai himself, had been dead fifteen years, and his sons, Sir Kaikhushrau Jalbhai and Sir Dorabji Jalbhai, were in London and Beirut respectively on business, but there were dozens of nephews, nieces, in-laws, cousins, with some of whom her father had done business, others whom Rustomji Jamshedji had mentioned during their talks. The Parsi women wore mostly shimmering saris like her mother's, with necklaces, earrings, bracelets, and brooches of diamonds, rubies, emeralds, sapphires, and pearls. Their men wore mostly daglas and paghris. The Englishwomen wore mostly gowns or dresses with bare shoulders and less jewelry than the Parsis — many of the Englishmen wore uniforms with decorations almost as bright as their women's jewels. Her mother saw someone she knew and excused herself. Rustomji saw them seated by themselves and called them to meet his company. Her father moved like a robot, but Granny couldn't keep still, clutched her sequined handbag in one hand, brushed at her dress with the other as if to smoothen wrinkles, swayed from side to side in a quick excited motion.

Rustomji introduced them to his friends: Teddy Wentworth, an Englishman of about thirty years, in a waistcoat and pinstripe trousers, with a narrow head of flat, striated, immaculately combed, dark brown hair, parted down the middle, which shone in the light; Helen Dastur, perhaps in her mid-twenties, in a long green dress with a long slit at the neck, her hair, so pale it was almost white in the light, held in a loose bun by a diamond barrette, the only piece of jewelry she appeared to be wearing; and Naju Cama, Rustomji's sister, perhaps in her thirties, one of the few Parsi women in a gown, with a diamond choker around her neck, diamond earrings, and a diamond on her finger.

Granny didn't like Naju Cama; she wore too much powder, trying to appear fairer than she was; her nose was as sharp and narrow as Granny's own, but her mouth was long and thin and her diamonds made her appear aloof as if she slept in a bed of ice. Recalling that Naju's first husband, who'd married her for her money (so the story went), had died mysteriously, Granny found it easy to believe (so, again, the story went) that she'd poisoned him.

Helen she liked immediately — the simple gown, the single piece of jewelry, her undivided attention when someone spoke, made her appear so vulnerable that even Granny felt protective. She'd heard about her; her mother, of Norwegian and English parentage, had been a governess in the employ of her father, a Parsi — a married man. When her mother had become pregnant, her father had sacked her denying all complicity. Her mother had died when Helen was nineteen and she'd lived since as a governess herself with all the sympathy and ostracism that the peculiarity of the position demanded. Her features were tiny and delicate like a child's and her skin just as smooth. She had gentleman callers because she was attractive, educated, intelligent, and a finer conversationalist than most Parsi women of her time. She'd have enjoyed the company of women equally, but unmarried women were too busy looking for husbands and married women looking after their husbands to consider socializing with her. Besides, mean minds speculated that her callers were after meaner satisfactions than affection and camaraderie though she lived much too humbly to support their speculations.

The women remained seated, Helen smiling with curiosity, Naju expressionlessly, when they were introduced, but Teddy Wentworth got to his feet. To her horror, Granny saw her father join his hands and bow his head ever so slightly as if he were about to say "Saebji" in his humble manner, the way he did

when he felt overawed. It might have been all right to greet
Rustomji that way, but an Englishman would only think of him
as typically Indian. She thrust her hand forward immediately
and spoke clearly. "How do you do?"

Teddy Wentworth snatched his glance from father to daughter, giving no other indication of surprise. "I say, so this is May-
her," he said, shaking her hand. "Rustom is an old fox. He said
nothing about how charming you were — how very charming."

Rustomji chuckled. "I do not like to boast."

"Stuff and nonsense. You've been hiding her from me. You
spoke of her as if she were a footnote. I find you guilty of
keeping secrets from me, Rustom."

Again, Rustomji chuckled. Teddy continued to hold Granny's
hand. She smiled broadly, amused that he'd mispronounced her
name. He spoke with no emphasis, but made his point unmistakably with the slowness of his speech, reminding her of the
times she and Nawaz would "tawk such haw-haw English" for
fun. Then her father put out his hand suddenly as if he didn't
know what else to do, and spoke hurriedly, "How do you do?"
and Teddy released her hand.

There were still a few minutes before the play so they all
sat down together. "I was just saying," Teddy resumed, "that I
really prefer Dickens to Shakespeare. How anyone can take
fairies and love potions seriously in the twentieth century is
beyond me. And his tragedies are all so bleak. But Dickens
always leaves me entertained and edified."

Helen leaned forward. "But if it's realism you're after, you
should really read Ibsen or Shaw or Trollope. Dickens's characters are so flat you could pass them through the crack under
a door." She spoke quietly, with assurance.

Naju cut off the ensuing laughter abruptly. "I still say
Shakespeare was the best. He had such a deep understanding
of human nature. He must have been such an intelligent man."

She looked around the company as if she'd said the last

word on the subject, but Rustomji replied with a chuckle. "I wish *I* had said that, Naju."

His irony wasn't lost on the company, but Helen turned to him for Naju's benefit. "But she's right, Rustom. He also understood how to fit his characters to his plays. If Hamlet had been in Othello's place there would have been no tragedy. He would not have smothered Desdemona so thoughtlessly. And if Othello had been in Hamlet's place there would have been no play either because he would have killed Claudius in the second act."

Before anyone could respond, Granny said, "Lord Melbourne told Queen Victoria not to read *Oliver Twist* because it dealt with paupers and pickpockets and other such things of which she should not be thinking." She had lost the track of the conversation because she'd been searching for an intelligent response to Teddy's preference for Dickens.

"That's very interesting," Teddy said. "I don't believe I knew that."

Granny was flushed with excitement for having contributed to the conversation, but it was time to go back to their seats. "It's been a pleasure meeting you," Teddy said. "Perhaps we can resume our conversation during the interval."

Granny smiled, shook his hand, debated whether to reply "Perhaps" or "I Would Like That," said "Perhaps," and followed her father back to their seats. Teddy was an unexpected bonus. No one had spoken to her that way before, certainly no man had, and she'd never dreamed that someday an Englishman might. His hair was brown, he was well groomed, well spoken. She was relieved she'd worn a dress after all instead of a sari as her mother had wanted. She felt she'd impressed Teddy by appearing to be more of an Anglo than she was. She looked forward to the interval now as much as she'd looked forward to the play itself before. When it came, Granny was disappointed to see Naju coming toward them alone, but her disappointment vanished when Naju invited her to a moonlight picnic on the beach after the play. Teddy was to be there and some of the other young folk. Granny and her mother were delighted, but her father, in deference to propriety, said it would be all right only if Rustomji would be responsible for her. Naju waved his objections aside. "With Rustom one can never be sure, but *I* will be there. It is settled, then." She spoke with a smile and an emphasis that made Granny think she might have misjudged her after all.

Toward the end of the evening Granny didn't know which was the more magical, the finery of the assorted fairies and lovers on stage or of the socialites in the garden of whom she felt increasingly a part, particularly when Naju came to her when the play was over. Naju's smile, still as flat as before, now seemed so generous that Granny felt ashamed for disliking her before. "Rustom cannot come just now," she said to her parents, "but he said for you to take the carriage home. Meher can stay with me just now. Rustom will see her home later."

Her parents left with large smiles. After they'd gone Naju said to Granny, "I'm afraid we cannot go just yet. I must stay here until the guests start going home. I hope it won't be too much of a bother for you. Then we can go to the beach."

Granny was tired, but too excited still to care. "Not at all," she said as graciously as she could. "Not at *all*. *Per*fectly all right."

"Good. I knew you would understand."

Granny smiled, feeling she'd said the right thing. She looked for Teddy and Rustomji and Helen then, but couldn't find them. Naju said they would meet them later at the beach; Rustomji couldn't be bothered saying goodbye to anyone and had taken his friends with him for company — "but someone has got to do the dirty work." Naju smiled as if she'd made a joke. Granny didn't find it funny, but smiled effortlessly as if no matter how tired she felt she'd shifted into a higher gear than she'd used before and, however different it felt, she knew she'd done it well. It didn't matter that Rustomji would be the only person she knew at the picnic, that there would be Englishmen and Camas and their friends who might know one another more intimately than she knew any of them. She felt as if her strangeness itself made her special, as if the more of herself she withheld the more special she would appear. Until she met the others she would content herself to cultivate her strangeness just saying goodnight to the guests who came to thank Naju for the entertainment. She was sure they must all be wondering who she was and why Naju had taken her under her wing.

"Shall I send for some port? or some sherry?"

Granny had never drunk wine, but didn't want Naju to know it. "Some port would be nice," she said.

When the bearer brought her a glass, Granny sipped the port carefully as if it were hot like tea. Naju smiled knowingly, but not so Granny could see.

After an hour, the crowd had thinned and some of the lights had been turned off allowing the moon to grow in ascendancy, particulary by the gazebo whose pearly dome shone like a half moon itself. Granny and Naju had a moment to themselves for the first time since her parents had left. "I'm afraid this is going to take longer than I thought," Naju said. "Come along, my dear. Let me take you to the meeting place while we have a few seconds. The others should be waiting for us now. I'm sorry you had to wait so long. You must be so bored."

"Not at *all*," Granny said, getting up immediately from her chair. "*Per*fectly all right, really."

They walked in silence, Naju a step ahead of Granny, until there was no one within earshot around them. "Teddy really likes you," Naju said then. "He's really looking forward to tonight. Don't tell him I said this, of course — he'd kill me if he found out" (she flashed a smile at Granny, adding a laugh as if at an afterthought) — "but he said 'A chap could get serious about a girl like her.' You should be flattered. He doesn't say that about every girl he meets. Also, he doesn't usually like Indian women in dresses — you and I are the exceptions that prove the rule, he said." Naju gave Granny another smile from over her shoulder. "He says they look so exotic in saris he cannot understand why they would want to wear dresses at all. Personally, I think you impressed him with that thing about Dickens. He loves Dickens. How did you ever know that?"

Granny's smile was so broad it threatened to spring off her face. "It was in *Little Ladies* magazine. I get it from the library every month. I read it from cover to cover."

"That was fortunate," Naju said, turning face front again. "That really impressed him — and he's not easily impressed. He's not like so many of the English in India who are really paupers in England. They come to India because they would never get the same respect — the servants, the privileges, the salaries — in England. But Teddy is not like that. He is rich in his own right — he has a brother in the House of Lords. He was sent to India to be rounded out, sort of like a finishing school. He could have his pick of dozens of girls. That is why I say it is not to be taken lightly when he says he likes you. I don't think you can even begin to realize what a compliment he has paid you."

Granny said, "I liked him too, I really did," but her smile had diminished considerably as if she knew that whatever she said would prove inadequate to her feeling, as if the matter were more serious than a smile might warrant.

"If I were you," Naju said, still facing front, "I wouldn't waste any time letting him know it. He's a busy man. If you waste this chance you might not get another. I only say this because I want what's best for you."

Granny didn't know what to say.

They reached the sand. Naju looked around as if surprised not to find anyone. "That's funny. They should have been here by now." They waited in silence for a few seconds. "I'm sorry, my dear, but I must be getting back. I'm sure they'll be here any minute. I hope you don't mind waiting a bit."

"Not at *all*," Granny said, but she cut herself short before she could add it was Perfectly All Right. She'd used those phrases altogether too often that evening. Besides, she wasn't sure she didn't mind; something wasn't right; but she didn't know what else to do. "I'll be all right," she said with less enthusiasm.

"Are you sure?" Naju looked at her again, sensing her apprehension.

Granny was a bit lightheaded from the port, and afraid because she didn't know how it would make her feel next, but she nodded.

"They should be here any minute," Naju said. "Besides, it's a beautiful bright night. Nothing will happen."

Granny nodded again. "I'll be all right. Please don't worry."

"Bye-bye, then. I'll be joining you all a little later."

"Bye-bye."

Granny watched Naju until she was out of sight. She found beautiful the silvery shadows of the trees cast by the moonlight on the sand, the spangles on the sea beyond, but she didn't like the brightness. Nawaz had been killed on a moonlit night; Granny could still recall the splash of moonlight on the blue mosaic floor and Nawaz's pale motionless foot. She hid herself within the shadow of a thick coconut tree and took off her shoes which had filled with sand. She stood for a few minutes in silence, listening to the waves, drawing deep breaths of the sea air to counter the effect of the port, following the stream of moonlight along the sea to the beach where it widened and got lost in the sand. She was about to step out of the shadows to go back to Cama Hall on her own when she saw a figure approach and chose to remain where she was. It was a man; she couldn't see him clearly from behind the tree, even in the moonlight, but when he shouted, "Ahoy! Is anyone there?" she knew it was Teddy. She stepped into the light. "Is it Teddy?"

"Yes. Is it May-her?"

"Yes. What *is* the matter? Where *is* everyone?"

"I'm afraid there's been a mistake, a misunderstanding, actually."

"Oh? What is it?"

He was still coming toward her. She remained where she was.

"Naju was to bring you to the house. The picnic is at midnight. It's only eleven-thirty now. I'm afraid you've been waiting in the dark for nothing. I'm sorry."

They were standing next to each other by the time he was finished talking. He'd brought with him a smell with which she was unfamiliar but guessed to be spirits. She felt suddenly awkward to be alone in the night with a man. Her shoulders slumped, her gaze fell to a stone behind him, her body turned slightly away. "It's all right. Thank you for coming to get me. Let's go back."

Teddy shook his head, standing as firmly as before. "Actually, I thought we might stay here until the others came. It would only be time to leave again by the time we got back."

Granny felt it would be wrong to stay; Naju should have come back for her herself; surely she knew what being alone with a man, especially at night, especially in such exotic surroundings, could do to a young girl's reputation — but Teddy was an Englishman; she couldn't expect him to see anything wrong with his proposal. There was no way she could deter him from his argument except by exposing herself for the unsophisticated Parsi girl she was instead of the poised equivalent of the English girls to whom he must be accustomed. "All right," she said. "We can stay."

"Good. I was hoping you'd see it my way." There was a tremor in his voice which gave her courage to look at him. His white face looked waxen and translucent in the moonlight as if it might reveal blood vessels and bones to a sharper scrutiny, doughy as if it might be rearranged by kneading. He smiled, but his eyes appeared glazed. Granny wished the others were there already, but told herself that that was no way for a sophisticated young girl to behave.

Teddy put his hands on her waist and drew her to him. "May-her," he said, and the smell of the spirits was stronger, "Naju said some things about you — very flattering things."

She turned her face from his, letting her hands holding her shoes hang loosely behind her, her handbag wedged under her arm. "What things?"

"She said you were a modern girl. She said you liked to have fun." He leaned over and kissed her temple.

His lips felt cold — and unclean. She brought up her hands with her shoes against his chest to push him away, but he only circled her with his arms and held her more tightly. Her handbag fell; the shoes between them hurt her chest; his unrelenting pressure panicked her; his face so close seemed like a giant's. She tried to hit his jaw with her shoe but couldn't get enough leverage; she tried kicking his shins but her bare feet had no effect; she struggled but he only held her more tightly as if she were a sparrow in a captor's hand. The smell of the spirits got worse. She thought of screaming, but that seemed uncivilized; she thought how ridiculously she was thinking, but couldn't think differently. She relaxed momentarily as if in surrender; he leaned over to kiss her again; and she butted her forehead against his nose. He dropped her with a shout; she dropped her shoes and ran the way she had come, screaming "Rustomji! Rustomji!" as if his shout had given her permission finally to break her own silence, but he caught up with her easily, clamped a hand over her mouth, an arm around her waist, lifted her up, thumped her down, lifted her up and thumped her down again until she ceased to struggle, then whispered ferociously: "Do *not* — I repeat — do *not* make a scene. Naju told me some things. I'm sorry I believed her. I believe I owe you an apology. I'm sorry."

Granny shook in his arms; when he released her she fell to her knees crying. "I'm sorry," Teddy kept saying. "I'm afraid I've behaved like a cad. I thought you were something you're not."

She appeared not to hear him and continued crying. "I'm sorry," he said again. "Please don't make a scene. Nothing's going to happen. We can go back to the house as soon as you've tidied yourself up a bit."

She became more quiet then. "I'm sorry," he said yet again. "I'm going to get your shoes and your bag. Please wait for me."

By the time he returned Granny had adjusted her dress, wiped her tears, and was ready to go back. When they got to Cama Hall she pulled Rustomji aside. "Rustomji, I'm sorry, but I want to go home now."

Rustomji, surprised, argued. "But the picnic is only just beginning."

"Please, Rustomji, please."

There was a wild look in her eyes he hadn't seen before. Teddy intervened for her. "I say, Rustom, something happened. A misunderstanding, I'm afraid. A bit embarrassing, actually. Take her home. Let her explain it to you." He spoke in a low voice, but not surreptitiously. "May-her, be sure to tell him everything. Do not leave anything out on my account."

Rustomji said nothing but sent for his carriage. Granny said nothing once she saw he was taking her home. She didn't even look at him, too immersed in her confusion. She didn't understand Teddy's pendulum swings of character. Was the prince who had proven himself a bounder proving himself still a prince by asking her not to spare him? She felt silly like Titania caught with Bottom, the weaver in the ass-head — but Teddy wasn't Bottom, and she couldn't tell if he was wilier or nobler; if wilier he might still make her appear a fool, but if nobler she might appear a fool in contrast. She thought of Lady Flora Hastings, one of Queen Victoria's ladies-in-waiting, who'd suffered from a cancerous growth on her liver which made her appear pregnant; since she was unmarried a scandal had ensued, she'd been forced against her will to submit to a medical examination which proved she was a virgin, and a few months later she'd died of the cancer; even the Queen had suspected the worst because Lady Flora had been seen alone with Sir John Conroy on one occasion.

Once they were on their way home Rustomji asked her what had happened. It was a warm night but Granny shivered, pulled her shawl more tightly around her shoulders, and sat forward in her seat next to Rustomji clutching her handbag in her lap. "I think it might have been ... I had a lot of ... Naju gave me a lot of port to drink...."

She told her story as if she could hardly believe it herself. "I'm sorry I've been such a silly goose. I'm sure Teddy didn't mean anything. It was just the port ... if only Naju hadn't poured me so much port...." As her voice trailed off she was afraid to look at him, afraid of what he might be thinking.

"If Naju hadn't poured you so much port she would have done something else." Rustomji's voice boomed more exultantly than it had all evening. Granny looked at him in surprise. He was smiling. "It is good this thing happened. She has shown us her cards and she has no trumps. She has already played her strongest suit."

Granny said nothing but continued to look at him in surprise. "Naju knows I am thinking about marrying you. This was the only way she could think of to stop it — by tarnishing your reputation. The old she-devil is running out of tricks if this is the best she can do."

Rustomji chuckled. "It is no big mystery, Meherbanu. Don't look so puzzled. It's a simple story, really. The old man, JP, to make sure the name of Cama would continue, made it a condition that only male heirs could partake of his inheritance. If

Naju had a son he could legally change his name to Cama, but she is not getting married again, and she is too old to have children. She will always be well off, of course, but if I have sons it will mean she will have that much less." He chuckled again as if it were a good joke. "And, by God, sons I mean to have. If I had doubts before this has swept them away. I will talk to your father tomorrow morning. What do you think of that?"

Granny thought he should ask her first, but he seemed so pleased with himself, like a boy who'd had the last laugh, that she didn't want to quibble. "I'm very happy, Rustom," she said, sinking back into the soft seat of the carriage. It was the first time she'd called him Rustom as an equal instead of Rustomji in deference to his age. She was crying; he put an arm around her shoulders and she hid her face in his chest, but she was thinking of that swine, Naju, and an image wafted in the air of a large pink sow with fat white udders floating in the sky like a balloon wearing Naju's blue gown reduced to a tutu around its fat waist, her diamond choker around its fat pink neck, diamond earrings in its floppy pink ears, and a diamond ring pushed as far as it would go along its wiggly pink tail. It was at moments such as this that I knew that Granny was as intent as Bapaiji on dramatizing what she showed me to her own advantage — but, as with Bapaiji, I didn't care. We were all on the same side.

A Legitimate Heir

Granny sat in the verandah of Zephyr, the house in which she was to live the rest of her life. She was sewing an intricate pattern of birds, bees, butterflies, and flowers onto a baby's dress. The girls were in the nursery with the ayahs. Over the stone balusters she could see the sea lapping at the Scandalpoint rocks. She could also see Naju's carriage as it came up her driveway, passed the coconut trees at the far end, and around the landscaped center of roses and daisies and sunflowers. "Stanley," Granny called, and her Goanese bearer appeared before her.

"Yes, Memsahib."

"Najubai is here, Stanley. Bring her to the verandah."

"Yes, Memsahib."

Granny put down her work for a moment, stretched. She didn't see Rustomji as much anymore; he'd given up writing and painting and rejoined Cama Enterprises befitting his responsibilities as husband and father. She had everything she needed, was happy enough just to read, sew, organize the household, play with the girls, and entertain her all too infrequent visitors. The girls, first Pheroza, then Jalu, had both been named after Jalbhai Phirozshah, and Naju had sent them lavish gifts — clothes, toys, furniture, even jewelry. Granny had wanted

151

to send them all back; she couldn't forget what had happened on the night of the play; but Rustomji had persuaded her to let bygones be bygones. Naju was his sister, he explained; she had, however inadvertently, expedited their marriage with her machinations; and Granny was glad finally that she'd allowed herself to be persuaded. Naju helped with social obligations, had become her most frequent visitor, sometimes bringing friends with her on her visits.

"There you are, Meher, my dear, hard at work as usual. How are you?"

"Quite well, thank you. How are you?"

Naju put down a brown paper bag. "Oh, my dear, at my age, if one gets up in the morning one doesn't complain." They embraced formally, then Naju stepped back. "Let me look at you, my dear. Let me see how you're filling out."

Granny was wearing a blue house dress. She turned around selfconsciously. "I think I'm beginning to show already, even through this baggy old thing."

"That's a good sign, to show early, especially in your third pregnancy. It means the baby's healthy. I really did not think it wise of you and the old man to have tried it again. It's so unhealthy for old people, and the babies are so often born deformed."

Rustomji was almost fifty, but Granny was only twenty-two. Granny had questioned her jubilation when Jalu had been born, their second girl. Of course she'd said nothing, but Naju had hardly been her only detractor. There were women who'd never forgiven her for marrying Rustomji, as if she'd spoiled their chances, or their daughters', or even once a granddaughter's chance, and were glad she'd had two girls, but Granny was determined to disappoint them all. "They say the third time is the charm," she said to Naju.

"So they do," Naju said, "so they do — and three times the trouble sometimes in cases like this."

"That is such nonsense, Naju," Granny said. "Women have five, six, and seven children without any trouble. They go and have them in the bushes if necessary. I know what it's like. I've had two of my own. It's no trouble at all."

"Well, yes," Naju said, "of course, it's no trouble, if you want to breed like bunnies. I didn't mean that at all."

"Well, I don't know what you mean, then. Queen Victoria had nine children. I don't think you would say she was breeding like a bunny."

Naju just shook her head. "How you do go on sometimes, Meher. All I know is I'm glad you're doing so well."

Granny smiled, but barely, not to make her satisfaction too transparent. After Jalu had been born Naju had said, "You two billy goats have made enough hay now. You're getting much too old to be milking each other still." She imagined she'd been charming, but Granny had been shocked to hear her talk, as she later put it to Rustomji, like a guttersnipe. Rustomji had laughed, but in the privacy of their bedroom, curtained by darkness, he'd said, "Well, you old nanny goat, do you think Naju was right? or do you think we should try one more time?" Granny had held him tightly and spoken fiercely. "I think we should keep on trying until one of us is dead."

When Naju had learned that Granny was pregnant again she'd said, "Well, best of luck, old thing, but it's going to be difficult." She'd sent some sev as a celebration. "It's a little bit sour," she'd warned, "because I put something in it to help the pregnancy. My herbalist says it's guaranteed to give you a son. I put in more raisins to make up for the sourness. I'll send you some sev everyday. That way we'll be sure the baby is all right. You must promise you will eat the sev everyday."

The sev wasn't too sour, but Granny wouldn't have eaten it if Rustomji hadn't encouraged her. It made an old woman happy, he said, his sister, who had no children of her own, and maybe it would even help the pregnancy; so she did.

"Have you been eating the sev regularly?" Naju asked as she picked up her brown paper bag again. "We want to be sure of a healthy baby."

"Yes, don't worry, I have. Thank you."

"Good. Here, I brought you something I thought you could use. It's the purest 22-karat yarn you'll ever find." She pulled out a plump golden skein from the bag and held it up in her bony hand like an apple. Granny accepted it with thanks. "Don't thank me," Naju continued. "No one I know can weave a finer pattern than you, my dear. This is all I can do to help, just to bring you materials. I would go into the business if I were you."

Naju had brought her threads of silk and cloths of satin and velvet before. Granny felt ashamed again, as she always did when Naju did her a good turn, for the resentment she still harbored. She knew, of course, that Naju didn't mean what she said about going into the business; a Cama didn't work for money, but Granny often gave away pieces of her work — tapestries, carpets, shawls, stoles, handbags — and the appreciation she received enhanced the value of the time she spent on them. She asked if Naju would like tea. They moved into the sittingroom, Stanley brought the tea things on a tray, including a plate of assorted cream and fruit filled biscuits, before retiring to squat in the corridor outside in case he was needed again.

2

Arre God, had I not known Granny had lived into her eighties I would have thought she was dying. Her eyes rolled, wide as saucers, large milky tears trickled down her cheeks leaving milky tracks; her voice was like a child's. "Suffocating," she said, suddenly doubling over, "window." Someone opened windows, doors, but it didn't help. Granny, in convulsions, vomited a porridge black and bright with blood through chattering teeth.

Her tongue protruded like a sausage from her mouth, as black and bright with blood as her vomit, as if she'd vomit her tongue. Mom and Jalu Masi, restrained by ayahs, stood to one side, too scared to cry. Rustomji held Granny in his arms on the floor where she'd fallen, getting vomit on himself, until the convulsions stopped, then picked her up, one arm around her shoulders, one under her knees, put her in bed, cleaned her up, then himself.

Calendar pages flew across the vista.

Granny appeared, still in bed, but breathing comfortably again; the bed was ringed by Rustomji, Granny's mother and father, a doctor (I could tell by his stethoscope and black bag). Mom and Jalu Masi, held again by ayahs, adorned the hinterland of the image like angels in a landscape from antiquity. "She is going to be all right," the doctor said. "It is unfortunate, but these things happen. What is important is she is going to be all right."

"Thank God for that," Rustomji said, caressing Granny's temples. "I was afraid ... well, never mind. She is going to be all right."

"Yesyes," said Granny's mother. "She is going to be all right. That is all that matters." She sat caressing Granny's arm across the bed from Rustomji. Granny's father hovered behind like a servant.

"Of course," said Naju. "That is all that matters. Thank God, and thank you so much, doctor. My prayers have been answered."

Granny didn't say anything, but I could see her gazing at Naju, I could hear what she was thinking: *You prayed for me to lose my child. The story must be true that you poisoned your first husband.* But I was the only one who heard. Her eyes were narrow, full of irony, but Naju appeared oblivious, ascribing it perhaps to her condition.

Rustomji saw the gaze, but when Granny looked at him the irony disappeared. "We shall have a son," she said, and the sharpness in her voice, even bitterness, was shocking. "We shall have another child. We shall have a son."

Rustomji looked at the doctor questioningly. The doctor nodded. "She is young. No reason she cannot have another child, but there is plenty of time. No need to rush."

Granny ignored him. She spoke again with the same deep bitterness. "We shall have a child as soon as I am able. And it will be a son."

Naju shook her head as if Granny were a child. "I am not sure that would be wise, Meherbanu. The next time we might not all be so lucky."

Granny turned her ironic gaze again on Naju. "We shall have a son. We shall have a son if it kills me."

Naju looked away. The doctor pretended not to notice. "No need to talk like that," he said. "No danger of that. If anything, we are now better prepared, but you should wait a little while longer before trying again."

Rustomji looked bewildered. "Your health is what matters, Mehru, my dear," he said. "We have got two fine daughters. We do not need a son. We do not have to have a son."

Granny did not look at him. "We shall have a son."

Naju shrugged.

Granny continued without looking at Naju. "I could tell this pregnancy was different. I could tell from the beginning something was wrong, something inside me was shrinking. All that — headaches, nausea, diarrhea, passing blood — it was all different from the other pregnancies. I will know what to do if it happens again. I will not let it happen again."

She held Rustomji's hand which still caressed her temple and looked again at Naju — who looked away again.

"I am tired," Granny said finally, sinking under the sheets, closing her eyes. "I want to sleep."

Rustomji covered her up. "Sleep, sleep, my dear. Go to sleep."

More calendar pages crossed the vista.

Granny was still in bed, but sitting, her back to the head-board, a copy of *Madame Bovary* in her hand. Rustomji sat beside her. "Look, Rustomji," Granny said, pointing to a line in the book. "This is what I am talking about, the bitter taste in the mouth, like ink. That is what I was tasting. That is *exactly* what I was tasting. Also all the other symptoms, the dry mouth, the suffocating, just read and see for yourself, the whole page."

Rustomji took the book from her to read the page she indicated.

"I kept thinking of the taste, and I thought of the book. When I was vomiting that was the taste. The scene stuck with me because it is so vivid. All my symptoms were *exactly* the same. Now, what do you think?"

Rustomji continued reading the page in silence. When he finished, he closed the book and set it on the bedside table. "Meherbanu," he said soberly, his eyes on the bedsheets between them, "you must not repeat this to anyone. Do you understand? You must not say to anyone what you have said to me. Whatever you think, you must say nothing. Do you understand?"

Granny replied wildly. "But why must I say nothing? If she has aborted my baby, why must I say nothing? If she has tried to poison me, why must I say nothing?"

Rustomji shook his head, continuing to speak quietly, his eyes still on the sheets. "Meherbanu," he said, "people will say you are getting all your ideas from books. They will say your imagination is getting the better of you. They will say you are going crazy."

Granny continued as wildly as before, waving her hands in exasperation. "They will *not* say I am going crazy. They will remember the stories about her first husband. They will know she poisoned him as she has now tried to poison me. That is what they will say."

Rustomji looked at her sharply; his voice took on an edge. "Mehru, that is unadulterated balderdash. You are *never* to mention that again. Do you understand me? Never even to al*lude* to that poppycock again. Do you understand me?"

Granny's hair was loose around her head, giving her face a wild look to match her tone, Lear on the heath as she might have phrased it herself. Rustomji had never been so stern with her before. She shook her head as if to clear it of debris. "Rustom," she said, her tone suddenly subdued, "I don't care what others say. I only care what you think. Do you think I am going crazy?"

"It doesn't matter what I think," Rustomji said, still keeping his eyes from her, and Granny knew he didn't believe her. "What matters is what others will say."

"But what does it matter what others say if it is not the truth?"

"That is just what I am saying, Meherbanu. What does it matter what others think if we know what the truth is for ourselves?"

His logic was transparently specious, but that was not what concerned Granny. "You do not believe me either," she said. "Look, let me show you one more thing, Rustom. Look at this." She pulled out another book from under her pillow and opened it to a chapter titled, "Abortifacients." When he protested, she held up her hand. "First, hear me out. Then believe what you want. In this chapter, it says arsenic or mercurial poisoning in small doses can cause a miscarriage. I just want you to read it and think about what has happened."

Rustomji took the book from her, but closed it and set it down with *Madame Bovary* on the bedside table without reading it. "Meherbanu, you are not understanding me. It does not matter what is written in books. How can I explain this?" He shook his head again as if he were at a loss. "Let me put it another way. I have written books myself as you know, two novels, but people were stupid enough to believe they were thinly veiled stories about the Camas and there was nothing I could do to convince them differently. In exchange for this hardship — this scandal — the Camas have given me a position which has enabled me to support myself and my family in a style only dreamed of by most people. What you are suggesting would be an ingratitude of the worst kind. I cannot impress this upon you enough. This can go no further. These are not things to be explained to people. These are things to be understood among ourselves. What is important is that you are well. That is what matters. Do we have an understanding?"

Granny didn't know whether he believed her after all; perhaps it wasn't possible for him to believe such a thing of his sister, but that wasn't the important thing. "Maybe you are right, Rustom," she said, surprising him with her sudden acquiescence.

"I know it. I am right. Have faith."

"But we *must* have another child, Rustom. We *must* have a son. We *must*."

"No, my dear Mehru, not if it is going to kill you. No son is worth such a price."

"But there is no danger of that, Rustom," Granny said. "You heard what the doctor said. But it *will* kill me if we do not have a son. I will not be able to bear it if we do not have a son. Then Naju will have won. We must try and try and try again until we have a son. That is all I want in my life now."

"We will see, Mehru, my dear," Rustomji said. "We will see."

Granny shook her head. "Nono, Rustom, it is you who are not understanding me now. Let me put it another way. I shall do as you wish. I shall say nothing about Naju and the poison — but only if we never stop trying to have a son. Do we have an understanding?"

Rustomji stared, but Granny wasn't to be cowed. She returned Rustomji's stare fixedly. "And I will not be eating any more sev — or anything else from Naju's house. Do we have an understanding, Rustom?"

Still he remained silent, still he stared.

"Otherwise, I shall tell them exactly what I think. I do not care what they think of me — no, nor what you think either. If I am crazy that is all right with me. Do we have an understanding?"

Rustomji smiled finally, nodded. "Of course."

Two years of calendar pages flew by, bad years during which Granny's parents died in quick succession, but Granny didn't provide details. Instead, she followed through quickly to her greatest news, the birth of Soli Mama, in the same bed; her face shone and the hair on her pillow streamed from her head as radiant as rays. I heard her thinking again: her purpose in life had been fulfilled; she had provided the Camas with a legitimate heir.

3

On the morning of the day Rustomji died, Granny had thought about the differences in her children and how evident they were so early in their lives. Pheroza played the piano slowly, cautiously, as if she might be punished for each wrong note. Jalu played at a furious pace as if she knew that however she played the applause would be the same, and she didn't want her playing to get in the way of the applause. Soli, on the other hand, had no interest in playing the piano at all, stating with unusual emphasis for a five-year-old that he would rather just sit and listen.

In the afternoon Rustomji had a fatal heart attack.

In the evening Naju came with a party of about ten friends and relatives to bear condolences and make the funeral arrangements. She also brought malido and bhakhras from her kitchen. Granny's eyes widened. "I cannot believe what I am seeing," she said. "I cannot believe even you would be so entirely devoid of shame."

Naju raised her eyebrows. "What do you mean, Meherbanu? He was my brother, after all." She held out the basket in which she'd wrapped the sweets. "These have been blessed with special prayers. It is the custom."

Granny seemed frozen, her arms remained stiff by her side, her eyes yoked to Naju's; a silence descended on the entire party.

Naju held out the basket again. "What is the matter, Meherbanu? Why are you looking at me like that?"

Granny continued to stare at Naju, wary as a wrestler in the ring. "Stanley!"

"Bai?"

Granny kept her eyes on Naju. "Stanley, bring the waste bucket from the kitchen — right away!"

"Bai?"

Granny glared swiftly at Stanley. "What have you got? Cottonwool in your ears? Bring the waste bucket at once!"

Stanley dashed to the kitchen.

The party remained silent, staring at Granny, who turned her gaze back on Naju who continued to hold out the basket. "I cannot believe it," Granny said, "after all you have done, how you still have the gall to bring me sweets."

Naju frowned, began to withdraw the basket. "I do not know what you mean, Meherbanu. I know this is a difficult time for you, but it is really not necessary to be so melodramatic."

Granny began to shout. "Melodramatic! Melodramatic! Is that what you call it?" Her hands trembled by her side.

Naju stiffened. "Really, Meherbanu. If you do not like sweets you have only to say so. I only brought them because it is the custom."

"Only the custom is it, to put arsenic in your sev? Only the custom to abort my baby? Only the custom to kill what you cannot control? Is that what you are saying?"

Naju spoke carefully, in a monotone. "Really, Meherbanu, this would be slanderous if you had not lost your husband, but

you are not in your right mind. There are many people who
have been saying it for a long time — ever since you lost your
baby. It is very understandable, but I want you to know I am
your friend. I want you to know you can count on me for
anything I can do."

I began to understand what people meant when they said
someone was beside herself. Granny sputtered and trembled so
violently she fell out of focus, appeared to vibrate. Stanley had
reappeared with the waste bucket from the kitchen, but she
grabbed the basket of sweets from Naju's hands, emptied the
contents on the floor, and stamped on them smashing the
bhakhras to bits, flattening the malido like clay. "Get out! Get
out of my house, all of you! The only thing you can do for me
is to keep out of my way forevermore!"

Naju joined her hands. "I will pray for you, Meherbanu. I
can see you have need of prayers. This is a difficult time, I know.
I shall remember you in my prayers."

Granny had held herself back for Rustomji's sake for too
long, was no longer responsible for her actions. She spit as she
spoke, her lips flecked with saliva. "You killer! You murderess!
You are lower than a snake. I have no need of your prayers! Pray
for yourself, you swine of a woman!"

Naju took a deep breath. "Well, we shall leave — but I must
say those are strange accusations to be coming from someone
who couldn't see the truth when it was right under her nose."

Naju knew Granny was sensitive about her sharp and shining nose, but her meaning became clearer still when Rustomji's
will was declared. He'd established a trust for Helen Dastur.
Granny had enjoyed the company of the witty blond Anglo-
Indian on several occasions after she'd met her on the night of
the play. She knew Rustomji had sometimes visited her when
he had time from work during the day, but she refused to believe
(as the size of the fund persuaded many others) that there'd
been anything improper about the visits. She liked Helen, but

wished Rustomji had said something to her about it so she might have been better prepared.

Next I saw perhaps the strangest scene yet: Granny seated at the head of the long dining table, a ten year old Soli Mama to her left, a bowl of what looked like mutton stew steaming before them; she ladled a mouthful of the stew into her mouth, shut her eyes tight as fists, champed her jaws like those of a horse, wrinkled her brow until her forehead appeared like one great gash; her cheeks turned momentarily to glass, as did her throat and chest; I saw morsels of food swirl in her mouth like clothes in a dryer, sloshed by her tongue, packed and moistened by saliva, cut and ground by molars; I saw her gullet widen to accommodate the mush, juices rise like waves from her stomach. You might say I didn't get the picture at first, this clinical progress of her food, but I soon recalled the significant detail: Soli Mama was not to come into his inheritance until he was eighteen; and Granny, afraid Naju would find a way to poison him yet, became his food taster.

Word got around that the strain had been too much for Granny to bear, but Granny didn't care what anyone thought anymore. She sacked one of her servants when she learned he'd worked once for Naju, and didn't ease her vigilance until she'd ensconced herself in Cambridge chaperoning Soli Mama during his college years. Then she looked, as Mom put it, as if she'd fallen.in love. Jalu Masi, had she not been married to my incomparable Sohrab Uncle and living in Hong Kong, might have said she had the strength of a survivor in her face. After Cambridge, Granny took a month's vacation every year, mostly at her favorite hill station, Mahableshwar, but the seeds of her paranoia must have been deeply sown indeed for a four day delay at the Bagdogra airport to undo a four year rest cure in Cambridge.

The Episode of the Vase

Perhaps the last time Granny found the initiative to do anything was when Soli Mama got married. Among other things she sat at her dining table day after day for a month with the Bombay telephone book and went through it from A to Z by the dim light of her chandelier to make sure no one was left out. Naju, of course, was not invited. Two thousand guests came to dinner, governors, chief ministers, members of parliament. Granny prepared the invitations, planned the menu, hired the band. Soli Mama was the cornerstone of her existence; he'd been with her for thirty years, she was not entirely sure of his choice, but glad he was so sure himself, a vivacious girl of eighteen with the white skin and black hair you'd have associated with Snow White. He would only be moving downstairs from her, but for a mother as jealous as Granny had been of Soli Mama the distance was secondary to the weaning away process, the spur being to establish yet another generation of heirs for the House of Cama.

If there'd been any doubt about the deservedness of Snow White — or Farida Banker, to give her her proper name — it was put to rest by an incident which the family remembered forever after as the Episode of the Vase. Turning the corner from her sittingroom into the corridor, Granny almost tripped over her bearer of six weeks who had been squatting there. She drew herself back immediately, launched into a tirade. "Salo luccho, swine! How many times have I told you not to sit in wait for me like that. But that's what you want — let the old woman fall, let her die, then we will rob her blind — but don't try your tricks with me. I know your tricks, you cunning thieving sons of swine."

Granny's outbursts always dismayed me, whether directed toward her servants, toward salesmen in long narrow dress shops for hiding the best cloths from her after they'd cluttered their counters with reams of satins, cottons, rayons; toward maitre d's in quiet, dimly lit restaurants for hiding the choicest entrees on the menu; toward ticket agents in crowded places for hiding the best seats from her chauffeurs who stood in line for her. I felt more sadness than embarrassment, particularly when, sometimes in the middle of a scene, she would turn to Rusi and me with a sudden sweet smile and apologize to us — to no one else — as if to exonerate us from all culpability in the affair. We would nod silently, awkward in the spotlight, until she resumed her tirade and Mom or Soli Mama or whoever else might have been with us made entreaties to her rationality.

The servants didn't stay long no matter how well they were paid. I felt they stayed sometimes only because they recognized she was harmless, that her imprecations said more about herself than about them, that they were being paid for their endurance more than their work of which there was not very much. I felt sometimes they even pitied her, but could take only so much abuse themselves. "Arre, memsahib," the bearer said, getting to his feet, "what is all this talk? It is not so. I was only sitting."

"Salo soower swine! You dare to call me a liar! You think I cannot do without you? You are all like that, let us see how much the old woman will take — but you can get out. The old woman has had enough. I will not have you here for one more day."

The bearer shuffled and asked for his pay. She said she would get it from the bedroom if he would wait right where he was — but then the bearer acted unexpectedly. There was no reason for him to mistrust Granny, but he wanted to go to the bedroom with her. Perhaps he meant her no harm, perhaps he meant to take more money than she owed him, perhaps he meant just once for his will to prevail over hers; no one would ever know the truth of the matter, perhaps not even the bearer himself, because at that point they'd reached an impasse: she refused to go to the bedroom with him; he refused to let her go alone — at which point Soli Mama walked in inquiring about the lunch Granny had promised to send downstairs for himself and Farida. After she'd explained the situation, Soli Mama told the bearer, as Granny had, to wait and they'd get him his money, but the bearer, no longer even listening, chose to force the issue, picked up a frosted blue vase, threw out the sunflowers, brandished it like a weapon, and tried to edge them toward the bedroom, but Soli Mama adroitly slipped the two of them into the diningroom instead where the bearer followed them slowly, threateningly, around the long dining table.

It was during this slow stalk around the table that Farida came upstairs. When she understood what was going on she said to the bearer, "That is all? That is all that this is about? Then there is no problem. You come down with me, no? I will give you the money. You can come into the bedroom, you can come up to my cupboard, you can take the money out of my purse. That is not a problem at all." She spoke with a smile as if she couldn't understand what the fuss was about.

Soli Mama and Granny were too amazed to speak. The bearer said, "This is a good memsahib. She will not cheat me. She does not shout and swear like the other memsahib." Farida's snowwhite appearance had worked its magic. When she beckoned him with her hand, saying "Come with me, no?" looking uncannily like one of the coy young girls the bearer must have seen in so many Hindi movies, he put down the vase and followed her downstairs. At the bottom of the stairs Farida looked up to see Soli Mama and Granny staring down still speechless with disbelief. "Why are you two looking like two fishes?" she said. "Get inside, no? What is there for you to do now?" When Soli Mama and Granny had locked themselves into Granny's flat, Farida looked over her shoulder, past the entrance to the house as if she saw someone she knew, and, when the bearer followed her gaze, slipped quickly into her flat, slamming the door shut and bolting it.

This was an incident I'd heard about, but not seen before. The scenes were becoming increasingly familiar as they caught up with the present. The bearer had rushed in a rage at Farida's brother who'd walked right then into the driveway, who was, fortunately for himself, unfortunately for the bearer, stalwart enough to take care of himself. The bearer lost two teeth. He returned that evening with a knife, but Farida's father paid him off enough never to return.

2

Then came the painful scenes, the shameful scenes, toward the end: Granny, off limits to Soli Mama's three sons because Farida worried about her influence; Granny, shouting at her bridge partners for cheating, reduced to playing incessant games of patience; Granny, cruising Warden Road in her chauffeur driven Studebaker for gangas to stay overnight because she was afraid to sleep alone even with Soli Mama and his family and servants downstairs from her and a chowkidar at the gate; Granny, caring no more about herself, her flat, her furnishings, dressed in rags, roaming and stumbling aimlessly through her dusty cavernous cobwebby rooms, ill with the ailment for which she refused to see a doctor, pain from the illness hunched like a goblin in her face, arms raised heavenward in a wreath, a wishbone framing

.her head, yammering aloud: "Oh, God! Oh, God! Take me! Take me now! Take me away from all this! Why do you not take me away! Why do you wait! What is there left for me! Why do you torture me like this! Oh, God! Oh, God! Why do you torture me! Why!"

The last, finally reassuring, scene of her death: Granny, seated in a chair, talking to all three of her children (even Jalu Masi, after years in Hong Kong, called on a premonition by Mom), gathered around her in a protective triangle, perhaps even a newly burgeoning love, her head dropping midsentence to her chest — but not before each child appeared in a bubble floating from her head: Soli Mama sitting on a throne with a crown on his head; Jalu Masi in a luxurious couch in the stained glass light of a Tiffany lamp; Mom hovering like a helicopter, giant angel wings fastened to her back.

The last image, of Granny dying in the chair, head slumped forward, faded into a silhouette, framed by a bright glow, before the outline changed. The new shape, of a man, squat, dense, was familiar, but I couldn't place it until what I can only describe as an aura revealed its identity; it was Jalbhai Pherozshah Cama, JP himself. When he spoke I recognized his voice from the time I'd heard him speak, holding on to the chair he'd reserved for his friend while the uniformed English official tried to take it away.

"Let me clear up a few things first, Homi. Everyone is always full of praise for me, and usually for the wrong reasons. Bapaiji is cynical enough to think God is a kind of cosmic joke, Granny is bitter enough to think Him unjust, but both are wrong. They think they are in heaven but they are not; they are at what might best be understood as a waystation. Bapaiji admired my honors, Granny my worldly goods, but both admired the wrong things, the end product, not the means. Capitalism is fine, but without the human touch it is no different from totalitarianism. Let me be more specific: I was on a sightseeing tour in Jerusalem once, staying at the Mediterranean Hotel. The city was full of history, of course, and there were groves of peaches, pomegranates, apricots, oranges — I always bore in mind the possibility of transplanting new fruits and plants in India — but more than anything else I was impressed by the sight of some nails, reputedly the nails with which Jesus Christ had been crucified, embedded in a stone some twelve inches thick. The nails did not make a Christian of me, but they deepened my respect for Christianity and, as a consequence, made me a better Zoroastrian. Just the previous month I'd attended a piano recital by Hans von Bulow in Boston where he'd performed Beethoven's *Diabelli Variations* — one theme, thirty-three variations — but I had not been much impressed. I preferred the sonata form where a single theme is explored and developed to its fullest — but watching the nails I realized that variations too are a form of exploration and development. Christianity became relevant as a variation on the theme of Zoroastrianism. Each was profound by itself, but their conjunction provided a breadth neither possessed alone. The many religions of the world reveal the world in all its variety like the variations of a theme. Heaven is not a tangible place as Bapaiji, Granny, and your pappa have imagined, recreated to suit their own needs. It is a state of mind encompassing all these possibilities — but I have spoken enough, and presumptuously. Your memoscan has the potential to accomplish more than I could even imagine. Good luck! God Bless!"

MOM AND DAD

Froglegs

My head felt better, the needles turned to mere rubber mallets. My temples throbbed with dull beats on the heels of my hands as they held up my head where I continued to sit on the bathstool in the verandah. The cawing of the crows had stopped, but the commotion of traffic on Cooperage Road, the shuffle of the crowd, and the hum of the conversation, had increased. The sporting event, whatever it was, must have ended. The loudspeakers had been turned off. I must have been unconscious during Granny's revelations; otherwise, I'd surely have heard "Jana Gana Mana," the national anthem, marking the end of the program in the stadium.

A smell of frying potatoes wafted up to the verandah from the second floor. I recognized the Mehtas' cooking oil. They fried wafers, chips as I'd learned to call them in the States, every evening. Rusi and I had got into the habit of visiting them at that hour. No other wafers, not the O.K. wafers, not the Victory wafers, not the Coronation wafers, tasted as good. The smell of the wafers more than anything else told me it had to be almost seven o'clock, the Mehtas' dinner hour, and sure enough a sweet curry smell followed shortly.

My bedroom door opened, someone entered, switched on the light. I winced at the sound more than the light, a loud snap, someone cracking a knuckle. "Baba? Where is baba gone?" It was our ganga, Sunanda. She would doubtless call me "baba" even when I was an octogenarian with doddering step and quavering voice. She had worked for the family (for everyone in Mayo House, in fact) ever since I could remember. She came for an hour every morning to dust and sweep and mop. She would have visited the Patels on the fourth floor before us, visit after us the Mehtas on the second floor, then the Bannerjees on the first, and the Chibbers on the ground. She never aged. The work kept her fit. She hitched her sari between her legs, tied it in a knot, and stuffed it into her waist so she could squat comfortably as she covered each room on sleek brown haunches, first with broom in hand, then a rag periodically soaked in a bucket of water. Even her torso, exposed between the waist of her sari and the high rim of her choli, remained firm and trim. When Rusi and I had been young, the ayahs had taken care of us, but after they'd left (Rusi's ayah, Julie, pensioned by the family, to live with her son and his family in Goa; my ayah, Mary, being much younger, to a subsequent position) Sunanda had helped Mom with cooking, cleaning, light washing (the dhobi came once a week for the heavy wash), ironing, errands and the like on the days our bearer, Jairam, was off.

"Baba, where you are?" Sunanda couldn't see me where I sat in the verandah and I was too weak to say anything. I was only barely aware of her movements.

"Bai, bai, come quick," she said then (she must have seen me). "Baba is got up from his bed." I heard her scurrying from the room. "He is sitting on stool in verandah. He is feeling better, no?"

Suddenly, Sunanda and Mom and Jairam and Rusi were all around me. Mom put her hand on my back; I was still leaning forward and couldn't see her, but I knew her touch. "Homi, can you hear me?" she said, rubbing my back slowly. "You don't have to talk. You don't have to open your eyes. Just nod your head if you can hear me."

I raised my head from my hands, wanting to answer her, wanting to see them around me, wanting to stand up, but my head felt too heavy and I'd have toppled onto my hands and knees if Rusi hadn't caught me and, along with everyone else, helped me back to the bed.

"The heat must have made him weak, Mom," Rusi said, closing the doors to the verandah. "We don't know how long he's been sitting there. He'll be better when the room cools down again."

"Yes. Maybe." Mom was tucking me in again.

"Bai," Jairam was saying, "Bai, baba is better?"

"Arre, Jairam," Mom said, "what can I tell you? He got up. That is a good sign." She spoke conversationally, but with an edge as if she were afraid to hope for too much.

"Baba is better, hey-hey! Teep-Taap! I will make him soup like you showed me, bai, chicken soup. Baba will like my soup. Yesyes-verygood-hurray!"

I could just imagine him then, the tiny man with the large head, the embarrassed pleased smile, wanting to help but afraid to get in the way, skinny wiry limbs emerging from his striped shirt and baggy shorts. He'd been with us a long while, but more importantly he'd been with Mom during the time Dad had died which had led to a trust between them that time alone might never have established. We provided his board and lodging; he kept his things in our godown, sleeping there on a thin mattress on the floor, and visiting his wife and two daughters in Bandra on his day off every week. He wished his wife would move even farther so he'd have an excuse not to visit her at all. I understood she was a large woman, and though he gave her all his earnings she badgered him continually for more. He didn't care how infrequently he saw her. At first we had a bearer, a ganga, two ayahs, and a cook; but when Rusi and I became too old for the ayahs, Mom found it easier to retire the cook with the ayahs and teach Jairam a few things in the kitchen than to manage so many of them at once. Jairam couldn't have been better pleased, loved to show off his newly acquired skills. "I will cook curryrice, bai," he said. "I will cook lemon souffle for baba. He will like my cooking."

"Wait, Jairam," Mom said. "Wait. If baba wants soup I will tell you."

"Also curryrice, bai, also curryrice I have made. You said, no, my curryrice is good, no?"

"Yes, Jairam, but first baba must drink. If he cannot drink soup, how will he eat your good curryrice?"

"Yesyes. Bai is right. Bai is right."

"Now go to the kitchen. If I want the soup I will tell you. Sunanda, there is nothing more for you to do now today. Come back tomorrow."

After the two of them left I heard Mom pull one of the folding chairs to the bedside and sigh as she sat down. "He looks better, Mom," Rusi said, "not so white like before. He's going to be okay. He just had a relapse after the long trip — the doc said that he might, I told you, no? He must have been conscious to go to the verandah like that, no? I'm telling you, he's going to be okay."

I sensed he was standing beside her, both of them looking at me. "I hope so, Rusi, I hope so. Sssh!" The hum of the airconditioner worked to ease the throbbing in my temples. Mom put her hand under the covers and squeezed my hand. "Homi," she said, "if you can hear me, if I make any impression on you at all, give me a sign — nod your head, open your eyes, move your hand, anything."

I opened my eyes. The bedside lamp had been lit. Rusi put his hand on my shoulder. "Can you say something?" Mom said. "Can I get you something? anything?"

How can I explain the sensations? She couldn't see my eyes

were open. I was in limbo with access to eternal secrets; she was on a one-way thoroughfare heading toward death — or from which death is the only escape, however you prefer. I couldn't hear her as much as read her thoughts — not even read her thoughts (which implies a conscious effort) as much as think them with her, or perhaps a nanosecond later, as if I were hearing her thoughts. I opened my mouth to speak, but no sound came. I needed someone to hear my thoughts as I imagined I was hearing hers — but however bizarre the situation, I no longer thought I was going crazy. I understood that I'd stumbled upon a different mode of communication. "Would you like something to eat?" Mom said, "some chicken soup? Jairam's made some. It's quite good. There's also some sali boti."

I still couldn't see her lips move with the words, but they twitched as if something else were on her mind. Her eyes darted as if to avoid mine, and around her the entire panorama shifted. We were assembled at our four foot square dining table with the glass top, seated in the cane chairs in our regular formation, Rusi on her left, I on her right, and Dad across. The bearer (Peter, not Jairam who came later) had filled our water glasses, left a second bottle of cold water on the table, and cleared away the empty soup plates. "Did you like the chicken soup?" She was speaking to Dad; her lips twitched and she avoided his eyes; she'd prepared froglegs for the main course; she liked experimenting with exotic foods; Dad hated her experiments, but she persisted and was invariably stalemated in her attempts to make a gourmet of Dad.

The bearer brought the katchoubar and the breaded froglegs on a large blue dish. "What is this?" Dad said immediately, looking suspiciously at Mom.

"It's only chicken," Mom said, pretending to have difficulty spooning the katchoubar into her plate. "Try it."

Perhaps if she'd said simply "Chicken" or "Chicken. Why?" he might have believed her, but Mom was a lousy liar. She had to say "It's *on*ly chicken," as if it might have been something else; she had to say "Try it," as if he'd never tried chicken in his life. Dad saw through her right away. "It is frog's legs," he said. "Do not lie to me. How many times have I told you not to do this to me?"

Mom's eyes were wide like those of a child who couldn't believe her ruse has been discovered. "It's chicken! Try it. I'm telling you it's just like chicken."

Well, it had to be either chicken or just like chicken; it couldn't be both. Dad swallowed his glass of cold water in a single gulp, dumped his napkin next to the wooden napkin ring, noisily scraped his chair against the tile getting up, and shouted at Mom. "I wish you would not do this to me. Now, because of you, I will have to go hungry." Without waiting for her response he stamped out of the room.

Mom's eyes filled with tears. "I wish he would try it. I wish he would at least try it. How can he know he doesn't like it if he won't even try it."

Rusi and I were silent, not entirely convinced of the edibility of froglegs ourselves. "Mom," I said, "where's the rest of the frog?"

"I don't know," she said distractedly, dabbing at her eyes with a tiny lace handkerchief. "I think it might be too small to eat."

I picked at my froglegs, fantasizing that perhaps they didn't kill the frogs but merely amputated them and popped them back among the lily pads on crutches and wheelchairs.

"If he goes hungry it's his own fault," Mom was saying. "It's not my fault if he won't even try something new. You like the froglegs, don't you, Homi-Rusi? They're not so bad. They're just like chicken, aren't they?"

Rusi, nodding, was eating the froglegs happily enough — but he, of course, had drunk cowpiss just as willingly during our navjote. For me eating the froglegs meant more than merely eating an exotic food — I felt I was betraying Dad. If it tasted just like chicken why the hell didn't she just serve chicken and save everyone this bother, especially when she knew how Dad felt? It was a way Mom had of straitjacketing Dad and siding with her I felt I betrayed him.

I sometimes fixed myself a snack after dinner, usually buttered toast. It became an intricate process because I wanted the butter to melt directly on the toast, which meant I had to take it out of the refrigerator about half an hour before I applied it so it would be soft, and I had to butter the toast as soon as it popped — otherwise, the toast would cool and the butter would lie thick and yellow and pasty and cold instead of bright and fluid and warm. Since we had a two-slice toaster, one slice would necessarily be cooler than the other when it was buttered. I toyed with the idea of toasting just one slice at a time so I could butter each to perfection while the next was being toasted, but gave it up because it seemed a waste to use a two-slice toaster for just one slice at a time, too priggish even for me. I buttered quickly instead, ignoring all distractions. On the night of the froglegs dinner I'd just buttered six slices when Dad came into the kitchen. "Did you make those for me, Homi?"

He was grinning, as if he'd made a joke, but I couldn't smile. I knew I was about to be cheated out of my snack as I'd been before. What annoyed me even more than losing the toast was his manner, as if I were being entirely too humorless. "No," I said, "I made them for myself."

"Do you mind if I have some then? I didn't have any dinner, you know."

Of course I minded, but I couldn't tell him that. He was Dad, and everything we had in the house we had because of him. "No, I don't mind. You can have them."

"I'll take just two. Then you can have four. Will that be all right?"

My rage made me stubborn. I had to have all of them or none. "No, you can have them all," I said solemnly, without looking at him. "I'll just finish off the leftover froglegs."

I told Mom about it later and she must have said something to him because he never asked for toast again. He even stayed out of the kitchen when I made the toast — but that was not what I wanted either. I had pushed Mom between the two of us again. What I wanted was to be able to say No to him myself, but that was an understanding a long time coming.

I felt the tug back to the present like a muscle spasm in my head, back to Mom by my bedside — but a Mom as if I were seeing her for the first time, or rather more like an unexpected variation on a theme I'd taken for granted. Her lips, always small, sometimes gaily painted, were more pinched; her cheeks, always high, were heavier; her hair, stiff because of her permanent, and black, appeared soft and white; her skin, customarily well creamed, reflecting all light brilliantly, reflected only grey; the wells under her eyes, usually well powdered, were deeper, darker, glistening with tears. She spoke again, but again her lips appeared not to move. "Homi, please don't go. I need you. Please don't go."

She appeared to be concentrating intensely, as if to heal me by telepathy; I assumed Rusi had left the room. I thought my eyes were closed, but I could see her. I tried to return the pressure of her hand under the sheets, but couldn't be sure that I did.

"I have lost too many already, Homi." Her hand gripped mine more tightly. "When your dad died — he was the first — I said I needed time, everyone said I needed time, time and prayer, time and prayer. I thought it would heal me if I repeated it to myself — Time and Prayer, TimeandPrayer, Timeandprayerandtimeandprayerandtimeandprayerandtimeandprayerand — as if it were a prayer in itself. But then Mummy died and Bapaiji less than a month after her, and all three in less than one year — and then this horrible, horrible thing ... this horrible ... Oh, God!"

Ah, this mother of mine, always a little girl in the body of a woman, now the body of an old woman, always lovely to the world, even to Mr. Grouse, my curmudgeonly Physics teacher in high school who once remarked, "Some mother you've got there, Homi," watching her walk away, his mouth open, his eyes glazed, barely aware he'd spoken to me. I thought he looked silly, but I didn't know why. I knew it had something to do with my mother, but I didn't know what. When I told her about it she smiled like a six year old with a new doll. "Everybody says that," she said, refusing with a coy smile to elucidate further. She thought the world was her oyster and couldn't understand why her openhearted appeals were occasionally resisted. There we were, on the upper deck of a red lumbering B.E.S.T. (Bombay Electric Supply & Transport) bus, returning from a visit to the doctor (Great News! I'd been free of the calipers for a while; Mom and Mary had been exercising my leg; I might soon dispense even with my cane) and a shopping spree (bags on our laps, in our hands, at our feet). We would normally have taken a taxi, but perhaps Mom felt she had been profligate enough with her purchases. Dad, who took the car to work everyday, despaired of ever convincing her that she was no longer a Cama. A young man in a white shirt and shorts revealing dark sinewy workman limbs sat in front of us with a loud transistor radio tuned to a station playing Hindi film music. Mom's request was hardly overbearing: "Arre baba, turn that down a little bit, no? please?" There was even a cajole in her voice, in her expression, to appear less offensive, but the young man turned and said, "Arre wahwah, memsahib. You think everyone is your servant, to tell them what to do — but this is not your private motor with your private driver. This is a public convenience, for *all* of the people."

The man faced front again. For a moment Mom said nothing; then, with more dismay than anger, she said, "What a horrible, horrible man! Come along, Homi. We're getting off."

We picked up our bags and descended the stairs. The man didn't even look at us. "We can stay downstairs, Mom," I said. "We can't hear him so loudly from here." But Mom wanted to get off the bus altogether. We took a taxi the rest of the way home. Mom couldn't stop talking in the taxi about the "horrible" man; she just couldn't understand him; she'd done "nothing wrong." I understood that Mom was "right," but I also understood there had been more at stake than a loud transistor radio. Perhaps she worked it out for herself subsequently, but I cannot understand, even at this remove, how she could keep herself so ignorant for so long.

"Waitwaitwaitwait, Homi, you are not being fair to your mummy." It was Dad. I wasn't surprised, having expected to hear from him after Granny had finished. "It is you who fail to understand. You cannot discredit her anymore than you can discredit the system that made her; the world makes us in its own image. First her family shielded her; then I. If she is ignorant it is our fault, not hers. Everywhere there is a balance. You think she had nothing to worry about, but she paid for her security in ways you do not understand. After I died, after her mummy and Bapaji died, she was finally alone, no one to look after her; she had to learn to grow up after she had grown old. Bear with me, Homi. I have the advantage of hindsight over you — and your misfortune with your machine, your memoscan, has made it possible for me to reveal this to you. Bear with me."

Edinburgh

The face of the young man in front of me so resembled that of the young man in the pictures I'd taken on my arrival in Aquihana in a photo machine in a Woolworth's on Main Street, that just for a moment I thought it was mine: handsome, yes, quite handsome, though I say it myself, and so glabrous it might have been carved from marble, a big confident grin with perfect teeth, hair swept back with no part and flat as if he'd just taken off a cap (my hair in the photographs is longer, with sideburns reaching below my ears, a part on the left, and swept in a wave from my forehead), and eyes wide with curiosity (just like mine except that I'd inherited wells under my eyes from Mom).

Dad's face shrank then as if a camera were panning away revealing a torso draped in a tartan mantle secured on the left shoulder by a brooch, a tartan kilt with a leather pouch hanging in front, tartan breeches barely visible beneath the kilt, brown knee stockings, green flashes hanging from his garters, and black buckled shoes. In his hand he held a boat-shaped cap with two ribbons hanging behind it, and as I watched he put it on his head completing a picture we had of him in the family album. "This mantle, Homi," he said, touching it lightly, "as you call it, is a plaid. It is part of the Highland dress. At one time it was five feet wide and twelve to fifteen feet long. A Highlander could

pleat it around his waist and throw the loose end over his
shoulder just like a sari, he could draw it over his head in the
rain and roll himself in it to sleep at night. This leather pouch
is a sporran; the French called it a cache-sexe, but it is just a
purse; that's the French for you. These breeches are trews; if
Bapaiji had looked carefully she would have seen that the
Highlanders are not always naked under their kilts — when
King George IV paid a state visit to Edinburgh in 1822 he wore
pink silk tights under his kilt — but Bapaiji was more interested
in making fun than anything else. In retrospect, though, I think
it might just have been part of her strategy to get me back to
India — she was so afraid I might like Edinburgh too much ever
to return.

"This boat-shaped cap as you call it is a glengarry; sometimes a balmoral is worn with the Highland dress, but the
glengarry looks more authentically Scottish; the balmoral looks
too much like a beret, too French. These stockings are hose and
these shoes are brogues." Dad acknowledged me with a profes-
sorial nod. "Look, now, Homi. I want to show you something."

Dad was followed by the celestial camera on his way to a
Grundig radiogram (the same he'd had in his bedroom in
Bombay — that we still had). The walls were paneled, the room
spartanly furnished: an L-shaped desk, rotary chair on castors,
a large compartmentalized cupboard, green couch, unmade bed,
all duplicates of the Bombay furniture; also a fireplace against
the wall adjacent to the radiogram. Dad flicked a switch, a
record dropped, and bagpipe music filled the room. "Now,
Homi, be patient," he said. "It seems you have to be Scottish
to like bagpipe music — Bapaiji called it snakecharming music
— but it didn't take me long to acquire the taste. Actually, it
is sinuous music; Bapaiji was right, but not in the derisive sense
she meant. Two of the notes in the scale of the bagpipe are
quarter tones — that is why it cannot be used in a symphony
orchestra; that is why it has an oriental tone; that is why it

sounds like a snakecharmer's pipe which also has quarter tones like so many Indian instruments. I knew better than to take Bapaiji's remarks seriously, of course — or perhaps I should say I knew better than to take them personally.

"Anyway, let me get back to what I was showing you. Watch me now." He stood with one arm curved by his head, listening intently to the music. I watched his bare knees enviously; however much I resembled him my right knee would never be as healthy as his. He broke suddenly into a series of intricate steps executed on the same spot. It was a vigorous performance but also delicate, especially when he hopped on one foot while twirling the other in front of and behind the calf. "This is the fling," he said, executing another loop with his foot, "and the dance is called the Highland Fling. It's something I never mastered while I was in Edinburgh. There is an irony here, Homi. This is a victory dance; I wanted to dance it when my examinations were over, when your mummy agreed to marry me, whenever I received a promotion at work, but I had to die before I could do it well, when I had no victory to celebrate — well, maybe one. I died before Bapaiji; perhaps my only victory over her — but what good is a victory with no one to share the celebration? and what a cruel reason for a celebration. It is spiteful of me, and I know it, but I cannot help myself. She always resented me; I always blamed myself for her resentment and tried to make it up by being whatever she wanted, but that is not the way. People hate you if you go against their wishes, but they despise you if you don't; and a man may be hated, but only a coward is despised.

"Yes, it is an irony, but even the irony is double-edged. I thought my greatest satisfaction when I died would be her dissatisfaction, but I was wrong. I felt only loss. I want to reconcile the loss, and yet I have chosen to be here in Edinburgh, where I was farthest from her — but that is not the only reason, as she would have you believe. That is hardly the only reason, no! Edinburgh is beautiful — beautiful! I love Edinburgh. In this respect I suppose I am just like your Granny — her Cambridge is my Edinburgh, her Englishmen are my Scotsmen. Perhaps for you, though, never having lived in the United Kingdom, there is no difference between English and Scots. Of course, there is no reason for you to have given it any thought, but let me just clear up some things.

"The English don't care what anyone thinks, but the Scots have a more tenuous hold on their identity. They still bridle when their sovereign is called Elizabeth II because, as they rightly object, Elizabeth I was never queen of Scotland. It is impossible to be like the English because the English never want to be like anyone else, but to be like the Scots is to flatter them. The English have a dry sense of humor, but the Scots need a surgical operation to get a joke into their heads — but this same vulnerability makes the Scots more lovable. The English laugh at the legend of the Loch Ness monster, the Scots call her Nessie as if she were a pet. Common sense, you see, is less prized by the Scots than imagination — but you might as well say that England is to Scotland as prose is to poetry.

"Actually, the one time that comes to mind of the Scots aping the English proved disastrous for the Scots. In 1698, there was talk of merging the Scottish and English parliaments at Westminster — but the Scots hesitated to hack yet another notch into their sense of nationhood, and decided instead to found the colony of Darien on the Isthmus of Panama so they could reap the same benefits in raw materials and trade with the American natives and their Spanish conquerors as the English with their growing empire overseas. Unfortunately, most of the Scottish fleet was shipwrecked, the surviving colonists found only disease, starvation, and hostile natives in Darien, and the economic debilitation resulting from the Darien Expedition did much to hasten the union with England. I think you get my point. King James founded the University of Edinburgh in 1582, but omitted to endow it with any money so that for two hundred years it was accommodated in a dingy cluster of buildings. The City Observatory was built in 1792, but there was no money for a telescope. A civic war memorial to commemmorate Wellington's peninsula campaign was begun in 1822, designed to resemble the Parthenon, but it was left unfinished because once again funding ran short.

"Do not laugh, Homi. We Indians are the same. We spend hundreds of thousands of rupees on weddings and ceremonies and celebrations and live the rest of our lives like mendicants. Maybe that is why we got along so well for so long with the British. We were like children; they were our mothers and fathers — but how meager the common sense of the English appears against the wall-to-wall hearts of the Scots — and, to be fair to the Scots, an American professor discovered that next to the Jews the Scots exhibit the highest incidence of genius per head of population than any other race on earth: David Hume, Dugald Stewart, James Boswell, John Knox, Sir John Napier, Sir Walter Scott, Sir Arthur Conan Doyle, Robert Lewis Stevenson, Thomas Carlyle, Alexander Graham Bell, J. M. Barrie, James Craig, Charles Rennie Mackintosh, Robert Burns, Robert Adam, Adam Ferguson, Adam Smith...

"But I am talking too much. Instead of talking so much, all this bukbuk as Bapaiji would say, let me just show you what it was about Edinburgh that got me so excited in the first place."

Dad led me to a tall narrow latticed window which he opened with a flourish. "Look!" The pride in his voice, in his smile, rivaled that of any mother with her newborn. "Take a deep breath and look on the face of paradise."

I took a deep breath, a step forward, and looked, hoping I wouldn't have to fake my appreciation because I didn't want to hurt his feelings, but the sight filled me immediately with wonder. I saw first a castle like a crown atop a rugged rise of hill with a dry moat, a drawbridge, bronze statues in niches on either side of the gateway, towers, turrets, ramparts, a wide esplanade with a cannon, and a flag fluttering vigorously in the bright cloudless sky. "That," said Dad in a new deep rich voice, "is Castle Rock. You might have heard of the cannon on the esplanade, Mons Meg? It weighs five tons, it is known all over the world." He spoke as if he'd discovered Castle Rock. I found his joy infectious, listened attentively.

"There is a new and an old Edinburgh," he said. "First there was only the Edinburgh on the rock — the town sprang up around the Castle because it was best fortified that way. The houses were built, one squatting on top of the other, the first form of flats in a skyscraper, what you call highrises in America, because the only possible expansion was upward. The Edinburghers preferred to huddle on the slope of the Castle Rock despite the lack of sanitation because the base of the slope was covered by the unassailable Nor' Loch, a fetid marsh, providing invaluable barricades against the British; but in the early nineteenth century, when the threat of invasions became less imminent, the loch was drained and the Princes Street Gardens you now see before you was created in its place — but until then, since tunneled drainage was difficult in rock, the citizens poured buckets of excrement and waste from the windows each night, at the sound of the ten o'clock bell of the church of St. Giles, with perfunctory cries of 'Gardyloo' for 'Gardez l'eau' meaning 'Watch out for the water' upon unsuspecting passersby, to be picked up by cleaning men the next morning."

Dad couldn't tell me enough about the gardens. The flowers were set in beds which were changed ten to twelve times a year. The floral clock which embowered a quarter hour cuckoo was the first in the world and had some 24,000 plants within its 36 foot circumference. The recreational areas included a bandstand and an outdoor dancefloor. Of the numerous memorials, the Scott Monument was the finest, a statue of Sir Walter and characters from his works, tall and slender, appearing from the distance like a coronet carved in stone. A fantail of railway lines threaded the gardens and converged at Waverly Station, the second largest in Britain. The gardens reached the thoroughfare directly below me.

"This thoroughfare," Dad continued, "is Princes Street. As you can see the buildings are all on one side so the view isn't lost. To my mind it is the loveliest street in the world — and I am not alone in my estimation — but, comecome, I want to show you more."

I felt as if he lifted me by the seat of my pants for I was suddenly airborne. Spires, steeples, pinnacles, rows of chimneys lodged in rows of tiled roofs, rows of streets, hills, gardens, always the sea at the periphery, came at me in kaleidoscopic forms, at breathtaking speeds, always as if each perspective had been planned just so, but the civilized splendor was juxtaposed with perspectives of a valley with upthrusting crags and somber craters much like a moonscape. "The ordered spaces," Dad explained, "are from the New Town which was planned after the Nor' Loch had been drained, and the crags and craters are from the Old Town, behind the Palace of Holyroodhouse where the royal family resided and still does when it visits Edinburgh. There are five extinct volcanoes within the city limits. This is what I find so irresistible, this mix of elegance and savagery. Edinburgh is so manly, so noble — and I was impressed even more by the people than by the city or the country. They were so fairminded I could not believe it.

"But I am talking too much again. Your Bapaiji and even your Granny are better storytellers than I am. Let me just shut up and show you what happened."

2

Dad, young and lanky in a blazer and trousers as baggy as a sack, stepped into a cobbled mews from Mrs. Dowds's boarding

house. Mrs. Dowds thought he must be very clever to be studying engineering at the university and had fixed him a breakfast
of tea and bread and butter, haddock and eggs, allowing him as
many servings as he wished and even adding Dundee cake
which she knew he loved because she knew he had a very
difficult examination that Monday for which he'd been studying
all weekend, also because she felt sorry for these poor handsome
young men who journeyed so many thousands of miles from
their homes for the sake of an education. She admired their
determination and mothered them when she could.

Dad walked with the spring of a grasshopper. He'd stayed
indoors all weekend studying Applied Mechanics and it felt
good to be out again, particularly on such a sunny and bracing
morning. He looked at his watch and chose to take the scenic
route to the tram stop because he wanted to enjoy the magnolia
trees, the rhododendrons, poppies, primulas — and sheep, the
blackfaced Shropshire sheep which reminded him of the
blackfaced monkeys of Navsari. He'd been struck from the
beginning by the contrast between their dark faces and light fur
and written about them immediately to Bapaiji.

Edinburgh, like Rome, is situated on seven hills, and Dad
caught unexpected glimpses of the sea and distant countryside
along the way — but I could see something that he could not:
his tram had left by the time he got to the stop; he'd been too
busy studying the previous weekend to wind his watch; the next
tram wasn't due for half an hour. By the time he realized his
mistake (he asked two bicyclists in balmorals and kilts with the
reddest knees what time it was) it was too late.

The wonders of the countryside no longer entranced him.
He closed his eyes instead praying for the next tram to arrive
soon, when it arrived he prayed for it to hurry. When he got
off he dashed headlong to the examination hall, afraid he wouldn't
be allowed to sit for the examination. When he tried to explain
to Professor Macauley, the invigilator, about the weekend, the

watch, the weather, the old man shushed him. "Mr. Seervai," he said. "You are half an hour late. Why do you wish to make it later with your explanations? Take your seat. Begin."

Dad thanked him, thanked God, prayed for speed, and started his paper. When Professor Macauley said, "Gentlemen, please put your pens down," Dad put down his pen, but the old man continued in the same deadpan voice, "except Mr. Seervai. Mr. Seervai was half an hour late. Mr. Seervai may have another half an hour."

Dad looked at the old man in the tweed jacket and tie as if he were God. In Navsari, even at the university in Bombay, he might have been punished by having to take the examination again, or by losing the half hour, or even by a caning from Hormusji since he was the headmaster's son and had to set a good example — and yet what purpose did the punishments serve? It wasn't as if he had been purposely recalcitrant. He was full of admiration for the wisdom of the Scots, particularly for that of Professor Macauley.

Ratilal

"I had never liked the authoritarian streak in Bapaiji and Pappa, but I never imagined it questionable. They were my mamma and pappa. It was their duty to treat me as they saw fit — and mine to respect them for it. Nevertheless, an occasion rose once when I *knew* they were wrong, but I kept quiet. It was not my place, however contrary the evidence, to say anything.

"I spent much of my childhood playing with the dubro, Ratilal. Bapaiji let me play with him only because everyone else's house was too far away, but she told me never to go inside his hut — I might get a disease or, at the very least, get his servant smell. I entered it anyway, out of curiosity, a hut of mud and thatch, but only once because it was so dark I felt as if the walls were closing in on me. There were no windows, a cloth covered the doorway, and two sheets were laid on the earth floor of the inner of the two tiny rooms for beds. In the front room was a hurricane lantern, a wooden chest of drawers, a coal brazier, and rudimentary articles of cookware. On the wall was a picture of Hanuman, another of Rama and Sita — but you have been in the dubro huts yourself, Homi. They have not changed through the years.

"Ratilal dressed mostly in my hand-me-downs: shirts like parachutes on his twig frame, pants like brown paper bags falling to his knees. Most of the time we just fooled around, chasing stray goats to ride, catching squirrels in mouse traps for pets. Sometimes, he would imitate a clown he'd seen by crooking his knees (the clown had been a dwarf), walking bowlegged in circles, holding out his arms stiffly to the sides, clapping his hands periodically, shrieking meaningless phrases, 'Aar-phaar! Aaiee-oh-vaaieek! Vairy vairy good!' to an imaginary audience. I would parade behind him, imitating his motions and sounds, acknowledging the cheers of the imaginary crowd. Yesyes, Homi, your dad was also a kid once — but this is about Ratilal. His most hilarious antic was wrestling cockroaches.

"The cockroaches were two inches long, sometimes three, with long feelers waving as if they were drunk. We stepped on them without thinking when we saw them, but Ratilal made a production out of it. He would bend over the cockroach, stalking it as if it were a wild animal, calling, 'Hey, cutulut! Ho, cutulut! Vairy vairy good!' blocking its avenues of escape with a strategically placed foot or hand without actually touching the cockroach until he had it scurrying to and fro within a space of about a square foot. Then he would pick up the cockroach, fall on his back and hold it over him, writhing as if it were holding him down. Finally, grunting as if with a renewed effort, he would roll over on the cockroach and place it on its back on the ground. If the cockroach righted itself and ran he would hold it in place with a finger over its feelers before stepping on it with his bare foot and raising his arms in victory like Tarzan. I would applaud, and he would smile and parade around like a conqueror before cleaning up the mess.

"I was so entertained by his performance that everytime I saw a cockroach, instead of stepping on it I would block off its escape routes and call Ratilal to wrestle with it. At first he came willingly, but after a while he tired of it — and finally, the last time, he said he didn't want to do it anymore.

"I was too stubborn to let him off easily. Besides, he was

my servant, and I continued to demand that he come and wrestle with the cockroach until, sulking, he came — but instead of wrestling the cockroach he stepped on it, killing it outright.

"I flew at him in a rage. I was stronger than he was, but he was too scared in any case to retaliate against his master. I held him with my head against his chest, my hands pulling his waist toward mine in a bear hug. He felt pitiful in my hands. I was surprised to feel the thin sticks of his ribs against my forearms, the frantic thudding of his heartbeat against my forehead, to hear his breath in such shallow gasps, as if being a servant he could not also be human. It wasn't until he shrieked, startling me (we'd both been silent until then), that I dropped him. He fell on his knees with a sharp intake of breath and a groan, and his face twisted with terror as if I were a demon.

"Suddenly, aware of my power over him, I was frightened myself. He had felt so fragile. I could have broken him so easily. I got on my knees in front of him and hugged him, carefully, telling him how sorry I was.

"Years later, after I was ensconced in Mrs. Dowds's boarding house in Edinburgh, I felt I understood something that Bapaiji and Pappa had never understood, that Ratilal and all the other dubras and also all the shopkeepers and tradesmen and other sundry workers looked upon us as their mothers and fathers in much the way that we looked upon the English as our mothers and fathers — as India looked upon England as her mother and father. Nothing could be said, of course, but everyone knew it. Some accepted it with respect and benevolence, others with resentment, even hatred."

Baksheesh, Seth, Baksheesh

Dad's itinerent memory sparked one of my own from my days in high school when, in the wake of my recovery from polio, I had agonized continually over the meaning of life. I hadn't always resented the polio. I'd once imagined everyone was like me, but when I saw others play cricket and hockey, run relays, bicycle, even after I got well, I continued to resent that I hadn't always been well. The illness had prohibited me from too much. Einstein was wrong when he said that God did not play with dice; order was a fallacy, chaos the rule. The moon was full on the night in question. I was returning home from a movie, *From Russia with Love*, at the Regal Theater, which I'd seen with my friend Erach. We might have had a cup of tea at Chiquita's, but it was getting late. Actually, it was only ten o'clock, but whereas I lived around the corner Erach had a forty-five minute bus ride ahead of him to his home in flat 34 of Vasundhara by the Cadbury Fry building at the junction of Pedder Road and Warden Road across from the Mahalaxmi Mandir. I saw him off at the bus stop, but instead of going home I decided to drop in on Vijay who lived a little farther away in Colaba to see if he was up for some tea. I took a shortcut through an alleyway to save time. The alleyway was deserted, narrow, dirty, stank of fish (it was the path taken by the fishermen to bring their catches to the shops), and littered with fishheads, scales, bones; it was a mudpath full of puddles, rubbish, dung. There were no streetlamps, but the sharp black silhouette of a palm tree against the full moon and the model of the James Bond movie filled me with adventure.

Unfortunately, three bends into the alleyway the moon passed behind a cloud and everything became blacker than the face of a monkey. I refused to panic telling myself the moon would soon reappear, my eyes would get accustomed to the dark. I walked more slowly, afraid I might step into something or trip over something. The stench covered me like a shroud; when something crumbled under my foot I cringed imagining it was a fishhead; when something scurried over my sandaled foot I froze — I had forgotten about the rats. I walked a few more steps in the dark before I bumped into a low branch and came to a halt. While I waited, jumping at the least sound (the nasal cawing of a solitary crow, paper crackling under rats' feet, a bottle sent rolling), I felt, uncannily, as if someone were watching me.

When the moonlight returned, I breathed more easily watching the shadows recede to the sides of the alleyway. I took a deep breath and stepped carefully forward when something touched me from behind. I jumped violently around. Behind me were two upturned palms, hands without fingers, raised in a supplicatory attitude. A strangely familiar voice intoned, "Baksheesh, seth, baksheesh." I saw a black head, patches of wormy hair, ears reduced to rubberbands of flesh, a nose pushed so far back it might have been a gaping mouth; the face looked at me through eyes narrow as wire, appeared to be grinning. The skin on the torso shone in the moonlight as if it were covered with scales. The body was seated, crosslegged, on a square wooden platform on wheels. The legs appeared to be moving because bugs were crawling heedlessly over them. Flies whirred about his open nose. The figure made no attempt to brush away the bugs and flies, but continued to hold up decaying hands, to say in a hollow voice, "Baksheesh, seth, baksheesh."

I turned and ran the way I had come, crying with the fear that I might have caught his disease, down the middle of the road when I tripped over one of the charpoys on the footpath. Back home I went straight to the bathroom, turned on the red light for the geyser, and filled a bucket with scalding hot water. As I sat on the tiny wooden bathing stool, pouring water over myself from a brass tumbler, soaping myself over and over, scraping my skin raw with the pumice stone, especially where he'd touched my thigh through my jeans, I recalled I'd seen the leper and others like him innumerable times before, ragged cloths on their faces against the sun, swollen reptilian skin threatening to burst and spill pus. I'd even dropped baksheesh in their cups, though always with an inward shudder — they were lepers, as distinct from me as mongrels, lizards, vultures, even more so since they were diseased — but what did anyone do to deserve *that*? If *that* was the alternative, leprosy in a putrid alleyway, I would never again complain about polio in luxurious quarters — but I was suddenly afraid I'd caught something worse.

Rusi was still out somewhere, but Mom and Dad knocked on the bathroom door curious about my late night bath. When I came out I told them my story calmly. I didn't want to cry because I knew Dad wouldn't like it, but I couldn't help myself as I reached the end and my fear of the disease overwhelmed me.

Mom tried to hug me, but I pushed her away. Her eyes were narrow with anxiety, Dad's wide with amusement. "It is not so easy a disease," he said, "that you can catch it just like that in a jiffy, not like flu. Remember Father Damien? on the island of Molokai? It took him years to finally catch the disease. There is nothing to cry about. Be a man."

During the days that followed I found more opportunities to drop baksheesh in the leper's cup, actually a grimy soup tin.

It was the least I could do. I felt — as Dad had felt with Ratilal — that I was his mother and father. The felt relation said more about order in the universe than I could understand, but more than understanding I thought perhaps it was acceptance that determined one's peace of mind, one's relations with God. Everyone was someone's mother and father.

Land of Forefathers

"A wag said once that Yes, the Scots are intelligent: they leave Scotland the first chance they get. He was being facetious, of course, but it's true that the Scottish winters have the chilliest fingers and the standard of living has always been lower than England's, so after graduating from the University of Edinburgh I got a job in London, Assistant to the Chief Engineer of the Great Western Railway — but when Bapaiji visited I took her to Edinburgh to introduce her to Mrs. Dowds and her daughter. They knew about each other, of course, from when I had stayed there before. I thought they would enjoy meeting one another, but I was wrong, at least about Bapaiji. She had come to England to take me back with her, her friends had said I was never coming back because I had married a muddum — that is what they called Englishwomen, especially waitresses and landladies' daughters who they said were just waiting to snap up educated Indians — and Bapaiji wanted to show them I was still unmarried — but here, let me just show you."

Dad appeared smiling widely in a seersucker suit, cleanshaven, homburg in hand, carrying two suitcases which he set down introducing Bapaiji in a sari and sweater to smiling Mrs. Dowds in the foyer of her house. Behind them was a narrow gravel path which disappeared when Dad shut the door.

Before them stood Mrs. Dowds in a white apron. "At last," she said, beaming, holding out her hand. "So glad I am, to be meeting you at last, Mrs. Seervai. It's been a great pleasure, it has, having Adi stay with us. So proud of him, you must be."

Bapaiji smiled selfconsciously. She didn't speak English well, and Mrs. Dowds's enthusiasm overwhelmed her. "Howdo-do, Missis Dowdy," she said.

Mrs. Dowds laughed, but Dad's smile appeared tighter by a notch. Bapaiji may not have known English well enough to speak it comfortably, but she knew it well enough to know what she was saying.

A door opened behind Mrs. Dowds and her daughter Pamela came in. She appeared as happy as her mother to see Adi and Bapaiji, but her welcome was quieter, in her face and smile more than in her voice. She wore a blue dirndl; Dad's face turned rosy in her presence and you couldn't blame Bapaiji for imagining there was more between them than met the eye. "Hullo, Pamela. Howayou?" he said, smiling, forgetting to introduce Bapaiji until Pamela held out her hand herself — but Bapaiji merely smiled, ignoring Pamela's outstretched hand which she confusedly withdrew.

"Och! Mrs. Seervai, so tired, you must be, you poor dear," said Mrs. Dowds, rescuing the moment. "It's rest you'll be wanting, I'm sure."

Dad's smile widened again. "Yes," he said. "I am okay, but we were on the train five hours from London. My mother is a little bit under the weather."

"Well, let's be shaking a leg then instead of shooting the breeze. Your room's waiting for you, Adi, as always, and I've put your mother across the hall. Dinner's till eight, as always, so you've got plenty of time."

"Yes," said Dad. "That would be best. Come along, Bapaiji." He spoke Gujarati when he addressed her, put on his homburg again, picked up the suitcases, and led her up the narrow wooden stairs, carpeted down the middle, to their rooms above.

Dad set Bapaiji's suitcase on her bed because he knew she'd want to unpack first. "I will be in the room across the hall," he said. "After we have unpacked, we can rest and go to dinner. I will be back about half past seven."

Bapaiji didn't acknowledge him. She was inspecting the room, inspecting the desk with her finger for dust. "Waitwait. What is the rush? You have a train to catch?"

Dad stood in the middle of the room. "No rush. I just thought you might want to rest. That is all."

Bapaiji pushed the suitcase into the corner of the bed. "When I am dead," she said, "there will be plenty of time to rest. Comecome. Sitsit. I want to talk with you."

Dad joined her on the bed where she'd made room for them both. "What is it, Bapaiji?"

She nodded her head, patting his thigh when he sat next to her. "You like it here? in Edinburgh?"

"I like it very much. Don't you?"

"It is nice. Veryvery cold, but nice — but veryvery cold, do you not think?"

"That is why I went to England. It is not so cold in London as it is in Edinburgh. Also, you can make more money."

"You can make lots of money in Bombay, in the Indian Railways. I know the Maharajah of Baroda. He will give you any job you want. He owes me many favors. Also, with your degree you can have a job anywhere you want in India. You can have the best job. You can have servants, free travel, anywhere in India, so many benefits, just you have to ask. Also, India is land of your forefathers, you must never forget."

Dad laughed. He could afford to laugh. He was mostly in good spirits then, pleased with his prospects, eager to show Bapaiji around, understanding at last what she was saying. He'd wanted to be an aeronautical engineer; it was a new field, there were many opportunities; but Bapaiji had dissuaded him. He

was her only son; she didn't want him to die in the sky, refused
to understand that he wouldn't even need to fly; but now he
understood. Bapaiji wanted to ride in the deluxe compartments
of Indian Railways, she wanted the preferential treatment ac-
corded relatives of railway employees. "Yesyes, Bapaiji," he said,
"but India is all the time so hot, and all the time so chaotic. The
English are very good to work for. If something is not cricket,
it is not done."

"What you are saying, Adi? We have cricket in India. What
is cricket to do with this?"

Dad laughed. "It is just a way of saying, Bapaiji. It means
they have a sense of fair play, everything is on the table."

"What table? What you are talking? The cold weather is
making your brain cold."

Dad was speaking Gujarati, using English idioms. He laughed
again and explained.

"Arre, Adi, Adi, if you are so clever, I can also be clever,"
Bapaiji said. "You think the English conquered India playing
cricket? You think they didn't murder and cheat and pillage? If
they did in their own country what they did in our country, they
would all be in jail. And everything is on the table in India also:
land, house, job, servants, rickshaws. Whatever you want, I will
put on the table. What do you think? Come back, no, to land
of forefathers? Otherwise, you will never prosper. In a foreign
land, you can never prosper."

Dad didn't say anything. It was a matter to which he'd given
some thought, but about which he remained undecided.

"Listen to me, Adi," Bapaiji said. "I saw how that girl was
looking at you. She has whitewhite skin like a sheet of paper,
like a ghost, and her face is redred like blood, but what she is?
a landlady's daughter. What you want to do with a landlady's
daughter?"

"Bapaiji, there is nothing between us. She has a fiance. She
was only being nice. I saw how you didn't shake her hand."

"In India, young people have more respect than to hold out hands to older people like that."

"This is not India, Bapaiji. Here that is not a matter of respect. She was only being nice."

"That may be what it may be. She knows I am from India. She should have shown respect."

Dad laughed again. "Bapaiji, she was only being nice. She was showing respect in her own way. I will think about what you have said, but you are wrong about her. She was only being nice."

"Goodgood, maybe I am wrong about her, but just think what I have said. That is all I am asking." She patted his thigh again. "One thing more I have got to tell you."

"What?"

"The English are very nice people, yesyes, but not so nice to marry. All are getting, all the time, divorcedivorce. All the time they are getting divorce. Always they are getting divorce. If the wife is not looking good or cooking good they are getting divorce. If there is little bit dust on the shelf they are getting divorce. If they forget one birthday they are getting divorce." It was a new word in her vocabulary; she used it with fascination. "You must marry a Parsi girl, you must stay with your own kind. Otherwise, you will never prosper. Otherwise, definitely, you will get divorce."

Dad smiled patiently, getting off the bed.

Bapaiji remained sober. "It is not so funny. I knew once, a general, an English, his wife got a divorce because he was sleeping in his uniform — belt, boots, everything. You think I am making this up?"

Dad's smile broadened. "Bapaiji," he said, putting a hand soothingly on her shoulder. "Everyone is not the same. You should know that."

"I am not saying they are all the same, they are not all the same, but they are all different from us. They are all thinking differently from us. I knew another English, a governor's daughter, who made an arrangement on the ship to sleep with her steward — but only if he would not talk to her in the morning. Why? Because he was a steward and she was the governor's daughter. Sleeping was okay, but talking was not. That is your English for you."

Dad shook his head in wonder. "Bapaiji, how can you know such things?"

"Everyone knows. Just think about it is all I am saying."

"Okayokay, I will think about it."

Through the subsequent scenes, Bapaiji crushed all Dad's arguments as implacably as a steamroller, but Dad remained ebullient because he wanted Bapaiji to enjoy herself. When he took her on The Flying Scotsman, the first locomotive to do 100 mph, she said the locomotives in India were just as fast; when he took her to see the equestrian statue of Earl Haig erected by Sir Dhunjibhai Bomanji, a Bombay Parsi, on the Castle Esplanade she said the Parsis were the tiniest community in the whole world, but they were everywhere; when he took her to Mother India, an Indian restaurant, she said she could cook better in her own kitchen.

There was a blurry image of a woman with chestnut hair in ringlets, holding a pink parasol, standing beside an ill-at-ease Dad, frozen smile, stammering tone, shaky gestures. "You are lovely," Dad said. "That is all there is to be said about it. You are lovely." The woman said nothing, but turned her back on him. Dad waited; she came more sharply into focus; a smile spread slowly, ironically, across her wide white heartshaped face. Behind them I saw people feeding pigeons, a tall column: Nelson's column, Trafalgar Square. The woman turned to face Dad. "How very lovely of you to say that," she said, but her smile spread slowly, ironically, across her face, and her voice turned, as slowly, ironic, "and how very quaint." Dad lost his smile, turned as white as the woman, turned away himself. I could tell he would have preferred to have been a murderer than quaint. I understood the woman's name was Honoria Hobson, but my curiosity was not to be satisfied further. The image faded to a pink wash and Dad disappeared altogether to be replaced once more by his voiceover.

"There was no one thing that convinced me to return with Bapaiji, Homi, no single moment of truth — I showed her Edinburgh, London, Paris, Rome, Frankfurt — but slowly I realized that outside of India I would always be a stranger. Even with my superior education I felt inferior to Pamela, a landlady's daughter, because she spoke better English. That was one thing that impressed me immensely about your mummy, her convent school education. Even your Granny had had a convent school education — in fact, they had both been to the same school. They both spoke English as if they had been born to it even though they were Parsis. One of the things I requested when I got here was the ability to speak the King's English. The irony is, of course, that there is no one with whom I might speak it — and even if there were, the medium of communication here is thought, not language. You would understand me clearly even if, as Bapaiji said, I spoke Zulu."

The Two Girls Huddled Together
Like Monkeys

Rusi removed the pressure of his hand from my shoulder with a final reassuring squeeze. "Mom, I have to go. I'm meeting Paresh for dinner at Chiquita's, but don't wait up. I might be late. I don't know what we'll do after dinner."

Mom nodded without looking away from me. "I wish he would just open his eyes. I know he's all right — he even looks more peaceful today — but I wish I could establish some kind of communication."

"He got up by himself today, Mom. That's a good sign. He's gonna be okay."

Mom nodded again. "I know. You go have your dinner. I'll be all right."

"Attchha. Bye, then."

"Bye-bye."

As soon as the door clicked shut behind Rusi, Mom renewed her litany of "time and prayer." I tried again to return the pressure of her hand, to catch her eye, but even when I looked directly at her I must have appeared asleep — and as I continued to stare she seemed to shrink as I imagine Alice might have shrunk in Wonderland when she'd obeyed the command:

Drink Me. Her hair grew longer curling into ringlets which fell to her waist, her face turned fresh and smooth, and her expression changed from anxiety to a more restrained seriousness. She was sitting at one end of the side of a long table, ankles locked and dangling from the chair, a notebook open in front of her, a pencil held laboriously in her hand as she struggled to transcribe some lines in Gujarati. Across the table sat Jalu Masi, younger than Mom, hair cut so short she might have been a boy, but I recognized her eyes: bright as an early morning light with eyebrows perpetually arched in curiosity. Mom's eyes, by contrast, were sleepier, reflecting more of a late afternoon light. Jalu Masi also had a notebook open in front of her, but her pencil lay untouched to one side, her feet swung to and fro, and her attention was fixed on the man seated between them at the head of the table. "But Popatlal-Master," she said. "Why were you gone so long? Mummy says we will never learn any Gujarati if you keep on disappearing like this."

Dad spoke again. "Homi, do not be alarmed. I am in charge. I will be directing some sequences relating to your mummy since she is still alive and has no control over these things. Just put your trust in me."

Dad needn't have worried; I was beyond alarm; but I was glad he was still guiding me.

Mr. Popatlal, who taught the girls Gujarati, was a tiny man with a thick black mustache against a wheat complexion. His hair shone with grease, and his upper arms, revealed by his white shortsleeved bush shirt, were inclined to sag. "I have been away so long," he said in a singsong voice, "because I have been in jail. The British put me in jail for nonviolently disturbing the peace."

"You were in jail?" Jalu Masi's eyebrows shot even higher. "But Mummy says only bad people go to jail. Are you a bad people?" She sounded anxious as if she wished to be proven wrong. Mom said nothing, but she stopped writing in her notebook and her face wrinkled with disapproval.

Mr. Popatlal leaned back with a shout of laughter. "Nono, little Jalu, not to be so worried. I am not a bad people."

Mom spoke up seriously. "But Mummy says the British are good, and all my friends in school — Edwina Keegan and Pamela Wright and Abigail Barlow and Charlotte Colchester — are good. So if the British put you in jail, then you must have done something bad."

Mr. Popatlal raised his hands as if to calm them both down. "Yesyes, your mummy is quite right. The British are good, your friends are all good, but sometimes good people do bad things, when they have a bad system. You girls are lucky to go to a good school, a convent school, where you can learn good English and British History and all, but you have to hire a tutor like me to learn Gujarati, our own native language, and you learn nothing about our own Indian History except what the British are teaching you. Do you think this is good? that another country tells us what we should do?"

Mom looked scared as if she were defending something she didn't understand, but she replied stubbornly. "But they don't tell us what to do! We can do anything we want! If I don't want to take piano lessons at school, I don't have to. Many girls don't. But I want to!"

"That is good," Mr. Popatlal said, smiling to put her at ease. "That is very good that you want to take piano lessons. But the piano is a Western instrument. What I am saying is if you wanted to take sitar lessons the school should also have a teacher for you. Do you get what I am saying?"

"I get! I get!" Jalu Masi was kneeling on her chair leaning across the table toward Mom. "Popatlal-Master is right, Pheroza. Mummy was playing the sitar, but Daddy said not to play it because it was an Indian instrument. I heard him! I heard him! It's true!"

Mr. Popatlal raised his hands for quiet again. "Quiet, please, little Jalu, please, quiet." When Jalu Masi had settled down again, he continued. "I am not saying the British are bad, I am not saying your friends are bad" (looking at Mom, who appeared mollified by his solicitude), "but even the best people can have a bad system. It is a bad system for one nation to rule another. The British have ruled us now for too long. And with Gandhiji to lead us we will gain our independence again."

"Have you met Gandhiji?" Mom seemed for the first time to be interested in what Mr. Popatlal had to say. "Daddy says he is a great man."

"Yesyes," Mr. Popatlal said. "For him only I went to jail. And for him I will go to jail as many times as he wants. For him I will suffer beatings —"

Jalu Masi interrupted incredulously, eyebrows arched again. "The British beat you?"

"Yesyes, little Jalu, but not to worry —"

"If the British beat you, then the British are bad."

"Nono, little Jalu, they are beating everyone who is disagreeing with them — but what is a little beating when Gandhiji himself has suffered so much already for us all? I am willing to die for him today. He is the greatest man in the world."

Jalu Masi's eyebrows were still arched. "Greater than God even?"

Mr. Popatlal smiled. "No man is greater than God. Gandhiji is a saint, but he is still a man."

"Greater than Zoroaster?"

"I cannot say greater than Zoroaster. Zoroaster is, after all, your prophet."

Mom spoke again. "Greater than the King of England?"

Mr. Popatlal nodded his head. "Yes, I think we can safely say that Gandhiji is greater than the King of England."

Jalu Masi stood up on her chair. "The King of England is a bad man because he put you in jail."

Mr. Popatlal twirled his mustache with amusement. "Nono, little Jalu, this has been going on before he was born. He does not know how wrong it is because he takes us for granted. We have to show him — with nonviolence — how wrong he is. That is why I wear khadi always. That is my way of supporting home industries."

Mom's expression had turned, slowly, more forgiving. "What is khadi?" she asked, her eyes widening.

"Khadi is cloth that is woven in India only, with Indian materials only, by Indians only. It is one way to show our independence — not to support British industry."

Jalu Masi had exhausted her interest in the subject but she didn't want to get back to the Gujarati lesson. She jumped down from her chair. "I am going to bring our baby brother. He is so big now. You must see him."

"Arre, little Jalu," Mr. Popatlal said. "How we will teach you any Gujarati if you are always running? See, no, Pheroza has done two pages already. Come, sit, I can see your brother after the lesson, no?"

Mom recognized what Jalu Masi was up to. "Jalu, we have got to work first. Popatlal-Master can see Soli afterwards."

"But he is so cute, *soo* cute!" Jalu Masi said. "And afterwards he might go out." She dashed from the room before anyone could stop her. "Oh, Soaa-leee, Soaa-leee!"

Mr. Popatlal shook his head with exasperation, but he smiled. Mom got out of her chair. "I will get her back," she said, but Mr. Popatlal shook his head again. "Nonono, it is all right. She will be back. No need to interrupt your lesson also."

Mom glowered as she sat down again. She didn't like the lessons anymore than Jalu Masi, but she lacked Jalu Masi's knack for getting out of these things.

During subsequent lessons Mr. Popatlal related the great Indian epics to the girls, *The Ramayana* which chronicled Prince Rama of Ayodhya's rescue of his wife Sita from the demon king Ravana of Lanka with the help of the monkey god Hanuman, and *The Mahabharata* which chronicled the dynastic struggle between the five Pandava brothers and their cousins the hundred Kaurava brothers; he related stories about the great kings Chandragupta, Ashoka, and Akbar; he related fables from the *Panchatantra*, but they didn't learn much Gujarati until Mr. Popatlal was put in jail again and replaced by a new tutor.

There was a corollary to Mr. Popatlal's departure: Jalu Masi said to Rustomji, seated in a rocking chair reading a newspaper: "Daddy, can I wear ka-di?"

Mom was practising Bach's "Minuet in G" in the next room. Granny was not to be seen. Rustomji laughed but spoke patiently. "Why do you want a khadi dress, my dear, when you already have so many prettier dresses?"

Jalu Masi answered just as patiently. "Because, Daddy, Popatlal-Master wear ka-di."

"Popatlal-Master wears khadi because he is a nationalist, my dear. You are only a little girl, a very pretty little girl."

Jalu Masi ran behind Rustomji's rocker and stood on the rails, holding on with her hands, rocking him gently. "I want to be a nashulist, Daddy. Can I be a nashulist?"

Rustomji turned back to his newspaper. "No. You are a little girl. Why do you want to be a nationalist?"

She rocked him more vigorously, watching the reflection of the ceiling light on his bald pate move to and fro. "Because, Daddy, I want ka-di."

He was alarmed at the amplitude she'd set for the rocker. "Jalu, get off the chair at once. You will get hurt." He was too late. Pushing with her legs, pulling with her hands, Jalu Masi pulled the rocker over its edge and onto herself. Rustomji lay on his back with his heels over his head, afraid to move for fear of crushing her under him. "Pheroza, Pheroza," he called, but Mom was already in the room. "See if you can get Jalu out without hurting her," he said, but Jalu Masi had already crawled out by herself.

As soon as Rustomji had extricated himself from the chair

he called Jalu Masi and held her tenderly. "Are you hurt? Oh, my dear, are you hurt?"

Jalu Masi, eyebrows still high from the excitement and fear of her fall, said, "Daddy, ka-di, please?"

Years later, 1962, when Chou En-Lai betrayed Nehru's trust, amassed troops along the Eastern Himalayan border, began his invasion of India, I enacted a variation on the theme of Jalu Masi's protest. Prior to the news about the Chinese, Mom and Dad had bought me a pair of shoes from a Chinese shop — which I subsequently threw onto a rubbish heap far enough from our home not to be found.

2

Jalu always got her way. Mom was furious. Rustomji had bought her a khadi dress which she didn't even wear, but he wouldn't buy one for her. He said Jalu had paid the dues for her dress with her fall. Jalu had been grounded (the bark of a dog, Jalu Masi barking back, Mom telling her to leave the dog alone, Jalu Masi kicking Mom leaving a white splash of powder from her tennis shoe on Mom's grey convent school uniform, Mom preserving and presenting the spot like an exhibit to Rustomji), but Rustomji was taking Jalu with them on their excursion to the aerodrome that day. It wasn't fair!

Sunlight streaming through the window onto Mom's mattress in the sittingroom had awakened her before anyone else. During the hot season the ayahs dragged the girls' mattresses to the sittingroom every night. Hurdles of dried straw called khas-khas tatties spanned the open doors to the verandah from the sittingroom within reach of the chowkidar in the compound outside who flung water periodically through the night on the tatties to cool the air that passed through them into the house. A bucket of water was kept near the tatties in the house for the early morning when the chowkidar was gone. Mom had even gotten to like the mildewy smell of the water on the tatties. Her features wrinkled with resentment as she leaned on one elbow to look at Jalu Masi still asleep on the mattress beside her. She had no right to join them on their excursion when she'd been grounded. Mom got up from her mattress and went to the window where she could see Gopal bring freshly cut grass and oats in a bucket for Toby, their carriage horse, who shared the stable with his carriage. I recognized, not the stable, but the site (later the garage for Granny's creamy 1955 Studebaker and Soli Mama's steel blue 1961 Chevrolet).

Mom heard sounds of stirring in the house from where she sat with her face cupped in tiny fists by the window. She saw Jalu Masi move lightly and dashed into action thinking she might never have the chance again. Dipping her hands into the bucket of water saved for the tatties she flicked her fingers at Jalu Masi. Within minutes Rustomji, in blue pajamas, awakened by screaming, was striding into the sittingroom wiping sleep from his eyes. Jalu Masi was standing on the sofa pulling Mom's ringlets. Their pink and blue night dresses were soaked. "Girls, girls," Rustomji said, "stop it, stop it this instant! What is going on?"

"She started it! She started it!" Jalu Masi said. "She splashed me!"

"It was an accident!" Mom screamed. "I was splashing the tatti!"

"All right, all right, all right," Rustomji said, wiping his forehead wearily with his hand. "I don't want to hear anymore about it, not a word. If you don't stop, then no one is going to the aerodrome today."

"Daddy! She started it!"

"Daddy! It was an accident!"

"I *said, NOT A WORD!*"

The girls were quiet immediately. Rustomji rarely shouted and they didn't want to risk canceling their trip. However dangerous Rustomji said it was they both hoped someone would give them a joyride in one of the two-seater planes even for just five minutes, but the antagonism remained between them until Granny smoothed it away explaining to Jalu Masi that Mom had wet her accidentally and to Mom that she should be more careful.

The aerodrome canteen was crowded, but Rustomji found a table with a good view of arriving and departing planes. The cups, saucers, and plates on which they received their tea and toast were old and chipped. The square wooden table was rickety and covered by a cracked sheet of glass secured by a single hinge on each side. The wooden chairs, just as rickety, had seats woven with cane. Granny took Jalu Masi to the bathroom. Mom stared enviously at a family on the tarmac waving goodbye to friends boarding the stairs to their plane. She knew there was no chance of her getting a joyride but she wished Rustomji would at least let them get closer to the planes. "Daddy, why can't I go where that family is? They aren't in danger. Can't I even go as far as they are?"

Rustomji spoke gravely. "No, Pheroza. What they are doing is very dangerous. We are in the best place to watch the aeroplanes."

As if to bear out his words the family — two men and a woman with a baby in her arms — disappeared (all except the baby which fell to the ground) in a brilliant stippled arc of blood in the sunlight sliced by the propellors under the wing of an incoming plane. Rustomji held Mom immediately telling her not to look. Mom had registered only the color and the brilliance. She might have found the arc beautiful if not for the screaming that followed. Instead, her faith in Rustomji's infallibility soared.

A crowd gathered blocking their view. Jalu Masi and Granny returned while Rustomji was still holding Mom. "What happened?" Granny asked, her forehead wrinkling with fear. "What was all the screaming?" Jalu Masi's eyebrows were high on her tiny white forehead.

"An accident," Rustomji said. "I will tell you about it, but I think we should go. Let me get the bill first."

The silence among themselves waiting for the bill while everyone else made so much noise was too much for Jalu Masi. "But what happened? Tell me no, what happened?"

"An accident," Mom said, in a new voice that was calmer than she felt. "Don't look. I will tell you about it later." She held Jalu Masi tightly feeling as if her horrific vision had conferred upon her a responsibility to shield her baby sister from things of which she had no understanding. There was a sweetness about the two girls huddled together like monkeys, but Rustomji was too concerned with getting the waiter's attention to notice and Granny still too uncertain of the situation to smile.

3

The two girls huddled together like monkeys were separated. Jalu Masi disappeared along with Rustomji, Granny, and the panorama of the people in the airport canteen into a swirl of dust on all sides of Mom. Mom grew larger, older, until she appeared seated by my bedside again, and the dust swirl unwound itself slowly to reveal the familiar enclosure of my bedroom walls — but Mom looked more animated: the grey in her cheeks was rosy; the anxious wrinkled eyes were wide with hope. I thought she must have seen my eyes open, felt the pressure I'd returned with my hand, but when she spoke I understood her delight correctly. "Is it really you, Adi? Adi, are you there? Are you all right?"

She'd sensed Dad's communication through me, and when he spoke she sensed it again. "Yes, it is me, Philly, darling. I am all right — never better, in fact, except that you are not with me — but enough about me. I might not see you again for a long time and to carry on this exchange might harm you in the long run. It will unquestionably harm Homi. He was not meant to provide a medium between us. I am well. Homi will be well. Be happy."

The mallets in my head began pounding more thunderously even as he spoke. Mom stood up still holding my hand, her face turned heavenward. "I love you, Adi. I love you, my darling. Take me with you. Please take me with you."

"Not yet, Philly. Your time is not yet."

My hand slipped from her grasp, her face turned white, and she fainted falling across me in the bed. As she fell I felt her consciousness slip as if it were something tangible and spatter around me splashing and shivering like globules of mercury. One such globule opened revealing Mom and Dad thrashing fiercely against each other under a shining white silk bedsheet, but I pushed the image away; another revealed her in labor in a bed in the Saint Elizabeth Nursing Home on Napean Sea Road in Bombay about to give birth to me, but I pushed that image away as well; yet another revealed a fantasy so bizarre, involving feathers and dead fish, that it could only have sprung from a well too deep for even Mom to fathom with her consciousness — but I was too squeamish to explore even this image further. I scanned the other globules for an image with which I was comfortable.

First Class! Absolutely A-Number One-First Class!

Dad first saw Mom across the drawingroom of the King George V Hotel in Karachi, seated alongside Jalu Masi at the grand piano. A man with what might best be described as a patient face — confident, interested, implacable — stood by them in grey pants and a grey sleeveless sweater over a white longsleeved cotton shirt. He made requests each time one or the other of them finished playing and they complied, sometimes alone, sometimes with duets. At one point they asked him to sing. Dad trembled to hear him sing "Santa Lucia" in a deep voice which vibrated with the strength of a thousand double basses. He had no such talent himself to allow him entry into their circle. He noted with relief, however, that the man had his eye conspicuously on Jalu Masi.

"You like her, no?" said Mr. Gupta, the owner of the hotel, with whom Dad was sharing tea. "That is Pheroza Cama, the great-niece of our J. P. Cama. She is here on holiday with her sister and her mother and her brother." Dad had assumed Jalu Masi was the sister because of the resemblance. Now he followed Mr. Gupta's expression and saw Granny on a couch along the side of the room working on what appeared to be some rather fine embroidery, silk on gauze with beads. Soli

Mama sat obediently by in short pants, shirt, sweater, and tie, obliviously reading *The Hound of the Baskervilles*. "I know them well," Mr. Gupta continued. "They come here every summer for a fortnight. Come, I will introduce you."

"Who is that man with them?" Dad took a sip of his tea to cover his consternation.

"That is Sohrab Cama of the Shanghai Camas. JP opened branches everywhere, as you know, even in Shanghai. Our Sohrab is here just now looking for a Parsi wife — not too many Parsis in Shanghai, you know (Mr. Gupta winked) — but I think he is most definitely interested in the sister."

I'd recognized Sohrab Uncle the moment I'd heard him sing. I'd known him just briefly (he lived in Hong Kong, having moved with the business from Shanghai when the communists took over), but "Santa Lucia" had remained his signature tune and his voice was unmistakable. "Come, no?" Mr. Gupta invited Dad again. "I will introduce you."

Dad shook his head. He felt uncomfortable with the crowd around Mom. "No. I will do it myself. I will find the right time."

"Okay, but do not wait too long. They are only here a few days. You are leaving even before them."

Dad's smile looked plastic as if it had been glued on. Not only was Mom lovely — she still had the ringlets from her girlhood, but the rest of her had grown into a willowy young woman — but she reminded him of Honoria Hobson who'd also worn her hair in ringlets and treated him with such disdain when he'd worked for the Chief Engineer of the Great Western Railway in England. Mom was also dressed in a pleated grey skirt with a sweater much as Honoria had often dressed. It panicked him to think they might be alike in other ways. He was shaken from his reverie when the girls rose from the piano bench and joined Granny and Soli Mama with Sohrab Uncle. Wanting to make his presence known before they retired he clapped loudly. "Bravo! First Class!" he said, ignoring all the other guests in the drawingroom, giving Mom the tiptop sign with his thumb and forefinger. "First Class! Absolutely A-Number One-First Class!"

Mom ignored him after a single astonished glance, but Jalu Masi bowed her head like a trouper and Sohrab Uncle smiled and said "Thank you" in his deep voice. When they sat down Mom said "What a silly man!" but she smiled as if she were pleased, and though she didn't look at Dad she didn't try to hide her smile. She'd noticed him before following her around with his eyes, but looking away the moment she turned in his direction. She'd never have been so bold as to stare directly at him, but she was flattered by the power she felt when he scuttled so easily — she was used to being stared at; it was nice to create a bit of a stir upon entering a room; but she hated men who kept their eyes on her mercilessly disregarding her discomfort.

2

Mom usually went to breakfast earlier than the others. She liked sitting in the alcove with the rattan chairs and glasstopped tables, adjacent to the diningroom, from which she could watch the white-uniformed waiters setting the tables with the china tea things, the teapots nestled in their cozies, linen napkins folded in origami patterns. She liked watching the tennis games from the tall narrow windows of the alcove, listening to the chirruping of the squirrels and doves and koels while she sipped her tea and leafed through a book. Later, the hum of early morning would swell with the cheery wishes of the guests and the sweet smell of her tea would be enlarged by the smells of porridge, eggs, bacon, and fruit served expertly from steaming spotless cannisters of stainless steel with racks of toast, pads of butter among buttons of ice, and cutglass containers of marmalade and jam.

She rarely got much reading done but didn't mind. She'd brought with her *Pride and Prejudice* which she'd read before. She liked Jane Austen, but she'd read *Lady Chatterley's Lover* the month before and Jane Austen had receded into a hinterland of a child's world which she wanted to leave behind. She didn't understand Lawrence, but he filled her with daring; even his titles — *Sons and Lovers, Women in Love, The Virgin and the Gypsy* — challenged her; but of course she couldn't read the books in public. She could hardly even read them in private! What confounded her most was the mystery. Some things were forbidden, but she didn't know what and she didn't know why and she couldn't get their mystery out of her head. The man who had so riotously expressed his appreciation the night before seemed inexplicably related to the mystery. She thought he might have the key; but when she saw him coming she pretended not to notice, appearing to concentrate on her book though intensely aware of his presence.

Dad had prepared nothing to say and felt as if someone had stuffed a pillow into his lungs making it difficult to breathe, but he imagined if he thrust himself deeply enough into the situation he'd know what needed to be done. "What are you doing?"

His voice was muffled, his question so innocuous, even arrogant, most of all nosy, that it composed her again. She knew he was interested, but he didn't know she was. Her smile grew bigger, more confident, her tone sardonic. "Reading."

"What do you like to do?"

"I like to read."

"What do you like to read?"

She showed him her book.

"I haven't read it. I like adventure stories — like Kipling."

"This is the second time I'm reading it."

"What else do you like to do?"

"I like to play the piano."

"What else do you like to do?"

"I don't know. I like to read. I like to play the piano."

"What else do you like to do?"

He seemed unable to say anything else, but a huge grin remained on his face reminding her of the Cheshire Cat illustration by Sir John Tenniel. She didn't know his name, but felt it up to him to volunteer the information. She still found him silly, but liked the way he looked: his hair combed straight back without a part from his wide forehead, the black encroaching claw of a widow's peak in evidence already; his cheekbones high, his cheeks pink with the continual nip of the season; his face inclined to roundness, particularly with the wide fixed grin; his longsleeved grey sweater pulled back slightly to reveal the fine hairs on his wrists tinted brown in the sunlight beginning to stream into the alcove — and she was enjoying herself. It was the first time she'd talked alone with a strange young man. At nineteen she'd already received proposals of marriage from a dozen eligible bachelors but never spoken with any of them so informally. The proposals were always sent to her parents. However silly Dad appeared, his approach was decidedly more stimulating. "I've already told you what I like to do," she said, grinning in return. "What do you like to do?"

Dad pulled a four anna coin from his pocket. "Do you know how to play Up, Jenkins, Raise Your Hand?"

"Of course I know. Even a child knows that."

Dad flipped the coin. "You go first," he said, clapping his hands over the coin.

"I say Heads. Up, Jenkins, raise your hand."

It was tails. Dad looked gleeful as if he'd staged a coup. "Let us do it again," he said, wanting to be generous.

She lost again. "This is a silly game," she said, losing patience after she'd lost twice more in a row. "Don't you know anything else?"

Dad slipped the coin back into his pocket. "What would you like to play?"

"I don't like games," she said. "I think all games are silly."

His grin lost strength and his eyes fell to the floor. She felt he needed help. "What's your name?"

He looked up again immediately. The relief in his eyes gladdened her. His grin was replaced by a chastened hopeful smile. "I am Adi, Captain Seervai. I'm on leave from my posting."

An army man! He seemed suddenly more exotic. "Where is your posting?"

"In Ledo, in Assam, near the border. The Americans are going to help us build the Ledo Road which will give us direct access to the Burma Road. They are afraid the Japanese will have too much advantage if they capture the Burma Road, so we're trying to build a new access for our own advantage."

Mom's eyes widened. "Have you been in the fighting?"

"Nono, nothing like that. I am an engineer in the army, a civilian, building roads and bridges and other construction. But I saw some fighting once, an air battle. It was very interesting." He'd heard the sounds of airfire and imagined puffs of smoke behind the clouds, but he left that to her imagination knowing she would find it more interesting that way.

"My name is Pheroza," she said when she saw he was going to be silent again. "We're here on holiday from Bombay."

"Yesyes, I know all that." His grin returned, blindly self-assured as before, as if he'd staged another coup.

"How do you know?"

"Mr. Gupta told me. He is a friend of mine."

"Oh, yes, of course. You were with him last night. He's a good friend of Daddy's."

"Really? He is also a good friend of my mummy's."

When Granny and the rest of them came to breakfast they found Mom and Dad chatting so comfortably that Jalu Masi, her eyebrows ascending, said later, "Pheroza was sitting there, so cosmopolitan, as if she had known him all her life and she had only met him that morning!" Mom introduced him to everyone, and Granny, on hearing he had a degree from Edinburgh, invited him to join them for breakfast. Dad didn't understand Sohrab Uncle's connection with the family — he wasn't related closely enough to appear so intimate a friend — but it didn't bother him, particularly when he realized that his attentions were focused primarily on Jalu Masi.

3

A thick grey monsoon rain fell on Scandalpoint. The sea across Warden Road from Granny's house had engulfed the rocks along what passed for the beach. Rusi and I had often netted the tiny grey fish that swam in the pools among the rocks and brought them home to display in jars. The monsoon meant sweating constantly under plastic raincoats and socks that slid off your feet lodging uncomfortably in the toes of the tall rubber gumboots in which we lumbered like elephants all day at school. On schooldays we were always either barely dry, wet, or about to get wet — but the first rains, coming on the heels of the hot season, were always more than a relief, always a joy, as was the sudden profuse greenery with frogs and toads hopping about the paths and snails the size of golf balls in the shrubbery.

Scandalpoint wasn't quite as I remembered it — Ben Nevis and the other tall buildings along the sea were missing. So were many of the bungalows of Oomer Park behind Zephyr which was almost the only house and certainly the largest, appearing, with its red tiled roofs, red brick corners, pale stucco exteriors, large bay windows, and columned entranceway, like a mansion in a wilderness. The chowkidar, in his khaki uniform, sat on a wooden stool in the foyer, barely out of the rain, his danda hanging from his belt, occasionally moving his stool to avoid the rain when the wind changed.

A carriage came along Warden Road, turned into Granny's gate, and stopped at the entrance. The chowkidar stood at attention immediately. A footman descended with an umbrella from the front of the carriage. He opened the carriage door telling the chowkidar to ring the doorbell. A tall white-haired woman emerged from the carriage. The rain appeared to lessen as she stepped out with a gracious smile for her footman who held the umbrella over her. She was young, perhaps in her thirties, her white hair imparting dignity more than age. Her sari, bright with the colors and forms of spring, swirled around her like a spiral. She held it up slightly to keep it from dragging on the wet muddy ground revealing slender white ankles in slender green pumps encased in plastic to protect them from the rain, and walked with a lilt to the front door. When an ayah answered the chowkidar's ring the lady said, "Tell bai and seth that Mrs. Perin Cama is here to see them."

The ayah led Perin Cama into the sittingroom. Seth wasn't home, she explained, but bai was. She switched on the light (the monsoon filled all homes with a continual gloom), switched on the fan, and asked her to wait. Perin Cama settled comfortably, confidently, in an armchair. The ping pong of a Mozart sonata sounded from another room; there was a smell of roses. The music stopped and Jalu Masi popped her head around the sittingroom door disappearing immediately when she realized their visitor was looking at her. Perin Cama had no time to say anything but smiled broadly and was still smiling when Granny entered the room.

That was when they first heard of Sohrab Cama who was in Bombay from Shanghai for six months looking for a Parsi wife. Perin Cama had a letter from Sohrab Cama requesting permission from Granny and Rustomji for him to see Mom with a view to matrimony. Mom was seventeen then and in no hurry to get married. Besides, no one, she least of all, relished the idea of her moving to Shanghai. Granny was impressed by

'Perin Cama's appearance; "so tall and lovely, she was," she said later, "so welldressed, even coming in from that awful rain"; but she turned down Sohrab Uncle's request. "He might be a nice man, but what is all this going to Shanghai?" Still, they had a pleasant chat, and Perin Cama met both Mom and Jalu Masi over a cozy tea and biscuits while the downpour continued outside.

Six months later Sohrab Uncle still hadn't found a wife, but the Japanese had taken Shanghai forcing him to stay in Bombay. A year later Perin Cama returned with a request for him to see Jalu Masi for the same purpose. The biscuits and tea were trundled out again, and Granny laughed after Perin Cama left the second time. "That Chinaman must have the brains of a turnip," she said, "to think I would shanghai one of my daughters and not the other." But Jalu Masi defended him. "He's not a Chinaman. He's a Parsi, just like us. And what's wrong with going to Shanghai? Who wants to stay in stinky old India for all of their lives?"

"Jalu, you must not talk like that."

"But I don't care, Mummy. I mean it."

"Jalu!"

Many parents acceded to Sohrab Uncle's requests to "see" their daughters, even allowing him the unheard of luxury (for the time) of spending time alone with them, but he found no one to make him happy. He stayed in Bombay for six years, until the British had retaken Shanghai, and during that time although he never got to "see" Jalu Masi the way he wanted he met her at innumerable parties, and after a while it became customary for him to single her out for his attentions, and even Granny didn't mind because his attentions seemed harmless in the midst of so many people, she had already clarified that neither of her daughters was going to Shanghai, and she felt sorry for him alone and so far removed from his home. Besides, he was also a Cama, she liked his company (especially on their holidays when she felt she could trust him with many of the details), she loved his deep songful voice, and the girls loved to accompany him on the piano.

Joyride

A small crowd was emerging from a school building onto a road I didn't recognize. When I spotted Granny with Soli Mama, Jalu Masi, Mom, Sohrab Uncle, Dad, and Mr. Gupta I knew they must still have been in Karachi. There were posters on the side of the school building and I could tell even in the dark blue night that they were advertising a gramophone recital for Lehar's *The Merry Widow*. Granny was in front with Soli Mama and Jalu Masi, Mom and Sohrab Uncle close behind, with Dad and Mr. Gupta leisurely bringing up the rear. "But Mummy," Jalu Masi was saying, "it's such a nice night. You take the carriage if you want. We'll walk. The hotel isn't that far."

Mom held her purse in front of her as if she were about to jump up and down like a kangaroo. "Yes, Mummy, really. You take the carriage, but I'm not at all tired. The walk will make me nice and tired and sleepy for bed."

Sohrab Uncle didn't want to get in the way, but when Jalu Masi nudged him hard in his ribs he said in his deep voice in as responsible and manly a manner as he could simulate. "Yes, yes, do not worry so much, Aunty. They will be all right. We men will see to it, won't we, Adi?"

Dad and Mr. Gupta had been talking between themselves apparently oblivious to the conversation in front of them. When

Mr. Gupta had found the Camas were going to the recital he'd persuaded Granny that it would be a good idea to take Dad as well. It hadn't taken much persuasion since Granny was impressed with Dad's credentials: his family (even she had heard of Bapaiji), his education, his employment; but she had insisted that Mr. Gupta come along as well. "Of course, of course," Dad said. "We men will see to everything."

They had reached their carriage. "Well, all right," Granny said cautiously, "but only if Mr. Gupta walks with you."

"Oh, he will, he will, of course he will," Jalu Masi almost shouted. "Won't you walk with us, Mr. Gupta?"

Mr. Gupta smiled and said he would, so Granny got in the carriage with Soli Mama and was driven away. The crowd got thinner as more carriages drove away and more people went different ways. Jalu Masi was ahead of the group, not walking so much as swaying forward to a waltz rhythm. "The sky is such a midnight blue," she said. "Just as I imagined it in *The Merry Widow*. Isn't it lovely?"

Mom was more restrained in her movements, but she walked languidly, playing with her ringlets, humming the main theme of *The Merry Widow*, "*Dum* de-*dum* dum / *Dum* de-*dum* dum / *Dum*, *dee*, *dah*," over and over.

The road along which they walked had only a few people left. There were hardly any buildings; there was a park nearby; the crescent of the moon was sharply focused against the dark blue sky. "Everything was so beautiful and so decadent," Jalu Masi said, "so beautifully decadent — the music, the story, the people. I could watch *The Merry Widow* forever."

Mr. Gupta found it prudent to inject a cautionary note. "Yesyes, but nothing happened, remember? Absolutely nothing happened."

"Of course, of course, if something happened that would have ruined everything. I always want a happy ending — but the feeling is nice, such a feeling of danger without any real danger. Aaah, such bliss!"

She waltzed with herself, humming the melody along with Mom. Sohrab Uncle who'd watched her in silence until then began to sing the words. *"Lippen schweigen / 's flustern Geigen / hab' mich lieb! / All die Schritte / sagen bitte / hab' mich lieb!"*

"Oh, isn't he amazing?" Mom said twirling in a circle. "He even knows the German."

Sohrab Uncle tapped Jalu Masi's shoulder and joined her in her waltz when she turned while continuing to sing. *"Jeder Druck der Hande / deutlich mir's beschreib / Er sagt klar, 's ist wahr, 's ist wahr / ich hab' dich lieb."*

Mr. Gupta nudged Dad toward Mom with a wink. "Go, dance with her."

Mom was whirling on her axis, counting breathlessly, "*One-*two-three, *one-*two-three," her arms and ringlets wide and free. "You are spinning like a helicopter," Dad said. "Would you like to go for a real ride?"

"For a joyride?" Her eyes were wide. "Oh, yes, yes. Will you take me?"

Dad drew her to himself for an answer, lifted her off her feet, and continued to spin in the circle she had begun maintaining the *one-*two-three *one-*two-three rhythm of Sohrab Uncle's singing.

She liked the pressure of her chest against his as he spun her around — danger without danger. She didn't know Dad, but she was among friends.

Mr. Gupta smiled watching the billowing parabolas of the girls' skirts as they flew through the air. When Sohrab Uncle finally completed the song and Dad put Mom down she was laughing and dizzy. "You look so lovely," he said, whispering for fear of embarrassing her. He had to hold her to steady her, but her face appeared to grow brighter and she put a hand on his arm for support. "You really think so?" she said, also whispering. "Really?"

"I know it. I know it. You are lovely. That is all there is to it."

She smiled, pretending to stumble with dizziness, leaning against him the rest of the way back.

The hotel was quiet when they returned. Dad wanted to kiss Mom goodnight, but hadn't the courage. He said instead that he'd had a wonderful time. The girls went to their room; Sohrab Uncle, Dad, and Mr. Gupta to theirs, but no sooner had Dad entered his room than he heard screaming and came dashing back to the drawingroom. "There's a monkey in our room," Mom shouted. Jalu Masi screamed. "He has a big black face!" Dad grabbed a nearby vase and dashed to their room. The monkey was howling, dashing panicstricken around the room, upsetting clothes, lamps, toiletries, looking for the window. He found it just as Dad entered the room. Dad slammed the window shut behind the monkey and turned victoriously as the others came in. "He's gone," he said, laughing. "It was only a blackface monkey. We have many of them in Navsari. The way you were screaming I thought it was a gorilla."

"It was the shock," Mom said, shamefaced at the commotion she had caused. "We turned on the light and he was sitting on Jalu's bed."

"I went chhoo-chhoo to him," Jalu Masi said, "but he made a face like he was spitting. We're not all like you, Adi, growing up with monkeys in Navsari, like Tarzan or something."

Dad just laughed again. "Anyway, he is gone now and I have shut the window."

After the noise had been explained to Granny and the other hotel guests and they had all retired again Mom found a moment to thank Dad for coming so quickly to her rescue. "If there is another monkey, or a snake or an elephant, just scream and I will come again," he said.

She looked uncertainly at him as if she were afraid he was making fun of her, but he put an arm reassuringly around her shoulders and quickly kissed her cheek. "I am serious," he said, and he wasn't smiling anymore. He felt like a hero. "You can call me anytime and I will come."

There was, fortunately or unfortunately, no need for heroics for the rest of their stay in Karachi and as his leave drew to an end Dad still didn't know if he would be seeing Mom again. "May I write to you?" he said. "Maybe if I am in Bombay I can see you again."

They were seated in the drawingroom again around the piano with Granny and Soli Mama to the side. Mom could still feel his lips like feathers on her cheek. It had all been too sudden for her and she'd rationalized his boldness thinking he'd only be seeing her for a few more days, but she didn't know how to say No to him. "I suppose so," she said. "I'd have to ask Mummy."

"Oh, come on, Pheroza," Jalu Masi said, slapping her sister's arm impatiently. "Don't be such a nervous Nellie. He's not asking you to elope."

"If he were asking me to elope it would be stupid of me to ask Mummy," Mom shot back triumphantly.

Dad grinned as if he couldn't believe how smart he was. "Will you elope with me?"

Mom struck a pianissimo chord abstractedly with her left hand playing a motif with her right. Jalu Masi spoke instead. "Oh, where would you take her?"

"Casablanca, Samarkand, Damascus, Istanbul, Baghdad, California, Kilimanjaro, Atlantis, wherever she wants."

"Oh," Jalu Masi moaned. "Take me! Take me! I'm so tired of India."

Sohrab Uncle spoke as if on cue. "Are you really? Really?"

Jalu Masi gave him a look with narrowed eyes. Mom spoke up instead. "Adi, have you got a pencil and paper? I could give you our address right now."

2

On the train from Karachi Dad wrote letters. Mom heard from him from Delhi, Lucknow, Ranchi, Calcutta, and finally Ledo, his base in Assam. She could tell when his train reached a station because the handwriting got steadier. He wrote about his escapades in England: to save money he'd stuffed the bottoms of his pants into his socks to simulate plus fours; thinking Benedictine to be a kind of sacrament he'd emptied a glass in a single gulp and fallen to his knees with the shock; expecting a tent and acrobats and animals he'd asked a policeman at Piccadilly where the circus was. He didn't tell her about Honoria of whom she'd reminded him — though, he realized subsequently with relief, aside from the ringlets and the pleated skirts they had little in common.

Dad also wanted all the details of her life, what she ate, what she did, what she wore. If she'd written as often as he wished she'd have done nothing but write to him saying she did nothing but write to him. He wanted souvenirs, photographs, x's, among other reassurances that she thought of him. Mom found him just a little importunate but was nevertheless enthralled. "Do you know what he went and did?" she said to Jalu Masi on one occasion, her voice quick with excitement.

"What?"

"Well, it appears he's in charge of some Naga tribespeople and he asked one of the Naga men to show his overseer some track which was about a two day hike from where they were. The next morning he found *all* the Naga men had gone with the overseer, even the village chief, every single one of them — so he was left alone with all their women. So do you know what he did?"

"What? What?"

"He had a snap taken of himself with all the Naga women. Look, he sent a copy."

Dad, grinning so you could see all his perfect teeth, was surrounded by sturdy women with pale round faces and coarse black hair knotted loosely on their necks, dressed in calico and silk with dark cotton sashes around their waists over which some wore girdles of bell-metal discs. Their necks were laden with beads, their legs spotted as if with insect bites, and their calves constricted so tightly by bands of woven cane that flesh bulged over the edges.

The girls laughed over the snapshot. "So what does he say?" Jalu Masi wanted to know.

"He says I am not to be jealous of all his women. He says there's no need." Mom laughed. "He's such a silly — as if I could be jealous of them. He's always joking like that." But she didn't let Jalu Masi read the letter herself because Dad had addressed her as his dearest darling and filled the bottom half of the last page with x's.

3

Dad could not leave a new piece of work alone. He enjoyed merely visiting sites to see what he'd accomplished. It was still early in the evening; he'd already written Mom a long letter that day, didn't want to play darts or bridge with the others; the weather looked promising; so he packed three chapattis with cheese, two bars of Cadbury's Milk Chocolate, a water bottle, and set off in the army jeep for one more look at the airstrip he'd planned which had been constructed under his supervision the week before. The Army dak bungalow was soon behind him. On either side of the military bridle-road were miles of clay banks enclosing irrigated fields of rice. The rice crops gave way to millet as the road got higher and as he approached the foothills the vegetation grew denser with pussy willow, violets, peach trees, pear trees, cherry trees, black stemmed banana trees, and on the rim of the woods tree rhododendrons. Far to his right on the slope of a hill lay a village on stilts, huts built on platforms, the inner edge of each platform touching the ground, the outer edge ten to fifteen feet above, the stilts pointing in all directions as if the huts had been propped and underpinned many times without removing any of the worn out timbers. The earth beneath was inches thick with refuse in which chickens scratched and big black hairy pigs rooted. Dad had watched the inhabitants through field glasses. They wore cane helmets with folded cloths around their necks for protection against arrows, wrapped cloaks around their middles like cummerbunds, and carried shields made of hides stretched on oblong frames, bows, arrows, and long bamboo lances. It was like a scene from the movies and Dad reveled in its wildness. His favorite stretch of the drive was through an upcoming gorge where the pine trees made a bower overhead and the road narrowed to a barely perceptible path. A river, about fifty yards at its widest, flowed alongside the path, green as the forest under the sun, and black patterned with foam in the shadows of the tall cliffs on the other side. Dad stopped the jeep. He liked watching the big grey kingfishers and the multicolored butterflies in the sunlight while he ate — but first he anointed himself generously with insect repellent from a bottle he kept in the jeep. The biting dimdam flies were most prevalent in the early mornings, but he was taking no chances.

He sat on a flat rock overlooking the river for fifteen minutes, wishing Mom could have been with him. When he was finished eating he took out the snapshot she'd sent, which he had not been without since, and kissed it. Love at first sight wasn't just for the young; he was thirty-four; it was for anyone who wanted it. He put the snap back in his pocket, cleaned up, and got back into the jeep humming "The Merry Widow Waltz." It wasn't until the first time the ignition failed him that he realized he should have checked the petrol tank before he'd left the base.

If he pushed the jeep a little he thought he might get it to go for at least a little way. He didn't care whether he got to the site or whether he got back home that night as long as he got out of the forest before dark; but moving forward he had to push uphill, turning around was even more difficult, and he knew he'd never make it on foot in time. He kept trying to start up the jeep with a push, but by the time the night shadows began to descend he'd moved the jeep barely forty feet from where it had stopped. A harsh anguished cry, like that of a baby, sounded overhead, but he recognized it, even muffled by the fog, for that of the white cranes he'd sometimes observed through his field glasses standing four feet tall on twiglike legs. The desolation in their cries seemed an omen, but as it got darker even more innocent sounds — the splash of a kingfisher in the water, the rustle of the wind in the trees — became ominous. He understood he'd have to prepare for the night because no one would miss him until the morning. He left the jeep to look for a thick branch he might use as a weapon. He didn't know what to expect, couldn't calculate his chances of survival through a night in the jungle, but wanted to be prepared for the worst. He found a branch of substantial girth and swung it through the air striking a tree with a satisfying thwack, but as he turned to return to the jeep the sun disappeared and he couldn't see his hand in front of his face. He walked slowly, certain he'd reach the jeep if he only walked in a straight line, but after five minutes which felt more like thirty he realized it was a hopeless task. At first he thought the blinking lights around him were fireflies, but soon he realized they were eyes. Suddenly the branch in his hand felt as reassuring as a toothpick.

There was nothing to do but settle for the night. He found a wide tree and wedged himself as comfortably as possible between its roots, his right hand holding the branch, his left the penknife he used to cut his nails. Something scurried across his ankles, something furry brushed his cheek, something wet fell on his fist clutching the knife, but he didn't move afraid to set another, less manageable force in motion. He recited all the prayers he could remember under his breath, grateful that he was at least warmly dressed. He thanked God he wasn't married (Mom was too young to be a widow), but if he survived the night he vowed he'd marry her immediately. He thought of Bapaiji and Pappa and his own bapaiji and bapavaji and all the others living in the house in which he'd grown up, who'd called him their Lion of the Jungle. "Well, Bapavaji," he thought, amused by the irony himself, "what do you think of your Lion of the Jungle now?" It was his last thought before falling asleep.

When he awoke he wasn't sure at once that he was awake because his sleep was as black as anything he could see, but there was no mistaking the hot breath, the smell of rotten meat, and the unnerving vibration of a low purr, not unlike that of a cat's but magnified a hundredfold. The purr became a growl and Dad saw for the first time two narrow yellow eyes like candleflames in the dark. A black panther was standing before him its mouth open in his face, its head appeared as large as an elephant's, and its growl (it might have been just a cough) sounded like concrete cracking. Dad felt a chill in his head as if someone had driven a razor along his hairline and rolled back his scalp. His branch and penknife would have been no use even had he held on to them in his sleep. The panther put a paw on his chest; there was a cracking sound; Dad lost consciousness.

The next morning he was awakened by the sound of his bearer calling him. He answered weakly unable to believe that a party had found him so quickly. He was less than twenty feet from his jeep. He had a broken rib, gouges in his chest where the panther had stood. He was still shaken, but excited about the story he had to tell. Later he liked to brag that he'd found leeches and lice on his body even after three days of continual scrubbing.

4

Either Dad's sense of direction improved or else he'd had an off night when he got lost in the jungle. I recall a moonlight picnic on Government Beach when our entire party might have drowned if not for his instinct. Mom and Dad liked dinner parties, bridge parties, movies, concerts, Sunday morning social calls, and musical evenings at which some of their guests would perform music that they'd practised, but perhaps the most fun of all their social activities was provided by the moonlight picnics. Mom knew someone who knew the Governor of Bombay who could occasionally get us passes to the private Government Beach. During the hot season the night was the best time for picnics and the nights of the full moon were the best of the nights. About six carloads of us would arrive at nine o'clock on the beach with sandwiches of lettuce and tomato, sugar and butter, chutney, mutton or chicken with mayonnaise, chocolate biscuits, cheese straws, samosas, patrel, chicken patties, wafers, and lemonade, park the cars at the edge of the sand, and talk hopping from car to car, while the moon highlighted streaks of silver on the waves. Sometimes we'd walk along the shore, children like satellites around the grownups.

On one such occasion we walked a longer distance than usual, found ourselves in a cove, and stopped to sit and chat on the rocks. It was midnight when Minoo Sanjana said, "I think we had better be getting back. The tide is coming in."

Almost as soon as we set off there were doubts raised about whether we were walking in the right direction. "This beach looks much narrower than when we came," Mitha Shroff said. "I think maybe we should have gone the other way."

"I think you're right," said Jalu Daruvala. "I don't see our footprints. We must have made so many footprints coming, no?"

Dad took charge. "This is the way. Our footprints were washed away by the tide. That is why the beach is narrower."

"Are you sure, Adi?" Mukund Agtey looked doubtful. "I think we should at least try the other way. I think we might have got mixed up at the cove when we sat down."

"Yesyes," said his wife, Madhavi, "this looks completely different."

On one side of us were unscalable cliffs, on the other was the sea coming in. Perhaps the cliffs had been there on our way to the cove, but as the beach narrowed their significance became more grave. "Nono, I am sure, I am telling you," Dad said. "We do not have time to go any other way. Come on, let us hurry."

Everyone followed him but grudgingly as if they remained unconvinced. Mom kept asking, "But are you absolutely sure, Adi? How can you be so sure?"

After a while he stopped answering her. I thought it was because he was unsure of his direction, but as I realized later it was because he was afraid we might not reach the cars in time. We had removed sandals, shoes, socks. The water came to our feet, to our knees.

"If I find myself in heaven tonight," Zarine Jairazbhoy joked, holding onto her husband Ashraf's arm with one hand, her sari up to her knees with the other, as she waded through the surf, "I'll get you if it kills me, Adi." Dad just smiled, wading ahead, praying that the moon wouldn't go behind a cloud. There were some in the party who still thought we had a chance, but only if we turned back immediately, and he wanted to reach the cars before the consensus turned against him.

Dad's instinct had not failed. Some of the party had lagged far behind, but when Dad shouted that he could see the cars they redoubled their efforts. Everyone complained about how soaked they were as if it were a disaster, perhaps because they didn't want to think about what might have happened, but no one argued with Keki Paymaster when he said, "Better wet than dead."

Her Mona Lisa Smile

There was a bomb scare in Bombay; the Japanese were to bomb all major Indian cities; and all who had homes elsewhere moved temporarily. Mom was in Navsari when she received Dad's letter about the panther. She read it sitting by the pond in the front compound of Cama House, considerably less impressed than Dad might have wished. Soli Mama was perched in a nearby banyan reading *The Sign of the Four*; Jalu Masi rode a bicycle around the house looking for the densest thickets through which to plough. Granny appeared at the front verandah calling, "Pheroza, will you come inside for a minute? Daddy and I would like to talk to you."

"Coming, Mummy," Mom said, folding the letter and putting it in the pocket of her dress, too distracted even to imagine what Granny and Rustomji might have to say. She'd met and liked Bapaiji, was relieved she'd earned Bapaiji's approval, but the repeated visits were beginning to stifle her; Adi had become a context for everything she said and did. There was an undertext to his story about the panther, as if the story itself weren't as important as the impression he wished to create, as if he might have been importunate enough to make up the entire story to create his impression. "Yes, Mummy, what is it?" she said, entering the sittingroom.

Granny stood by the door. Rustomji sat upright in one of the reclining chairs. "Sit down, Pheroza," he said. "We want to have a word with you."

She sat on a wooden stool facing them both, wondering for the first time why she'd been called. Rustomji looked so solemn. "Yes, Daddy?"

"Tell me, my dear," Rustomji said, his eyes on the intricate pattern of the Persian on the floor. "Do you know where babies come from?"

Mom didn't understand why she was embarrassed, but she felt he wouldn't have asked if not for the letters she'd received from Dad. "Why," she said, gesticulating with her hands like a magician to cover her consternation, "everyone knows that. You get married and then God sends you babies."

Granny and Rustomji looked at each other. "Have you read this book?" Granny said finally, showing Mom *Lady Chatterley's Lover* which she'd been holding behind her all along.

Mom's head felt hot. She knew there was something wrong with the book, she knew she should have thrown it away instead of hiding it in her cupboard behind the old petticoats she no longer wore — but then she couldn't have returned to the illicit feeling she got from reading it. Again she was sure her predicament wouldn't have arisen if not for her letters from Dad. "Yes," she said, "but it's not such a good book, Mummy. If you're looking for a good book you should read *Jane Eyre*. That's a lovely book."

Rustomji cleared his throat. "My dear, did you understand what you were reading?"

Mom's customarily dreamy eyes flashed. "Of course I understood. What's there to understand? It's not Einstein's theory of relativity."

Rustomji and Granny looked at each other again. They might have expected such defiance from Jalu Masi. Mom would have been apologetic. Rustomji nodded understandingly. "I told you, Meherbanu. It's the expurgated version."

Granny gave Mom another book to read. "If you're going to get married," she said, "you should know what married people do."

Mom read the book Granny gave her, but it made her sick. "It's so unladylike," she said to Jalu Masi. "I can't believe ladies have to do that."

"Oh, my God," Jalu Masi said, "but that's like going to the bathroom together. What a thing to get married for! Much better not to get married at all."

"But it's got to be done," Mom said seriously. "Otherwise, how will the human race survive?"

"Well," said Jalu Masi, "if it's got to be done, it's got to be done — but still ... what a thing to do."

Mom was glad later that she'd learned about it the way she had instead of the way Dad had, from the goondas who loafed around the atash behram in Navsari, but what upset her more than anything was that everyone took her marriage for granted, taking her choice away from her, and Dad had not even proposed. Besides, she'd met him on only the one occasion in Karachi and already he expected her to write to him everyday, to send him photographs, to bob her hair like an English girl, to wear frocks and pants, to play the piano — or, if she had to wear a sari, not to show her tummy, not to wear tilas, not to wear bangles. When she saw him again in Navsari on his leave he kept touching her as if they were already engaged when all she wanted was to be left alone. She was glad for the custom which dictated that they had to be chaperoned by a grownup everywhere they went until they were engaged, but on his second visit, this time in Bombay, he said, "I am fed up with all these old people trailing us everywhere. You may be young, but I have no time to waste. I made up my mind a long time ago, when we first met, but you have not given me an answer."

They were seated on the wide stone steps leading to the wooden swing gate of the back verandah of Zephyr with its rows of balusters along the open walls. Granny sat in a rattan chair embroidering a stole barely out of earshot.

"You never asked me," Mom said, "so what answer could I give you?"

"In every way except words I have asked," Dad said. "I think we could have a nice life together. What do you think?"

"I don't know what to think. This is all nothing like I thought it would be."

He shook his head impatiently. "What do you want? If you want a formal proposal, like in the eighteenth century, I will get down on one knee and bow my head and kiss your hand like a cavalier. Is that what you want? Just tell me and I will do it."

She was terrified that he might make just such a spectacle of himself before Granny. It would have been the crowning humiliation to what she'd thought would be the most beautiful day of her life. "Nononono," she said. "I do not want anything like that. Now that I know what you want I shall have to think about it."

"Then think about it," he said, "but I have to go in a fortnight. I must have your answer by then."

Everyone said she should marry Dad. Granny said she was a very pretty young girl, but she would not be for long. Still, Mom hated the pressure, and after the fortnight could only say that she needed more time, but Dad said he couldn't wait another year for her to make up her mind. "I have had a very difficult year in Assam," he said, "and I want something more definite. It has got to be now or never."

She couldn't believe he was being so demanding. "If it's got to be now or never," she said, "all I can tell you is it's certainly not going to be now. I need more time."

When he saw how firm she could be Dad panicked, became suddenly contrite, blamed his impatience on the way he'd felt after the panther had broken his rib, told her to take as much time as she needed to be sure, such matters were not to be rushed.

After he left for Assam again Mom felt she had more power and liked the feeling of equality. Her parents still got proposals for her from young men or their parents who had seen her and knew who she was, but she recognized that her chances of getting to know them the way she'd gotten to know Dad were slender. When she wrote to ask how he could be so sure about the two of them he wrote back: "The dogs may bark. The caravan goes on." It was hardly what she wanted to hear, but they continued their correspondence and the next time they saw each other neither doubted they were to be married.

2

"Homi, are you there? I feel you tugging at me. There is no need to pull so hard. I'm not hiding anything."

Mom lay across me on the bed where she'd fallen, but I didn't question the nature of her communication. Of course, she was hiding things, but only unawares. She was unaware of the image i'd glimpsed of her fantasy with the feathers and dead fish. Monsters lurk in the recesses of everyone's subconscious; consciousness is a mechanism for keeping them at bay. If I dug deeply enough I would unearth not only her monsters, but mine, yours, everyone's; if I dug deeply enough I'd find we all have the same monsters; but I haven't the appetite for such revelations. In the meantime, a more persistent image presented itself: Mom taking a bath! behind an open door which nevertheless (thank God) shielded her from view. A dasturji stood in the room leading from the bathroom. According to the Zoroastrian marriage custom she was to be bathed by the dasturji, but modesty allowed her to bathe herself while the dasturji stood outside an open door. Dad was exempted from taking a bath because he was a navar, a ceremony he'd undergone which qualified him for the priesthood had he felt so inclined.

"On the day of the wedding, I was as unsure as I'd ever been about the whole thing, and your dad didn't make it any easier. First of all, he was late. Actually, he was just in time, but he'd circulated a rumor that he thought the wedding was to be at Albless Baug instead of Cama Baug. His pappa, Hormusji, was furious he'd made such a mistake. He didn't tell Hormusji, of course, but it was no mistake. He'd done it on purpose, for a lark. I was so scared, I felt I was marrying a stranger. It had been three years since I'd met him, but we'd spent only forty-two days together (he'd been counting); the rest had all been in letters.

"By the time I came out in my white wedding sari (I could have conjured the image myself of Mom in the shimmering silver sari, gold trim and embroidery, diamond necklace and earrings which Bapaiji had given her, from their wedding pictures with which I was familiar), your dad was already seated onstage behind the white sheet which separated our chairs. I was led to my chair, given a handful of rice to hold in my left hand, his hand to hold in my right under the sheet. According to the myth, when the cloth was removed, the first to throw the rice at the other would be the more loving partner in marriage. Our clasped hands were bound by a cotton thread, the priests recited prayers while the same cotton thread was wound clockwise seven times around our chairs, the sheet between us was removed — and, of course, he was the first to throw the rice, but I felt if he'd really loved me he would have let me be the first.

"But he was saving the worst for last. When he was asked by the dasturji if he would take me for his wife, he didn't say anything. When the dasturji said, 'Come on, Adi, what are you waiting for?' he said, 'I am thinking about it.' Even the dasturji got angry. 'Thinking about it?' he said. 'Is this the time to be thinking about it?' I was so embarrassed I couldn't even look up from my lap, but your dad answered as if he were playing a game. 'If not now, then when?' The dasturji shook his head. 'Come on now, Adi,' he said. 'Be serious.'

"I was scared and he didn't seem to care; he was like a hunter who had bagged his quarry; but later he explained it to me; he was so happy it had made him cocky; he'd thrown the rice first because he had wanted me to feel the more loved. I understood more than that: I think he might just as well have been cocky from relief. Gustave Flaubert said in every kiss there is always one cheek and one pair of lips; and both of us knew, at least in the beginning, that my contribution to our kisses had always been the cheek. In that light it all seemed quite funny, even to me, but even in the literal sense I was not a kissing person — at least, not in public. And sometimes I felt he was just trying to show everyone how Westernized he was, but I was afraid that if I let him get away with a kiss he wouldn't know where to stop."

3

Mom sat beside Sohrab Uncle on the top step of the same white stone steps, leading to the same verandah with rows of balusters on which Dad had threatened to get down on his knees to propose — but this time Dad was nowhere to be seen, the rattan chair on which Granny had then been embroidering her stole was empty, and Mom had told Jalu Masi to stay away. The war was over — for which everyone was glad, but it meant Sohrab Uncle would finally be going back to Shanghai. He still spent time with them, but he still hadn't proposed to Jalu Masi. Mom smiled, shaking her head, recalling Dad's suggestion that Jalu Masi pretend to have lost something dear to her, a brooch, an earring, and cry about it to Sohrab Uncle; when he approached with a handkerchief for her tears she could put her head on his shoulder and he'd understand. Mom's ringlets had spread into a wild black mane pouring down her back. Sohrab Uncle wore a sweater, white pants. Mom couldn't lose her smile; once they'd put the wedding behind them her smile had become a constant, and she'd blossomed into marriage as if into a new and luminous skin. To see her was to fall in love, to hear her wish was to fulfill it; her laugh would have launched a thousand ships, her smile have lit a thousand and one nights. She didn't look at Sohrab Uncle as she spoke, but kept her Mona Lisa smile. "Sohrab, do you want to marry my sister?"

Sohrab Uncle looked sharply at Mom. His thin curly hair had already begun to recede, his eyes seemed to grow larger behind his spectacles. "Of course. I thought she knew that."

Mom still didn't look at him, still kept her smile. "How could she know? Have you asked her?"

"She said No when I asked her. I didn't ask her again because I was afraid she would say No again."

"That was five years ago. And you didn't ask to marry her, you asked for permission to see her. Well, you've seen her now. Are you going to ask her to marry you?"

Sohrab Uncle's eyes still seemed large behind his spectacles. "I was going to ask her before I left. She is the only girl I have wanted to marry of all the girls I have seen. If she said No again I was going to go back by myself, but I thought she didn't want to go to Shanghai."

"That was Mummy. Jalu will go wherever you want."

"But I couldn't take her if Mummy didn't want her to go."

Mom was enjoying herself. She continued smiling as if she knew something he didn't. "Arre, you men are all so stupid. That was five years ago. You can call my mother Mummy as if you were already married to Jalu, but you're still too afraid to ask her to marry you. Mummy used to call you That Chinaman, but she doesn't anymore. She likes you."

Sohrab Uncle's eyes resumed their normal proportions. His

grin stretched like a crescent moon across his face. "If what you say is true, then I am the happiest man in the world."

"It's true," Mom said, looking at him for the first time.

4

Bravo! Well Done! I wanted to cheer, applaud, bounce, float, fly. Mom had played a fine Cupid for the finest of men, my Sohrab Uncle, what can I say? I'd met him on only two occasions: one, when we'd visited Hong Kong; two, when they'd visited Bombay. He didn't like to travel, I was too young to travel as I pleased, but I remember him well — generous, kind, considerate, centered — that is, if you can trust the impressions of first a five-year-old, and then an eight. Yes, he had thinning hair, a bulbous nose, swarthy complexion, but even Granny, a stickler for pale English complexions, didn't hold that against him — but let me cut the blather, let me get specific:

FIRST: I was five years old, with Mom, in Hong Kong, on the mainland peninsula of Kowloon, where Sohrab Uncle, Jalu Masi, and their daughter, my four year old cousin Zarine lived. Dad was to join us later. Rusi was too young and had been left behind with Bapaiji. We lived on the top floor of a four-storey residential building. A quirk of architecture made it necessary to walk through the kitchens of residents on the first, second, and third floors to get to the top floor. We passed by Chinese women every morning, in Mandarin collars and pants, with pigtails and smiling faces. Sohrab Uncle told Zarine and me to wish everyone Good Morning on our way down. He would converse with them at a leisurely pace, perhaps about the weather, perhaps about their health, perhaps about their relatives. I didn't understand, I didn't want to understand, I wanted to be away, particularly if they were discussing my limp, but I hobbled dutifully along at Sohrab Uncle's pace despite the cloud of selfconsciousness through which I struggled.

Once, seeing my chance (Sohrab Uncle was still packing his briefcase, Zarine finishing a glass of milk), I shouted, "I'll meet you downstairs," and rushed from the door, hopping madly down the stairs, waving my cane as if for balance, ignoring the ironers as if I were in too much of a hurry to acknowledge them. I waited almost ten minutes on the busy street, watching the narrow shops lining both sides, the advertisements in the pictographic Mandarin script, the rows of laundry perched among rows of ferns along the faded facades of residences over the shops, coolies hefting bamboos on their shoulders with cargo weighted at each end, rickshawwallahs in conical hats scurrying on wiry calves, before Sohrab Uncle came down with Zarine, spoke sternly. "Did you wish everyone a Good Morning on your way down?"

I mumbled something noncommittally.

"That is not good enough, Homi. I want you to go back up the stairs and wish everyone Good Morning. Take your time. There is no hurry. We will be right here waiting for you."

Dad would not have made me do it. He would have said goodhumoredly, "If the boy got around it let him go," but Sohrab Uncle wasn't Dad. He grew suddenly more honorable and just — not that Dad was dishonorable or unjust, but less inclined to push unless he were pressed himself, prone to let things slide; and he might have lost my respect for letting me so willfully have my way.

SECOND: During the same visit, Jalu Masi and Mom sat side by side in front of Jalu Masi's long dressing table, Jalu Masi in a light blue silk sari on which voluptuous blossoms had been handpainted and a darker blue satin blouse, Mom in a shimmering sari of gold and a gold satin blouse, each putting the finishing touches to their makeup in the glare of fluorescent lights over the three way mirror in front of them. Sohrab Uncle sat on the bed pulling on his socks and shoes. "The Rachmaninoff Second is my favorite," Mom said. "I can hardly wait."

"It's everyone's favorite," Jalu Masi said good naturedly, waving her hand impatiently. "I prefer the fourth. I like all those clumps of notes."

"Yes, but the second is so irresistable." She began to hum the theme, "*Da* de / *Da* de / *Da* da / *Da* da *dum*...."

"We all know how it goes," Jalu Masi said, interrupting her. "It's so easy to follow, but the fourth is more avant-garde."

Mom's eyes opened wide. She'd forgotten that Jalu Masi liked to be contrary sometimes just to be provocative, but Sohrab Uncle knew what she was up to and came to Mom's rescue. "*Sum mare luccica,*" he sang in his deep voice, "*L'astro d'argento.*"

"Here we go again," Jalu Masi said, grinning. She knew what he was doing. "Quiet, Sohrab," she said. "We're having a discussion."

"When I hear you having a discussion," Sohrab Uncle said, looking up from his shoes, "I will be quiet." He turned back to his shoes, singing loudly, "*Placida e l'onda / Prospero e ilvento.*"

Jalu Masi raised her eyebrows, staring at his head bent over as if she might smack him, but Mom interrupted, not understanding that they were playing. "Oh, let him sing, let him sing. I never get tired of listening."

"I just wish he'd learn some new songs," Jalu Masi said. "That one's had it."

She sounded exasperated, but Mom noticed with relief that she was grinning. She wished she could pick up on what was going on more quickly. Sometimes she felt so silly.

Sohrab Uncle had barely finished his verse before I saw myself in pajamas, limping into the room without my cane up to Mom at the dressing table, squinting in the light. "Goodnight, Mom. I just came to say Goodnight."

Mom stared as if she couldn't understand why I was there. It was the fourth time I'd appeared to say Goodnight. "Yesyes," she said. "Goodnight. Goodnight."

I sat by her while Sohrab Uncle put on his tie.

"Don't you think you should be going to sleep, Homi?" Mom said. "It's way past your bedtime."

I felt strange in the apartment in Hong Kong without her. I didn't want to sleep with her bed empty next to mine in the dark bedroom we shared with Zarine. I wanted to stay with her in Jalu Masi and Sohrab Uncle's bedroom. I wanted to leave with her when she left. I said, "Yes, of course. Goodnight."

"Goodnight."

I sighed deeply. "Goodnight, Jalu Masi. Goodnight, Sohrab Uncle."

They said Goodnight. Sohrab Uncle looked thoughtful. "I don't think he wants you to go, Pheroza," he said after I'd left the room.

"Oh, but I do so want to go!" Mom looked alarmed as if she were afraid he'd order her to stay. "He'll be all right. He likes the amah. He'll be all right."

As if on cue, I reentered the room and sat by her again. "Goodnight, Mom. I just wanted to say Goodnight."

"Homi, what is the matter?"

"Nothing. Why?"

"Maybe you should stay, Pheroza." Sohrab Uncle spoke kindly. "I think the boy wants you to stay."

Mom's voice was high with uncertainty. "But I can't stay. I have a ticket."

"We can get another ticket another time. I think the boy needs you tonight."

Mom seemed caught between desire and maternal duty. "There's nothing to be afraid of," she said to me. "We've left you and Rusi with Mary and Julie so many times in Bombay. The amah is right there in the next room if you need anything. She's very nice. There's nothing to be afraid of."

I remained silent.

"He's still new here," Sohrab Uncle said. "I'm sure if this were Bombay he'd be asleep by now."

Mom's eyes relaxed, her shoulders slumped. "I suppose you're right. I suppose I should stay." I hugged her and our embrace and expressions provided a tableau sentimental enough for a Mother's Day greeting card — but I knew she would not have stayed if not for Sohrab Uncle. I remember watching the Hong Kong harbor tilted at a crazy angle from the train to Victoria Peak, I remember the dense floating fishing village of Aberdeen where everyone lived on junks with sails like batwings, I remember the ferry onto which Sohrab Uncle drove his Fiat every morning to cross the harbor from Kowloon to Hong Kong Island where he worked — but best of all I remember Sohrab Uncle looking grave, kind, determined, saying, "Maybe you should stay, Pheroza. I think the boy wants you to stay."

THIRD: I was eight years old, struggling over long division homework at my desk that I'd been set by Miss Sandra Rodrigues, my fourth standard teacher, a slim olive-complexioned young woman of Portuguese descent from Goa with whom I was infatuated. I was convinced she'd said that a thousand divided by ten was ten and, consequently, I continued to get the wrong answer to the problem. I hated to ask Dad's help for anything because he shouted if I didn't understand everything immediately. Sohrab Uncle spent an hour trying to shake me from my delusion, going over the multiplication tables, laws of arithmetic, calculations from first principles. I understood him, I'd long understood the solution, I was after all a certified genius, but I couldn't understand how Miss Rodrigues could be wrong. "She is the teacher, Sohrab Uncle," I said. "How can the teacher be wrong?"

"Ask her again tomorrow," he said patiently. "You will see that there has been a misunderstanding."

"But maybe there is no misunderstanding. Maybe you are both correct."

"If we are both correct then ten would equal one hundred, and that is impossible."

"But maybe not."

"Just ask her tomorrow."

It wasn't the first time my infatuation had ruled my logic, and it wasn't the last. Sohrab Uncle was right, of course. I'd misunderstood Miss Rodrigues. The legacy of the circumstance wasn't mastery of long division, certainly not of infatuation, but a consolidation of my image of Sohrab Uncle as solid, patient, dependable.

The Greater of His Two Loves

A whirlwind of images followed, literally a whirlwind, my newly beautiful Mom appeared to be spinning, often with Dad, always with the smile, while the landscape swirled around them. I recognized some of the places, Delhi, Srinagar, Gulmarg, Calcutta, Darjeeling, Poona, Bangalore, Mysore, Ooty, having seen them myself, but the ones I did not recognize were revealed by snatches of conversation, municipal buildings, signposts, Kathmandu, Kanpur, Nagpur, Ladakh, Lucknow, Lahore. The swirl generally included in the hinterland tea parties, swim parties, garden parties, cocktail parties, dances, clubs, concerts, movies, shows. At one point, Dad came rushing through the swirl, handsome in his major's uniform, cap in hand, hair black and shining, to find Mom in an orange sari, dark satin blouse, hair parted down the middle, a rose entwined above one ear, sitting at her dressing table in a bedroom, ready to take his arm; but instead of giving her his arm Dad froze as if stopped by an invisible hand. "Philly, what are you doing? What are you thinking?"

Mom eyebrows rose, but she smiled. "What do you mean? What do you think I am doing?"

"You know damn well what I mean. We have got so little time as it is."

Mom lost her smile. "But we can go. I am ready."

"Do not be silly. How can we go with you looking like that?"

"Like what? I always look like this."

Dad removed the rose from her hair. "Do not pretend you do not know what I mean, Philly. People will think I have married a damn dancing girl or an actress or something. Go on and change. Hurry up now. People are waiting."

She knew what he meant, had known from the start: he liked her best in western dress, hair parted on one side, heels high in pumps. She was flattered by the attention he paid her dress, but sometimes felt invisible, no more than a doll to be dressed and exhibited, an ornament for his arm. She disappeared for a few minutes, returned in a long evening dress, still shaking her head, but seeing his smile, his arm extended, she smiled again though not without irony, and took his arm.

A moment later, she shimmied out from behind a table of youngsters dressed like themselves, an equal mix of foreigners and Indians, and with a toss of her head, a roll of her shoulders to the beat of the music (a brass band was playing "Anything Goes"), took the arm of the uniformed gentleman who'd asked her to dance, flicking a glance at a table of GIs from which had issued a volley of wolf whistles. Almost as soon as they'd begun to foxtrot, another gentleman, in a doublebreasted suit, cut in on them, and Mom swirled from one pair of arms to the other as if she'd been choreographed. The music changed to "Putting on the Ritz" and Dad cut in on the doublebreasted gentleman, but again almost immediately another uniformed gentleman cut in on him saying, "No, Major Seervai, you are privileged to be the husband. You must let others do the dancing," and Dad surrendered his prize with a smile and a bow.

I moved backward and upward to provide myself with an overview of the party, and the couples on the dance floor appeared to make kaleidoscopic patterns as they waltzed, reflected in the chandeliers above. There was a neatly landscaped garden nearby, with a swimming pool, and as the night grew deeper couples strayed from the dance floor into the garden where some of them fell giggling, fully dressed, into the pool. When Mom moved to the garden to investigate the squeals and the splashes she was astonished. Brigadier Tarapore said, "Do not look so disapproving, Mrs. Seervai. They are only having fun. You should join them."

Mom flashed him a look, afraid he might toss her into the pool himself. "I'm not disapproving," she said. "I'm just a little shocked."

Brigadier Tarapore nodded, smiled, and raised his glass in a toast. "To your charming wife, Major," he said, turning to Dad, who grinned and raised his own glass. "Cheers!"

In the Ford, going home, Dad said to Mom, "You know what, Mrs. Seervai? My wife was the loveliest girl at the ball." She smiled, and was about to say something, when the idyll was shattered by screams, "Hare Ram, Ram, Ram! Jaane do, oh, God, let me go, mujhe jaane do!"

"Oh, my God," Mom said, her face suddenly as small as a child's. "What do you suppose that could be?"

"What do you think?" Dad said angrily, stepping on the accelerator. "More repercussions of that damn Jinnah's Direct Action Day. We are so close to Independence and he has got to spoil everything. Mark my words. Gandhi is right. Pakistan is a stupid idea. It will come to no good. This is only the beginning of a long tunnel of trouble."

Again back, again up, across narrow streets where, by day, Chinese cobblers might have peddled wares among Muslim tailors and Hindu storekeepers, across rows of shacks of cardboard and corrugated metal within which families slept in rows, to a dung-encrusted stench-filled flyridden alley, where a man lay on the ground in the dark, goondas kicking him, beating him with lathis and dandas. Blood spilled from the man's mouth, and from around the corner came more goondas, blades unsheathed. The first stabbings drew arcs of blood as the long knives rose and fell. I remembered the time from my high school history: almost four thousand dead in the streets; six thousand including those dying in the hospitals; twenty thousand including those merely shot and stabbed and hacked and burned. Communal gangs had terrorized Calcutta: men's limbs were torn from their bodies as their families watched; lathis were stuffed into women's vaginas, wrenched upward tearing the women apart; pregnant women were cut open, left to die next to their unborn babies.

I drew away again, unwilling to absorb the details, back to the Ford with Mom and Dad. "Oh, my God," Mom was saying. "When will it end? When will it all end? How much killing will it take?"

"If anybody can do anything about it," Dad said, "Gandhi can. Let us pray he survives his fast. No telling what will happen otherwise."

Mom shook her head, looking more troubled than I'd seen her yet. "I feel like Marie-Antoinette sometimes," she said. "We have such a good time, but all around us people are getting killed!"

"I know what you are saying," Dad rejoined. "We are like Nero fiddling while Rome is burning — but there is nothing we can do about it. There is absolutely not one damn thing that we can do about it. Might as well enjoy life while we can. Calcutta is not the best place to be in these times. Tomorrow, it might be our turn."

"Don't be silly, Adi. You mustn't even say such beastly things. We must keep on praying for the best."

Gandhi survived the fast which brought an end to the atrocities and Mom remembered her old Gujarati teacher, Popatlal-Master, who'd gone to jail for Gandhi. Gandhi was more than a man, a saint, the most Christlike figure in the world; she liked to think she would have gone to jail for him herself, but she was no Bapaiji. She didn't think even Bapaiji would have gone to jail — except maybe for the publicity, for the column in the newspaper.

When Independence came, Mom and Dad were in Nagpur. They'd been invited to Government House for the midnight inauguration, August 14, 1947, of the new governor. The Durbar Hall was floodlit; the British officers, civilian and military, wore medals, decorations, tailcoats, top hats; their ladies wore gowns and jewelry; there was a band in attendance. Mr. Pakvasa, the first Indian Governor-to-be, was late. Dad fumed; such unpunctuality had been unheard of during the Raj. Finally, some sadhus arrived, wearing dhotis, smeared with saffron from the waist up, took their places onstage, and performed puja, preparing the way for Mr. Pakvasa who made his appearance shortly in a kurta, dhoti, and Nehru cap. Some of the British snickered, some of the Indians looked embarrassed, but then the Union Jack was lowered, the National Flag was raised, "Jana Gana Mana" was sung for the first time in public, Nehru held his tryst with destiny in Delhi, Mountbatten became the first Governor-General. Mom huddled against Dad in the crowd, tears trickling prettily down her cheek. "I'm so proud," she said, turning to Dad. "I'm so proud." Dad, grinning with pride himself, held her closer sneaking a kiss to the side of her head.

It has been said, for every birth there is a death, and perhaps for the births of nations the deaths are multiplied a millionfold. I recalled again the high school history. Millions migrated, Muslims from India to Pakistan, Hindus from Pakistan to India, many with no more than the shirts on their backs, by foot, by bullock cart, by train, and more than a million died in the ensuing carnage. A train arrived in Pakistan, A GIFT FROM INDIA scrawled on its side, packed with the corpses of murdered Muslims, men, women, and children — which prompted Muslims to respond in kind. Mom's tears developed into a monsoon and a deluge of blood, flooding the carnage in a crimson wash. "Jana Gana Mana" dissolved into a squawk of feedback over the loudspeakers, rose into a wall of lamentation. On a thin mattress, on a hard floor, in a dark house, somewhere in Calcutta, Gandhi curled like a worm on his side, shoulders shaking, weeping silently, this was not the conclusion he'd dreamed for his nonviolent revolution.

2

Mom and Dad were in bed. Mom, pregnant with Rusi, lay on her side, her back to Dad. Dad lay on his side, a hand on Mom's shoulder. A blue nightlight embedded in the headboard cast a pale blue mist over their heads. Through the wall, in the next room, I could see myself, a baby in a cot (yes, I have passed by my birth; it wasn't momentous, no lioness whelped in the street, no grave yawned to yield up its dead). On the floor, next to the cot, Nancy, my first ayah, snored lightly on a bedroll. "What is it, Philly?" Dad said. "Tell me what is the matter?"

Mom said nothing, tried to shake his hand off her shoulder, but Dad's grip only tightened.

"Is it that same problem we talked about still? Is that what it is still?"

"Yes."

"Still?"

"Why should I change my mind? The circumstances haven't changed."

"But, Philly, I have explained it to you. If I leave the army we will give up so much. I will be giving up a pension for which I have worked already so many years, for which I will be eligible in only a few more years. I will be throwing away everything I have worked for. We will also be giving up so many privileges: house, servants, travel —"

Mom interrupted sharply. "That's just it! I can't believe you would even bring it up. I'm tired of moving around all the time.

I want us to be settled. It was all right when we were young, but we're having our second child. Children need a stable environment. I don't want to bring up our children like gypsies, constantly moving from one post to another."

"Philly, what do you mean we live like gypsies? We live very well — and it is because of the army that we live so well. If not for the army, I could hardly give you all the things you want. What do you mean?"

"I don't care how you put it. I hate all this traveling. I want us to settle down. Bombay would be the best place. You can begin again as a civilian. We mustn't let an army pension hold us like a prison."

"A prison! How can you call this a prison? I thought you were happy here. Besides, I am past forty now. I am not a young man. It will not be easy to get jobs."

Mom said nothing. Dad's hand now lay on her shoulder like something dead.

"Something else is the matter, isn't it? It is not the army. I have been in the army since before we met, but this is only a recent development."

"If it's a recent development, it's only because Homi is a recent development, it's only because Rusi is going to be an even more recent development."

They were so silent for a while I could hear the nightlight buzz between them. When Dad spoke again he sounded tired. "One more thing you should think about, Philly. It is because of the army that we meet the people we meet. When Bapaiji got me into the Maharajah's employment in Baroda I was so bored. I had a bungalow and servants and good wages, but there were not many Englishmen or Parsis around, mostly just vegetarian types. The social life was like nothing to what we are now accustomed. We would have to start out all over again. I think you would like that even less."

Mom sensed his weakening. She almost turned around.

"Bombay is not Baroda. There are plenty of our type of people there. We would soon find our place. Besides, Mummy is also in Bombay, and she needs me now, especially with Jalu in Hong Kong. She is getting old."

"Soli is there for Mummy in Bombay. She does not need you as well."

"Soli is a man. It's not the same thing. Men are useless where these things are concerned."

Dad pursed his lips, shut his eyes, said nothing; his hand slid off her shoulder.

"If you will not do this for me, Adi, I will have to ask Bapaiji to help me. I do not want to do it, but you will force me to do it."

Dad's mouth opened, but he said nothing. He'd given up a job he'd loved in London for Bapaiji, who'd got him the Baroda job as she'd promised, but Bapaiji had enjoyed that job more than he because she got to travel in the luxury railway carriages at the state's expense. He'd escaped during the war, from Bapaiji as much as Baroda (much to Bapaiji's fury), because the army had need of engineers and he'd volunteered his services without asking her permission. After the war she'd written to his commanding officer that it was time for him to resume civilian life. Dad had insisted he wanted to stay and for once prevailed over Bapaiji — but despaired of prevailing alone against both women. His voice turned small, bitter. "It is not for the children at all, is it? It is for yourself, isn't it?"

Mom's shoulders stiffened. "What *non*sense! It is *not*! And what if it was? If I am happy, the children will be happy."

Her indignation was transparent. Dad knew he was right. "And what about me? What about my happiness? Am I not the one doing the work?"

"That's your job, to do the work — and it's my job to look pretty for you. Do you suppose I enjoy dressing up just to please you all the time? But I do it — because that's my job."

Dad said nothing.

"And if I'm happy, you will be too. Don't I make you happy?"

Still he remained silent. She laughed, but he couldn't bring himself to smile. He remembered his loneliness before he'd met her — and since my birth, the birth of his oldest son, the loneliness had crept over him periodically. He was afraid to lose her — and now he knew he would give up the army which he loved, against his better judgment, for Mom, the greater of his two loves. She turned to face him, smiling; he knew he could have put his hand on her shoulder now, but no longer wished it.

A week later, when he told Mom of his decision, her ankles developed wings, she flew smiling into his arms; she'd won the battle, proven herself more than an ornament for his arm, she'd begun to affect his life, to have a say on her own. He smiled, relieved to hold her close again, but his smile was toothless, the corners of his mouth arced downward, and I recognized a look on his face I'd known through childhood, but which he'd not yet shown me from his perch in Edinburgh, Eternity.

3

At first, everything was black, then a black rectangle getting gradually lighter at the edges. The rectangle revealed itself to be a black stick in the head of a snowman, ostensibly its nose, and more black sticks appeared sunk in its head for eyes. As my field of vision broadened I saw a blue field of snowmen, and as it broadened farther it became an army of mashed potato men with toothpick arms sitting in Mom's large blue serving dish; the black sticks of their eyes and noses were cloves. Next to the mashed potato army sat a companion dish in which white rice provided the head, shoulders, back, and tail of a sheep, and pink slices of roast lamb the face, legs, and torso. I recognized Mom's handiwork; she brought a Japanese imagination and delicacy to the presentation of her meals at dinner parties. She'd developed from a gangling girl, all arms and legs, to an efficient and radiant hostess — for which Dad, not without some justification, took credit.

Sure enough, as the field broadened farther I saw her and Dad, recognized many of their friends though younger than I'd known them and moving more quickly — far more quickly than possible, like a movie being sped toward its conclusion. The lamb disappeared amid a flurry of cutlery, the snowmen appeared to levitate themselves onto the plates of the guests with the suicidal urge of salmon scaling the falls. When the action slowed it was to focus on Dad heaping his plate with baked Alaska, Mom touching his arm. "Adi, please put that back. You know what the doctor said."

I could see it already, the beginning of the end: at five feet eight inches Dad weighed one hundred and ninety pounds, had too much sugar in his blood. He didn't look at Mom. "It's all right. It is just for one evening."

"One evening can ruin your diet for the whole week, and you know it. That's your third serving already." She grabbed the plate out of his hands.

They stared wildly at each other for a moment before Dad grabbed his plate back. "I don't tell the doctor what to eat. Why should he tell me?" He looked around, expecting a laugh, but when none was forthcoming resumed eating.

Mom looked around as well, the party might have become a court of appeal. "He's allowed *exactly* two thousand, two hundred and ninety calories a day. I might as well give up. He's upset my schedule for months. There are almost a hundred calories in each spoonful of baked Alaska."

Dad just grinned, shrugged, gobbled another spoonful. "She's always nagging me. She's getting more like her mother everyday."

Granny's reputation for eccentricity was no secret. Mom took a deep breath, spoke with lungs filled to capacity, released each syllable with a puff of air, eyes filling with water. "I am *not* a nag. I am *not* like my mother. I'm only telling him for his *own* good. It's only because I *care* about him."

Dad grinned again. "If I am fat, it is only because I am trying to keep up with you."

It was a silly joke at best though it carried less of a sting in the ignorance of the fifties. Mom, fat with Rusi, dashed from the room. Dad gobbled another spoonful. Gool Paymaster, perhaps the most sensitive of their friends, stood close to Dad, spoke softly. "Maybe you should go to her. She is right, you know. She only does it because she cares."

Dad turned away. "Arre, what does she know?"

Keki Paymaster spoke as considerately as his wife. "She's upset. You should go to her. She's your wife, after all."

Dad laughed. "She's also a woman. It's her privilege to get hysterical now and then." When no one laughed he continued. "We go through this all the time. She will be all right in a minute."

Gool Paymaster spoke again in the same patient tone. "Well, Adi, I hope you won't take it amiss then, if I go to her. I think she needs someone to be with her." She didn't wait for a response, but left the room looking for Mom.

Dad finished his plate; the guests followed his lead; and shortly Mom returned with Gool Paymaster as if nothing were the matter though she didn't speak to Dad for the rest of the evening. Dad smiled gamely through it all, but you could tell from his eyes, suddenly dull, without focus, that he'd lost another battle.

4

Dad was still at his last posting with the army, in Poona, when we settled in Zephyr, on the ground floor, with Soli Mama and Granny on the first — and the troubles began immediately.

Nancy, my ayah, took me to visit Granny daily — but Granny didn't like Nancy, her reasons were immaterial, she trusted no one, and insisted Mom give her the sack.

Mom complained that she was pregnant, that Dad was in Poona, that she trusted Nancy, that I liked Nancy, and surely that counted for more than her own dislike. Granny wondered whether she meant to take her mother's side or her servant's. Mom wanted to know who would take care of me when she had to go to the hospital. Granny countered that the first child was the responsibility of the maternal grandmother, the second that of the paternal. It was the custom, and Granny had hardly been responsible for Mom's first pregnancy, but Nancy was sacked, and Bapaiji summoned from Navsari. Images poured again: letters flying back and forth to disrupt Bapaiji from her 'busy schedule; Bapaiji taking the train finally to come to Bombay; Bapaiji installed in Zephyr in my room, my sofa her bed; Bapaiji in an evening sari taking me by the hand to Granny's rooms upstairs, me barely two, before my first haircut, hair light brown and streaming like a girl's; Bapaiji ringing Granny's doorbell, the door opened by Granny's servant, Granny standing imme-diately behind, also in an evening sari, frowning. "Yes, Banu, what is it?"

She didn't invite us in, nor take a step back, but Bapaiji pushed me forward and shut the door behind her. Granny spoke English, but Bapaiji replied in Gujarati. "Arre, Meherbanu, I was just taking Homi to the park. Then I saw your car and thought this is the time you go for your drive, is it not?"

"And if it is, what is it to you?"

Bapaiji's eyes narrowed, but otherwise she ignored Granny's impertinence. "I thought we should all go for a drive. It will be nice for Homi, with his two grandmothers, and the wind and the sea air will also be good for him. Also he likes your Studebaker very much."

Granny knew I liked to ride in the car, but she knew Bapaiji liked it even better, and she resented Bapaiji for using me as her excuse for a drive. "I shall take Homi for a drive sometime when you are not here. When you are here he is your responsibility, not mine. Do not think I do not see through your scheme. I know just what you are thinking."

Bapaiji's eyes widened; she thought she had learned to expect the unexpected from Granny, but apparently she had more to learn yet. "Arre? What am I thinking? It is no big mystery. I am thinking we shall both go for a drive with our grandson. What is there to be thinking?" Granny remained silent, but something seemed to be roiling within. Bapaiji felt sorry for her, something was wrong with the woman, she had psychological problems; she put her hand on Granny's shoulder. "Chaalo. We are both dressed and ready. Homi is ready. The car is waiting downstairs. Let us go."

Granny spun away from Bapaiji, dislodging her hand. "Do not touch me! Who are you to touch me? You are just a Dhondi from Navsari, hardly even a Seervai, and you dare to touch a Cama! It is insupportable!"

Granny kept talking, but Bapaiji's eyes had narrowed again and hardened. She was at least as much a Seervai as Granny was a Cama, before which Granny had been a mere Motiwalla, a jeweler's daughter, but she said nothing. She didn't understand everything Granny was saying because she continued to speak in English, to shout in English, but finally raised her hand, palm thrust forward, shouted herself: "Bas! Enough! I have had enough!"

Granny shut up as if she'd been slapped, eyes as wide as Bapaiji's had been a moment earlier, watched as Bapaiji practically dragged me to the door and down the stairs again — at which point she began shouting again.

When the time came for Mom to go to the hospital Bapaiji took her in a cab; Granny stayed home though her Studebaker and Soli Mama's Chevrolet were both parked in the driveway.

She was repentant by then, but never apologized. The full force of Bapaiji's anger wasn't evident until later: she refused to set foot in Zephyr again, not only in Granny's rooms but ours as well; we had to move just so she could visit us again; Dad was happy enough to move into a place of his own, particularly since Bapaiji insisted on paying for the flat; Mom didn't complain because she knew that when Soli Mama married he would want the ground floor for himself, but she hadn't anticipated that Bapaiji would buy us the flat in Mayo House on Cooperage Road (where I was lying in bed) halfway across Bombay greatly reducing the time we were able to spend with Granny.

Nehru and Lady Mountbatten Had an Affair

Mom was driving the black Morris Minor down Hughes Road, called Hyujiz Road in Bombay. We kept two cars for a while because Mom didn't like driving the big Ford, which Rusi called the Humpty Dumpty after the eggshell curve of its rump — but she could barely claim greater control over the smaller Morris. She liked its smaller size, stickshift between the two front seats; it was like a toy, she said, but Rusi said it had a face like a cockroach.

It must have been deep in the afternoon, very likely a Sunday afternoon, when Bombay napped, because Hughes Road was silent, and except for a few strollers uninhabited. Rusi rode in the passenger seat in front, Julie in the back. He appeared about six or seven years old; it must have been during one of my many illnesses. There was no traffic on the road, but Mom swerved suddenly and swiped one of the parked cars on her right. She was doing perhaps twenty, she didn't even dent a fender, but paint chipped, and in the quiet Sunday afternoon the collision sounded like an explosion.

A man appeared almost immediately from one of the neighboring buildings. Mom got out of the car, waved him over. "Are you the owner of this motor vechicle?"

The man looked puzzled, nodded.

"I'm sorry. I'm the one who hit your vehicle. It was an accident."

"Yesyes, whatelse? I am sure that it was," the man replied politely.

A policeman arrived and Mom waved him over as well. "Over here, over here," she said. "It's nothing. We've had a little accident, but it's no one's fault. Let me explain."

She spoke as if she were in charge of an investigation. "It's a shame how dusty the street is," she said. "I've been meaning to write to the Chief Minister about it. I was avoiding the dust when I hit this gentleman's vehicle. If the streets had been swept this wouldn't have happened. I was afraid the dust would clog the engine."

The men exchanged looks. The policeman shook his head. "Arre, memsahib, this dustbust will not work. Dust cannot hurt your motor. This sahib can take you to court if he is wanting."

Mom's authoritative manner changed abruptly. "No! That he cannot do! My husband has a very high blood pressure. Something like this could give him a stroke — it could paralyze him — maybe worse." She turned to the owner of the car, suddenly griefstricken. "I'm sorry. It was an accident. I really thought the dust would be bad for my vehicle. I thought the wheels would sweep it into the engine. Can't we settle this quietly somehow?"

Rusi couldn't understand why she kept calling the car a vehicle. The man examined the damage, confabulated with Mom, and they came to an agreement. Back on the road again, Mom smiled triumphantly. "They were only men," she said to Rusi, "so helpless." She made him promise not to "breathe a word" of it to Dad; it would unnecessarily raise his blood pressure. Rusi nodded, but his face twitched uncontrollably. I understood how he felt though he couldn't have himself, and neither could I at the time, and perhaps neither could Mom. The secrets we kept from Dad (Rusi and I with Mom), made us cozier among ourselves, but cordoned us off from Dad, making him a stranger in his own home — but to be fair to Mom, Dad would have fired first and asked questions later. By the time he noticed the scrape on the Morris, she'd almost forgotten the incident herself. "I think it must have been when I was parking on Marine Lines, when I was visiting Silloo Dadabhoy. There's a tree on the footpath so big it practically comes onto the road. Someone should really do something about it."

2

Mom's lilywhite lie, "There's a tree on the footpath so big it practically comes onto the road," was born to keep Dad's red rage at bay.

I didn't want to dwell on the scenes that followed, particularly not now I had seen Dad as a lovelier man than I'd known, but they had to be faced. Singly the scenes meant little, but cumulatively they provided a sad mosaic, of Dad mad, perpetually redfaced, fists knotted, emitting a white hiss, inhaling and exhaling like an Olympic runner through flaring nostrils, signaling the boiling lava about to erupt like a bull signaling his charge. His arms rose in a steeple of frustration, sometimes descended, hanger in hand, on Rusi's behind bent over his knee (polio exempted me from such ministrations). As I watched the images were cartoonized, perhaps my subconscious working against the ugliness, flames belched from his mouth, his finger pointing accusatively swelled to the size of a banana in my face, his eyes narrowed turning yellow and convex like a cat's, his teeth obtruded like fangs, his tongue lashed words like a whip. The occasions were banal: he might have tripped over my cane left lying against a couch, lost patience with Rusi while explaining a calculus equation, stumbled on one of Mom's secret purchases, found a beggar too importunate, a servant too un-

manageable, neighborhood kids too loud, a roast underdone, a
souffle overdone, it didn't take much; the cause was inside, not
outside, as I could see now in ways I could not before. He
fought little battles vehemently because he'd lost the big ones
irrevocably, and his rage appeared directed at us not for what
we'd done but for what he'd failed to do himself, which understanding shed an ironic light on his recurring phrase, "This
hurts me more than you." Too many ugly words, shouted too
often, had left almost too indelible an imprint: DAMN! STU-
PID! IDIOT! I AM ASHAMED OF YOU! STUPID BOY!
BLOODY FOOL! WHEN WILL YOU LEARN! HOMI! RUSI!
HOMI! RUSI! DAMN! DAMN! DAMN! BLOODY FOOL!
WHO DOES HE THINK HE IS! COMPLETE IDIOT!
THINKS HE'S TOO DAMN GOOD FOR US! DRIVING
ME CRAZY! SHEER CARELESSNESS! HIS OWN DAMN
FAULT! HOMI! RUSI! I'M TELLING YOU FOR YOUR
OWN DAMN GOOD! DON'T COME RUNNING TO
ME! NOT MY FAULT IF YOU WON'T LISTEN! DAMN
FOOL! RUSI! HOW MANY TIMES I HAVE TOLD YOU!
BLOODY DAMN FOOL! STUPID IDIOT BOY! STUPID
BLOODY DAMN FOOL BOY! DAMN! DAMN! DAMN!

Not how I wanted to remember Dad, Not how I wanted
to remember Dad, Not! Not! Not! Not! and I scanned the
images quickly searching for one to vindicate his temper.

3

When I saw Dad shake hands with Dr. Mistri, our dentist, also
a friend, he was heavier still, his widow's peak more prominent.
He smiled, but as he left the office, walked down the corridor
past the frosted glass windows, past the wooden shingles bearing various names and degrees in white block letters, past the
plaster walls covered with red expectorations of paan to the lift,
his smile dropped abruptly and his eyes glazed over with dis-

appointment. He looked like a child who'd been cheated. Philly had been right. She'd told him not to give away his services freely. They needed money; but he'd said Mistri was a friend, that he'd have done the same for him — but he hadn't. Dad had drawn up blueprints for a bar in Mistri's sittingroom, found the materials, supervised the construction, without charging him. Mistri had fixed him the first drink at the bar. "Anytime you want a drink, come on up," he'd said. Dad wasn't a drinking man, but he'd needed a filling for a tooth. The filling wasn't expensive, but Mistry shouldn't have charged him after the work he'd done, and he was damned if he was ever going back. The man had no sense of honor.

It wasn't the first time something like this had happened. He'd done work for the Desais and the Vazifdars without charging them, but they'd charged him for work done in return. He didn't mind losing their friendship; not a friendship at all, but the illusion of a friendship; but he was beginning to think he'd missed the big picture. Perhaps honor had nothing to do with it, perhaps honor was a fiction which had been perpetrated to take advantage of those who believed the fiction, perhaps men of the world understood this and he would never be such a man — Bapaiji understood this and he could never be like her. Was it honor that kept him apart? or just pride? foolishness? Was there even a difference?

It was a hot day. His bush shirt clung to his back, heartshaped with sweat, as he got into the Ford and drove to Napean Sea Road where Mom was to wait for him. She was visiting Mr. Gokhale, the Chairman of the Reserve Bank. When the Chairman had learned that she planned to visit Kashmir that summer with Rusi and myself he'd insisted that she visit him first so he could inform her, looking at the latest reports (the Defence Minister was his good friend), if it were safe (he'd heard the Chinese might be making advances again at the border). Dad had been surprised at Mr. Gokhale's concern. He'd warned

Mom to be careful. She'd pooh-poohed him as always. "He's
the Chairman of the Reserve Bank. What's he going to do to
me? He's just being nice."

Perhaps she was right; much as he hated to admit it, she'd
been right about Mistri. He hoped she'd be on time. He'd never
been able to convince her that it was rudeness, not the privilege
of a lady, to keep others waiting. She'd never been able to
convince him that a lady lost respect if she treated a social
engagement as if it were a military detail.

Mom was heavier too, but she spread her weight evenly
unlike Dad who concentrated his in his stomach; whereas Dad
looked simply heavier Mom looked more womanly. Her hair
was short, waved like Debbie Reynolds's, and her lightblue
shortsleeved cotton dress was dark at the armpits. She waited
for Dad at the gates of Mr. Gokhale's mansion. Adi had been
right. Men were all the same. There'd been a British brigadier
at their hotel in Calcutta who'd flattered her with conversations
of Keats and Shelley and Byron every morning at breakfast for
a month, attempted to force his way into her suite when Dad
had been at work, and left as soon as she'd started screaming.
There'd been Mr. Rao, a friend of a friend, who'd invited her
to meet his family who spoke no English, from whom she'd
accepted two glasses of wine and almost passed out before she'd
torn herself from his embrace and hailed a taxi home (she
should have known better; any woman who drank wine in the
daytime, particularly in the absence of her husband, might as
well have branded herself a prostitute). There'd been others.
Adi had warned her but she'd assumed, always erroneously, that
if she felt nothing but friendship for a man he couldn't possibly
feel anything more for her. The British brigadier had been thirty
years older, Mr. Rao of an entirely different class, the chairman
was, well, after all, the chairman — but in this one respect they
were all the same. He'd told her she was lovely, kissed her hand,
told her to think about it, he was a powerful man, he could help

her in many ways, he could help her husband, and he'd shown her a private bedroom behind his office! She couldn't believe he'd propositioned her after she'd spent such delightful evenings with his wife and children who lived on the other side of the mansion, but she'd held on to her indignation because she was afraid of what he might do in retaliation and left his office immediately. He'd offered to have her driven home, but she'd told him her husband was coming and she preferred to wait at the gate. She wished he'd come soon but she hated to tell him what had happened.

Dad was surprised to see Mom at the gate with the guards instead of in one of the wicker chairs in the garden or on the porch by the driveway, but he was too obsessed with what he had to say himself to notice her distress until she spoke. "You'll never believe what happened," she said, getting into the car.

Dad didn't say anything.

"I can hardly believe it myself. I still can't believe it."

The wonder in her voice, almost shock, caught Dad's attention more than what she'd said. "What? What happened?"

"Just drive. I'll tell you."

Dad's fist tightened on the wheel as he listened to her story.

"He said we were all grownups now. He said his wife knew. He said he could help you. He even has a bedroom behind his office — with a bed! I still can't believe it."

Dad stopped the car. "The swine! The bloody swine!"

Mom, more in a state of bewilderment now than indignation, looked at Dad as if she were seeing him for the first time. "Adi! I will not have you swearing like that!"

Dad stared at her so piercingly that she was afraid. "Are you crazy?" he shouted. "The man has defiled my wife, and you are telling me not to swear at him?"

The way he said "my wife" made her feel as if he were talking about a third person. Usually, when she told him about the passes other men made, he was angry with her for being so trusting; sometimes he laughed (she'd never come to harm and made the stories seem amusing); she'd grown less trusting with the years and could barely remember the last time an incident had occurred — but she didn't know what she found more surprising: Mr. Gokhale's behavior or the violence of Adi's reaction. "You can swear if you like," she said, unsure what to say, embarrassed by her uncertainty, "but no one was defiled and no one was hurt. I just never want to see that man again."

Dad stopped the car. Mom looked alarmed. "What are you doing, Adi? Why are you turning around?"

"I am going to give that swine a piece of my mind. Chairman or no, I am going to tell him exactly what I think."

"Adi! No! Don't do anything foolish now. He's a powerful man. He could hurt the business."

Dad shouted without looking at her. "Damn! Woman! Whose side are you on?"

Mom remained silent while Dad drove back the way he'd come, through the gates of the mansion, and up the driveway. Later, when he told her about Mistri, she understood that her story had stoked longburning coals, but at the time she'd feared his mood as much as the possible repercussions of his actions. The guards and servants knew him from previous visits so they let him through. Dad knew his way around so he strode directly to Mr. Gokhale's office and pushed the door open violently. Mom followed, hesitantly at first as if she wished to slow Dad down — but when that didn't work as if she couldn't resist the vacuum in his wake.

Mr. Gokhale was alone at his desk. Dad didn't stop until he'd picked up a paperweight from the desk and slammed it down. "I say, Mr. Gokhale," he shouted. "I want to know who the bloody hell you think you are treating my wife like a bloody tart."

Mr. Gokhale rose from his desk. I recognized him immediately, his long trim torso in the dark brown Nehru jacket, his thin angular handsome brown face, his greasy grey hair combed

flat and straight back on his head. I'd exchanged comics with
his son at school. I'd wondered why Rusi and I had suddenly
been forbidden to talk to him, not even to get back an issue of
Plastic Man he'd borrowed.

"Now, now, Mr. Seervai," Mr. Gokhale said in his soft voice,
"we are civilized educated men, is it not? I do not know what
you are talking about, but let us discuss it calmly. Otherwise,
nothing will come of it. Why do you not sit down? Mrs. Seervai,
will you not come in?"

Mom was standing at the door as if she were on guard. She
looked at Dad for a cue, but he ignored her. "I will *not* sit down,"
he said, still shouting, "and you know *exactly* the hell what I am
talking about."

Guards came rushing to the door, looking at Mr. Gokhale
for instructions. He held up his hand and they waited at the
door. "Mr. Seervai," he said sternly, "I am willing to discuss this
calmly — but if you do not lower your voice I will have to have
you ejected. Please sit down."

Dad sat on the chair that was indicated. Mr. Gokhale dis-
missed the guards with a wave of his hand. "Mrs.Seervai," he
said, indicating a chair, "please?"

"What about the door?" Mom said, not sure what to do.
"Shut it."

Mom shut the door and found herself a chair next to Dad's.
Mr. Gokhale continued. "Now, what can I do for you?"

Dad spoke with less fury, but no less urgency. "I want to
know what the bloody hell you mean behaving like a bloody
swine with my wife."

"I do not know what you mean. I have always treated your
enchanting wife with the utmost courtesy and civility."

Mom felt nervous. Mr. Gokhale appeared so sure of himself. Perhaps she'd misunderstood his intentions — but then she
remembered. "There's the door to the bedroom, Adi — with
the bed," she said. "He showed me the bed."

"It is a room to which I retire when I am tired," Mr.Gokhale said. "I was just showing Mrs. Seervai around. Nothing unusual in that."

Mom appeared so nervous, Mr. Gokhale so selfassured, that Dad began to doubt Mom. The Chairman didn't look like a man with anything to hide.

"I think there has been a misunderstanding," Mr.Gokhale said. "Perhaps that is all, is it not, Mrs.Seervai?"

"There was no misunderstanding," Mom said, panicking. "He tried to kiss me. He said his wife didn't mind. He said he could help you."

Dad's moment of doubt vanished. He couldn't believe the effrontery of the man, to be so clearly wrong and so clearly conscienceless. The wild look came back into his eyes. "Now, now, Mr. Seervai," Mr. Gokhale said. "We are men of the world, is it not? Our Nehru and Lady Mountbatten had an affair" (pointing to a portrait of Nehru on the wall garlanded by marigolds). "Are you thinking Lord Mountbatten did not know? He was looking at the big picture. This is happening all the time — and, after all, what does it signify? two bodies rubbing? I can get you big commissions, government contracts, the Brindavan Buildings."

Dad's mind went blank again. There were those phrases again: "men of the world," "the big picture," "happening all the time." Were they just excuses for shabby behavior? or was that the way of a sophisticated civilization? and the Brindavan Buildings would be a lucrative commission. "If I have offended Mrs. Seervai," Mr. Gokhale said quickly, "I apologize. I never meant to offend her, only to flatter her. I am sorry if I did otherwise."

Mom shuffled uncomfortably in her chair. Dad could see she was ready to go, but if he left feeling bested then everything he believed would remain continually at stake. He got up. "*Your* Nehru had the affair," he said. "*My* Nehru won us independence." He picked up a lamp from the desk and threw it on the floor. The shade flew, the bulb smashed, the door opened, the guards came in. Dad took Mom firmly by the arm and led her out. Behind them they heard Mr. Gokhale say, "Nothing to worry — an accident, that is all."

Back in the car, as soon as they were outside the gate, Mom kissed Dad quickly on the cheek. "You were wonderful, just wonderful — especially when you said that about *his* Nehru having the affair and *your* Nehru winning us independence."

Dad grinned, feeling better than he had in a long time. "Someone had to teach the bloody swine a lesson."

"Do you think they really had an affair?"

"Who knows? Who cares? It was cheeky of the swine to compare himself with Nehru at all. He is not fit to tie his shoelaces."

"He *is* a swine, isn't he?" Mom said, her eyes wide at her own daring.

"A bloody swine!"

"Yes, quite right, a bloody swine."

She said it as if it were a title, but it was a wonder she'd said it at all.

4

It was late at night, raining, Dad hadn't returned, we were worried, Mom, Rusi, I, the servants — well, Mom was worried and the rest of us took our cues from her. She'd called friends enquiring about him. When we heard the Ford ramble up the driveway, it was ten-thirty. When Dad stepped out of the lift and shut the door behind him, Mom sprang forward. "Adi, where have you been? Oh, my God, look at you! You're soaking wet!"

Dad seemed hardly to hear her, even embarrassed at the fuss. His hair was wet, plastered to his forehead, over one ear. He ignored me and Rusi altogether. "I'm all right."

"But you're soaked," Mom said. "Where have you been?"

I remembered the occasion because Dad had been soaked mostly on his right side; his left had been almost dry; and I'd commented on it. "He's only soaked on his right side," I'd said, as if that made it all right — and I repeated it along with myself as I watched myself say it again.

Mom touched Dad's right and left sleeves. "Homi's right," she said. "What happened, Adi? Are you all right?"

Dad headed down the corridor toward their bedroom. "I am all right, just tired. I am going to bed."

"Would you like some tea? or coffee? Anything hot?"

"Nono," Dad said, disappearing around the corner of the corridor. "I am all right. Really."

"Homi-Rusi, go to bed," Mom said. "There's nothing more to be worried about."

She didn't have to tell us again. We were already in our nightsuits.

"G'night, Mom."

"G'night, Mom."

"Jairam, you can go to sleep also. We will not be needing anything more tonight."

"Goodnight, bai."

"Goodnight."

"I'll be right with you, Adi. I have to call Gool and Havi and Khorshed to let them know you're all right."

That had seemed a curious night, particularly for Dad's half-wetness, but we'd lost our curiosity by morning. I'd imagined he'd walked alongside a building which had shielded his left side better than his right — but now, as Mom followed Dad to their bedroom, my curiosity swelled.

"Adi, are you really all right? You look pale. You're not well."

He was sitting on the bed, getting it wet. He'd made no effort to remove his wet clothes.

Mom continued feeling how wet he was; water continued

trickling down his face. "Adi, you must change immediately, or you'll catch cold."

Dad remained silent and still, but a sheepish smile beginning to play on his face as he acknowledged her attention.

"Adi, what happened? Why are you only wet on one side? Where have you been?"

"I went for a drive," Dad said finally. "Ended by parking on Marine Drive, just watching the rain on the sea."

"But why? And in this weather?"

"I wanted to think about some things."

"What things? And how did you get so wet?"

"It was raining."

"But you were in the car."

"I kept the window down, only the driver's side."

Mom's eyes widened, her mouth formed a small o. She rubbed Dad's wet side with a towel, removed his wet shirt and sadra. "Adi, my darling, what is the matter? Tell me, what is the matter? Why would you do such a thing?"

"Philly, I...." He looked at Mom, his eyes as wide as hers, his mouth as small. He looked scared as a little boy, and as helpless. I hated to see it, there was shame in his face, as if he'd failed her. He took a deep breath. "I ... don't know what to say, Philly. I ... don't know what we are going to do?"

"What do you mean, Adi? Do about what?"

"About money, for our expenses, for the boys' education, for everything. I am not young anymore. I cannot get jobs anymore like I used to. I do not know what we can do. If Bapaiji would let us sell the land, we could get a good sum. This is a good time to sell. But you know how she is. How you can sell the land of forefathers? You have no shame? If you husband your resources properly there will be no need to sell the land. Still, you have not learned the value of a paisa, but you spend like you are the son of a maharajah."

There was a bitterness in his voice as he mimicked Bapaiji.

I knew what he was talking about. The land he wanted to sell belonged to him, but Bapaiji lived in Hill Bungalow which was on the land. The Seervais owned other houses in which she'd have been just as comfortable, but nothing short of a World War could move Bapaiji if she didn't want to be moved.

Mom continued to towel Dad, help him remove his pants. When he was dry she brought him a fresh sadra and his pajama bottoms. After she'd helped him on with them she held his head to her belly, standing beside where he sat on the bed, caressing his head. "There are many ways, darling," she said. "If money is the only problem, there are many ways we can economize. I can give piano lessons. That would bring in enough for the household expenses. We have money saved. A scholarship is virtually guaranteed for Homi's education, and maybe for Rusi's as well depending on how well he does. Soli might be able to help us getting a job. After all, he is a Cama, and he is my brother, and we've never asked him for a thing before. There are plenty of ways, darling, if it's just money."

Dad remained where he was, not responding to Mom's ministrations. "I hate to tell you about these things, Philly. I hate for you to worry about these things."

"That's just plain ridiculous, Adi." Her voice got much sharper. "That is just plain stupid. You must tell me about these things if they worry you. I'm your wife."

Dad nodded as best he could with his head in Mom's embrace. I could tell from his expression in the crook of her elbow that he felt chastised. "You are right, Philly. I feel better already just telling you. Something will turn up. I think I am still feeling bad about the Brindavan Buildings. I would have got that if not for that swine Gokhale."

"We did the right thing there, Adi," Mom said warningly. "There was nothing else to be done."

"Of course, but it's a shame that swine like him have so much power."

"Yes," Mom said with a smile, "but look at it this way. He wanted me — and you've *got* me."

Dad put his arms around her. "Right you are. The swine can keep his Brindavan Buildings. I got the better of the bargain."

Dad slept well that night, but Mom, nestled within his left arm, couldn't sleep. She'd known for some time that she'd made a mistake yanking him out of the army. He'd never again been as happy, working longer hours for less pay as an older man. He'd never stopped missing the army, the free housing, the privileged accommodation, the constant travel. She'd been wrong; it had been more important for him to be happy than for them to be settled. The added responsibility of a family had not helped. However patient he was with her, he was always impatient with his sons. Had he been a happier man he'd have shouted at them less. In all their travels — England, Scotland, France, Japan, Africa — he'd never wanted his sons with them, and aside from the one trip on which they'd taken Homi to Hong Kong they'd always traveled alone. The vacations she'd shared with her sons had all been without him. She'd read something about Sigmund Freud recently, and wondered if there were not something to be said for the Oedipus Complex. His own mother, Bapaiji, had treated him so aloofly that he thought she made too much fuss herself over their sons. He wanted the mothering from her that he should have got from Bapaiji, and he envied the attention she gave his own sons. He'd never have admitted it, of course, perhaps he didn't even understand it. He was not a contemplative man, not even a reader. If something was wrong, he liked to fix it; if he couldn't fix it, he threw it away; and he was frustrated that he could neither fix nor throw away his sons, but she'd been too young to know better herself.

Soli Mama was able to help Dad get jobs, the wolf was kept far from the door, a forest away, maybe two, but the jobs were arduous, construction sites under the hot Bombay sun all day, and Dad hated being indebted to anyone, particularly Soli Mama, his wife's kid brother — but by that time he was in his fifties he had diabetes, high blood pressure, an ulcer; and worse was to come.

The Towers of Silence

Mom appeared grey and lost walking along the long dark hospital corridor her hands clasped in an attitude of prayer before her, looking as if she didn't know where she was. A nurse touched her arm, spoke kindly. "Mrs. Seervai, you must make an effort to look more cheerful. He depends on you, you know."

Mom seemed surprised to see her there. "I know, but I can't help it."

The nurse spoke firmly. "You must help it. He notices nothing, he appears unconscious all the time, until you come into the room. Then his eyes follow you everywhere. Last night I held his hand because he was reaching out and I didn't think he would know the difference, especially in his state and half asleep in the dark — but he threw my hand away with so much force I couldn't believe it."

Mom's eyes opened wide. "Did he really?"

"Absolutely! Even practically unconscious, he knew it wasn't you, don't you see? You've got to be strong for him, don't you see?"

"Yesyes, I suppose I do." She spoke gazing blankly ahead of her. "I'll try. I'll do my best."

The nurse smiled giving her arm an encouraging squeeze. Dad was asleep. He hadn't been shaved recently. His head looked scraggly on the pillow because his hair was longer and whiter than I'd ever seen it. Mom sat quietly by his bedside in the artificial afternoon darkness created by the curtains. Less than a minute later he raised his hand toward hers. She took his hand, smiling as soon as she realized he was awake, surprised to see his eyes still closed. "Hello, Adi," she said in a level voice.

He opened his eyes.

She leaned forward, smiling. "You know what I was thinking, my darling?" she said. "I will be fifty years old this year. Now we can both grow old together."

His head moved slightly to one side as if to deny what she'd said. She leaned closer still to hear what he had to say. He spoke slowly as if each word were a hurdle. "You will never grow old, my darling. You will always be nineteen, always like when I first saw you."

She nodded, losing her smile, not knowing what to say.

"You have one bad habit," Dad whispered. "You have always made me wait; and I know you will make me wait even longer after I am gone."

Mom shook her head, losing her smile, dropping her gaze, drawing a deep breath to keep from choking.

"I do not mind waiting," Dad continued, "but you must not let yourself go. Otherwise, I will not recognize you, and I will have to settle for one of the other angels fluttering around me there."

Mom understood that he spoke breezily of the things that mattered so little because he'd relinquished all other controls to God, but she shook as if invisible hands had grabbed her. She withdrew her hand to find her handkerchief and dabbed her eyes. Dad appeared bewildered. "What is all this, Philly? I have told you: you must be the merry widow when I am gone."

She wished he'd stop telling her. She hated it when he reminded her of the old days. When he'd hummed the theme once she'd cut him off with a kiss.

"You must marry again if you wish, Philly," Dad continued. "You have been well taken care of. There is nothing to cry about."

That was how he talked, as if the important thing were that she was taken care of. She was the sole beneficiary of life insurance payments, stocks, the Seervai properties in Navsari, various other assets and savings that had accumulated over the years. I was already in Aquihana on a scholarship. Rusi remained an unsettled element, but strongwilled enough to know what he wanted and how to get it. She'd meant to talk to Dad about Bapaiji, but Bapaiji herself had warned against it. "It will make him worse," she'd said. "Some things you have to live with, however painful." Something had happened, of that Mom was sure, but she didn't know what, and she didn't know how she might find out — but Dad spoke then as if the question were written in bold type on her face. "Mamma was here," he said, suddenly smiling broadly.

His smile as much as his prescience took Mom by surprise. "Who?"

"Mamma — Bapaiji."

She'd never heard him call her Mamma before.

"You called her Mamma?"

"She is my Mamma."

"Of course, of course. When was she here?"

"About a month ago."

"A whole month? Why didn't she come back?"

"I told her not to come."

Mom didn't know if she should ask the obvious question.

Dad continued smiling, but no longer looking at Mom. "It was the first time she ever did anything I asked."

"She would have come back if you had asked."

"I know it."

"She would have done anything."

"I know it."

"She would still do anything."

"I know it."

Mom had nothing to say. Dad spoke again finally. "I wanted to make a point."

"Yes?"

"Bapaiji has many accomplishments."

"Yes?"

"My Mamma, Bapaiji, has many accomplishments."

"Yesyes, Adi. What is your point?"

Dad appeared to be enjoying himself. "My point?"

"Yes, what is your point?"

"Only this: all accomplishments demand a sacrifice."

"Of course, but what are you saying, darling? I don't understand you."

"It is simple, Philly. I was the sacrifice. I was the sacrifice for her accomplishments."

Mom shook her head despairingly. "Nono, Adi darling, you must not talk like that. You were no one's sacrifice."

Dad was not to be swayed; he lost his smile; his tone got stern. "Do not say that. I am dying. This is no time for pretty lies. I am so sick of pretty lies. Sometimes I think I am dying of pretty lies. I was the sacrifice. At least, grant me that much."

"If you say so, Adi. Of course, if you say so."

"Not if I say so, Philly. That is the way it was. That is the way it was. Nothing to be lost by admitting it."

Mom just nodded.

Dad's tone mellowed again. "I want you to tell her something."

"Of course, darling. Anything."

"Tell her that her accomplishments are also mine. Because I was the sacrifice, her accomplishments are also mine. Will you tell her that?"

"Of course, Adi, of course. I will tell her."

"Also tell her that I was proud of her accomplishments. I,

too, was proud of her accomplishments. Will you tell her that?"

"Of course, Adi, of course."

"Thank you."

He took her hand then and closed his eyes. When his hand went limp in hers she leaned over him to see if he were asleep, murmuring continuously, "OhmyGodmyGodmyGodmyGod-myGod!" When she understood, her knees buckled and she fell across him in a faint in the bed.

2

My first memory of the Towers of Silence, the dakhma, is of vultures hidden within palm trees over the rocky cliff along-side Gibbs Road leading from Kemp's Corner to the Hanging Gardens and Kamala Nehru Park on Malabar Hill. Julie was taking me and Rusi, who was still small enough to be carried, to the park. The panorama of Marine Drive from the Naaz Restaurant on the hill, arcing alongside the sea was breathtak-ing, people and cars and buildings the size of matchboxes by day, and bejeweled by lights by night giving rise to Marine Drive's best known sobriquet, the Queen's Necklace. The vultures surprised me because I couldn't see their bodies and from where I stood their bare skinny s-shaped necks growing into flat bald heads and hard hooked beaks resembled nothing so much as snakes. Julie explained they were vultures because the Towers of Silence were nearby. Snakes didn't stick out like that from trees.

Zoroastrians feed their dead to eaters of carrion — earth, fire, and water being held too sacred to pollute with putrefying flesh. Within the stone walls of the tower, open to the sky, are three concentric slabs of stone. The outermost, the widest, holds hollows scooped in the stone for men; the middle, nar-rower, is for women; and the innermost, the narrowest, for children. A drainage system allows liquids to seep into a central pit. The bodies are picked to the bone in less than thirty minutes. The birds have grown so tame through the centuries that they wait for the priests to administer the last rites before they descend. More to the point, whereas a claim can still be made for arcana in this verdurous enclave in the heart of industrial Bombay, it can no longer be made for privacy. Sights restricted by religious edict only to Zoroastrians, some only to Zoroastrian males, are now available to anyone who can secure a vantage point in one of the multistoreyed residential buildings that so profusely dot Malabar Hill, and complaints continue to mount against the presence of the Tower when some of the less than considerate vultures litter the balconies of Mr. Kumar, Mr. Kapur, or Mr. Srinivasan, with disembodied fingers, ears, and other such appendages.

RUSI

Maybe If I Had Been a Quadriplegic

With the night came silence, disturbed only by the infrequent whirr of a car passing along Cooperage Road outside, the cawing of a solitary crow, the twang of a weaver's distaff hefted on his shoulder as he made his way home. Normally, I couldn't possibly have heard these sounds over the hum of the airconditioner, but I was tapping into ultrasensory apparatus of which I'd been unaware before. I heard next scrunching footsteps along the gravel driveway of Mayo House. I thought it might be Rusi returning from his dinner with Paresh at Chiquita's, and knew I was right when I heard the lift ascend and its outer door (also the front door to our flat) unlatched. I had just heard the cuckoo call ten times (Mom must have brought the clock to Bombay after Bapaiji died). The door to the bedroom opened. "Arre, Mom, are you feeling okay?"

Mom was still sprawled across my stomach where she'd fallen on the bed just as she'd fallen across Dad when he'd died. Rusi shook her gently by the shoulder. She jumped. "Adi! OhmyGodmyGod! No!"

Rusi shook her more firmly. "Mom, it's not Dad. It's Homi. Are you feeling okay?"

She stared at him, eyes wide as if she were afraid. "It *is* Adi, it *is!*" She pulled her shoulder away from his hand. "Leave me alone. Why are you shaking me like that? What have I done?"

Rusi backed away with an openhanded gesture. "Mom, it's only me, Rusi. I just got back from dinner. You were fallen on the bed. You must have been dreaming."

Mom sat slowly on the chair as if she were trying to absorb what he said. "I was, you know. I was dreaming, I must have been — everything about Adi, until he died."

"Yes, a dream, that is all."

"But no, Rusi, I talked with him. I could swear I actually talked with him." Her voice was soft with thought, with puzzlement. "He said he was all right. He said Homi was going to be all right, but if we kept talking Homi might get worse, so we stopped. I don't know what to think. Maybe Homi became a medium for us. It's so strange."

Maybe I'd been a medium, but maybe also I'd tapped into my own genetic memory, a subdivision of my collective memory. For the first time since I'd succumbed to the memoscan I wanted to be well, back in Aquihana, continuing my experiments, to get to the bottom of the mystery. Rusi spoke stoically. "Go to bed, Mom. You must be tired. I will stay with Homi for a while."

"Yes, maybe you're right. It's all so strange." She touched my forehead softly and walked as if she were in a daze from the room. At the door she turned. "If something strange happens, Rusi, come and get me. You will know what I mean."

"Yesyes, ofcourse-ofcourse — but nothing's going to happen."

"Yes, that's what your Dad said."

"Dad's gone. Dad's not here. I told you no, the doc said he might have a relapse after the trip? But he's going to be okay."

Mom just nodded, shut the door behind her. Rusi leaned over to look at me. I thought my eyes were open but he sat on the chair Mom had vacated as if I were asleep, leaned back, clasped his hands in his lap, and shut his eyes. I was immediately barraged by what I can only describe as emanations of his thoughts — *arre? / again? / what is ... / some things never change / I'm telling you / always ... / hell! / man! / you only / bloody hell! / always you ... / I swear!* — the barrage was more annoying than painful, like a tune that would not be placed, or if placed would not be put out.

"Comecome, Homi. Do not be so stubborn. I can place the tune, I can put it out, whatever you want, but first you must let me help you."

Dad was back. "Help me with what? I don't need any help."

"Yes, you do, just like with Mummy. You are not an island, whatever you think. I can unscramble Rusi's thoughts for you like I unscrambled Mummy's. You can order your own thoughts, we can order ours for you, but you need help ordering those of others. It's a little bit like unscrambling a language — and, like Bapaiji said, we can make you understand even Zulu. So just relax. Let me do the work."

I was feeling much better, enjoying the show, so I shrugged, gave myself into his care, and the emanations continued.

"I swear, Homi, this is too much. What does a bugger have to do in this family to get a little attention? I mean, you're my brother and I love you and all that, but it was no bloody joke being your brother. Maybe if I had been a quadriplegic, or had leprosy or leukemia or something I might have stood a better chance, but maybe not even then. You had not only polio but all that light brown hair like a European when you were born — how could I compete? It wasn't enough I had an IQ of 120 because you were a certifiable genius. Your IQ couldn't even be properly measured, two hundred and something it was. Bapaiji never even taught me Gujarati because you didn't want to learn it — and then she got mad because I couldn't speak it. Let's face it, yaar, you were one maha spoiled bugger, spoiled rotten, never even bloody spanked because of the polio and everything, always the favorite. I was always left out from things

because I was too young. They took you to Hong Kong, but
they left me in Navsari with Bapaiji — but even when I grew
older I was always too young. You got all the new clothes, new
books, everything new, and I got them later, never mind they
were old, never mind our tastes were different. Everyone said
of course you were going to America and made a big fuss at the
aerodrome and everything, but I had to do all my own correspondence, and even Mom didn't come to the aerodrome when
I left, just my own friends. Of course, Dad was dead by then
and she was going a little cracked herself, but still she could
have come.

"And now I'm making a life for myself with Jan, finally
someone who gives a damn about me first — I mean, hell, we're
having a baby — and what happens? Homi has an accident with
his machine, Homi has to be brought back to Bombay, Homi
is back where he belongs, centerstage, and who cares about Rusi
or his wife or his baby?"

Yesyesyesyesyes, easy for Rusi to complain — but polio was
no bloody joke either, no bloody picnic. I was four years old,
two weeks after my first tonsillectomy, my throat was still sore
when I woke that morning, I had a headache, I got up to go
to the bathroom, fell with the first step. My right leg hurt too
much to stand, as if someone were bending it the wrong way
at the knee. I screamed for Mom, vomiting on myself through
the screams, screaming through the vomit.

I got used to the calipers and the cane; I got used to resting
month after month through the school year without being
detained a single term because I was still able to pass the examinations; I even got used to the painful bending exercises
with which Mom and Mary helped me; I understood that I was
lucky to have been less severely affected than possible (some
polio victims had to live in iron lungs); I understood that
poliomyelitis was derived from the Greek words "polios"
meaning "grey" and "Myelos" meaning "marrow" and the Latin

suffix "itis" meaning "inflammation of" (inflammation of the grey marrow of the brain and spinal cord) as if understanding that I understood why I'd been struck rather than a million other kids — but I didn't understand that I'd been rendered fundamentally different until three years later.

We were playing French cricket rather than cricket in the Back Gardens as a concession to me because in Frenchie the batsman doesn't have to run. At such times polio seemed a boon because I got to bat for both teams without fielding for either. Someone had left a bicycle with a tiffin in the back standing by the giant banyan, and a resoundingly hit but unfortunately placed ball spilled an unknown luncher's repast (rice, dal, sliced onions, curds) at my feet, and all the erstwhile players fled, bounding over the old and easily negotiated enclosing wall.

I hobbled panicstricken toward the gate, which appeared to move as quickly away from me as I moved toward it, when Rusi hissed me toward the wall and helped me hand and foot over it. No one was caught; someone lost a tennis ball; someone else lost a lunch; but while the misadventure was recalled with glee by the others for days my right leg appeared to get ever skinnier. I laughed as if I'd been an equal partner in the mischief, but I wished I could have flown with their ease, their fat muscular sausagy legs, as light and bloated as balloons, as they heedlessly scattered, scampered, scrambled over the wall.

"Let's face it, yaar, Homi, you were a maha spoiled bugger and a maha sore loser on top of it. Everyone treated you like a prince, but you only took it for granted. I swear it, yaar, you took too much for granted.

"I mean, we played chess every day of the summer hols — because you only wanted, not me — and one game out of maybe sixty I beat you and you went thupthup, and slapped me twice, and never wanted to play again — talk about a sore loser. Who would play with you then? But you yourself lost interest then, even in your kitefighting — which was a pity because you were the best bloody kitefighter on Cooperage Road. You just stood by the balcony all day and one by one, sometimes even two by three, cut off every bloody kite that came near. You had a too-good wrist action for anybody."

I had forgotten my kitefighting days, how proud I'd been of my hands, callused by manja, the glass-encrusted twine, used to bear kites aloft; how I'd enjoyed crossing the manja of a kite already in the wind with mine and sawing it until it snapped and the erstwhile sovereign kite, its authority usurped, drifted on its torn plumage to a rooftop, or fell like a tarred arrow spinning to the ground. My too-good technique consisted primarily of keeping my kite on a short twine, below the stratospheric arena, until I'd tested the wind and established my control. However unpredictable the wind, the best kitefighters learn to use it to their advantage. During the finest moments the two kites tangled, spiraling furiously around each other, circling like cobras joined at the neck.

I remembered precisely when I'd lost my interest in kitefighting. I'd been ten, rooting wildly for the Loyola House team against the Xavier and Britto Houses in the 1500 meters relay at the Annual Campion School Sports Meet, when my cane had slipped and I'd fallen between the wooden tiers, ten feet to the ground. I'd fallen on my side and lain, unmoving, suddenly aware that there were two spectacles being enacted, suddenly watching (at a second remove) the spectacle of which I'd just been a part. I might have broken my bones, or, had I fallen from the highest tier, been killed, and no one would have noticed or cared till the end of the race. I was unhurt aside from a few bruises. I was shocked less by my fall than by the ferocity of my friends urging on their respective champions, a ferocity I'd shared just moments earlier. Their passion was like a drug. I didn't care who won the race after all; the victory was too small a compensation for the narrow selfabsorption it demanded; there were finer uses for such concentration and angst; but recalling the thrill of the kitefights I wanted once more to leave my bed, head back to Aquihana, and pursue the thrill in a different arena, with the memoscan again. I'd disengaged myself too long from the challenges ahead, but I was still too weak to do more than absorb what Rusi was showing me.

"Okay, Homi, so I got your drift about the sports meet, but who could understand the words? angst? selfabsorption? second remove? Mom said you were a genius so we let it go; Mom said you had polio so we let everything else go; maybe if we had had it out more you would have learned something more about people — but the worst thing, what I felt most sorry for, was not the genius or the polio but how Mary used to really give it to you. If you did something wrong, dhaar, she'd give you one, and if you tried to explain, dhaar, she'd give you another. She just kept going dhaardhaar until you shut up or somehow got away — and there, for whatever reason, Mom always took Mary's word over yours."

Mary was too clever to let Mom catch her. She scarcely needed an occasion to smack me, rap me, thump me, ostensibly to discipline me, but the occasions seemed prompted more by her whims than my fractiousness, and it was difficult for Mom to accept the word of a highstrung imaginative boy against that of a responsible indispensable ayahcumhousekeeper, especially since one night when she and Dad were attending a concert, Mary had persuaded Jeckie, our bearer, with whom we later learned she'd been conducting a liaison, to hide in the godown in the dark and sing Goanese songs in a spooky voice to scare me into finishing a dinner of prawn curry with rice (I hated prawns). Mom smiled when I told her there was a bogeyman in the godown, but she did stop serving me prawn curry on the assumption that it affected my imagination. I uncovered the deception a while later when I heard Jeckie sing to himself as he dusted the sittingroom; he had a naturally spooky voice, tuneless and sibilant; but I couldn't prove a thing.

Later, after Dad had given Jeckie the sack (something to do
with Mary), I found a way to get back at her. I told her Jeckie
wanted to meet her at the gate downstairs, and to wait for him
if she didn't see him right away because he was going to buy
cigarettes. She didn't believe me (it was April Fool's Day; we'd
been playing pranks all morning), but the possibility was too
enticing for her to resist. She was gone an hour before Mom
realized she was missing. When I told her what I'd done she
smiled, but said it was a naughty joke even for April Fool's and
Mary had waited long enough, so I called to her from the
window, "Mary! April *Fool!*" so that everyone would hear. Mary
stormed back, her single long black plait, knotted thickly at the
tip, wagging furiously with her gait, thumping her back like a
club; her black triangular face as cold as that of a praying mantis.
She ignored me until Mom and Dad had left for the evening;
then, twisting my arm behind me, calling me a liar, threw me
on my stomach, and beat me across the back and shoulders with
my own cane until Julie stopped her. I didn't report the in-
stances to Mom anymore (Mary had ingratiated herself too well
for her to believe my stories; Mom would tell Dad who'd say
sparing the rod spoiled the child and I was already too spoiled
for my own good), but I never tired of devising schemes to
embarrass Mary — until the occasion of my ninth birthday.

It was my turn to retaliate in our continual feud. The latch
on the bathroom door was broken and Mary had warned me
not to come in while she was taking a bath. I gathered my guests
by the door and pushed it wide open with my cane. Mary sat,
naked, on the bathstool, a brass tumbler in her hand with which
she poured water over herself from the brass bucket. She
screamed at the congregation tittering before her (gauzy party
dresses, starched shirts and shorts), threw the tumbler at me
narrowly missing my knee, and slammed the door shut again
— but not before I'd noted the shame in her eyes (unfocused
as if by rendering her audience invisible she became invisible

herself), and the blackness of her torso (of course, she had black arms and legs, but I'd imagined her torso as pale as my own, as pale as the palms of her own hands, the soles of her feet). I coupled her shame with her blackness and associated them with Disney's Goofy who had the only other black torso with which I was familiar. The world divided into people with pale and goofy torsos, and I felt sorry for her as if her blackness, her goofiness, were a secret I'd unfairly exposed. When she paid me back later for her embarrassment I felt I deserved her blows, and responded less rationally than before, striking instead at Rusi because he'd beaten me at chess, at Julie because I knew she wouldn't hit me back, and at my cousin Zarine when she visited from Hong Kong because she was a girl, enhancing Rusi's estimation of me as one maha spoiled bugger. It was a stupid stupid cycle: Mary struck me, I struck someone else, she struck me again for striking someone else, I struck someone else again for being struck by Mary for having struck someone else, ad nauseam.

Yes, I was a maha spoiled bugger, but I was surprised that it still affected Rusi. I'd always envied him: being the favorite I fettered myself with standards to uphold of which he was always free; his ayah was Julie, not Mary — kindly, grey, soft, round, wrinkled Julie who unrolled her bedding alongside his bed every night so that she might cushion him with her body if he fell out of bed in his sleep. (He was four years old before he realized that Julie wasn't his mother. He went into a sulk for weeks upset with both Julie and Mom. Julie's face wizened as if she'd lost a son.) Best of all his friends constantly dropped by, often bearing gifts, a battered guitar, a barely audible radio, a damaged cassette player, old records, psychedelic shirts. I'd often wished for his Tomsawyerness. He was only six at the earliest such occurrence I can recall. Mom had planned one of her musical evenings; she'd even typed copies of the program for everyone. I introduced the evening, playing under duress,

"The Anniversary Waltz" on the harmonica, one of the things
I had to do to set a good example. A punch was served, Havovie
Sanjana sang Schubert's "Die Forelle" to a piano accompaniment, Khorshed Bhagat played *The Goldberg Variations*, an inter-
val followed with cheese wafers, patrel, bhajias, sandwiches, the
Paymasters played *The Kreutzer Sonata*, Gool Paymaster played
Liszt's *Hungarian Rhapsody, No. 2*, and Mom wound up the
proceedings with Chopin's *Ballade in G Minor*. "Arre, Rusi," Adi
Joshi said when Mom had ducked into the kitchen to see about
the coffee, "and what about you? What are you going to do for
us today?" "Yesyes," said Nergesh, his wife, "it's your turn now,
Rusi. What have you prepared for us today?"

Rusi had recited nursery rhymes in the past, turned som-
ersaults. Perhaps everyone's favorite of his antics had been when
he'd sung "How Much Is That Doggie in the Window," sup-
plying the barks, the parrot squawks, even humming for the
"bowl of little fi-shies." He'd drawn more applause than
Beethoven that evening. "Yesyes, Rusi," Aloo Chibber said.
"What are you going to do for us this evening?"

Rusi surprised everyone by jumping from his chair, falling
to his knees on the blue and red rug Mom unrolled for special
occasions, holding up his hands, and chanting loudly, "Hare,
Ram-Ram-Ram, Ho Ram-Ram-Ram, Ho-hai-ho-hai Ram-
Ram-Ram-Ram, Ho Ram, Hai Ram, Hare Ram-Ram-Ram."
His eyes were shut and he swayed from the waist. Everyone
stared in silence not knowing what to make of it. Dad said, "Get
up, Rusi. What are you doing? You mustn't be so foolish," but
Mom, coming in from the kitchen, understood what was going
on. "Arre, the Mehtas hired professional mourners yesterday,"
she said. "Someone died in the family. I was explaining it to him
just this morning." The guests encouraged him to continue his
caterwauling over Dad's remonstrance. Rusi was canny enough
to wait until Dad left the room before he went up to Adi Joshi
and said, "Mom said the mourners got money for their mourn-

ing." He collected a rupee and five annas in one and two and four anna bits. I sat rigidly thinking he'd cheapened himself, wishing I could have done the same myself.

Stupid Bloody Bawaji Bastard

I didn't know how long it had been since Rusi and I had left Aquihana for Bombay, but Rusi must have been tireder than he'd thought because he'd slumped in his chair by my bed, his mouth a little open, his hands trailing the floor. I hadn't known him with his untrimmed beard which gave his face a wild grimy cast, but his thick curly black hair, the hollows under his eyes, the tiny upturned bump of his nose, and the full sensuous lips unhidden even by the beard, were comfortingly familiar. I wanted to touch him, to say I was sorry for the trouble I'd caused him, but there was no time for recriminations. The dark turned to light around him, my room into Santa Cruz Airport, his beard disappeared, along with his wiry locks, and I appeared beside the shaven and shorn Rusi waiting with the Hartleys (American friends, Penny's parents, but more about them later), to welcome Mom and Dad back from their visit to England and Scotland in 1959. I hadn't thought of them much while they'd been away, but on the day of their return I imagined mawkish scenes of reunion (Mom running to me with open arms, Dad following with the confidence of Napoleon). Instead, Mom patted my head lightly, patted Rusi's head, said "Hi, Homi-Rusi" in an anglicized voice I didn't recognize, held her chin higher than I remembered, her shoulders more squared, and

talked almost exclusively with the Hartleys. I was so bewildered
by the change in Mom that I hardly even noticed Dad.

She continued to be a stranger during their first weeks
home, appearing younger, moving more briskly, carrying herself
more erectly, dressing more advantageously — which was fine,
even better, because people stared, and that made us, Rusi and
me, feel special — but she also paid less attention to us. "Man,
she thinks she's English," Rusi said. "It's gone to her head."

At first, not wanting her to resent us for making her seem
older than she looked, we stayed out of her way, but gradually
we grew to resent her nonchalance. She didn't appear to appreciate the effort we made to stay out of her way, and one night
Rusi found his own way to let her know — but this was a time
of which I was unaware because we had separate bedrooms.
Mom popped her head into Rusi's bedroom. When she saw he
was still awake she told him to go to sleep and began edging
into the corridor again, but Rusi seized his chance. "Mom, why
do you walk so funny?"

That held her back. "What do you mean? I don't walk
funny."

"Yes, you do. You walk like a duck."

"I do not," she said, appearing embarrassed, a little angry,
in the yellow claw of light encroaching from the corridor.

"You do," he insisted, leaping from the bed to the far end
of the room, switching on the light. "You walk like this," he said,
waddling enthusiastically across the room, saying "Quack, quack,
quack" until he was standing directly in front of her.

Her eyes widened, her breath came more quickly. "You *stop*
that *right this minute*, Rusi," she said, "or I'll tell your dad — and
you know what *he*'ll do then."

We knew what he would do. He'd paddle Rusi with a hanger
saying it hurt him more than it hurt Rusi (to which Rusi had
once responded saying he couldn't be sure of that, assuring
himself only of a heftier paddling); Mom, suddenly remorseful

at Rusi's wailing, would beg him to stop; Dad would stop, angry
with Mom for making him appear a bully, and accuse her of
getting to be as crazy as her mother; which would make her
angry in turn with him — and in the subsequent quarrel Rusi's
misdemeanors would walk into the wings.

"I wouldn't tell Dad," Rusi said. "That would only raise his
blood pressure, and maybe give him a stroke."

Mom's eyes, already wide, widened until they crowded all
other features off her face. I thought she was going to scream,
maybe have a stroke herself. Instead, she slapped Rusi, hard,
without warning. I think her shock was even greater than his
(she'd never struck either of us before). Her eyes narrowed as
if the light were too much, as if she were in pain, and her hand
dropped limply, as if in reproach. "Now *look* what you made
me do."

Rusi didn't say a word, didn't even move to nurse his
scalding cheek. I felt strangely triumphant along with him.

"That was a *hor*rible thing to say," she continued, looking
contritely away.

She'd forgotten from whom he'd learned it. "I'm sorry,
Mom," Rusi said — which was all that was needed.

She hugged him tightly. "That was a very naughty thing you
said, Rusi," she said. "I hope you know that."

He said nothing, and she continued to hug him, until he
finally hugged her back.

"Just don't do it again," she said. "You made me very angry.
I would never have slapped you otherwise."

Rusi said nothing, but continued hugging her — after which
incident her Englishness exited, her wavy black hair, delicate
features, widely arched brows, all appeared slowly to resettle,
become more recognizable; her shoulders softened, her chin
fell, and her upper arms swung more easily. Of course, she'd
have reverted to her old form in time, but I saw for the first
time how Rusi had provided the impetus.

2

A familiar caterwauling enveloped me, whoops and hollers, the
eleven-twenty to eleven-forty morning recess during which
hordes of Campionites exploded from doorways, thundered
down stairways, barreled through hallways, jostled, hustled,
shoved, and goosed their way into the canteen lines. Not for
me, not with my leg, but I saw Rusi forging ahead, doing a breast
stroke through the crowd, arms flashing, legs kicking, waving
a rupee note, yelling like a madman, "ONE PACKET OF
WAFERS! ONE PACKET OF WAFERS! ONE PACKET OF
WAFERS! ONE PACKET OF WAFERS!" amid other cries of
OVER HERE, ONE PACKET OF SAMOSAS! and
HEREHERE, OVERHERE, TWO PACKETS OF DOUGH-
NUTS! and OVERHERE, OVERHERE, THREE COKES,
TWO SAMOSAS! and more cries of ONE PACKET OF WA-
FERS! ONE PACKET OF WAFERS! ONE PACKET OF
WAFERS! ONE PACKET OF WAFERS! when someone yelled
from behind him, "WATCH IT, YOU STUPID BLOODY
BAWAJI! MISTER ONE PACKET OF WAFERS! I'M TELL-
ING YOU, YOU BETTER WATCH IT!"

It was Tonto, but I almost didn't recognize him. He was
larger than Rusi even then, but tinier than I remembered. When
I'd known him, playing lead guitar in Rusi's band, Just Folks,
he'd grown into the biggest kid in his class. His name was
Babu Mathur, but we called him Tonto because he had a dog
named Scout.

Rusi yelled back. "WHAT DID YOU SAY?"

"I SAID, 'WATCH IT!'"

"WATCH WHAT?"

Tonto stopped and turned to confront Rusi. The throng
parted to provide an arena. "DON'T PLAY DUMB, MAN,"
Tonto shouted. "YOU SHOVED ME."

"I did? I didn't mean it, yaar. Who can tell in this crush?"

"Just watch it," he repeated, turning his back on Rusi, but growling loudly "stupid goddam bawaji."

I flushed on my pillow, pink as salmon myself with the slur, and cheered with the choir of goths when Rusi shoved Tonto again from behind.

Tonto turned. "What, man? Are you a stupid bawaji or what?"

Rusi, still smiling innocently: "Arre, what do you mean, yaar? Are you imagining things or what?"

"Did you bloody shove me or did you bloody not?"

"Arre, that depends. Did you bloody call me a stupid bloody bawaji or did you bloody not?"

"If the shoe fits, you stupid bawaji, you wear it," Tonto said, shaking his head pityingly.

"Arre, Tonto," Rusi said, smiling innocently. "Be cool, man. Take it back. This is maha uncool, man, totally uncool."

Tonto, fists on hips: "Who is going to make me?"

Rusi, shrugged. "Not me, yaar, nono, but if I have to...."

The choir of goths was already chanting: "O-VAL! O-VAL! O-VAL! O-VAL!"

The Oval, alongside the Rajabhai Tower, Bombay's Big Ben, was farther from the school than the Back Gardens, but large enough for many simultaneous games of hockey, cricket, football, out of sight of the authorities, ideal for fights among the students.

"You wanna go to the Oval, you stupid bloody bawaji bastard?"

"No time now, yaar," Rusi said. "It's almost time to go back."

Tonto and others set up a chorus: "COWardy CUStard! COWardy CUStard! COWardy CUStard! COWardy CUStard!"

Rusi shook his head pityingly. "No time now, but if you want to fight let's go at one o'clock. Fight to the finish. What do you say?"

One o'clock was lunchtime. They'd have an entire hour then. "One o'clock," Tonto said. "Be there!"

"One o'clock," Rusi said, holding out his hand to shake Tonto's in a gentleman's agreement, but Tonto ignored his hand and Rusi just shook his head pityingly again.

At one o'clock the same choir gathered to escort and cheer its champions on to the Oval, but surprisingly the fight ended quickly, surprisingly because even then Tonto was larger than Rusi, but Rusi had a monomaniacal technique. He rushed Tonto as soon as the signal was given, gripped his hands over the small of Tonto's back, pulled Tonto's hips toward his own, and pushed against his chest with his head, putting pressure on Tonto's spine. Such fights generally ended when one of the combatants either gave up, verbally submitting to a nelson or a bearhug such as Rusi was exerting, or was laid on his back with the other astride his stomach pinning his shoulders with hands and knees. Tonto gave way, falling on his back to shake Rusi's hold, pulling Rusi with him. Rusi lost his grip, but charged again as soon as they were standing again, to secure the same grip. They appeared like a whirlwind with heads, fists, elbows, and knees flashing through the dust. A canvas shoe, Tonto's, dislodged, jitterbugged away from the melee. From within the melee, I saw closeups of Tonto's nose, kneecap, and fist, and the landscape careening, reeling.

The second time Tonto gave way falling on his back to shake Rusi, Rusi was ready for him. Instead of losing his grip he gave it up voluntarily, surprising Tonto while Rusi scrambled up his torso and pinned his shoulders with his knees. "Do you take it back?" he said, sitting heavily on his chest.

Rusi was choking Tonto subtly with his knees, and Tonto, panicked, hoarse, said, "I take it back. I bloody take it back."

When Rusi let him up he demanded, immediately, a second round, which Rusi granted, with the same outcome.

When he demanded a third round Rusi felt sorry for him.

The crowd was jeering him; he'd lost his pugnacity; it was just bravado that kept him going. "Only one more," Rusi said. "Three rounds and that's it."

"Let's cut the bloody talk, man" Tonto said. "Let's bloody get on with it. Let's go, man. Come on, let's go."

The third fight was the shortest. When it was over, Tonto said, "You win wrestling, man, yeah, but I'll beat you boxing. Let's bloody box, man. Come on, man, if you wanna bloody box." His eyes darted from side to side as he feinted at Rusi with his fists.

Rusi didn't want to fight him anymore, particularly since he'd made his point. Ignoring his fists, he said, "I'm not a bloody boxer, man. You'd win boxing. Let's forget it."

It was easy to be gracious. He'd beaten Tonto so clearly that no one believed Tonto could have outboxed him. "Great fight, Roos," someone said as the crowd began to disperse. "Congrats, man."

Amid the congratulations, Rusi went to Tonto and shook his hand. "Great bloody fight, man," he said. "Thanks."

Tonto smiled, nodding his head as if he'd planned his own defeat. "Yeah, sure, okay, my bloody pleasure. You're bloody okay," he said, adding "for a bawaji" under his breath.

"What was that?"

"Nothing, yaar, bloody nothing."

Rusi tweaked Tonto's ear, Tonto grinned, and they walked out of the Oval, itching from the grasscuts they'd received, into the beginning of the best friendship of their schooldays.

I envied once more his wholeness. Polio had made me special, exempted me from fights, but also from friendships. I wondered how I would have fared in a world where everyone had been stricken by polio.

I hadn't known about the fight, but I remembered the day from what happened that evening. The Bombay Symphony was performing an All Beethoven Concert (the Prometheus Over-

ture and *Pastoral Symphony*); and Mom and Dad were determined to infuse us with culture if it killed us. Rusi didn't mind
the music, but hated keeping still, and squirmed continually
from grasscuts and bruises throughout the overture. Dad, sitting
at one end of our foursome (then Mom, then myself, then
Rusi), was unaware of his discomfort, especially since Mom
swayed and bobbed her head puppetlike to the music herself,
but at the end of the overture Mom leaned across my seat and
whispered, "What's the matter, Rusi? Why can't you sit still?"

"I fell down the stairs in school today," he said, "all the way
from the top. I just *ache* all over."

I didn't believe him, but for the wrong reason; it was a ploy
for Mom's attention, annoying because it worked, she reached
across me and touched his arms, legs, ribs, to check whether
they were broken, his head for a temperature.

"It was no big deal," he said hastily, "maybe it was just
halfway down. You don't count the stairs when you're falling,
you know."

He and Mom stared at each other for a moment. I couldn't
believe she still believed him.

"I'm okay, Mom, really. I just kind of *ache*, you know."

Mom didn't have time for a more thorough examination.
The *Pastoral* was beginning. I found it more stimulating visually
than most other works, and as the strings advanced, springing
gently, twirling, I conjured images of a meadow, a shepherd with
a crook, a boy (his son) with a flute, sheep in a cluster, lambs
gamboling, a wolf in the forest beyond the pasture (but he,
unlike Prokofiev's wolf, never came out), and I was surprised
to see that Rusi had conjured similar images for himself floating
in a bubble over his head in the auditorium — but feeling an
itch on his calf he scratched madly and the entire picture dissolved. By the time he was finished scratching he'd lost too
much of the movement to catch up and imagined instead Dad's
pants. Just before we'd left the house Mom had noticed that

they were wrinkled. "You can't go out in those pants, Adi," she'd said. "Why don't you wear your blue ones?"

"They're dirty," Dad had said, laughing to humor her. "Don't worry. No one's going to look at my pants."

"That's what *you* think. *Everyone* will notice." She was serious. "Take them off. It'll only take a minute for Julie to iron them. We've still got time."

"We haven't got time," Dad said. "If Julie's going to iron them, she's going to have to iron them with me in them."

He looked at Rusi and myself, expecting a laugh, but we merely looked at each other. "That's the trouble with this family," Dad said. "No one's got a sense of humor."

Rusi and I laughed, but later.

"How does it hurt you to laugh at his jokes?" Mom had asked us once, "and it would make him feel so good."

"They're so *stu*pid," Rusi had replied. "It would bloody well hurt us to bloody laugh."

"Rusi!"

"Sorry."

You Think This Is Bloody Communist Russia You Can Just Walk into My Room

The *Pastoral Symphony* gave way to *Sgt. Pepper's Lonely Hearts Club Band*, the auditorium to Rusi's bedroom, its walls covered with posters of Joplin, Hendrix, The Doors, The Beatles, Dylan, Gracie Slick, and (just for the hell of it) Frank Sinatra. Rusi sat on the bed strumming chords on his guitar and singing softly along with "Lovely Rita." He wore flared blue jeans that almost hid his feet, a white kurta almost to his knees, his hair was bunched untidily in a ponytail, wisps of hair on his upper lip, on his chin. There was a knock on his door which he ignored. The knock sounded again, but he continued strumming and singing to himself. The door opened and Tonto came in, also wearing a kurta and flared jeans. A flap of his straight black hair fell over the left lens of his spectacles, but he was never so unhip as to push it aside — and wisps of hair adorned his upper lip and chin. "Arre, Roos, what is this? You heard me knocking or no?"

Rusi continued to ignore him.

"Arre, listen, no? This is important, yaar — about the amplifier."

Rusi scowled at him, still strumming. Tonto picked up the latest issue of *The Beatles Book* lying on the desk and began leafing through it.

When the song ended and the cock crowed to introduce "Good Morning, Good Morning," Rusi looked up. "Did I say you could come in? Where did you learn your manners?"

Tonto put down *The Beatles Book*. "Arre, Roos, don't be like this, yaar. This is bloody important."

"Ask me if I bloody care. You think this is bloody Communist Russia you can just walk into my room?"

"Arre, sorry, yaar, Roos, but Bunny bloody says he's going to sell the amp to bloody Chitku if we don't come up with the bloody bread by Friday. What are we bloody going to do?"

Rusi turned back to his guitar, strumming and singing to "Good Morning, Good Morning," "'Nothing to do, it's up to you / I've got nothing to say, but it's okay.'"

"Don't be so bloody cool, yaar, Roos. What are we bloody going to do?" Tonto's voice was getting shrill.

Rusi put the guitar aside. "Don't get so shook, yaar. We'll get the bloody cash is what we'll bloody do."

"Five hundred bucks? From where? I bet you haven't even got a bloody ten chip note on you."

"It's so bloody hot, yaar, Tonto. Get me a coke from the fridge. Get yourself also. It's too bloody hot even to talk."

"Damn the bloody coke! Don't be so bloody cool, yaar, Roos. What the bloody hell are we going to do, no?"

"I'm going to get a coke. You want a coke?"

Tonto shrugged helplessly. "Yeah. Sure. I'll take a bloody coke."

"Go get it then. Get me one also while you're there."

Tonto went to the kitchen to get the cokes. When he got back "A Day in the Life" had just started and Rusi was strumming and singing again. He put Rusi's coke down next to him, sat at the desk with *The Beatles Book* again, and drank his coke. Even after the last heavy percussive chord had sounded and faded away he said nothing. "Attchha, I'll tell you what," Rusi said. "Make sure Bunny keeps the amp till

Friday.   Tell him I'll have the cash for him by then
for sure."

2

Rusi peered around the door into Mom's bedroom. "Mom, you
got a minute?"

Mom was at her dressing table before the three-way mirror,
rows of lipsticks, perfumes, sprays, powders, other cosmetics.
The fluorescent light atop the middle mirror was lit. She wore
a grey satin petticoat, a grey satin blouse, painting her fingernails
red with the tiny brush adjoining the nail-polish cap with a swab
of cotton wool ready by the bottle in case her hand slipped. "Yes,
Rusi, what is it?"

Rusi sat on the bed. "Mom, you know how much Gran gave
Homi on his birthday?"

Mom looked up from her nails. "You know perfectly well
how much he got, Rusi. Why are you asking me?"

"Just answer, no? How much did he get?"

"A hundred and one rupees, like he always gets."

"And how much did I get?"

"Fifty-one."

He appealed to her rationality with an openhanded gesture.
"So, you only tell me, Mom. Is that fair?"

Mom went back to her nails. "It's because you're younger,
Rusi. You know that."

"But I'm only one year younger. Is it fair?"

"But Rusi, *I* always give you both the same. *I* don't play
favorites."

"But Mom, just answer my question, no? Is it fair what
Gran does?"

"Arre bawa, if you must have your answer, then no, of
course it isn't fair — but what can I do? It's your gran's money.
I can't tell her what to do with it. If you feel so strongly about
it, then *you* tell her."

Rusi picked at the nap of the candlewick counterpane. "Mom, I can't talk to Gran. You know how she gets. She might start shouting like a madwoman. Even Bapaiji only gives me fifty-one rupees."

Mom's hand slipped and she used the cotton wool. She didn't like it when anyone called her mother crazy, not even Dad. "I told you, Rusi, it's because you're younger. That's the tradition. It's not anything personal."

"But it's not fair."

"Then ask Bapaiji, no? At least she won't shout at you like a madwoman."

"Bapaiji's too stingy. If it wasn't traditional, she wouldn't give me even fifty-one rupees."

"Oh, very nice. So one grandmother is a madwoman and the other one is stingy. Well, it's no wonder, if that's how you feel about them, that they don't give you any more — but I really don't see what I can do about it."

"I thought you could make it up. That would only be fair." He continued to pick at the nap.

Mom looked up from her nails. "Rusi, I wish you would stop doing that. You've ruined one counterpane already."

Rusi stopped. "It's not bloody fair."

"What did you say?"

"It's not fair."

"That's better." Mom replaced the cap on the bottle of nail polish and waved her hands to dry her nails. She knew he was right, but she didn't know what to do about it. "Get me my purse from the cabinet in the cupboard," she said finally. "I'll give you a hundred rupees. Then I don't want to hear anymore about it."

"Mom, a hundred rupees? You owe me at least a thousand rupees to make it up."

"Arre, and then what am I going to do for money?"

"You can get more from the bank, no?"

"Arre, but I also have a budget to maintain. If I just went to the bank every time I wanted money we'd be stoney broke."

"Then at least five hundred, Mom. I need five hundred for an amp by Friday."

"Rusi, I'm not going to bargain with you. If you keep this up you won't even get the hundred."

"It's not fair."

"If you don't think it's fair then I'm sorry, but that's the way it is. The way I see it I'm giving you a hundred rupees that I don't even owe you. Is that fair to me?"

Rusi took the key from its hiding place under the wrapped bundle of clothes on one of the shelves of the cupboard, unlocked the cabinet above the shelf, took the money, and replaced the key. "Can I have some rum?" he said, referring to the bottles of cooking sherry and rum which Mom kept on the bottom shelf of her cupboard to use in desserts.

"Only a little."

Rusi took a long draft drinking straight from the bottle. "Thanks," he said with a grin, replacing the bottle.

3

There was Rusi, the hundred rupee note in his pocket, poking through books with lurid covers at the Empire Book Stall, *The Temptress*, *The Hellcat*, *The Things Men Do*, until he found what he was looking for, *The Kama-sutra of Vatsyayana*, which he bought along with the latest issue of *Playboy*; there was Rusi cutting pictures out of the *Playboy* and phrases out of the book, "The Long-Suppressed Oriental Manual," "The Art and Technique of Love," "The Ancient Art of Love," "Kama-sutra," "The Hindu Ritual of Love," "Complete and Unexpurgated," "The Arts and Rites of Love"; there was Rusi purchasing blank cassettes and pasting the cutout pictures and phrases onto their cases; there was Rusi, walking from the Gateway of India with its high

Gothic arches, along Apollo Road with the Arabian Sea on one side flush with motorboats and launches, and the palatial facade of the Taj Mahal Hotel on the other, to the Radio Club where Dad had designed and supervised the construction of their swimming pool, and back, soliciting American tourists, Bill and Jeanne Dietsch, Val and Sonny Fach, Paul and Linda Koptak, Robin and Susan Blench, with the tapes saying "Heavy shit, I'm telling you" to the men and "very instructive, very educational" to the women, "very hot, one hundred and twenty-five degrees, and only one hundred and twenty-five rupees each," handing each of them flowers that he wore in a garland around his neck; there was Rusi showing Tonto five hundred rupees, two new colorful kurtas, a new pair of felt pants, and a hat with a brass buckle in front and a blue feather sticking out from the side.

Look at His Hair, Like a Gollywog

Mom wore a smart pleated blue skirt with a white blouse, Dad
a white bush shirt and grey pants, as they walked from the
Ford through Breach Candy (what I now call Americatown
because of the American consulate, club, and kindergarten
school where Rusi and I had been enrolled), past Bombelli's
restaurant and pastry shop, Chimalker's, and Readers Paradise, into a lane and into the foyer of Aquamarina, one of the
new skyscrapers (sixteen storeys), up the automatic lift to a
door bearing the plaque DR. ARMAITI (AMY) BHATIA,
where they rang the doorbell and were admitted into her
sittingroom. It was obviously her home but also, evidently, her
office. The doctor, a thin Parsi woman dressed in a sari, hair
in a bun, smiled, and asked them to please sit down, speaking
with a distinct American accent. "I noticed you have both your
names on the door," Mom said, "Armaiti and Amy. Do you
have a preference?"

"Well," the doctor said, sitting on a tall straight chair across
a coffee table from the couch holding Mom and Dad, "they
called me Amy when I was at the University of Chicago. It's
easier for them, of course, than Armaiti. Then it was picked up
by some of my friends here. But my clients usually call me
Dr. Bhatia, or just Doctor. Your Rusi calls me Doc."

317

"My, my!" Mom said, raising her eyebrows. "It certainly didn't take him long to make himself familiar."

"Nono, not at all," the doctor said. "He was very refreshing, a joy to talk to."

Dad, sunk low in the upholstery of the couch, stared at the embroidered carpet under the coffee table, smiling weakly.

"Well," said Mom, her eyebrows still high, "that's certainly nice to hear, but hardly what we expected."

"Well, then, tell me. What were you expecting?"

The doctor leaned forward. Mom sank back into the upholstery, her surprise turning to consternation. She looked helplessly at Dad. Dad struggled to lean forward in the couch, to put himself on an equal footing with the doctor. "Well, Doc — you do not mind if I call you Doc also?"

"Not at all, Mr. Seervai."

"Well, it's like this. Rusi has been behaving very strangely and we were at our wits ends what to do with him. I was sure that someone like you, with your foreign degree from America, would see what was wrong from the start."

He smiled knowingly at the doctor as if there were nothing more to be said, but she said, "Well, that's why I wanted to talk with you and your wife. I've had two sessions now with Rusi, and I find absolutely nothing wrong with him. He's quite your normal teenager. In fact, I found him quite entertaining. Clients like him make me feel I should be paying them for the session."

Dad's face dropped, as if he'd been betrayed, but he said nothing.

"So, tell me, Mr. Seervai, what do you find so strange about his behavior?"

Dad sank back into the couch, staring at the wall. "What is so strange? Look at his hair, like a gollywog, never combed, always dirty. When I tell him — nicely, not shouting — to cut his hair, he just combs it a little. What am I supposed to do?

He is too big to spank now. And look at his clothes, even a girl would be ashamed to wear his clothes."

"He's young. It's how youngsters express themselves today. Selfexpression is healthy."

Dad shook his head. "I don't know what you mean. I never selfexpressed like that."

Mom bound into the conversation as if she'd had a sudden insight. "That's not true, Adi. You were the same. I've seen pictures of you with the walking stick, in the bowler and tails. You looked quite silly yourself then."

Dad looked sharply at her as if he couldn't understand why she was there. "I did not look silly. I was in U.K. Everybody dressed like that there."

"But that is precisely my point," the doctor said. "It doesn't matter where you are. Styles may change, but clothes always remain a form of selfexpression. You carried a walking stick, Rusi grows his hair. What's the difference?"

"What's the difference? I'll tell you what's the difference. He gives away flowers on street corners like a jaripuranawallah. Don't give me What's the difference. Even his friends are all the same."

Dad meant Tonto, "that damn actor's boy" (Tonto's dad made documentary films).

"But this is the Beatles generation. Flower power is in. Everyone is like that."

"Our other son was not like that. He was interested only in his studies — and look where he is now — in America! But who will take Rusi, looking like that?"

"Adi, Homi was a special case. You have to admit that."

"Of course he was a special case. Why do you think they took him? But who is going to take Rusi?"

"Lots of universities will be happy to take him, Mr.Seervai. They don't care how he looks, only about his scores."

"He's not doing badly in school, Adi. His marks are not all that bad."

"They take everything into account. I'm telling you, they take everything into account."

Mom looked at the doctor; the doctor looked at Dad; Dad looked at the carpet. "Let us go," he said finally. "I have wasted my money."

Mom smiled apologetically, getting up. "Thank you, Doctor, for your time. I hope we haven't been too much trouble."

"Not at all. If I can be of any more help, please give me a ring." She held out her hand. Mom shook it gingerly, but Dad ignored it. He didn't even look at her. When they were outside again Dad said, "We should not have sent him to a woman doctor. They are too emotional, especially where boys are concerned."

2

"Arre, Homi, what is this? What is going on? Mom was right. Something maha strange is going on that I am talking to you like this, but it is a good thing. This all needs to come out in the open. Actually, I tell you, Homi, it was lucky Dad sent me to the Doc. After he died she only told me, nobody else, how to apply for admission to the U.S. universities, what to do about SATs, ACTs, all that. She was a solid help, even gave me recommendations. I applied only to universities in Chicago because she knew people in Chicago. I got entrances to the University of Chicago and Northwestern University as well, but I chose the Illinois Institute of Technology because they gave me the most aid.

"Still, before that, before Dad died, things got pretty bad for a while. I mean, I don't know exactly what happened when he saw the Doc, but after he came back he just stopped talking to me. Mom said I should apologize but I said For what. She said For your dad's health, but I said What about *my* health? She even gave the Doc a ring again to set up another appointment for me, but the Doc said she couldn't help me because I didn't have the problem — Dad had the problem. Mom told me all that only to butter me up so I would speak to Dad, but I told her that wasn't going to solve the problem, so then she just let it go.

"In the meantime I concentrated on developing the group, Just Folks. We got pretty good, actually, and we got quite well known in Bombay before I left. The trouble was, when Dad died, the day of the funeral, I was committed to a concert. Mom went crazy, I tell you, telling me to cancel the concert and how could I sing when Dad had just died and all — but I had booked the hall myself, the sponsors were counting on us, the advertisements had been paid for, the tickets were all sold out, the group was counting on me, how could I let them all down? I told her I would be at the funeral, but I would have to leave early — and that's what I did. It was touch and go, yaar, touch and go. I changed clothes in the taxi going to the auditorium. The driver got a maha shock, I tell you — I was wearing my dagla from the funeral when I got in the taxi and my Davy Crockett shirt when I got out, from Clark Kent to Superman or something.

"Anyway, the next day, in the papers they wrote, 'Dad Dies, But Son Carries On,' 'The Show Goes On,' 'The Biggest Trouper of them All,' 'Rusi Seervai Sings Through His Tears.' I don't know where they got all that from, like it was a maha big thing, like I was a bloody hero or something — but at least it made Mom feel better. The thing is, after Dad died, something changed, you know. I started thinking about my future and all, I started thinking about coming to America."

Chicago

A row of palm trees rushed by before sinking and shrinking from view, blending into a green and brown patchwork which continued to sink and shrink until its outline grew visible, the dogleg that was Bombay, licked by a flat blue surround, disappearing with distance into the straight line of the Malabar Coast, India to the right, flat as a map, still sinking and shrinking until the flat blue drum of the sea merged with the blue and white fleece of the sky. In time the patchwork grew visible again, more gridlike than before, buildings reaching like beanstalks into the sky, earth rising and expanding to meet the wheels of Rusi's plane. I saw him debark carrying a shoulderbag and guitar in its case, met by a brisk bright bony woman, friend of Dr. Bhatia, who introduced herself as Chris Hahn, pumped his hand vigorously, grabbed his shoulderbag from his hand, cut a swath through the crowd to the baggage terminals, and drove him from O'Hare to the campus.

He marveled at the plush interior of her Datsun, the automatic shift, the airconditioning, the perfect reception on the radio, "Bridge Over Troubled Waters," "Instant Karma," "Mama Told Me (Not to Come)," "Band of Gold," "Hey There Lonely Girl." He wanted to make a good impression, but had already committed his first faux pas on the flight asking the air hostess for a cup of tea. Instead of a kettle brewing tea under a cozy and a strainer she'd brought him a pot of hot water and a tea bag. Not wanting to trouble her again for a strainer he'd ripped the bag open, brewed the leaves in the pot, decanted the tea into his cup, managing all maneuvers with a flourish, a cosmopolitan young man aboard a transatlantic flight, but wished he'd kept a lower profile when he saw a young lady across the aisle from him soak her teabag in the pot before pouring it.

He remained silent much of the way to the campus awed by the sights. When they came to Lake Shore Drive he wanted to say it was like Bombay's Marine Drive, but didn't. Lake Shore Drive had six lanes, the inner drive had four more; Marine Drive had altogether only four lanes. Chris Hahn drove at over seventy miles an hour; Dad had never driven over forty on Marine Drive. Bombay might have had more people, but they seemed to be going in circles; Chicago had more cars and all seemed to be going straight to the moon. Bombaymen spoke with a lilt, Chicagoans with command. God might have been everywhere in Bombay, but Chicago might have been God Himself. Besides, there was nothing in Bombay to compare in size to the black steel and glass John Hancock Tower, big black Xs buttressing its facades, antennae like horns on its head in the sky, resembling, eerily, what might have passed, in the twilight, for a postpostpostcontemporary, Twenty-first Century, Castle Dracula.

The dormitories hadn't opened yet for the semester and Chris drove to a YMCA on the south side of the loop, put down six dollars for a room, wished Rusi luck, apologized for her abruptness, but she had a drive of a couple of hours home to Champagne yet for the night. He thanked her, tired from traveling for almost a day but too excited to sleep. He was in America!

He was in America, but not the America he'd envisioned, neat rows of houses, California girls, Mickey Mouse, Batman, Woodstock. Hearing a rumble outside the window he raised the shade to see a train negotiating a bend in a track on an elevated structure passing directly by him, a giant worm in the night light. The tall flat massive ratty facade of a dark brick building faced him across the tracks, framing garish yellow rectangles of light; a fire escape crawled like a snake up its side.

The sight depressed him; the floor of his room creaked; the couple in the next room were quarreling; he couldn't lock his door, and latched it instead securing the chain because he felt stupid asking how to lock the door. He recalled Dick Whittington arriving in London expecting streets paved with gold, but consoled himself: things had looked better on campus.

Too excited to sleep he left the hotel to get something to eat. The concrete pavements were as wide as Bombay roads, but cracked and dotted with shrubs and shards of hard green glass. Neon signs flashed advertising parking, x-rated movies, burlesque shows, hotels, restaurants. He entered Dawg Lovers, drawn to its logo (Pluto with a sausage torso), wanting a genuine American hot dog, and sat at a corner table by a greasy window trying to get the attention of the cashier — but the cashier, a young muscular black (negro, as Rusi knew to call him), only scowled at him. He was aware in the harsh light of the naked yellow bulbs that all the customers were blacks, but they seemed bold, unlike the Uncle Toms he'd anticipated from what little he knew of them. He wondered what he would do if they refused to serve him until he saw someone place an order at the counter and followed his example. He hardly tasted his dog, feeling he'd entered America through a warp, that he was continually to be challenged as his expectations were continually shattered.

Morning found him optimistic again. Taking bags and guitar to the lobby he asked the concierge to get him a cab. Anxious to be away from the Y, on campus again, he waited with his bags in front of the building. It was no less depressing outside than the night before, but the sun was shining. He felt hot and conspicuous in his corduroy jacket, but it was easier than carrying it along with everything else. He watched so intently for his cab that he didn't notice a figure shuffle up to him until the figure spoke. "Wouldja like t'hear some po-try?"

The voice was guttural, almost unintelligible. The man hadn't shaved, smelled of garbage. His forehead and cheeks were red, cracked with dirt. He carried an old shoe in one hand and limped on his unshod foot — but that was what Rusi expected of poets. Besides, he felt like a guest, and if his host, however unsavory his appearance, chose to be hospitable, he didn't want to appear ungracious, and he had time until his cab arrived. "Sure," he said.

The wino (it didn't take Rusi long to recognize him for what he was) pulled out a sheaf of papers from his coat and started to read. Rusi couldn't understand a word, his cab arrived, the meter started ticking, but he couldn't cut off the wino politely. Finally, he picked up his bags, said "Thanks, but I have to go," and got into the cab.

The wino spoke through the window. "Whatdja think of the po-try?"

Rusi looked ahead as if he'd forgotten the recitation already. "It was okay."

The wino gripped the window with his hands to keep Rusi from raising it. "I think it's better than anything Shakespeare ever wrote."

Rusi still looked ahead. "Everyone has got his own opinion."

The wino thrust his head forward. "I want a quarter for my reading."

Rusi looked at the wino again. "Arre, yaar, I asked you to read? Why should I give you a quarter?" He told the cab driver where to go, but the wino put his elbow over the window. "You give me a fuckin' quarter or I'm gonna break this fuckin' window."

Rusi looked helplessly at the cabbie who jumped out immediately with a baseball bat. "You break that fuckin' window and I'll break yo' fuckin' haid."

It was not the kind of help Rusi wanted. "Here," he said, giving the wino the quarter he'd so desperately earned. "I don't want any trouble."

As they drove away the cabbie said, "You shouldna done that. He wouldna done nothin'. He was jus' drunk."

"It's okay," Rusi said. "I don't want any trouble. This is my first day in America."

2

The quadrangle of nine fraternities was constructed in a U, the three largest houses in the base, arms toward the road, constant motion of students threading the glass and brick shoeboxes like ticker-tape. Light and sound percolated from one little kingdom to the next, but the similarities made it difficult to tell where one ended and another began. Couples in clinches decorated dens, basements, livingrooms, hallways, stairways, bathrooms, bathed in red lights, blue lights, green lights, strobe lights, pounded by Creedence, Zeppelin, Chicago, Santana, Joplin at a hundred decibels, seeming so nonchalant that Rusi was afraid to watch, feeling out of place, imagining they knew something he didn't. He'd had some experience as Just Folks had gained popularity, but either the girls had proven too unsophisticated at the crucial moment, or he'd proven too prudent himself — but the rules were different in America.

Males on campus outnumbered females twenty to one, but during Rush Week the fraternities scouted incoming freshmen for pledges, and girls (sisters, cousins, friends, girlfriends and their friends) came to the parties from all over Chicago. He'd attended the parties with Faisal Ahmed from Karachi and Rajiv Dua from Delhi, freshmen he'd met on his first day, but their presence provided too comfortable a refuge to mingle and he'd chosen finally to go alone. Sitting in a corner of the Tep (Tau Epsilon Phi) House he watched the girls in jeans, shorts, miniskirts, culottes, haltertops, afraid his difference would make a difference to them, imagining they would not notice the difference if only he moved fast enough.

Deliberating for more than an hour, accumulating courage from draft after draft of beer, he found one girl too muscular, another too cheerful, another too smug, before rising suddenly, walking to the next girl he fancied, and forcing himself to speak before he could find her in any way unworthy. "Hi. How're you doing? Howzit going? I'm Rusi Seervai, from Bombay — India. What's your name? You want a drink?"

The girl jerked her head back so suddenly her ponytail snapped in front of her. "Oh, hi. No."

"No, what? You don't want a drink?"

"No. No, thanks."

"What's your name?"

"Diane."

"Diane what?"

"Diane La Fontaine."

"La Fontaine? Like the chap who wrote the fables, like Aesop? I know him. Hi, my name is Rusi Seervai."

"Hi."

"When is your birthday?"

Her eyes, which had been widening, narrowed as she regrouped. "October 2nd."

"What year?"

"1952."

He circled her waist with his arm. "Oh, yeah, a Virgo — or is it a Libra?"

She moved firmly away from him and spoke clearly. "I can stand very well by myself, thank you."

He mumbled something, left the Tep House, ducked into

an adjacent fraternity, the Tee-Eck (Theta Xi) House, took a deep breath, another draft of beer, and scouted the room at leisure, focusing at length on a girl to the side of the room wearing tight blue jeans, a black top, and a black satin neckband which made her appear nightclubby. He approached her, cautioning himself to slow down, adjust his pace to hers, allow the conversation to breathe. "Would you like to dance?"

She appraised him coolly, hair in a pageboy lightly brushing her shoulders as she swayed to the music. "No."

She was smiling, which meant she hadn't turned him down completely. "Why not?"

"The music isn't right."

Mary Magdalene was singing "Everything's Alright" from *Jesus Christ Superstar*. "What's wrong with the music?"

"It's in 5/4 time. You can't dance to 5/4 time — at least, not a slow dance — at least, not unless you're very good."

"Why not? They're doing it."

She smiled again. "If you can call that dancing."

If she hadn't smiled he might have found her too superior. "You have studied music, yes?"

"No."

"But you know something about it, yes?"

She looked down at her hands, still smiling. "I'm a singer."

Rusi chortled. "What? Really? No kidding? Me too!" When she looked at him he continued. "No, really! I am a singer. I had a band, Just Folks it was called, in Bombay. I'm from Bombay, India. No kidding. Really? You are a singer?"

Her eyes grew softer as if she were amused. "Just Folks? I love the name."

"Pun intended!"

She laughed. "Of course!"

"So, tell me," he said. "What's your name?"

"Maureen."

"Mau-reen." He spoke her name thoughtfully, he might

have been tasting a wine. "It is a good name, Mau-reen. You are the first Mau-reen I have met. Hullo, Mau-reen."

She said nothing but continued to smile.

"I say, Maureen. I have got an idea. Why don't we go to my room? I have a guitar. I could sing for you."

She looked at him cautiously.

"Only sing, nothing else. You can also sing. What do you say?"

She nodded. "Okay."

Walking back to the dormitory he couldn't stop talking, about his band, about Tonto, about how "maha" the Beatles were, "too bad, yaar, that they broke up."

She stopped him once. "What is Yaar?"

"Just a way of talking, like Man. Means nothing."

She didn't understand everything he said, but listened without interruption, watching him as if for a fitting, smiling all the while.

He locked the door when they got to his room praying his roommate, Tim Joseph from Alaska, wouldn't be back for a while. Beds lined the longer walls of the short room, desks at their heads, dressers at their feet, closets flanking the dressers, the door between the closets, windows across the room from the door. He lit Tim's reading lamp (the dimmest light in the room) turning it toward the wall, removed his guitar from its case, sat on the chair by his desk, invited her to relax on his bed, began with the last song he'd written. "I always like the last song best," he said — but as he finished he realized she hadn't been listening. She'd slipped off her shoes and lay in bed propped on an elbow playing with the zipper of her jeans, continuing to zip herself up and down when he was finished. "Is something wrong?" he said, afraid to wake from what seemed the best dream of his life.

She watched him closely. "My zipper's stuck."

He didn't understand how it could be stuck if she kept zipping it up and down. "You want me to fix it?"

"Do you think you could?"

"I could try."

He knelt in front of her, zipping her jeans up and down. When he was sure there was nothing wrong with her zipper he unclasped the hook at her waist. "You fixed it all right," she said with a giggle, wriggling out of her jeans as he pulled them down.

3

He had to sneak her out later because it was long past visitation time, but made plans to see her again the following day as they walked to her car, a green Falcon. "We also have a Ford," he said, "a 1948, a Humpty Dumpty I call it. This is your own? not your dad's? I can't believe it."

She smiled. "This one's an oldie. Dad was going to trade it in, but I convinced him to let me have it. It's no big deal — not like you. You have *servants*."

"Everyone there has servants."

"Everyone here has a car."

"Still, I can't believe it."

"Can I give you a ride back to the dorm?"

"Sure, sure."

He didn't want to stop kissing her goodnight. When she left he didn't want to go to bed, and roamed the campus, marveling at the wide streets, the flashy cars — and Mau-reen, most of all Mau-reen. "This is America," he repeated over and over as if he couldn't believe it, unable to stop grinning. "This is America. I am in America. I am in America. Rustom Adeshir Seervai is in America."

4

He was ten minutes early for his rendezvous with Maureen in the dormitory lounge, but after forty-five minutes he wished he'd taken her phone number. She might have had an accident;

she might have misunderstood their arrangement; she might have thought he'd meant the following day, Sunday, not Saturday, because Friday had slid so imperceptibly into Saturday when he'd asked her — but she was leaving for Valparaiso University in Indiana on Sunday. She couldn't have misunderstood. She had a brother at the Tee-Eck House where he'd met her, but he hesitated to approach him about his sister because some of the fratboys resented his presence — but after he'd made a round of all the fraternities in vain he went back to the Tee-Eck House and asked a group congregated in the doorway for John.

The group got suddenly quiet looking at him. "John who?" one of them asked loudly as if he were addressing a child.

"John, Maureen's brother. Maureen was here yesterday. She said her brother is a member here."

"John Blunden, he means. He's in the basement. I'll get him."

Rusi raised his hand. "It's okay. Not to worry. I can go."

The fratboy glared. "I *said*, I'll get him."

"Attchha — I mean, okay."

Rusi waited by the narrow border of gravel that circled the house, ignored by the others, until he thought he recognized someone coming out of the house, an ROTC haircut, a T-shirt at least one size too small. "Hi, Nick. How're you doing? Howzit going?" he said, holding out his hand.

The newcomer ignored his hand. "I'm not Nick. I'm John Blunden. What do you want?"

Rusi swore under his breath. They all looked alike. It was not the first time he'd made such a mistake. "Sorry."

"What do you want?"

"Is Maureen here?"

"Who wants to know?"

"I had a date with her for tonight. She never came. I thought there might have been an accident."

"Maybe she didn't want to come."

"Then she would have called, no?"

"No. If she didn't want to call she wouldn't have called, *no?*"

Rusi felt embarrassed, wondering what Maureen might have said. He took a folded note out of his pocket. "Would you please give her this when you see her? It's my address and phone number."

John Blunden took the note, tore it three times in half, let the pieces fall to the ground. "I said she didn't want to come."

Rusi's mouth dropped; he turned and left, muttering "Bastard" under his breath when he was sure he couldn't be heard, as angry with Maureen as with her brother; she could have called him if she wasn't going to come. The dormitory number was available through the exchange.

Jan Schultz

As Rusi turned into the hallway from the stairs on the third floor of East Hall he took a deep breath — someone was fixing a sign to his door with scotch tape, her face hidden by a curtain of dark glossy hair that fell forward in line with her jaw. Her long brown legs took his breath away. He still couldn't hide his awe of the big beautiful American girls who swore so cheerfully, defied authority so wilfully, dressed so immodestly, and slept so readily with their sweethearts. He tried not to think of Maureen, immersing himself instead in his books, but there were occasions such as this when he couldn't help himself. "Hi. How're you doing? You looking for me?"

The girl looked up. "Are you Russy Seervai?"

Her forehead was so wrinkled with concentration, visible even from the distance in the dim light of the hallway, that he was sure she hated him. The cut of her hair shaped her face like a diamond, her head was perhaps too small for the thick sturdy trunk of her body, but he marked her expression with regret because her sleek muscled legs filled him with admiration. "Roo-si Seervai, yes. Something is the matter?"

"If you're Russy Seervai, there is."

He looked at the sign she had posted on his door:

RUSI SEERVAI
is
a SCAB!!
Send Him Back
Where He Came From!
J.S.

Rusi felt a chill but he didn't know what he'd done. "What is J.S.?" he asked.

She stood by with her arms crossed, as tall as himself. "Jan Schultz. That's me."

"What is a scab?"

"You are a scab."

"Why am I a scab?"

"Because you take jobs from people who need them."

Rusi washed dishes with Manolo Carillo from the Philippines and Roman Hudec from Czechoslovakia in the cafetaria for ninety cents an hour because the job had been advertised on the dormitory bulletin board. He needed the money and hadn't realized they'd displaced other workers until Manolo had said that he hoped they would stay on strike until he'd added enough to his savings for an engagement ring for his girlfriend, May. "If they need the job they can have it back," Rusi said. "I'm only keeping it for them until they come back."

He'd spoken sincerely, wanting her to like him, but he must have said the wrong thing. "Ha. Ha. Very funny." She turned and walked away.

Rusi took the sign down. The encounter had shaken him because he didn't wish to offend anyone. He felt more vulnerable in Chicago than in Bombay. When his roommate came back Rusi pointed to the sign. "Is it bad to be a scab?"

Tim said, "It's a word, like cat or dog. You can't help it if you're a scab."

Rusi shook his head. The words were no comfort, but Tim couldn't help it; he was being literal as were many of the engineers; they took pride in their literalness, as if it made them manlier. He was also so meticulous he took his clothes folded to the washing machines in the basement insisting they kept the crease better that way. Rusi changed the subject to another which had been puzzling him. He had seen posters all over campus, on bulletin boards, on trees, on walls, of a cowled figure with legends that read, "THE PHANTOM SLEEPS," "THE PHANTOM LURKS," "THE PHANTOM HIDES," "THE PHANTOM CREEPS." "Who is this phantom?" he said. "What is this all about?"

Tim spoke ironically. "The phantom's Rettaliata," he said.

Rusi's eyes widened. "Rettaliata? No kidding? *The* Rettaliata?" Dr. John T. Rettaliata was the president of the university.

"Sure," Tim said, turning away as if there were nothing more to be said.

"But why? What does it mean?"

"It means the student body's unhappy with him. We have no communication with administration. We know nothing about what they think. In the case of Rettaliata, no one can even remember when he was last seen!"

Tim's voice jumped momentarily as if with outrage, but he kept his ironic smile and Rusi remained as bewildered.

"So? What's that got to do with anything?" he said. "We're here to study. As long as the classes are there, what is the problem?"

Tim shook his head, never losing his smile though he'd stopped looking at Rusi. "That's not enough. We've got to take a stand. The whole country's up in arms about what's happening in Vietnam, and our administration pretends it's not even happening."

"In Vietnam? Why should we pretend anything's happening? What's it got to do with our education?"

"No one's pretending things are happening. They *are* happening. Don't you read the papers?"

"Of course, but that's Nixon's business. He's the president. We're students. We have our own business."

Tim shook his head as if it were too much to explain, and Rusi despaired of understanding Americans. They appeared to use a kind of shorthand; even when he understood the words something was lost in the overtones. He hesitated to speak too directly because he felt himself too easily misunderstood, too easily drawn into explanations that would have been unnecessary in Bombay. He called it Ethnic Anxiety as if naming the problem were the same as solving it.

2

Rusi didn't like dishwashing, particularly when some bored student had squeezed a whole orange into a glass or glued five plates together with mash potatoes and gravy and he'd have to pry out the orange, unglue the plates. Besides, he didn't like to think he was a scab — it made him feel even more unclean than the work, unworthy even to talk to someone like Jan Schultz who looked at him as if he were a lizard when their paths crossed. He found himself another job, cashier at the campus drugstore on weekends, and the next time he saw Jan he burst into a broad grin. She was across 33rd Street from him, heading for the women's dormitory. "Jan, I say, Jan," he shouted, jumping up and down, waving his arms like a windmill in a gale. When she failed to respond he dashed across the road, but not all the honking, screeching, swearing, and apologizing that followed prompted Jan to turn her head. "I say, Jan, wait up a bit, will you, no? I have good news," he said, catching up with her on the tarmac in front of the dormitory. "I swear," he said, grinning, running backward beside her, "a chap could get killed and you wouldn't even bloody notice."

She didn't look at him. "I notice the things worth noticing."

"I say, but listen, no?" Rusi, still running in reverse, struck his heel against a curb and fell heavily backward. "Oooof!" Jan had her keys ready and would have left him without another word, but couldn't resist a smile, a shake of her head.

"I have good news," he said without getting up, raising his hand as if he were making a point in a debate. "Wait up, no? Niagara Falls will still be there tomorrow."

She waited. "What is it?"

He crossed his elbows over his knees, still seated on the ground. "Let us go to The Bog for a coffee and I will tell you." The Bog was a coffee house on campus with a jukebox.

"I don't think so. I don't have time." She fitted her key to the door.

"Wait, wait. Let us just go to the side then, out of the way of the people traffic."

He got up and led her over to one of the linden trees by the entrance. "What is it?" she said again. "I really have to go."

She seemed so uninterested that his news seemed anticlimactic even to him, but he managed to keep smiling and said, "I am not a scab anymore. I thought you would like to know."

Her brow wrinkled, but the skin on her face flattened as if someone had tightened it a notch. "Why would you think a thing like that?"

"Arre, when I was a scab you made a sign for my door. Now, when I'm not a scab anymore, you don't even care?"

"Look, Rusty ... "

"My name is Rusi."

"Sorry. Rusi. Look, this is nothing personal. I just don't like foreigners coming here and interfering with the American process. If workers go on strike you can be damn sure it's because they're getting ripped off by the establishment, and people like you don't make it any easier."

She started to walk away, but Rusi caught her arm. "Yesyesyes, and how am I supposed to know this? For you I am just a foreigner, something to occupy your free time to make you feel important, something to talk about when you go back to your own kind. For me, what a country this is — *everybody* is a foreigner! Even their names are like from novels, Maureen and Tim and Diane and Jan — but the true American, the first American, was the Indian, no? And I am an Indian, no? So, you only tell me, who is the American and who is the foreigner?"

He smiled, his eyes on the ground as if he were embarrassed by his own feeble joke, but hoping she'd at least acknowledge his effort. She ignored it altogether. "Let go my arm," she said.

"Go, go," he said, letting go. "No one is holding you."

3

Rusi appeared in a sequence of images: seated before a terminal with a Fortran manual, composing a flowchart; performing with a guitar for a small group in a coffee house, his thick curly black hair kept out of his face by a leather headband; skipping like a fool in a long coat and top hat through a parking lot at night during the first snowfall of his life; ordering pizza from Connie's, fried rice and egg rolls from Shanghai's late at night with Rajiv and Faisal and others in the dormitory; crossing Jan's path without saying a word, keeping his eyes on her while she looked in the opposite direction; seated in a pink and orange bowling cubicle with Faisal and Chuck while Tim rubbed his hands to dry them over the air vent and wiggled his fingers.

"He thinks he's a surgeon," Rusi said, and Chuck laughed.

Faisal laughed as well, but without Chuck's irony.

Tim grinned, wiggling his fingers at Rusi. "You guys ready for a vasectomy?"

"Ooh!" Chuck said. "He's getting snippy!"

Rusi grinned. "I'd say by the scoresheet the vasectomy's over."

I peered over his shoulder. Faisal and Tim were ahead of Rusi and Chuck by eighty-four points.

"Man, we're *cream*ing you guys," Faisal said, bouncing in his seat, clapping his hands. "We're beating you guys hollow!"

Tim looked ironically at Faisal. "Did you say *we*?"

"Boy, that Faisal sure do get excited," Chuck said.

"Children will be children," Rusi said.

"Pay no mind, Tim," Faisal said. "Pay them no mind. Just give us another strike."

"Maybe," Tim said, picking up his ball, "if you'll let me concentrate."

"Shut up, you guys," Faisal said. "Let him concentrate."

"*Us* guys?" Chuck said, turning to Rusi. "How do you like them apples? *You* shut up, Faisal."

Tim was the only one of the four to own his ball and shoes. He balanced it with his fingers in the holes as if he were testing its weight, and cantered in place limbering up for a run.

They were familiar with his minuet. He would spring to his toes, spring forward three steps, his arm would swing in a wide arc backward, a wider arc forward, he would touch the ground with his fingertips for balance after releasing the ball, and fix the ball with his gaze from his three-pronged stance as if he still had control, until it hit the pins.

"Hell," said Rusi. "He thinks he's a ballet dancer."

"A bally dancer," said Chuck. "What a hoot! Klondike Tim, the bally dancer."

"Shut up, man!" Faisal said. "I'm telling you: Shut up! Can't you just let a fellow bowl in peace?"

"Hey! Don't tell me to shut up," Chuck said. "Sheesh! *You*'re the one making all the noise."

Tim released the ball and held the ground with his fingertips; Faisal yelled STRIKE! even before the ball hit the pins; Rusi shook his head in wonder; Chuck didn't even bother to look. He was doodling on the back of the scoresheet, a stick figure, a cowboy hat, the face hidden by a bandanna like a rustler's. Chuck shaded in the bandanna and wrote in a snake of letters across the page: RETTALIATATA-YATATA-YATATA-YATATA-YATATA-YATATA.

Tim returned to the seat by Chuck. He took his own strikes more in stride than Faisal. "The Phantom strikes again," he said wryly.

"You got that right," Chuck said.

"Did you mark his strike?" Faisal said. "Did you mark his strike? I swear, we're giving you guys such a licking — the licking of your lives. World War II is a picnic compared to what we're doing to you guys."

"Vietnam's no picnic," Tim said sharply. That was when I noticed his ROTC haircut, in sharp contrast with Rusi's and Chuck's long hair.

"I'm not talking about Vietnam," Faisal said. "It was just an expression."

"You can't *not* talk about Vietnam anymore," Tim said. "It's everywhere."

"C'mon, man," Faisal said. "We're here to study. For us that's everything. The rest is government business."

"Not for me, it isn't," Tim said.

"But you *chose* to be in ROTC."

Tim ignored Faisal. "You coming to the meeting?" he asked Chuck.

Chuck grinned. "To the meltdown, you mean. You betcha."

"How about you?" Tim said to Rusi.

Rusi agreed mostly with Faisal; he couldn't understand how students spoiled with stereos, tape decks, bicycles, even cars, could be so antiestablishment, give the cops the finger; many were afraid for their lives, of course, but it got more complicated; the face of patriotism in America was changing in the face of a growing mistrust of government, and even those in no danger of their lives protested; Rusi had been willing to give

Nixon the benefit of the doubt even when he'd ventured into Cambodia after promising to initiate the peace process in Vietnam, but the Kent State killings had bewildered him. "I think so," he said. "Yes, sure."

"All right, Rusi!" said Chuck.

"Right on, Rusi!" said Tim.

Faisal said, "I have a math test coming up."

The bowling alley was in the basement of the auditorium building, and as I watched the entire alley rose as if in an elevator, the sound of falling pins faded first to an echo before disappearing altogether, two calendar pages swept across the hazy panorama like leaves in a breeze, Rusi and Tim and Chuck appeared in different stages of dress and toilet before the auditorium materialized around them, filled quickly to capacity, overflowed into the aisles, and a buzz of expectancy muffled all conversation. Microphones were available throughout the hall whereby students might ask questions of the famous phantom of the campus, the president of the university, Dr. John T. Rettaliata, standing behind a lectern onstage. The situation appeared topsyturvy to Rusi, students questioning authority, and he almost expected the hooded humpbacked phantom of the cartoons all over campus in place of the Rettaliata at the podium.

The first question came from an architecture student, complaining that on Fridays the Freshman architects had a drafting class from nine to noon, a history of architecture class from noon to one, and another drafting class from one to four, leaving no time for lunch or any other form of rest. The president refused to say what he thought himself, suggesting instead that the question be addressed to the head of the architecture department.

The next question asked what he thought of the U.S. involvement in Vietnam, which he deflected saying it was a personal matter.

The next question dealt with the computer school, the next again with Vietnam, the next with the gym, the next again with Vietnam, and again, and again. Most of the students posed their questions deferentially, but Rusi was amazed that they posed them at all, as if the president were on trial. He understood that it had something to do with the meaning of America.

He couldn't always follow the questions — the accent was still occasionally troublesome — but understood that Rettaliata was answering questions relating to academic and administrative affairs, not to political. "I cannot answer that," Rusi understood him to say, "because my politics are my own business and I cannot saddle my administration with the burden of my personal point of view."

The students wanted him to go on record with a statement for the university against the war. "I cannot speak for all the students," he said, repeatedly. "I cannot speak for all the staff. They cannot all be of one accord. I can speak only for myself, but that is no one's business except my own."

Each of his responses to Vietnam deflected the question for a while, allowing once more for parleys about academic and administration policy, until someone repeated the question again, and someone else again, and someone else, and again. Finally, the embattled phantom spoke heatedly. "I cannot speak for anyone else, but as for myself, I think President Nixon is doing one hell of job and he has my full support in everything!"

The audience rose like a sea in a storm, perhaps eighty percent leaving the hall. Chuck and Tim left. Rusi stayed to see what would happen next, but when Jan passed him along the aisle he followed her out. He said nothing until he saw she was headed back to the women's dormitory. "I say, Jan," he said. "Wait up a bit, I say."

She said, "Oh, hi, Rusty," as if she were surprised, but he knew from the casual way she looked at him that she'd known he'd been following her.

"My name is Rusi."

"Sorry. Rusi."

"But you can call me Rusty if you like. I like it."

She smiled. He felt as if they knew each other well, as if she'd ignored him so determinedly for two semesters that they'd become a part of each other's lives.

"That was quite something, no? what happened just now?"

She stopped smiling. "Yes, wasn't it? Now I have to think about changing schools."

"I say, no — not seriously."

"You heard what Rettaliata said. That's as good as a statement for the school."

"Yes, but you can't do that."

"Why not?"

"He's not worth it."

She said nothing, but looked at him closely as if she'd expected him to say something else.

He shrugged as if she'd backed him into a corner. "And I would miss you."

She didn't look at him. "But you don't even know me."

"I would miss seeing you on the campus. I would miss getting to know you. I would miss being ignored by you."

She remained silent, but smiled again. Her face appeared to recede into a soft focus. He stepped closer, squeezing her shoulder. "You are very pretty."

She pulled away, grinning broadly. "That doesn't give you a license to touch me."

His eyes grew wide. "Don't be so paranoid. I was only saying what I think."

She laughed. "Just kidding."

He took a deep breath. "Oh, yes, my dad said Americans are great kidders. It's true."

"Tell me about your dad."

"He's dead. He died before I came."

"Oh, I'm sorry."

"It's okay — but would you like to get a coffee in The Bog. We can talk better there."

"Seriously?"

He knew from the way she was grinning that she was kidding him again. "Seriously, you bet your bottom dollar."

She had a funny laugh, as if she were choking, but he found it charming.

"Let me get a sweater," she said. "It's getting chilly."

"I won't budge. I'll be right here." His heart beat, budda-budda-budda, like a machine gun. He was cold himself, but didn't think of getting a sweater, afraid he might never see her again if he missed this chance, but he needn't have worried. She returned with an extra sweater.

4

"After that, Homi, I swear, things moved so fast I still can't believe it. We spent nights just talking, having coffees. Her grandparents, German Jews, were killed by Nazis. Her father got lost in New York when they came. Her mother lives with her older brother and his family near Gary in Indiana. He is a financial analyst which means he gets paid — and this is what *she* said — even when he loses money for his clients. She doesn't like to go home, she said, because they are all so bourgeois. Arre, I said, he's making money, no? he's feeding his wife and kids, no? (also the mother, she said) then what is the problem? She is in liberal arts — what is she going to do for her mother? When she has no answer she turns the subject to me: why am I in computers? Arre, but that is what I want. Arre, she says, but I am only asking. I swear, when she uses our Indian slang like that I feel I would do anything for her. I cannot tell her enough about India. She says biculturalism is the best thing because it armors you from the abuses of patriotism — which are nationalism, insularity, myopia, that sort of thing. She's not a liberal arts major for nothing, yaar.

"She got pregnant almost right away — you know how it is, yaar, no stopping these Seervai hormones. I said we could get married or have an abortion or give the baby for adoption, whatever she wanted. She wanted to get married. I said, Are you sure? She was sure. Someone in the dorm had said "Now she's going with Indians, soon it's gonna be blacks," and she'd over-heard her. It was an asshole thing to say, but she said it had concentrated her mind beautifully. She didn't want to sleep with anyone else again, not blacks, not whites, only me! I said to her that some people wore their Americanism like a badge, but she slipped into it as easily as into a pair of blue jeans. She said her liberal arts was finally rubbing off on me.

"One development I thought was ironic actually — for a child to be born Jewish the mother must be Jewish, but with us it is the father who must be a Zoroastrian. We talked about it — no bar mitzvah for the child and no navjote, only love, a good education, what else? the rest will take care of itself.

"When Dean Shipley called about what happened to you she wanted to come to Aquihana with me, but I said it wouldn't have been a good time. She was in the middle of a summer class, and there was nothing she could have done for you anyway — but she can't wait to meet you, my genius brother who is such a faltu chess player — and also Mom. I think you will like her, I think she might even beat you at chess — but I'm warning you: if you slap her, I will not be held responsible for what I will do to you. That was always your trouble, no resilience. They said you had trouble with some girl. You kept calling her name, Candace. I wish you had written to me what you were up to. It might have helped — but now no regrets. You are going to be an uncle! Think about it. Why do you want to throw it all away?"

I did not want to throw it all away. I wanted to meet Jan. I wanted to be an uncle. I wanted to hug my beautiful bearish bearded brother as he sat slumped in the chair by my bed, exhaling the occasional buzzing breath of sleep — but I couldn't shake the mass of clay I'd become. I shut my eyes instead, matching the rhythm of his sleep with mine, making a bridge of our breaths.

HOMI

Penny

I had synchronized my breath just once before as I synchronized it now with Rusi's, on the only night I'd spent with Candace — on the only night I have spent with any woman — fitted to her back, preparing to sleep. I could think of nothing more precious after the hundred and more butterfly kisses I'd spent on her hair and shoulders (the first had made her giggle as if we'd been adolescents again after the adult business of sex, but the next had put her into a quicker sleep than I'd thought possible), while I remained with unblinking eyes unwilling to sacrifice even a few such magical moments, holding a lovely naked woman, so trustingly asleep, in my arms, until my eyes felt reptilian with the strain and I found a new comfort, tracing her breaths with mine, falling instantaneously asleep myself. But though I traced Rusi's breath with the same assiduity I couldn't fall asleep. I thought instead about Candace, about what my friend Dale Schweppenheiser might have told Rusi about her, and the room dissolved once more, focusing its new configuration on her face, her thick wavy ocherous hair spreading like the rays of the sun as I remembered it on her pillow at the Come Back Motel between Aquihana and Tunkhannock, her eyes shut so tightly that creases multiplied in their corners and her pale brows vanished amid the furrows which etched her forehead. This was the sight for which I'd wished to freeze time, the moment to which I'd so finely tuned the memoscan, for which I'd been willing to sacrifice science, life, wisdom, on the altar of a feckless woman's vanity — but the moment was glorious and I wanted to enjoy it one more time, uninterrupted one last time by Arabs in the desert.

I roamed one last time from her eyes closed but not in sleep, past the sugar and spice bump of her nose, the dark open cavern of her mouth sheltering the thick red undulating wedge of her tongue, the soft round jut of her jaw, the long narrow tunnel of her throat, the hard ridge of her clavicle converging over her wide flat heaving breastbone, the pale flesh and pink swollen tips of her breasts — but as I maneuvered for a wider angle, two tawny brawny hairy arms (not mine) flanked her shoulders, two tawny brawny hairy thighs (again, not mine) straddled hers, and her long white arms garlanded a short thick neck (as they never had mine) knotting themselves at the wrists.

A horrible sight: another man in my place, a ridge of thick black hair crawling like a giant worm from the dome of his back and shoulders, spreading like a delta over the small of his back and the paler globes of his buttocks, beneath which ... the hard brutal work of pistons and valves, sweat running like grease, the wet slap of his dark heavy hairy balls against the soft white pads of her buttocks — but it couldn't be, it couldn't be, not only because I didn't want it so but because I had no memory of such voyeurism, and without memory there is no recollection.

I should have noted the differences from the start: the pillowcovers at the motel had portrayed bouquets of roses, now the covers were white; the motel had offered a bed as wide as the ocean, now the bed was a narrow mattress on the floor; the motel room had smelled of roses, now the room smelled of armpit and groin. I didn't understand. I didn't understand at all. Arabs had interrupted my recollections before, which Bapaiji had explained — but how to explain this present and uglier pornography? The throbbing returned to my temples, the needles resumed their weave in my head. I had to do something to counteract the effect. If you returned with determination to a hated dream you could alter its outcome; disfiguring a hated image you controlled it, a mustache on a pretty woman, horns on a handsome man. I imagined the tuft of hair at the base of the intruder's spine growing fleecier, becoming a wagging wedge of tail, becoming the coarse grimy flanks of a black and white goat with spindly forelegs on her ribcage, its horned head, its yellow slitted eyes — but I couldn't shut out the rising swell of her moans, his grunts, until I found the bathroom across the untidy clothes-strewn floor, entered, locked myself in, turned on shower, faucets, exhaust, and repeatedly flushed the toilet.

How could it be? An issue of *Cosmopolitan* on the bathroom floor provided the answer. It was dated October 1971, weeks *after* my admission to Aquihana Hospital, weeks *after* my misfortune with the memoscan, even weeks *after* we'd flown to Bombay on September 5. I was not only *not* recollecting anymore, but projecting into the future. I was watching her in the present in her bed in Aquihana from mine in Bombay despite the separation of thousands of miles and a time difference of nine and a half hours (afternoon light played on her blinds; night blacked out my windows). Over the white noise provided by the running water and air I pieced it together. "For us," Einstein had said, "the distinction between past, present, and future is only an illusion, albeit a stubborn one." How can I be more specific? A chair becomes visible when it reflects light from a source (sunlight, electric, candle) onto the retina of an eye. If the eye could follow the rays of light reflected from the chair faster than the speed of light it would see the chair *before* it appeared, it would see the chair in time as if time were a fourth dimension — but this is nonsense because the speed of light is absolute, impossible to exceed, barely possible to approach; the traveler, approaching this velocity, 186,000 miles per second, finds space contracted, time expanded, and achieving this velocity (a hypothetical situation at best), space and time collapsed into one, no more the geography of here and there, the history of now and then; the traveler is everywhere, always; ironically, you achieve this velocity only to find there is nowhere to go; you are constantly wherever you want to be. This absolute state might be compared to the ocean in which a drop of water becomes not lost in the ocean but the ocean itself — or to the collective unconscious, the repository for the record of the universe, resident in all sentient beings, adjunct of individual memory, into which I'd unwittingly tapped when I'd probed the vault of my own memory, stranding myself in limbo between the absolute and the commonplace, in which diffuse state I could drop in at whim and will on the unsuspecting universe.

Her moans were becoming perceptible again, rising gradually, rhythmically, to a crescendo, until she was screaming how much she loved it (it, not him), and he was shouting so all Aquihana might hear, calling her a slut, a cunt, the best goddam fuck in the world, as if he were complimenting her. How pallid my feathery I Love Yous must have sounded in contrast. The weave tightened in my head, I climbed into the shower, drew the curtain, turned the water to cold.

How long I waited I cannot say, but it seemed no more than a few minutes before she, still naked, came smiling into the bathroom, stoppered the bathtub, and started the water. None of my machinations (the closed bathroom door, the running water and air, the drawn shower curtain) was evident to her. We were together, but our distances from each other were relative — I was halfway around the world from her, she was halfway across the room from me.

I withdrew the shower curtain, stepped out of the tub, turned off the faucets. Her goat lover had left, fled rather (his large dirty white rumpled handkerchief still lay on the floor), as if he were sure enough of his plumbing not to indulge in the softer, less lubricious kisses of afterlove (my afterlovemaking had taken longer than my lovemaking), as if anything more than the stark brutal friction he'd provided were pretentious, apologetic, unmanly, and she, so summarily accommodating his churlishness, appeared to be rebuking the ardor I'd shown in my time.

An additional, less subtle rebuke awaited me yet: next to her bath oil in the medicine cabinet stood the sandalwood elephant I'd given her, faded from its wash in the washing machine when I'd forgotten to remove it from my pants, given to me by Adi Ghadiali, Bapaiji's sweetshop sweetheart for whom Dad had been named, when our rickshaw had developed a flat in the Mota Bajar and he'd plied Rusi and me with sweets. A white cloud appeared over her head like a thought balloon in a comic strip, with a caricature of my naked self, smiling pathetically, right leg like a hockey stick. My face in the caricature filled with chagrin as she laughed, threw the elephant in a waste basket under the sink, sprinkled bath oil in the water, and settled in the tub.

Some things remain inexplicable; where physic stops metaphysic steps in; an act of faith accomplishes what an act of will cannot. I didn't think I could have turned her shower nozzle to HOT in my phantom state, but I did, provoking a shriek from a suddenly standing Candace scrambling to turn off the water. I didn't think I could have retrieved the elephant from the waste basket and tossed it on her suddenly scorched shoulders, but I did, provoking a sonata of screams which promised delightfully never to end.

I might have left her satisfactorily on that sweet cacophonous note (notes, actually), but a framed mother and daughter portrait on a worn wooden dresser, standing apart from lotions and lipsticks, caught my eye: a skinny smiling pretty girl Candace, blond curls to her shoulders, waisthigh to a skinny smiling plain woman in a plain dress, her hand on Candace's shoulder. For the first time I became curious about her family. Did her plain mother imply a hunk of a father to account for Candace's own looks? Why wasn't her father in the picture? Had he been one of those incorrigible charmers I'd read about? Had she known him? Was he still alive? Was her mother still alive? Had their instability contributed to her wildness? I'd have pursued the questions, but the picture dissolved into another, girl Candace dissolved into another girl, Penelope Hartley, Penny, my own dear darling Penny, also skinny smiling pretty, blond curls to her shoulders, seated on our sittingroom couch, posed amid smarmy, swarming, oily, disheveled, grubby, grinning little males, as apparently heedless of them as they were of the other girls, her pink and white face inclined capriciously toward a naked pink and white shoulder (her daring pink and white party dress was held up by just one strap). We'd met romantically, been linked romantically, and parted romantically.

The picture had been taken on the occasion of my sixth birthday party, but even as I watched Penny's head began to bob in the picture as if she were in a rowboat on the sea; the oily boys remained, but the panorama around her, our couch, our sittingroom, faded into the terrace of the Breach Candy Nursery School littered with the colorful baggage of kindergarteners — a jungle jim, a pedal-powered car, a stuffed elephant as large as some of the children, and behind everything the classroom in which I was the youngest pupil by nine months. Penny's bobbing head appeared to get larger, closer, laugh more loudly. "Are you scared?" she shouted. "You look scared."

She was tall, a year older than me, the daughter of an American diplomat. We were seated at opposite ends of a green rocking boat, she rocking it with all the strength of her plush pink limbs, I with my leg stretched forward in its calipers, my knuckles white where they gripped the sides of the boat, more than a little seasick but stubbornly refusing to acknowledge my panic to my peers. According to the game we'd invented whoever panicked first had to cede his seat to the next challenger. I'd entered the boat with Penny because I liked her and because I didn't think any girl could outrock me even with my halfleg, but she was rocking the boat to an amplitude I hadn't believed possible, springing to her toes with each crest and slamming herself down toward each trough. I knew I'd be all right as long as I kept pace with her rhythm, but she kept changing her rhythm and I was afraid she'd soon either tire me out or catch me by surprise. Fatso Kapoor, who also liked Penny and wanted to get in the boat with her, edged himself in front of the crowd, shouting, "Scaredy Cat! Scaredy Cat! Homi is a scaredy cat! Homi is a cowardy custard." I bristled; Penny held the trough down a moment longer than I'd anticipated; I flew like a javelin in an arc. Fatso chanted rhythmically, "*De-Fea-Ted! De-Fea-Ted! Ho*mi is a *wea*-kling, de*fea*ted by a *girl*." I was unhurt, but too dazed to retaliate — but Penny wasn't. Jumping from the boat she clenched tiny hands and drummed soft fists indiscriminately on Fatso's head, back, shoulders, arms, whatever he presented to defend himself, until he ran away. Then, making mewling noises, she came to where I lay on the floor, cradled me clumsily in her arms.

So it began, my first, my only love affair before I came to America. I was five, she was six, we rode on horses made of sticks. We became so inseparable that by the time we graduated to the first standard in the domed and arched Walsingham House High School, originally Cutch Castle, Fatso Kapoor had perpetrated the rumor that we were married under the mistaken assumption that I'd be embarrassed into relinquishing Penny. Instead, felicitations followed: Penny, tying my shoelaces in the vast entrance hall to the school for everyone to see, while I leaned against the glass showcase displaying an immense stuffed Bengal tiger; Penny, fighting boys, monitors, prefects, teachers, so we could sit next to each other in music class, striking

instruments (her tambourine, my triangle), accompanying
Mrs. Somack playing "The Merry Peasant" and "The British
Grenadiers" on the piano; Penny, offering me my first apple pies
and peanut butter sandwiches on Saturday afternoons at the
Hartleys' residence on Napean Sea Road; and, most felicitous
of felicitations, sitting with Penny in her bedroom, eating food
out of her mouth, feeding her food from mine, bananas, tarts,
ice cream, licking and sucking each other's tongues and faces.

The summer came to an ugly end: Penny, descending the
schoolbus, flaxen hair flying as she turned her head for a final
(too prophetic) goodbye, flashing her last big happy sweet last
lover's smile before the rush across the street to meet Erica, her
English speaking ayah whom she called Nanny; a screech, a thud,
a scream, Miss Bean (responsible for the children on the bus)
shouting, "Do not look. Nobody is to look out of the window."

How does a six year old cope with the loss of his sweetheart?
He puts himself in quarantine, he lowers his resistance, he
searches out toxins as if they were grail, he dreams of a
reunitement (pupal angels in a Hansel and Gretel heaven). In
the two years that followed I contracted mumps, jaundice,
chicken pox, typhoid, two kinds of measles, three kinds of flu;
I underwent a second tonsillectomy, an appendectomy; I had
yet to run through cholera, small pox, tuberculosis, and whooping cough, but something I read and someone I met so exposed
the selfindulgence of my quarantine that even the most be-
nighted eyes (mine) began to see.

I had resigned myself to a bedridden life, a diet of rice,
chicken stock, and water, when I read an article, "Explorer of
the Human Brain," in the July 1958 issue of *The Reader's Digest*
(I remember the date because I kept the issue and took it with
me to Aquihana where it must be even now among my other
effects), about Dr. Wilder Graves Penfield who used an electrode to probe the brains of epileptics to determine the root of
their affliction.

The patients were administered local anesthetics so they could immediately report the effects of each probe. Dr. Penfield successfully located the ridge of tissue which, when removed, cured or greatly improved the condition of the epileptic in seventy-five percent of the cases — more importantly (from my perspective), not only was he able to identify the areas of the brain cortex controlling toes, elbows, eyelids, et cetera, in this way, but he also established a link with memory which he postulated was stored in the temporal lobes. During one of the probes, a middle-aged housewife from New Jersey exclaimed that she seemed to be giving birth to her child all over again, and proceeded to report, vividly, the sights and sounds of the delivery room as if the events were taking place again before her eyes. During another probe, a young South African suddenly found himself back in a family gathering, the piano playing, his cousin telling a joke, and insisted it was happening all over again even though he knew he was with Dr. Penfield in Montreal. During yet another probe, a young woman found herself in the livingroom of a house in which she'd lived with her family more than fifteen years ago; the march from *Aida* was playing on the phonograph; when Dr. Penfield removed his probe the music stopped, when he applied it again it started again. What I understood better than anything else was that Penny was not as irrevocably lost as I'd imagined; she was trapped — retrievably! — in my brain; but by that time I'd already contracted a case of hydrocele, a seepage of fluid into one of my testicles until it was more than twice as large as the other making it impossible for me to sit or walk comfortably. It was not serious, essentially a question of draining the testicle with a syringe, a stay of no more than a week in the hospital, but I'd had enough of hospitals and so had Mom and Dad, so when Mary suggested a healer of whom she'd heard miraculous things we chose to visit him instead.

Dad drove us out on a Sunday morning in the Ford, Mom in the front seat, Mary and myself in the back, through the city, past Byculla, Dadar, Bandra, Thana, Borivli, the most distant suburbs, until we were alone on the road (actually, a dusty cow path). Dad parked the car to one side because Mary said cars weren't allowed beyond that point. We still had about half a mile to go, but we'd come prepared with a wheelbarrow since I could hardly have walked the distance on my own (my leg, my testicle). Mom, Dad, and Mary took turns pushing. It was a pleasant walk — a beach on our left, coconut trees, cool salty air (we'd gotten an early start) — but I felt foolish sitting in the wheelbarrow and was relieved when Mary pointed to the healer's hut in the distance.

The hut was of mud, the roof conical thatched with palm leaves, built on a step, one round room with two windows facing each other, a writing table with drawers in which herbs and powders were kept, a wooden chair with a cane seat to go with the table. The healer sat in a lotus position with his eyes closed in the middle of the room, ash on his face, necklaces of beads of many colors and the kernels of fruits around his neck, naked except for his dhoti, praying — or, perhaps, meditating. His ribs showed clearly (like those of fakirs who appear too weightless to be harmed when they lie on beds of nails), but the long black hair coiled on his head, the perfect posture perfectly still, and the detached expression on his face made him appear the healthiest person in the room. He looked old, wise, but perhaps that was only the ash on his face. We learned later he was just twenty-five years old.

He never opened his eyes, and spoke with us through an intermediary, but when he learned of my medical history he said he couldn't help me because I didn't want to be helped, I wanted to be sick. When Gautama Siddhartha, the Buddha, had witnessed old age, disease, and death, he'd renounced earthly pleasures to better understand the will of God, but confronted with the death of a small girl I'd sought only to escape from life. Amazed at his clairvoyance I acknowledged what had once been true, but (without going into the story of Dr. Penfield's experiments) submitted it was true no longer.

The healer nodded, said he believed me, I had gifts it would be a shame to waste, prayed (or meditated) for perhaps five minutes to vanquish my demons, gave me dry leaves (all through the intermediary; he himself barely moved) to wrap around my testicles, and said I should return in a week.

The leaves were prickly on my testicles, but I wore them stoically. We returned to the hut every week for a month for more prayers and leaves by the end of which time the fluid in my testicle had vaporized and I could walk normally again — or as normally as my leg would allow. When Dad broached the subject of his fee the healer said he would lose his powers if he accepted money, but he gave Dad a list of charities to which he might donate if he felt inclined.

Penny: Corollaries

First Corollary: Granny had a friend who lived in one of the tall buildings that had sprung up in the Sixties from which we could look into the sprawling shapeless Breach Candy swimming pool, so large it had islands built into it, appeared more like a lake than a pool, and was constantly occupied by American and European women in bikinis any of whom might have been Penny had she lived — each of whom, I sometimes imagined, *was* Penny, who'd broken with me the only way she knew how, by faking her death.

I didn't reveal my hypothesis to anyone, but asked Mom to find someone who might take me swimming in the pool (membership was restricted to Americans and Europeans, but Indians were allowed as guests). She suggested the CCI (Cricket Club of India) pool where we were members, but I insisted on the Breach Candy pool and she didn't argue because the doctors had said, at all costs, to encourage me for the sake of my leg, to be more physical. She asked the Hartleys, Penny's parents, if they'd take Rusi and me. Rusi didn't want to go, but Mom overruled him; Mom didn't go ("I can't swim!" but actually she had a horror of appearing in a swimsuit); neither did Dad ("I do not much care to swim," but actually he had a horror of being with me and Rusi without Mom).

The occasion was an embarrassment for all concerned. Indians were allowed as guests, but only in the small, rectangular, indoor pool. The Hartleys argued for us in vain, Rusi refused to enter the pool (he might have been piqued but all he said, complacently enough, was "I don't feel much like swimming") and sat in his costume on a bench by the pool while the rest of us determinedly had our fun. I couldn't imagine Penny in the indoor pool, but I couldn't let the Hartleys down after their trouble, and entered the pool feeling vaguely unclean, vaguely compromised, wishing I could have been like Rusi, but feeling also vaguely responsible for the fiasco.

Second Corollary: Penny had cast a longer shadow than I'd imagined. I was only beginning to distinguish its murky penumbral outline because it had barely appeared to touch me in the wake of my selfimposed quarantine: not when I'd been ordered to kiss Yasmin Shroff for the camera; not when Mom and Dad had taken Rusi and myself for weekends to Juhu Beach along with the Jairazbhoys and their daughter Nishat; not during my boyhood dances with Kamal Malani; not during my first dates with Lalita Raman; but increasingly after I arrived in Aquihana, Pennsylvania — and most especially now, back in my Bombay bed reliving the past. I had loved and lost once, a blond girleen, whom I'd imagined I'd found again in Candace.

Third Corollary: I'd almost forgotten the following corollary, five years later, when I was eleven.

Mom: Why do you want a sister?

Me: No reason. To play with.

Mom: You have Rusi to play with.

Me: Yes, but I want a sister.

Mom: Why do you want a sister?

Me: No reason. I just liked doing things with Penny.

Mom: What did you do with Penny?

Me: Nothing. We just goofed around in her bedroom, you know.

Mom (after a pause): Whatever you did, Homi, don't do it
again.

Me (defiantly): I can't! She's dead.

Mom: You know what I mean, Homi. Don't do it with
anyone else.

Me: Why not?

Mom: It's naughty.

Me: Why is it naughty?

Mom: I thought you said you didn't do anything.

Me: I didn't — we didn't!

Mom: Didn't what?

Me: Nothing.

Mom: Good.

Me: Why can't I have a sister? I promise not to do it again
if you get me a sister.

Mom: Promise not to do what?

Me: Nothing.

A MONTH LATER

Mom (giving me a book, *How Shall I Tell My Child*): These
are the facts of life, Homi. Your dad and I think it's time you
learned them. Read pages 109-115. If you have any questions,
ask me.

FOUR YEARS LATER

Me: Mom, Remember when you gave me that book to read,
about spermatozoons and eggs and everything?

Mom (with a silly smile): Yes?

Me: So, did you and Dad do that to get me?

Mom (fluffing an already fluffed cushion): What do you
think?

Me (almost screaming): No, Mom! Tell me!

Mom (still smiling sillily): Arre bawa, what's the fuss about?
Everybody does it. I thought you understood.

Me: But did *you*? Did *you* do *that* with *Dad*?

Mom: Of course, we did. It's okay if you're married. How do you think we got you?

Me: How could you do that? I just don't understand how you could do that. Did you do it again?

Mom: Of course, we did. How do you think we got Rusi? I thought we explained that to you, Homi, when we told you about the facts of life.

Me: You explained nothing! Nothing! You didn't tell me you did *that* with Dad!

Mom: Well, we did. You don't have to get upset. It's okay if you're married. Marriage makes it all right.

I'd said nothing, but felt betrayed; she'd been on Dad's side all the times she'd pretended to be on mine, sharing secrets with me but sharing her biggest secret with Dad — and beyond the Oedipal rage, another festered, against marriage for so mechanically making it right. I felt pushed into the presence of two emperors, each with no clothes.

Aquihana

I was flanked by images of Dad: he stood on a dais to the left of my bed before a microphone, before congregated Radio Club members, accepting tribute from grateful Radio Club officials, for whom he'd designed and supervised the construction of a swimming pool. Mom sat with Rusi and myself behind him, Mom grinning the widest, Rusi bored, myself awed. In the Humpty-Dumpty Ford, returning home, Mom kissed him lightly on his cheek, Rusi and I raised eyebrows at each other in the backseat, I in surprise, he ironically.

He also stood grinning with Mom at the foot of my bed. "Would it be okay if I cat-eared your books?"

"What?"

"Is it okay if I cat-ear your books? Your mummy said you didn't like it when I dog-eared them."

"Oh, come on now, Adi. You're just being silly. That's not even funny."

I had complained to Mom about the way Dad dog-eared my books because I couldn't tell him myself. As much as I wanted to span the gulf between us I didn't know how. I didn't laugh, but I said, "Could you, maybe, just mouse-ear them? I'd appreciate that."

He laughed delightedly, delightfully, saying to Mom, "He's

all right. The boy is all right. He's got a sense of humor all right."

To the right of my bed, he strode confidently across Cooperage Road, the image of an erect goodlooking man in his fifties marred by what followed, a taxi, appearing suddenly with a blaring horn, sent him scurrying penguinlike to the sidewalk. I wished he hadn't run, I wished he'd magically arrested the motion of the taxi, a wave of his hand like the wave of a wand, and maintained his confident pace.

I'd watched the incident from the window of his study where I was reviewing the elevation of a factory he was designing. He'd disguised the chimneys to resemble the funnels of a ship. I didn't usually criticize his work, but I was disappointed with him that day for running across the street. As soon as he joined me in the study, I said, "Why do you have these chimneys looking like funnels?"

He seemed surprised, but pleased that I'd asked. "I thought it would look better, don't you think?"

"But it's not a shipyard," I said impatiently. "It's not a dock, it's not a wharf, it's not for nautical goods. Why funnels?"

His expression faltered as he realized my interest had been a trap. "It was commissioned by the Indian Navy," he said. "I thought you knew that."

"I didn't know," I said, mumbling, suddenly confused, "but still ... funnels are so obvious."

He wouldn't look at me then, his pleased expression looked glued on his face, his eyes flinched, and watching him through my prism of time and space my heart shriveled to the size of a pea. How much sharper than a serpent's tooth to have a thankless child — or, at least, an ignorant child — but let me also give you my perspective. Let me defend myself.

I resented our resemblance, particularly in the early pictures taken in Edinburgh and London, as if he'd usurped my father's place, taking credit for my scholastic accolades as if I were a prize tomato he'd cultivated, robbing from the meaning of my life to give meaning to his own, making me first his trophy, and only incidentally his son, as if he'd chosen finally to forgive me for the sickly boy I'd been instead of the son he'd deserved. He'd wanted me to attend the University of Edinburgh where he was an alumnus, but the university not only provided no scholarships for foreign students but required of them triple the regular tuition. His next choice was Harvard where I was offered a full scholarship, a grant to cover all expenses, and eighty hours of credit on the strength of my college boards and the Bachelor of Science degree from St. Xavier's College in Bombay (Princeton, Yale, and MIT, among others, offered variations of the same enticements) — but for the first and only time (he died shortly after I left) my resentment became concrete. I combed the College Handbook, A through Z, looking for acceptable universities of which he'd never heard. Aquihana University, among the A's, was the first to accept me, the one I accepted.

Aquihana University was an institution on the make. I'd have been admitted with a much muddier record than the one I presented. The administration wanted to develop an international reputation and amply compensated for its lack of prestige with its excess of attention to foreign students, accommodating them into the homes of Pennsylvanian students, particularly during holidays, so they'd feel less like strangers. I was met at JFK Airport in New York by Dale Schweppenheiser who'd volunteered to be my official Big Brother. I was afraid he would find me unhip, but his hair (uncombed, but short), his clothes (unlike Rusi's), and his grin reassured me from the beginning. "Hi, Homi," he said, as if we'd met before. "You look just like your photograph."

I'd sent him a photograph but was sensitive enough, even then, to think he'd recognized me by my barely perceptible limp. "Hello," I said, extending my hand. "How do you do? Are you Dale?"

"At your service, Brother Homi. How was the flight?" He took my hand in both of his. Later I understood he called me "Brother" because he imagined I was his brother in Christ, but at the time I thought he was speaking as a member of the university's Big Brother program. "A little long."

He grinned. "No kidding! We should get moving. There's going to be a lot of traffic getting out." He insisted on carrying all my bags. "You're a guest here, Homi. I know you're just going to love it at good ol' OW."

"OW? What is OW?"

"A-U, Aquihana University, better known as OW."

It was three o'clock in the morning. For the next thirty minutes we found ourselves in lanes which moved as if the cars had locked bumpers, but the luxury of Dale's car, as amniotic as an airconditioned room, inured me against all discomfort. "You can sleep if you want. We have a long drive ahead. We can talk in the morning."

"Nonono. I want to see everything. Who knows when I will come back to New York."

"We can come back for a weekend if you like, but you must be tired. You can lean your seat back if you want."

"Thanks, but still." I must have been more tired than I thought because the next thing I knew we were on a mountain road along a valley carpeted with green, creeks and waterfalls glittering in the sun. "Good morning, Brother Homi. Welcome to Pennsylvania."

Nothing seemed real: my life in Bombay culminating with the festive sendoff at Santa Cruz Airport (a party of thirty, a coconut broken for good luck, garlands of marigolds) seemed a dream; my brief passage through New York even more so; the alternating alpine vistas from the car, as if veils were being removed with each bend in the road, like shimmering visions — but this, finally, was America! I hadn't thought I'd ever get there. "Good morning," I said, feeling flushed.

Dale kept his eyes on the road, grinning. "For someone who wanted to see everything you sure slept a lot," he said.

I shrugged. "This looks like Daniel Boone country, all these trees like big Christmas trees."

He held his head high as if he'd created the trees himself. "Actually, you're not far wrong. Daniel Boone was born around here, near Reading, but then he moved on to Kentucky and Missouri."

I felt comfortable enough with Dale already to remain silent. "Sugar, Sugar" was on the radio, and "Honky Tonk Woman," "Get Back," "In the Year 2525," "Bad Moon Rising," and "Aquarius." The road became less mountainous; we crossed creeks through covered bridges, passed orchards, log houses, stone houses, barns larger than the houses, and fields of corn, pumpkins, strawberries, and cows. A blue Volkswagen appeared ahead of us, puttering so slowly that we'd barely seen it before Dale caught up with it. I didn't understand why Dale began honking (there was room enough to pass the Volkswagen with ease) until he told me to read the Volkswagen's bumper sticker: Honk If You Love Jesus. I became newly aware of the white cloudshaped sticker on Dale's dashboard which said Jesus Saves in red toy letters. "Jesus loves you, Brother," Dale shouted as he passed the Volkswagen. The man in the car, with a beard like a leprechaun's, removed a pipe from his mouth. "He loves you, too, Brother," he said in a deep voice.

"Nice fellow," I said as we pulled away from the Volkswagen.

Dale laughed. "This is Pennsylvania, Brother Homi," he said, "the land of universal brotherhood."

I nodded slowly, smiling. "What about you, Brother Homi? Are you saved?"

"From what?"

"Have you accepted Jesus? Have you given yourself to Jesus?"

"You mean, like a Christian?"

"Yes, like all true Christians."

"Nonono, I am not a Christian — true or false. I was born a Parsi. My religion is Zoroastrianism — but I am not devout. I believe in God, but not too much in any one religion."

Dale knew of Zoroaster, older than all the prophets (so some theologians argued) of the Old Testament, and of his religion which (so the same theologians argued) had influenced Judaism, and, consequently, Christianity, and, indirectly, Islam. Unaccustomed to Americans, I wasn't surprised that Dale had heard of Zoroastrianism, but when the subject arose on subsequent occasions most Americans thought only of a blackhatted, blackcaped, blackgarbed figure from a previous century in California who'd brandished a sword and whip — but Dale was studying theology, and his understanding of the aspects of Zoroastrianism which had influenced the west outstripped my own. The Wise Men from the East, the Magians, had been Zoroastrians, come in accordance with one of Zoroaster's prophecies. Jews had been.influenced by Zoroastrians, first as exiles in Iran during the Babylonian occupation of their homeland, later as subjects of the Iranis after Cyrus the Great had vanquished the Babylonians and allowed the Jews to return to their homeland. Until their contact with the Zoroastrians, said Dale, there was no mention in the Jewish texts of Satan, of a Savior, the last judgment, resurrection, free choice, and the immortal soul, among other similarly familiar notions, all derived from Zoroastrianism.

2

A voice sounded, as if from Rusi, as he continued to lie slumped in the chair by my bedside, but it was no longer his voice; it was deeper, more resonant than any of the voices I had yet heard — but even that is not strictly true since I wasn't hearing voices in the conventional sense as much as sensing them. I was too distracted at first by the intonation to listen to the words, but soon recognized the Yatha Ahu Vairyo prayer:

Yatha ahu vairyo atha ratush, ashatchit hacha, vangheush dazda manangho shyaothananam angheush mazdai. Khshathremcha Ahurai a yim drigubyo dadat vastarem.

They are blessed who follow the Truth because they are loved by Ahura Mazda. They are blessed who work not for themselves because they work for Ahura Mazda. They are blessed who give to the poor because they know the will of Ahura Mazda.

It was the prayer with which Ahura Mazda, also known as Ormazd, the Wise Lord, had hurled Angra Mainyu, also known as Ahriman, the Demon of the Lie, back into the darkness from which he had emerged at the end of the first of four periods of three thousand years each, the twelve thousand years which spanned the history of the world. Bapaiji had recounted the cosmogony to me. It was not until the end of the first quarter that Angra Mainyu had discovered the light, and rushed to annihilate it only to be beaten back. During the second quarter Ahura Mazda had created the sky, the water, the earth, the plants, the primal beast, and the primal man in that order. During the third quarter, Angra Mainyu, recovering from his confusion, had sprung like a snake through the vault of heaven, shattered the order of the planets, polluted the water, filled the earth with serpents, scorpions, lizards, and toads, poisoned the plants, and brought illness unto death to the primal beast (a bull) and to the primal man (named Gayomard) — but plants grew once more by Ahura Mazda's decree from the marrow of the bull, from its semen appeared more fish, birds, and animals, from Gayomard's members came the metals of the earth, and from his semen, Mashya and Mashyoi, the parents of human-

kind. The battle was joined between the two forces until the
end of the third quarter when Zoroaster was born.

I tried to visualize the events fully, but could see no more
than a brilliant white ball of light, yellowing and reddening
toward the edges like the sun, with a play of flashing fingers
within, accompanying the narrative which I gradually realized
was Bapaiji's (I was still not accustomed to her new deep intonation). "Do not ask too much, Homi. Some things not even
the dead can show you. Maybe after you perfect your memo-
machine you will find out the truth for us all. We cannot even
be sure of the date of Zoroaster's birth. Scholars have said it
might have been any time between 6000 and 600 BC — but if
one is to believe the story of the four periods of three thousand
years then he could not have been born much before 1000 BC,
because at the end of the fourth period of three thousand years
Ahura Mazda is to triumph irrefutably over Angra Mainyu, and
that has not happened yet. We know that he was born in western
Iran, perhaps in Azerbaijan, perhaps Rayy, perhaps Shiz, perhaps
somewhere else, to Porushaspa and Dughdova. We know of his
miracles, of his ten year pilgrimage in the Elburz Mountains
during which he was tempted by Angra Mainyu with palaces
of gold and the kingdom of the world, and of his struggles to
bring the revealed word of Ahura Mazda to the world — but
perhaps the more relevant of these details, apart from his teach-
ings, relates to his posthumous sons. Zoroaster had taken a wife,
Hvovi, and fathered three sons and three daughters, but on
three other occasions his seed had been sown through three
virgins at thousand year intervals during the fourth and last
period of three thousand years, Ukhshyat-ereta, Ukhshyat-
nemangh, and the last Astvat-ereta, the Saoshyant, the final
Saviour, to be born fifty-seven years before the end of the twelve
thousand years."

3

The farmhouse seemed to spring right out of the ground, reminiscent of Hill Bungalow in both ricketiness and the country sweet smell of dry dung. My room was the third floor landing, with a draft and a noticeable tilt from front to back, but the floor tilted just enough to invite a tumble into the bed. The space was musty, but cozy: the bed tucked into the far wall; roof beams sloping toward the wall so there was barely room to sit without bumping your head; a low dresser laden with towels. I wanted only to ingratiate myself with my hosts.

Mrs. Schweppenheiser hovered like a hen. I might sleep if I wished, I might shower, or I might partake of the breakfast she'd prepared. Neither she nor Mr. Schweppenheiser could keep from smiling, but he remained laconic through the introductions merely nodding his head when he shook my hand. "I think I'd like a bath first," I said. "After that breakfast sounds great."

Dale's older brother was named Broderick, called Bro Brod, for Brother Broderick. He'd just returned from work, cleaning in a canning factory. He was taller than Dale, stouter, his hair much longer, more tousled, his arms more corded with muscle. "Welcome to America, Homi, by gum. Welcome to America."

They all seemed to shout. It was the American way, I soon realized, to shout, to be direct, the consequence perhaps of the spaciousness of America compared to India, the sparsity of its population. "Thank you, I must say it all feels like a dream just being here. You cannot know what it means for me to be here."

Broderick couldn't stop grinning any more than anyone else. "What does it mean?"

"It is everyone's dream to come to America. I cannot explain it. Your daily life is my dream come true."

"Well," said Mrs. Schweppenheiser, still grinning, "we're very happy to be here too. Now what about that bath?"

It was late for breakfast after the bath, but the breakfast was a repast sumptuous enough for lunch. The table, covered by a gay tablecloth, filled the entire kitchen. I lost track of the number of cats and dogs slinking continually from room to room. The farm was actually on the outskirts of Watsonburg and the wide kitchen window revealed trees and rolling meadows (no houses) lit by the sun and birds unlike any I'd seen. "It seems so wild around here," I said, "like a frontier."

"Thet it is," Mr. Schweppenheiser said. "We're always on the lookout fer weasels'n possums in the henhouse. If they git in there they just bite their heads off, the hens' heads. Whut d'you think o' thet?"

It was the first thing he'd said to me and he looked expectant as if he were afraid his effort might have been wasted. I raised my eyebrows. "No kidding."

He made a sound deep in his throat as if he might have been laughing. "No kiddin', nossir. Jus' las' month I surprised a possum early in the mornin' in the henhouse. He got away but I had to pick up them chickens, no heads and blood all around. Whut d'you think o' thet?"

"Sounds pretty wild."

"Now, then, Pa," Mrs. Schweppenheiser said, "not at the table. Let the boy eat."

"Jus' lettin' him know, Ma. Jus' lettin' him know. He asked."

There were eggs, milk, pancakes, waffles, toast, butter, jelly, bacon, pork chops, potatoes, tomatoes, onions, corn, strawberry shortcake, apple pie, peach pie, and cream. "Everythin' you see," Mr. Schweppenheiser said, "was grown on the farm. You name it, I grown it — milk's from the cow, the Missus made the butter, and the pork's whut it is cause it's cornfed. I bled the pig myself, strung 'im up and slit 'is throat, and grew the corn that fattened 'im too. Whut d'you think o' thet?"

I was impressed but Mr. Schweppenheiser continued to look at me so expectantly that I couldn't think of anything to say. Mrs. Schweppenheiser said nothing except to urge me to more helpings of everything. "You're a growing lad," she said, beaming into the shortcake she passed me once more. "You've got to eat. That's real shortcake — not your shortbread or your sodabread, not your sponge cake neither. It's richer. I put in three more egg yolks, and a half cup more sugar and milk."

Va-Va-Va-Voom

One Sunday afternoon Mr. Schweppenheiser took me to the fire station to show me off. "He got polio — an' he's from Hindia, Bhombhay, land of the Zorroers. Whut d'you think o' thet?" I entertained the firemen by writing their names in Hindi, and when someone produced a mouth organ by playing "Your Cheating Heart," "Sixteen Tons," "Swanee River," "Spanish Eyes," "Beautiful Dreamer." "Heven in Hindia," Mr. Schweppenheiser said, "whut you got? American culture."

I spent five days in Watsonburg, hardly enough to exhaust the resources of the Pennsylvania backroads, but I was impatient to get to the university. I was sorry to leave the Schweppenheisers, but consoled myself I'd be seeing them in less than three months for Thanksgiving. The panorama didn't change from Watsonburg to Aquihana. Even the towns were much alike, each with a Main Street, barber shop, movie house, Post Office, library, hardware store, grocery store, Woolworth's, schoolhouse, clinic, court house, firestation, stuccoed office buildings, and side streets wide with elms and two-storeyed farm houses. Aquihana had a longer Main Street than Watsonburg (fifteen blocks to six), a hospital with a research laboratory (part of the reason I'd chosen the town), and, of course, the university.

It was a four-hour drive; Dale was at the wheel, Broderick

in the back seat, I in the passenger. He pointed to the university's administration building, Carter Hall, as soon as it was visible at the top of the hill leading from Main Street, a structure of rose-colored brick with a four-columned portico and clock tower, shadowed by elms. Behind the hill the rest of the university sprang into view, but before we got there Dale stopped the car and honked. "Yo, Candy!"

He was looking at a blond girl walking along the sidewalk across the street from us toward Main Street. Broderick nudged me from behind. "It's the slut," he said, but he wasn't even looking at me. His eyes were like flames and he was grinning, leering actually, at the girl.

What registered? A blond girl — a woman, actually (she was older than Dale), but I was too inexperienced myself to think of her as a woman. Besides, her face was fat like a child's when she smiled, and her eyes shy and roving when she talked. Had I seen vestiges of my own lost childhood darling Penny in her even then? Was unconscious memory so much a master of one's will? All I knew for certain was the hush I felt as when one enters a place of worship or recognizes a moment of destiny.

What else? A white dress, the miniest of miniskirts, the goldenest limbs of summer, a bright tender mouth cleft with a hint of cruelty, a foreshadowing perhaps of madness behind the hallowed facade, or, more simply, a defence against the world.

"Oh! Hi, Schwep," she said, stopping momentarily and waving before walking on.

Dale got out of the car. "Yo! Wait up, Candy! I want you to meet some folks."

Inside the car, still leering, Broderick spoke sibilantly. "Yess, yess, yess, yess, yess, yessssss!"

I didn't think Candace would turn around, but when Dale began running after her she chose to meet him halfway and walked back to the car with him.

"This is my brother, Broderick, Bro-Brod. I told you about him" (she nodded; Broderick remained crouched, leering, openmouthed, speechless in the back seat) "and this is Homi. He's from Bombay, India. He speaks Hindi and he's a bona fide genius. I'm his Big Brother. Folks" (looking at us), "this is Candace Anderson."

Candace seemed to affect everyone's balance. I might have found Dale patronizing, but I found myself wanting to impress Candace myself and was happy to let Dale do it for me. "Hullo," I said, and, unable to choose among the greetings I'd brought with me and the new ones I'd learned I used them all. "How do you do? How is it going? I'm fine. How are you doing?"

She smiled — it seemed, especially for me. "Nice meeting everyone," she said, "but I have to be going."

"Ciao," Dale said. I nodded, wishing I'd grown the mustache that Mom had talked me out of the year before. Broderick remained frozen in his stance like a lizard. No one said anything until Dale got in the car again and revved the throttle. Broderick spoke then as if the sound of the throttle had broken a spell. "Va-va-va-Voom! All right, Dale babay, brother mine: All Right! She can work my mojo anay-time!"

Dale responded sheepishly, keeping his eyes determinedly on the road. "She's a charming girl — a little lost, but quite charming."

"Charming! Yes, charming!" Broderick hooted. "If she was any more charming she'd be the whore of Babylon. Tell him about the celebration, Brother Dale. Tell Brother Home about the celebration."

There was a ministry on campus called the Community of the Spirit which held services weekly in the minister's livingroom where the communicants sat in a circle on the floor, passed around bread and wine, and sang hymns and songs some of which had been written by the minister, Jay Rochelle, himself, who also strummed a guitar accompaniment. On the one occasion when Dale had persuaded Candace to attend she'd passed around a joint after the bread and wine. Jay had either pretended not to notice or let it pass goodnaturedly as something that would not recur. "She was just having some fun," Dale said. "We were all just having some fun."

The long ride seemed to have gotten to Broderick. He was rocking gleefully in the back seat. "She was just having some fun," he said, mimicking Dale. "Come on, Brother Dale. She's a slut. She puts out. Tell Brother Home what she does for a living."

I didn't expect Dale to answer, but he seemed as fascinated with Candace's life as Broderick. "She's a barmaid at the Inn Different. She's real popular down there."

"Yeah! Real popular! What else? What else?" Broderick shook Dale's shoulder from behind.

"She's a model. She poses for the art classes on campus sometimes."

"Without a stitch! Without a goddam stitch! In front of the whole goddam class! In broad daylight! Hoo-Whee! Tell him, Brother Dale! Tell Brother Home what else!"

"What else? What else is there to tell?"

"About how she lives with her boyfriend, about how she sleeps around, about how he always takes her back!"

"Well, Bro-Brod, I don't know about that. That's all hearsay."

"Where there's smoke there's fire, Brother Dale! Where there's smoke there's fire!"

Dale seemed to be getting tired of the exchange. "You know what it says in the Good Book, Bro-Brod. Let he who is without sin ... "

"Cast the first stone! Come *on*, Brother Dale! I'm not here to cast stones! I wanna be her acolyte!"

Neither Dale nor I responded, not to his words, not to the thunderous laugh that followed, and Broderick soon subsided, as silent as he'd been noisy before. His girlfriend of two years had married a virtual stranger just that spring. He'd decided to drop out of school and work until he was more sure of what he wanted to do. He'd come with us only to drive the car back. Dale said he was actually better off without the Wagner Girl but Broderick, whatever he said, was yet to be convinced himself.

"Would you like to come to our Community of the Spirit sometime?" Dale asked. "I think you might like it."

"You don't have to be a Christian?"

"Everyone is welcome."

"Yes, maybe, if you don't have to be a Christian."

Manasni, Gavasni, Kunasni

The foreign students at OW (all six of us) were treated like dignitaries. During my first summer the administration even scheduled a class just for my convenience so that I might graduate at the end of my second year — not preferential treatment, they said, merely their way of expressing appreciation for their finest student ever, confirming my notion that I'd chosen the right university after all (would Harvard have been so accommodating? even to Einstein? and I was hardly that). There were plenty of activities available on campus, but I was too selfconscious to take part until Dale took me to one of the celebrations of the Community of the Spirit where I met Julie Clooney. She felt sorry for me (Dad had died, I hadn't resources for the trip back), took me to a Carroll's outside Aquihana for a burger (she had her own car), and gave me my first goodnight kiss, a rubbery business which nevertheless awakened the sleeping monster of my flesh.

What can I say about Julie? She was tall, sensitive about her height (wore flat shoes, walked with a crouch), liked me, leaned against me a lot, had a soft large chest, receding chin, long wavy chestnut hair, wanted to be a teacher, was a devout Christian, had a car, liked me, let me kiss her, let me touch her breasts, took me home to meet her parents for Christmas in Allentown, they liked me, I liked them, devout Christians who asked polite questions about Zoroastrianism.

What about me? I still thought about Candace Anderson, but on the few occasions our paths crossed could never think of anything to say to her except "Hullo. How are you? How do you do? I am fine. How is it going?" She never offered conversation herself, and after a while her presence made me so awkward I avoided her when I saw her coming and, if I were too late to avoid her, ignored her as if I hadn't seen her. Julie talked even when there was nothing to be said because it made us both more comfortable. Candace never ceased to affect me when I saw her, but I didn't otherwise think of her though she once provided a bone of contention between Julie and me. We were on our way to The Angus (the best steak in Aquihana) where Julie was taking me for my birthday, when she crossed our path and I went through my customary barrage of greetings. She barely smiled, but Julie looked at me curiously. "I didn't know you knew her."

"I don't, not really, only hardly, a little bit." I told her how Dale had introduced us.

"Leave her alone," Julie said. "She's not good."

I was surprised at her presumption. "Dale said she was a little lost. He wanted to help her. I thought I should be friendly."

Julie had attended the celebration to which Dale had brought Candace. "If Dale thinks he can help her he's a little lost himself. She's a ... she's not good, Home, dear, and he knows it."

It was the hour following twilight; the dim distant streetlamps cast lush conflicting shadows behind the elms; there was no sound but the champ-champ-champ-champ of our footsteps in relief against the rustle of the trees; Candace had faded in the semidarkness behind us, but I was afraid she might still hear us. Julie looked at me as if being "not good" were the saddest thing. "That's hearsay," I protested. "Besides, Christians should show a little charity."

Julie gave me a sharp look. Perhaps she understood immediately, as I did later, that it was an indirect way of piercing her
hypocrisy, because though she deflected what I'd said, she spoke
with a gentler tone. "I think you meant chastity, didn't you,
Home, dear?"

"Maybe," I said, disinclined to argue, thinking about the
imminent dinner and the many kindnesses she'd shown me.

                                    2

I spent my first Thanksgiving with the Schweppenheisers and
my first Christmas, but I spent my first Easter with the Clooneys
in Allentown, and the next Thanksgiving, Christmas, and Easter. I heard from Rusi in Chicago during my second year at OW,
but was too involved with my research to do more than acknowledge his letter. One circumstance in particular had convinced me that my arrival in Aquihana had been fated. I could
hardly understand Dean Shipley's excitement when I mentioned my interest in Dr. Penfield's research on memory. He
stared at the *Reader's Digest* article I'd brought with me from
Bombay as if I'd given him a million dollars. "You have absolutely got to meet Dr. Edward Horvath," he said, speaking as
if he'd discovered gold. Dr. Horvath was a lecturer on campus
and Head of Research at Aquihana Hospital — but, uncannily,
HE HAD WORKED WITH PENFIELD HIMSELF AT
MCGILL UNIVERSITY IN MONTREAL!

I impressed Dr. Horvath sufficiently over the course of my
first year to be granted unlimited access to the research facilities.
According to Dean Shipley, Dr. Horvath had said that I worked
intuitively, that sometimes he didn't think I knew what I was
doing until I'd done it, but he wanted to take the risk of giving
me a free rein. "We'd be burying our heads in the sand," Dean
Shipley told me later, when I couldn't stop thanking him, "if
we did anything else." I could only beam and repeat endlessly,

mindlessly, "Thanks. Thanks. No kidding. You will not be sorry. Nosirree, Bob. No kidding."

I soon justified their enthusiasm and mine with a crude working model of the memoscan which enabled me to electrically stimulate the brain of Magic (our mascot, a white rabbit, donated by a passing magician whose new wife was allergic to rabbits), using a non-invasive technique, an x-ray instead of the electrode which Dr. Penfield had applied directly to the brains of his patients during his research on epilepsy. I was able to bob Magic's tail, cock his ears, twitch his legs by making appropriate adjustments. I was able to explore, localize, and record the functions of his brain (a matter of developing a series of cross-sectional graphs of its brain using a mathematical model I developed which I hoped soon to computerize). I was able to produce only gross movements; finer movements required finer tuning of the x-ray itself, a finer wavelength which I hoped to induce using a diffraction grating or a laser. My primary interest lay, of course, with the invisible rather than the visible consequences of the stimulation, the retrieval of memory rather than the vulgar display of twitching limbs. To this end, with Dr. Horvath's help, I explored and recorded a series of graphs of my own brain. The graphs were necessarily rough, the memories predictably unclear (I couldn't see what I remembered as much as feel the attendant emotions as I tracked the imprint of my life on my brain). I could confidently pinpoint only two occasions on the graphs even though they'd remained a jumble of images — Penny's death, and my arrival in America. It struck me that Candace had already impressed herself on the convolutions of my brain as frequently as Julie — but not that her influence might have been yoked with that of Penny, certainly not that I should let her influence my plans to marry Julie.

Marriage! I thought I knew what it meant. What did I know? I had my degree. I had a research scholarship. I always received all the grants and scholarships for which I applied (Dean Shipley saw to it personally). I had known Julie for almost two years. I knew her family. Everyone liked everyone else. I thought I understood Julie's needs. I thought she understood mine. What did we understand? I don't think it would be presumptuous of me to speak for her. Neither of us could think of anything that might have interfered with our plans. We took each other for granted — mistakenly so. Where shall I start? These are painful recollections.

It was a moonlit night — in May. We drove out of Aquihana (my request) to an isolated spot along the road where we some-times parked when we wanted to be alone together. I thought it would be the perfect spot to propose. She wore jeans and a blue sweater (she knew I liked her in sweaters). She wore her hair in a ponytail (she knew I liked to undo it). I'd been careful not to use too much Brylcreem because I knew she didn't like it. I was surprised how nervous I was, but after I suggested driving to our spot I could think of nothing to say. I couldn't even follow what she said. When she parked the car I felt something was expected, but I couldn't think what. She was looking at me with eyes wider than usual as if she were waiting for my response. "I'm sorry," I said. "What did you say?"

She gave a short laugh. "I said, Home, dear, that you haven't been listening to a word I've said."

"I've got something on my mind, something I want to ask you."

Her eyes became cloudy as if she knew what was coming. "Yes?"

"Let's take a walk. It's a nice night. We can talk while we walk."

"Attchha."

She knew it amused me when she spoke Hindi, but I couldn't even smile. I took my shoes off instead. I thought it would be romantic walking without shoes. When she asked me why I was taking off my shoes I shrugged. "It's a nice night."

"There are stones outside."

"I don't mind. In India, we sleep on beds of nails."

She didn't laugh at my feeble joke.

There was no sign of life except for the sound of the crickets and a house in the distance with one bright yellow square of light. On either side of the road along which we walked were fields, occasional trees, highlighted in silver as far as I could see. "Look," I said, squinting my eyes, "when the wind blows through the grass you can almost imagine you're at the seashore. It looks like the surf when the tide comes in."

Julie squinted gamely. "Yes. I see what you mean."

The glow and the shimmer were unearthly, and at some other time I might have been happy just to watch in silence, but stones were cutting into my feet and I was aware of other important things that needed to be said. "Look at that house," I said, pointing to the sole visible form of inhabitation in the distance. "Isn't it amazing to think that someone actually lives there, so far away from everything else."

She looked at me as if I were becoming less familiar. "It's not so amazing," she said. "It's not that far away. I'm sure they have a car. What are you trying to say?"

I shook my head as if I were clearing it of a spell. "I don't know why everything gets so difficult. I want to marry you. Will you marry me?"

I couldn't look at her, but I knew she'd stopped walking. She turned me around from behind, held me tightly against her wonderful bosom, kissed my face repeatedly until it tingled. I kissed her back, tasting wonderful salty tears. "Crying? Why? Does this mean Yes or No?"

She laughed. "Yes! Yes!" She cried some more. "I'm so happy."

"I love you."

More kisses.

"I should have bought a ring. I wasn't thinking."

"It's all right."

"Here, take this instead — just for the time being." I thrust my sandalwood elephant, my good luck charm for so many years, into her hand.

She took her hand away. "That's sweet of you, Home, dear, but no. It's all right, really. We can get a ring later."

We walked back to the car arm in arm. I felt I was sailing on ballbearings. "Suddenly there's so much to be done," she said, "but first things first. We must get you baptised as soon as possible."

The stones began cutting into my feet again. I knew what she meant, perhaps I'd even feared it, but I said, "Baptised? Why? What do you mean?"

She clasped her hands around me from the side, kissed my ear. "You know what I mean, Home, dear. You're not a Christian. You have not taken Jesus into your heart."

I held her tightly, but I felt myself shrinking from her already. "Why would that make a difference?"

"Why? Well, I couldn't marry a heathen, Home, dear. You understand that, don't you, dear?"

"I am not a heathen. If you thought that why didn't you say something before?"

"I thought you understood. You came to all the celebrations. You said you enjoyed them. I thought it was only a question of time."

Yes, yes, yes, YES, of course, and YES again, the misunderstanding between us became increasingly clear, but remained insoluble. I was a Zoroastrian, but not as devout as I might have been because I did not wish to close myself off to what other religions had to offer. That was why I had attended the celebrations. In Hinduism, Rama was the eighth avatar of Vishnu, Buddha the ninth, Jesus the tenth. I liked that. Gandhi had conducted prayer meetings for Hindus, Muslims, Christians, Sikhs, Jains, Jews, Parsis, whoever chose to attend. I liked that. It didn't make me a heathen. I thought she'd understood that about me. I tried to make her understand one more time. She listened patiently, but a patronizing patience. Her face lost its contours appearing like a moon itself in the silver light. I felt as if I were choking. "What about the children?" she said.

I might have thought she was still trying to meet me halfway if not for the flatness in her voice, as if nothing I said would make a difference, but I tried anyway. "In one of the Zoroastrian prayers," I said, "there is a phrase: Manasni, Gavasni, Kunasni. It means good thoughts, good words, good deeds. Zoroaster teaches that good thoughts are necessary, good words are preferred, and good deeds are the most desirable. We have to show our children, by our example, to do good things and let them make up their own minds what to believe."

"It doesn't mean a thing what you do," Julie said, looking pointedly in front of her, "if you don't believe in Jesus."

"I'm not saying I don't believe in Jesus — but I believe in others also. Jesus would not want me to cut them all off. He is not such an egotist. He is Love. We must teach our children about Jesus."

She gave me a sharp sideways look. "And also about the others?"

"Why not?"

She was silent. In the car I massaged my feet. The gravel on the road had made ribbons of my socks. She pretended not to notice. How different was the ride back. I talked about my feet; she kept silence. As we passed the WELCOME TO AQUIHANA sign she spoke again. "If you love me, Home, dear, you will do this for me." She spoke gently, tremblingly, looking at me as if she were afraid I might strike her. "Would you do it, just for me?"

I couldn't look at her. "How can I do it? It would not be real. How can you even want such a thing?"

"It would become real, given time. It would be all right with time. You'll see, Home, dear. Please? For me?"

A song I'd always hated, but she'd always loved, "Julie, Julie, Julie, do ya love me?" was on the radio. She turned it off. I could only shake my head for a while. "I'm sorry," I said. "That I cannot do."

On the Wings of a Dragon

I couldn't believe it; it made no sense; I was no heathen; something else had to be the matter; I was Indian; I had a bum leg; I wasn't sexy; I could have believed any of that, all of that, but I was no heathen; that was a red herring. I understood Rusi's phrase: Ethnic Anxiety. During the following month I lost ten pounds, I couldn't sleep, I couldn't work, but when I called Julie (she was back in Allentown for the summer) she was unwilling to talk unless I saw things her way, and that I couldn't do. It was inevitable that I'd meet Candace again (I wanted her, Julie didn't like her, Aquihana is a small town, I was ready for her) — and this was the recollection which I'd wanted repeated ad infinitum, for which I'd invented a tripwire mechanism for the memoscan.

I think of my interlude with Candace as a weekend because it took place on a Saturday night, but it was hardly even one night. I scouted the places I'd seen her as often as possible, until I saw her again on Willow Street. I'd imagined I'd know just what to say when I saw her, but nothing could have prepared me for the way I felt as she came toward me, her face shaded by the streetlamp behind her, her tranquil walk as if she were propelled by air, hips swaying like a bell. An electron microscope trained on my heart would have revealed a thousand minuscule elves working a thousand minuscule pumps. "Well, well, well, well, hullo, hullo, hullo! I'll be darned if it isn't old Candace. How are you doing, Candace? How is it going? What's new with you? Fancy meeting you here."

She walked right by me as if she hadn't seen me. I thought perhaps I hadn't spoken loudly enough and shouted after her retreating back. "I say, Candace. Hullo, I say. Hi! How is it going?"

She continued walking, and I might have let her go thinking at least there'd been no one to witness my humiliation, but I couldn't contain the rage of another rejection. "I say," I said, stalking after her, "you don't have to be so bloody rude. You don't have to treat me like a bloody beggar just for saying Hi. It's not going to bloody kill you to say Hi back."

She turned just as I caught up with her. "What do you want?" Her jaw trembled, her eyes were wide.

I hadn't expected her to be scared. I replied with a chastened tone. "Nothing. Just saying Hi. It just got me mad when you kept on walking."

She searched my face as if for a clue before she spoke. "Do I know you?"

I didn't know what was worse, that she might deliberately ignore me or that she might genuinely have forgotten me. I rationalized: it was dark, the light behind me. "I'm Homi Seervai. We were introduced once, by Dale Schweppenheiser, on the hill going up to Carter Hall, about two years ago. Don't you remember?"

As I watched the unfolding of the scene yet one more time, the scene which I'd already played back for myself countless times, I became aware of an additional texture underlying its fabric, Candace's perspective presented as clearly as if it had been my own. I felt her envy, anger, frustration as if it were my own. I understood that she'd wanted to attend OW, but had disqualified herself because she didn't think she was good enough.

She found it easier to hold the students in contempt. It was promising that I understood how Candace felt because it indicated that instead of blindly tracing my memory once more I was bringing my own faculties to bear on what I was seeing, it indicated a positive prognosis for my malady. "I remember Dale," she said, smiling. "Such a sweet boy. How's he doing?"

I wished she might have thought of me as wistfully. I would have preferred to have been remembered as a man than a boy, but I'd have been content to have been remembered at all. "Dale's fine. He's in Watsonburg again for the summer. We had just come in for the fall semester. His brother Broderick, Bro-Brod, was with us. He told you I was from Bombay. Dale was to be my big brother. You *must* remember."

"I remember now," she said, still smiling, but now I felt she was smiling for me. "You were the brain."

"The brain, yes, that's me! I'm so glad you remember."

She continued to smile. The lamplight gave a sheen like a halo to her hair, a texture like gossamer to her jacket and skirt, a dusky glow to her downy legs. "Is Bombay in the Middle East?"

"Nono, in India, on the west coast — like Los Angeles. Calcutta would be our New York — on the east coast. Culturally also they are alike. Calcutta is intellectual, Bombay is more frivolous."

"Oh, of course. India. That's even more exotic than the Middle East."

"Exotic?"

"My astrologer said an exotic would come into my life. She must have meant you."

The qualitative difference between being an exotic for Candace and a heathen for Julie escaped me entirely. "Yesyes, you might call me an exotic," I said instead, delighted at my good fortune. "For an American, of course, I am an exotic. We consult astrologers all the time in India. I believe strongly in astrology."

"Me too, but most Americans think it's weird — but not me. I believe."

"My exgirlfriend thinks I'm a heathen," I said, anxious to let her know that I'd been around, that I was free — anxious to learn that she was free as well, that she had nothing against heathens. "That was why we broke up."

She laughed, but when she said nothing I persisted. "Do you have anything against heathens? Do you think they are funny?"

"Oh, no, I love heathens. I'm a heathen myself — at least, I think I'm a heathen. Christians are so damn sanctimonious."

It was my turn to laugh. "I know what you mean. My exgirlfriend was a Christian. You knew her I think — Julie Clooney. She met you at one of the celebrations on campus. We passed by you once, right here on Willow Street, about two months ago. Do you remember?"

She shook her head.

"It doesn't matter," I said, finding it somehow appropriate that Julie had remembered Candace so determinedly while Candace hadn't remembered her at all. "What about your boyfriend?" I said, getting back to my point. "Does he mind that you're a heathen?"

She narrowed her eyes as if she saw through my ruse. "Who said I have a boyfriend?"

"I just assumed. Everyone on campus is so mad about you. Is your boyfriend a heathen?"

She shook her head, still sizing me up with her eyes. "Who's everyone?"

"Everyone! When you model. They like to talk."

She kept staring, but said nothing.

"It doesn't matter," I said. "It's not my business if you have a boyfriend."

She nodded, barely perceptibly. "I have a boyfriend." She laughed again, and the image of someone I'd never seen emanated from her, a scruffy bearded man with a large balding head, soft round belly, in a dirty undershirt, red and white striped boxer shorts. Surprised, I recognized him from a description Candace had given me later of his pale eyebrows like foam and his face the color of a Bud lite. Even had I known his exact appearance, I wouldn't have admired Candace less. I might have pitied her more, but hindsight diminishes her appeal considerably, that she would consort with so unappetizing a man, that she had so little regard for herself as to live with him as his lover. "So," I said, "where are you going?"

"To the Inn Different, where I work."

"Oh, you're working tonight?"

"No. It's my night off, but Biff's working. He's tending the bar. I'm just going to keep him company."

"Ah, this Biff is your boyfriend?"

She hesitated before answering. "Not really. He thinks so, and it doesn't make any difference to me so I let him think what he wants — but I'm thinking of leaving him."

"Leaving him? But why? Is he bad to you?"

She laughed. "Nah, but he's a jealous fuck. I can't go anywhere without telling him." She stopped laughing. "Still, I suppose that means he loves me — if he's jealous."

"But nonono," I said, glad to have won her confidence, wanting to ingratiate myself further. "If he is jealous it means only that he doesn't trust you — and if you do not have trust how can you have love?"

She said nothing. I elaborated. "If he is a jealous fuck it means only that he is jealous — and that he is a fuck."

She laughed again. I felt worldly talking to her like that. She'd already broadened my horizons. "I say," I said, "I have an idea. Why don't I show you my experiments? It won't take long. Biff won't even miss you. No need to tell him anything. What do you say?"

She said nothing, but appeared to be thinking. I told her about Magic, how I'd mapped his brain so I could make him do what I wanted merely by training the memoscan appropriately.

"But that's cruel," she said. "Poor little rabbit."

"But he is not hurt at all. This is a non-invasive technique. That means no surgery. There is not even the need for an anesthetic. It is completely painless." When she continued to hesitate I said, "Come on, Candace. Biff will not know. You only said you wanted to be free. What do you say?"

I don't know how much she understood of what I said about the memoscan, but I convinced her. "Is it far? Should we take my car?"

"Not too far, maybe twenty minutes walking. You know where the Aquihana Hospital is."

"That's more than twenty minutes. Let's get my car."

"Okay. Let us."

We walked in the direction from which she'd come to a blue Thunderbird convertible. "Get in," she said. "It's open."

There was a clutter of newspapers, empty Budweiser cans, a large half-empty bag of Wise Owl potato chips. I cleared a space for myself on the seat and wedged my feet between the cans and papers. "Sorry for the mess," she said. "I hate to throw garbage on the street. You know how some people think the street is their garbage can? I'm not like that. I wish I was. Then I wouldn't have such a messy car."

"It's not a problem," I said, wanting to put her at her ease. "I'm quite comfortable. Let's go."

She drove as if gangsters were chasing her, but I pretended not to notice. The top of the car was down and all I could see were the striations of her lovely blond hair behind her and the imperious tilt of her chin against the wind. "Lovely name you have," I said. "Candace. It suits you."

She missed the compliment, or pretended to. "Folks call me Candy. I'm used to it — but I prefer Candace. It's more cosmopolitan."

"Yes, of course, absolutely, it is! Candy is like sweets, for children — but Candace! A princess could be proud of a name like Candace. Incandescent Candace! It is so appropriate."

"Much better than Candy Andy," she said with a grin. "My last name's Anderson."

I laughed, as if she'd been witty. "Candy Andy! Ha! But I prefer Incandescent Candace. Suits you better."

She smiled approvingly, but said, "Well, thanks, but I'm really more of a Candy than a Candace."

"But nonono. Maybe you are a Candace and you don't even know it yourself."

She continued to smile. "Maybe, but I don't think so."

"Arre, but you must think so. You have to believe in yourself first, no? Otherwise, why should anyone else?"

"Maybe. I never thought of it like that."

"But you must. Otherwise, why should anyone else?"

She looked at me sideways, a ribbon of hair flying across her face, as if I'd said something unexpected, but then she laughed. "You're right ... What did you say your name was?"

"Ho-mey Seervai."

"Homi. Yes, you're right, Homi. From now on everyone is to call me Candace — and don't you forget it." She laughed again.

There was a touch of mockery in her laugh, but I took it for worldweariness. I thought only that we were kidding together, that my name was on her lips; and my face burned with a temperature of a thousand degrees. "I would never have called you anything else anyway."

I was glad it was a Saturday night. The research labs would be empty. I wanted neither to share her presence nor to explain it to anyone. The only person to see us was the guard who knew me and waved staring at her all the while. It was dark. She seemed scared, following me silently, but I left the lights off gathering power from my familiarity with the place in the dark. There was someone in the adjacent lab, but I closed my door so we wouldn't be disturbed. She relaxed when I got Magic out of his hutch and let her hold him. Her baby talk while she cuddled Magic made me proud as if we were parents. I showed her the maps I'd graphed of Magic's brain, the adjustable metal plate which would cover his head, the cathode ray tube which would generate the electrical impulse, the memoscan whose screen would guide us through the graphs of Magic's brain. At first she playfully refused to give Magic up to me as if she knew I meant to harm him. I considered that she might have been inviting me to wrestle her for Magic, but didn't dare to take her up on it choosing instead to explain once more how innocuous the procedure was. She gave him to me then, eyes downcast as if I'd scolded her. I took him back, furious with myself for being such a prig, but during my demonstration (Magic twitching ears, nose, feet, tail, as I directed) her eyes grew wide as if she were a child at a birthday party and I the magician. "Wow!"

After we'd returned Magic to his hutch she began looking at me as if I'd suddenly come into focus, as if I were newly a contender. "Tell me *all* about India," she said. "It must have been so different growing up there."

I felt uneasy as if her question were a mask for something else. I didn't understand it then but from the sanctuary of my bedroom in Mayo House I saw clearly what she'd been thinking: the two of us naked on the floor of the lab, she astride me — but a me with a different body, flabbier, a complexion the color of lite beer, curls of flaxen hair like foam around the nipples, Biff's body! She'd imagined me with Biff's body because she hadn't given enough thought to how my own might look. "Where to begin?" I said in answer to her question. "I think of America sometimes as the land of unlimited orange juice — OJ as you call it. In Bombay, my grandmother's bearer spent hours squeezing oranges so my brother and I could have one glass of orange juice, only one glass in the whole week. Here you can get readymade, easily, as much as you want — anything you want, with so little trouble. Everything is so easy."

She smiled as if she hadn't heard a word I'd said. "Is there some place we can lie down?" she said.

"You are tired?"

She nodded, still smiling.

"There is the lounge."

"Will you lie down with me?"

I pretended to check the lock on Magic's hutch. "I am not tired."

"That's not what I meant."

I knew what she meant, but she had a boyfriend. From my perspective, she might as well have been married. My suggestion, stealing a few innocent moments in the lab, was mere hijinks; hers suggested irrevocable betrayal. Besides, I'd never slept with a woman. "They might see us in the lounge. There is no privacy."

"What about your place?"

I didn't want to take her to the dormitory. I didn't want anyone to know. "That's no good. My roommate will be there" (I didn't have a roommate). "What about your place?"

"Someone might see us. They might tell Biff."

I shrugged, smiling weakly, as if to say Well, we gave it our best shot, but more than anything else I was relieved.

"What about a motel?" she said. "Would you spring for a motel?"

"You would not mind going to a motel?"

"No, not if it's the only choice."

I said nothing.

"What's wrong? You don't want to?"

We hadn't even kissed. I couldn't believe it made so little difference to her. Her shamelessness galled me, but I confessed to her instead that I had no experience in such matters, from which point, of course, there was no going back. I rationalized that the love of one good man might do her good.

We got back into the Thunderbird and she raised the top. She suggested the Come Back Motel where she'd been before when she'd had "absolutely no other place to go," but she wanted me to get the room because she didn't want to be seen. Subterfuge wasn't my style, but after Julie had left I wasn't sure anymore what was. I was silent for most of the ride, but she couldn't stop chattering: I can't believe it's your first time (laugh); it's such a nice night we could just go by the roadside (suggestive smile, sidelong glance, shake of the head from me); but no, not for your first time, of course not, we want everything to be just right (snicker, laugh), but it *is* a nice night for a fuck, so warm, don't you think? (big smile, nothing from me); I was thirteen my first time, it feels so long ago I can't even remember what it was like before (laugh, guffaw, laugh); I just can't believe it's your first time (laugh, guffaw, guffaw).

"I don't think it's so funny," I said, more for something to say than to shut her up, more to make an observation than to appear disapproving, but I was hardly convincing, even to myself.

"I'm sorry," she said, immediately concerned, "I wasn't laughing at you. I was laughing *with* you. It just seems strange to me, like you were still learning how to walk or something, especially after you'd had a girlfriend for so long."

I thought about my leg. Even when I walked normally I felt as if I were perpetrating a deception, as if I had to hide from everyone that I would always be learning how to walk, as if polio had rendered me fundamentally different. I hadn't felt that for a long time, but after Julie had left the old insecurity had returned as if it were a conscience warning me of my limits. "She was a Christian," I said.

"I know," she said, sympathetically squeezing my knee. "I'm sorry."

She might have meant that she was sorry that Julie was a Christian, but I preferred to think she'd spoken without irony. "It's all right," I said. "I'm just nervous."

"Nothing to be nervous about," she said. "You'll see." She leaned over to kiss my cheek and my heart soared as if on the wings of a dragon.

I switched on the light the moment I entered the room. She followed me in, dimmed the light, and shut the door. I took in the wide bed, blue counterpane, azaleas hanging in a pot from the ceiling, roses climbing the walls, roses sweetening the air. From the window came strains of the Bee Gees from someone's car radio: "How Can You Mend a Broken Lover's Heart? How Can You Stop Rain from Pouring Down?"

In my nonchalance, I attempted to ignore her, but she pushed me gently back on my back on the bed, held up her finger telling me to stay, and proceeded to strip as naturally as if she'd been alone. Our roles from the lab were reversed. I became the child, she the magician, the moment she threw off her jacket and slippers, pulled her dress up over her head, pulled down her panties. I felt privileged just sharing the room with her naked person, and hardly moved when she turned to me, holding out her arms, undulating her shoulders. Her breasts were smaller than I'd imagined, but proportionate with her slim limbs, her sleek torso, flushed, and capped with swollen conchlike nipples. "I want you to remember me like this," she said, placing one foot on the bed, spreading her thighs, showing her pink plump pudendum, turning and bending to show rosy plump swaying buttocks, turning again slowly, placing her foot again on the bed, combing blond pubic hair, almost invisible in the amber light, with her fingers.

A pungent piano introduced the next song, Carole King's "I Feel the Earth Move," and Candace's movements quickened as she bumped and ground on the floor. "Sweetie-pie," she said. "If you wanna get something outta this, you're gonna have to do something. Otherwise, it's not gonna be any fun." Her eyes were narrow and hard; she spoke without mirth, but her voice was as molten as French horns in four part harmony.

I slid out of my clothes in bed. My senses that night were so skillfully woven that I hadn't imagined such a dense fabric possible: the smell of herbs in her hair, of cloves in the soft sandpaper of her armpits, the taste of salt, the texture of silk in the web of her pubic hair, the smell of rainwater and earth, the texture of peachskin in her complexion, the taste and the smell of a pungent cheese in her feet, the continual moan of the ocean as heard through a shell broken periodically by the shrieks of seabirds. I was quieter, hardly daring to enjoy myself, afraid to disrupt my fortune as if it might have been a house of cards, afraid to bring her suddenly to her senses, aware that Biff's place had been usurped by a pretender with a puny leg, but after I'd satisfied her curiosity about my polio she kissed and caressed my leg — my twice naked leg, because it was uncovered, because it was a stilt leg — as if it were a talisman, and I breathed more easily.

"Nice," she said, giggling when it was over as if she were suddenly shy. "You're a sweet fuck, gentle, very nice, nicer than Biff."

"Really? How?"

She giggled. "I just told you. You're sweet. You're also better looking. Biff's fucking ugly."

I snuggled behind her as she described Biff, fitting myself to the curves of her body as we lay on our sides, enfolding her in my arms, hardly daring to believe what she was saying, kissing her to sleep, tracing her breaths with mine until I too was asleep.

The idyll was over. When she awakened me she was slipping into her dress again. "It's almost three o'clock," she said. "We've gotta go. Biff's gonna kill me."

I was too chagrinned by her disappearing nakedness to hear what she said. "C'mon," she said. "I never intended to go to sleep, but you were so sweet with your kisses."

"Forget Biff," I said. "I will take care of you. I mean it."

She laughed. "Don't be silly. You're sweet to say that, but it'd never work."

"Why not? I ... I love you. I will make it work. You will help me."

She slowed down. "Look. You're sweet. We had a nice evening, but it's over. I'll give you a ride home, but that's it. There's nothing between us."

"Arre, but how can you say that? After what has happened, how can you say that?"

She spoke patiently, as if I were a child. "Nothing happened. Absolutely nothing happened. We had a sweet evening, but it's over. I'll give you a ride home, but I might never see you again — and that's okay, because we had a nice time, but it's over. Let's not spoil it now."

I couldn't think of anything to say. I got dressed. She drove me to the dormitory, smiled, kissed me goodnight. I said, "I love you." She smiled. I was sure that she felt guilty about Biff, but that after she'd had time to sort it out for herself she'd come back to me. She frowned when I pressed my phone number into her hand, just in case, but smiled again when I followed it up with my sandalwood elephant "for remembrance's sake," thanking me then, and kissing me once more, quickly.

2

The denouement came the next Saturday evening. After a week of inactivity, of impossible hopes raised and dashed with each ring of the telephone down the hallway in the dormitory, I decided I had to see her again and headed for Willow Street to take up a vigil by her Thunderbird. I was so immersed in what I planned to say that I almost missed her, but there was no mistaking the swinging bell of her behind when I looked up and saw her about to turn the corner onto Main Street. "I say, Candace, wait up, old girl," I shouted, running after her. "It's me, Homi. Wait up, I say."

She stopped a moment but, recognizing me, continued

walking, so that when I caught up with her we were on Main Street, brightly lit and crowded. She walked briskly; it was difficult for me, out of breath from my dash, to keep up with her, but I matched her stride as well as I could. "Slow down, I say, Candace," I said. "Where's the fire, I say? I have something to tell you."

She looked at me briefly as if she couldn't understand why I was there, a concession for which I was grateful, before accelerating her pace. "What do you want?"

"Slow down, no, and I'll tell you. I have to tell you something."

She stopped. "What is it?"

Nothing was as I'd imagined. There were people around, it was bright, I was puffing like a locomotive, feeling more like a recalcitrant schoolboy than a courting lover, but I didn't know when I'd see her again. "I say, Candace," I said (puffing, puffing), "that night we spent" (more puffing), "it was the happiest night of my life" (still puffing, puffing), "the most beautiful ..."

"Look," she interrupted, "no hard feelings, but it was nothing like that for me, understand? Nothing happened!"

I hated to think there were others listening, but there was no help for it. I tried to keep my tone confidential despite the puffing. "How can you say that? You were there. You know what happened. You were there. You said I was nice — gentle."

She held up her finger, once more the magician and I the child. "Look, there's nothing more to be said. Nothing happened and that's how it's going to stay, okay? Let's not spoil a good thing, okay? Don't be a shithead, okay? Now leave me alone."

She turned to leave, but I caught her wrist to make her stay. She yanked her hand to free herself. I wouldn't let go, but she caught me off balance and yanked me ahead with her hand. I stumbled; I might have recovered, but she tripped me with her foot. I like to think it was accidental, but the evidence of the memoscan is against me. I fell to the ground on my side; she got out of the way as I fell. Dazed from my fall, I heard her shout as she walked away. "Leave me alone, dammit! Just leave me alone!"

Someone came to help me up, but I waved them on. I didn't want to talk to anyone. I think I was crying. It seemed women were always leaving me, but this time I didn't waste time moping. I set about directly refining the memoscan. If I couldn't be with Candace in the way I wanted, I'd be with her the only way I could, repeatedly reliving the memory of my night with her until it became my whole life. I didn't know whether I'd die of dehydration (attached to the memoscan I'd have no access to water), or of a debilitated brain (the convolutions in which the particularized memory was stored would deepen with re-peated use, slicing the brain as incisively as a lancet, causing unpredictable dysfunctions) — but I didn't care because in either case I'd die the happiest of deaths, constantly reliving the happiest moments of my life. I chose the fourth of July weekend to carry out my plan to give myself an extra undisturbed day in the lab, hung a Do Not Disturb sign on the door for insur-ance. I didn't think, as suicides do, of leaving a note of expla-nation, because I wouldn't have called it suicide. I thanked God instead for providing me with so benevolent an alternative as the memoscan.

Epilogue

When I fell on the sidewalk the needles in my forehead felt as if they were pulling threads of blood like rivers behind them from temple to temple. It was perhaps the strongest attack yet, but my comprehension of its etiology gave me the courage to wait out this one final attack. I had thanked God for His gift, then set about abusing it. The potential of the memoscan, by slipping from conscious memory to unconscious, the Memory of the Soul as Bapaiji had put it, where all things are written, began only then to dawn on me. I'd been given the power to probe the memory of elephants, to fathom the windsong of whales, to discover no less than the equation to the universe which Einstein had sought, return to the dawn of man, the dawn of time, and I'd chosen instead to perish romantically — foolishly, pathetically — denying the world wisdom for a selfish, selfdestructive love. I might have killed myself had not a doctor forced the door in answer to my screams, broken the cycle into which I'd locked myself, and freed me from the memoscan.

The crowing of a cock outside told me it would soon be dawn. I would soon be talking normally with Mom and Rusi and everyone else, but my brush with the collective unconscious had shown me a way to control the past, at least in my imagination, and I wanted to exercise that control one more time to prove to myself that I was finally the master, no longer the slave, of what I chose to see. Tableau: Bapaiji, Hormusji, Rustomji, and Granny in tall stately chairs in a row on the porch atop the stoop of Hill Bungalow in Navsari, posed as stiffly as in the portraits in Bapaiji's sittingroom; behind them Mom in a sari, Dad in uniform, Jalu Masi and Sohrab Uncle beside Mom, Soli Mama and Farida beside Dad, and Jalbhai Pherozshah Cama hovering protectively over everyone; children ranged on the steps, Rusi, Zarine, Penny, Cyrus, Anand, Erach, Vijay, among other childhood friends; behind the family the Paymasters, the Bhagats, the Jairazbhoys, the Chibbers, the Davers, the Agteys, the Amberkars, the Shroffs, the Sanjanas, among other friends; around them, hovering like archangels, ancestors, old men and women, in pious robes and saris, dating back centuries to Yezdigard III, Khushrow II, Noshirwan, Shapur II, Darius, and Cyrus, the shahanshahs eran ud aneran; all impatient, stiff, angry with the person who'd assembled them, kept them waiting, but as I rose from my bed, the focus of all their gazes, their poses relaxed, their faces broke into smiles, and everyone got up to give me an ovation; behind them, above them, all around them, a light like a halo, ethereal, ineffable, the presence of Zoroaster conferred a blessing. I'd done it: I'd brought them all together in one place at one time, made a whole of the scattered pieces.

The cock crowed again. As a child I'd entertained a recurring dream of a forest beyond the Back Gardens filled with chickens running from a fox in the night. I was afraid for the chickens, but just when it seemed the fox would catch them a cock would crow, it would be morning, and the fox in retreat. The fox *never* caught the chickens.

Rusi was still in the chair, but slipping, jerking in his sleep as if he'd soon fall. I got out of bed, set him up from behind, kissed the top of his head. He woke with a start, shaking his head to clear it. "Arre, Homi? Are you okay? How are you feeling?"

I couldn't stop grinning. "I'm fine, but I have to open the window." I walked across the room. "The airconditioning's making me so claustrophobic."

Rusi leaped to his feet; opening the door behind him, he shouted, "Arre, Mom, come quickly, no? See for yourself what has happened. Homi is okay again." He walked slowly toward me as if I were a ghost, but he was smiling.

There was the noise of a chair toppling over within. Outside, the cock crowed repeatedly, and the sky became lit, as if with a wash, veined by the first streaks of pink.

Glossary

Achu Michu: Blessing performed during weddings by the in-laws respectively of the bride and groom.

Ahriman: The Evil One, Satan, also known as Angra Mainyu.

Ahura Mazda: The Almighty, the Wise Lord, God, the Creator in the Zoroastrian cosmogony, also known as Ormazd or Hormazd.

Amah: Ayah, nanny (Chinese term).

Arre: Catch-all expression to preface indignation, surprise, anger, or other emotions.

Ashem Vohu: A short prayer on the theme of truth.

Attchha: Okay.

Avestan: One of two ancient Irani languages, the other being Pahlavi, in which the sacred books of Zoroastrianism have been written, and in which the Zoroastrian prays.

Ayah: Nanny (Indian term).

Baba: Boy baby or child.

Babu: A native, untutored.

Bai: Madam, what a servant might call the mistress of the house.

Baby: Girl baby or child.

Baksheesh: Tip, gratuity, money for a beggar.

Bania: Shopkeeper, merchant, money lender.

Bapaiji: Paternal grandmother.

Bapavaji: Paternal grandfather.

Bawaji: Slang for Parsi, which, depending on the context, might be used affectionately or derisively.

Bearer: Houseboy.

Bhajia: Deepfried snack, filled either with potatoes, onions, or other vegetables.

Bhakhra: A sweet.

Bhel Puri: Mixture of grams and cereals with sweet and spicy sauces.

Bidi: Home grown cigarette.

Carom: Game played with flat round counters on a board with corner pockets.

Chai: Tea.

Chaipi: Tea drinker, used derisively in the sense of a bum or drunk.

Chana: Gram.

Chapatti: Unleavened bread, made of wheat flour, baked on a griddle.

Chappals: Leather sandals, generally with open heels.

Charpoy: Rope cot or bed.

Chhabar: Water splashed indiscriminately creating a mess.

Choli: Blouse worn with a sari.

Chori: Beans, often served with kharia.

Chowkidar: Guard for a private residence or single building.

Chula: Stove; also a pot with hot coals used by channawallahs to keep over their channa and sing warm.

Collector: District Officer, collector of revenues.

Dagla: White satin overcoat to be worn on special, especially religious, occasions by Parsi males.

Dagli: White cotton overcoat, lighter than the dagla, with bows instead of buttons in front, but serving the same purpose.

Dak Bungalow: Post house.

Dakhma: A Tower of Silence where the Parsis commit their dead.

Darbar: Court of the Indian king.

Dastur: Zoroastrian priest.

Dekchi: Large pot used for cooking.

Dhimmi: Non-Muslim who remained in Iran after its conquest by the Arabs.

Dhobi: Washerman, launderer.

Dhoti: Cotton cloth worn by men around the waist, loins, and thighs.

Dubras: Tribe of people indigenous to the west coast of India.

Fakir: Ascetic, a member of a set of religious mendicants.

Fehnta: Stately, semi-conical, custom-made, hat, to be worn with a dagla or dagli, dropped in favor in recent years for the readymade paghri owing to its complicated construction;

also because fehnta-makers have disappeared owing to a slackening in business.

Ganga: A working woman, primarily a laborer.

Ghora Gari: Horse and carriage.

Gujarati: Language of the state of Gujarat on the west coast of India, also the adopted language of the Parsis.

Hindi: National language of India.

Hindu: Follower of Hinduism.

Hisab: List or calculation or sum.

Housie-Housie: Bingo.

Hu-tu-tu: An outdoor game in which teams line up outside the opposite borders of a narrow arena. Each team sends out a member in turn to tag one of the members of the opposite team and to return to his own team without being pulled over the line into the opposite team. While he is in the arena the member must hold on to his breath and demonstrate that he is doing so by muttering Hu-tu-tu-tu over and over without pausing to breathe. The opposite team is not allowed to touch him until he has tagged one of them.

Irani: Iranian.

Jaripuranawallah: Ragman, ragpicker.

Jizya: Tax levied on all non-Muslims who chose to remain in Iran after its conquest by the Arabs.

Katchoubar: Salad primarily of thinly sliced onions, cucumbers, and tomatoes, sprinkled with cilantro and lemon.

Khadi: Home grown cloth.

Kharia: Goat legs, trotters.

Khas-khas Tatti: Screen made of grass matting, hung across doorways, and sprinkled with water to cool temperatures in the hot weather.

Kiddy-kiddy: Game with two teams in which one team bends over against a tree or wall in a long line arms locked around one another's waists, while the other team leaps atop them from behind as boisterously as possible and stays for a count of ten, the point being to get the team holding them up to give way.

Kurta: Long cotton shirt.

Kusti: Cotton thread, one of the articles of the Zoroastrian faith, to be tied around the waist over the sadra, the other article of the faith, while reciting certain prayers.

Lhega: Loose white pajama-like cotton breeches.

Looban: Conical container with a narrow opening at the top in which sandalwood is burned so that its smell may permeate the house.

Maha: Great, as in Mahatma (Great Soul), but also used in a slang sense to indicate, for example, a great time.

Maidan: Park, garden, or field used for recreation, spelled more phonetically as "my-daan."

Maiji: Madam, used respectfully.

Malido: A sweet.

Mama: Mother's brother.

Mamaiji: Maternal grandmother.

Mamavaji: Maternal grandfather.

Manja: Glass-encrusted twine used in kitefighting to saw and cut through the opposing kite line.

Marere-mua: May the swine die (a curse).

Masi: Mother's sister.

Matka: Round earthenware vessel in which water might be stored.

Mehndi: Orange cosmetic applied on the hands of women.

Mem Sahib: Madam, used respectfully; also Bai.

Mithai: Sweets, pastries, desserts.

Mota Bajar: Big Market.

Motabawa: Big Bawa, used respectfully.

Muddum: Corruption of Madam, used derisively to indicate an occidental woman.

Mussalman: A native word for Muslim or Muhammadan.

Navar: Ceremony, only for Zoroastrian males who have had their navjotes, who might wish to study for the priesthood.

Navjote: Investiture ceremony whereby a Zoroastrian child is officiated into the religion, wherein he is initiated with the sadra and kusti.

Paan: Betel nut.

Paghri: Hat, not unlike a brimless derby, to be worn with a
   dagla or dagli; also a white cotton head-dress, not unlike a
   turban, worn by priests.

Pakadav: Indian name for Catching Cook or Tag.

Parsi: Name given to the Iranis who fled from Iran to India.
   The name comes from Pars, one of the Irani provinces.

Patrel: Spicy, pulpy snack.

Pehlwan: Strong man, wrestler, weight lifter, or gymnast.

Pinjda: Literally a cage, also a wire mesh cupboard used as a
   pantry.

Puja: Hindu prayer ritual.

Puri: Light fried wheat cake.

Raga: Traditional melodic pattern in Indian music, an
   improvisation on the pattern.

Saakar: Unrefined sugar.

Sadra: Loose white cotton garment worn as an undershirt, one
   of the articles of faith of the Zoroastrian religion to be worn
   at all times, around which is tied the other article of faith,
   the kusti.

Saebji: Parsi greeting.

Sahib: Sir, same as Seth.

Samosa: Triangular deepfried snack filled with ground beef and
   potatoes.

Seth: Sir, what a servant might call his master.

Sev: A sweet.

Sing: Peanuts.

Tala: Traditional rhythmic pattern in Indian music.

Talao: Well, pond, lake, or other similar small body of water.

Tandaroosti: Health prayer.

Tila: Decorative red dot placed on the forehead for festive
   occasions.

Tonga: Two-wheeled, two-seater carriage drawn by a pony.

Wadi: Neighborhood enclosed from the rest of the town or
   village by doors which were closed during feuds and sieges.

Wah-wah: Expression which might be used to indicate
   admiration or praise as well as facetiousness, analogous to
   Wow!

Yaar: Meaningless slang term, used primarily as filler, analogous to "man," "you know," and "bloody."

Yatha Ahu Vairyo: A prayer which gains its power, to smite the "violators of truth," by repetition.

Zoroaster: Greek form of Zarathustra, the prophet of the religion of Zoroastrianism.

Phoenix Fiction titles from Chicago

Ivo Andrić: *The Bride on the Drina*

Jurek Becker: *Bronstein's Children*

Thomas Bernhard: *Concrete, Correction, Extinction, Gargoyles, The Lime Works, The Loser, Old Masters, Wittgenstein's Nephew, Woodcutters, Yes*

Arthur A. Cohen: *Acts of Theft, a Hero in His Time, In the Days of Simon Stern*

Jean Dutourd: *A Dog's Head*

Wayne Fields: *The Past Leads a Life of Its Own*

Bruce Jay Friedman: *A Mother's Kisses*

Jack Fuller: *Convergence, Fragments, The Best of Jackson Payne*

Randall Jarrell: *Pictures from an Institution*

Margaret Lawrence: *A Bird in the House, The Diviners, The Fire-Dwellers, A Jest of God, The Stone Angel*

André Malraux: *The Conquerors, The Walnut Tree of Altenberg*

Dalene Matthee: *Fiela's Child*

R. K. Narayan: *The Bacheler of Arts, The Dark Room, The English Teacher, The Financial Expert, Mr. Sampath—The Printer of Malgudi, Swami and Friends, Waiting for Mahatma*

Morris Philipson: *A Man in Charge, Secret Understandings, Somebody Else's Life, The Wallpaper Fox*

Anthony Powell: *A Dance to the Music of Time* (in four *Movements* with three novels in each volume)

Peter Schneider: *Couplings, The Wall Jumper*

Paul Scott: *The Raj Quartet* (in four volumes: *The Jewel in the Crown, The Day of the Scorpion, The Tower of Silence, Division of the Spoils), Staying On*

Irwin Shaw: *Short Stories: Five Decades, The Young Lions*

George Steiner: *The Portage of San Cristóbal of A. H.*

Richard Stern: *A Father's Words, Golk*

Stephen Vizinczey: *An Innocent Millionaire, In Praise of Older Women*

Anthony Winkler: *The Painted Canoe*

Christa Wolf: Accident: *A Day's News*

Marguerite Yourcenar: *A Coin in Nine Hands, Fires, Two Lives and a Dream*